SHOOT THE MOON

ALSO BY AVA BARRY

Windhall

Double Exposure

SHOOT THE MOON

AVA BARRY

PEGASUS CRIME
NEW YORK LONDON

SHOOT THE MOON

Pegasus Crime is an imprint of
Pegasus Books, Ltd.
148 West 37th Street, 13th Floor
New York, NY 10018

Copyright © 2025 by Ava Barry

First Pegasus Books cloth edition February 2025

ISBN: 978-1-63936-821-1

10 9 8 7 6 5 4 3 2 1

Printed in the United States of America
Distributed by Simon & Schuster
www.pegasusbooks.com

For my dad,
John David Arthur Barry,
the most creative person I have ever known.
Everything I write is for you.

ONE

We had just passed El Matador State Beach when my car started to over-heat. It was the middle of June and the temperature outside had already climbed above a hundred degrees. The air conditioner had stalled some-where around Malibu, but that wasn't necessarily any cause for alarm: my car was a 1970s Datsun, and the cooling system was fickle at best. When smoke started to curl out from under the hood, though, Lola shot me a warning look.

"Pull over."

"We're almost there," I said, keeping an eye on the road. "Twenty min-utes, tops."

Below the bluffs, sea stacks rose from the ocean like prehistoric animals. When I was younger, they had reminded me of elephants sinking to their knees, but now, I only saw danger. Waves crashed against the rocks, then splintered into mist. Far too strong for any swimmer.

"Rainey," Lola said, alarmed. "Your car could catch fire. Pull over. I'll call the Delmonicos and let them know we're running late."

"All right, all right."

I hit my turn signal and slowed down to ease onto the side of the road. I didn't have to look at Lola's face to know that she was pissed. She had offered to drive out to Oxnard that morning, but Lola had already spent the week driving all over Los Angeles to see a range of clients, and I wanted to cut her a break. Summer was always busy for the firm; the heat made people crazy, impulsive.

"I just had the car serviced last week," I offered, risking a glance at Lola. Her mouth was set in a thin line.

"Really?" Lo sounded skeptical. "Where?"

I paused. "Floyd had a free afternoon."

Lo slowly turned her head to look at me, then raised an eyebrow. "*Floyd?* Floyd is out of prison?"

Floyd was a petty criminal whom we had befriended a few years back. He had been an unlikely source of information on a case we were working, and he quickly realized that by helping Left City Investigations he could make a nice legal income. The problem was that Floyd was easily bored, and when the opportunity arose to make a quick buck, he rarely resisted. Floyd was a good-natured thief, but boastful, and he couldn't keep his mouth shut to save his own life.

"Floyd," Lola said now, nodding. "Okay. We can talk about Floyd later. Right now, though, we need to call a tow truck to take us into Oxnard." She took out her phone and squinted at the screen. "I'm not getting a signal. You?"

I took my phone out of my pocket and tilted it toward me. "No. Nothing."

"Okay." Lola slipped her sunglasses on. "I saw a fire station just past the last bend. You stay here and keep an eye on your phone, just in case you get service."

It was only eleven o'clock, but already the day had stretched into hot taffy. It was our first time meeting the Delmonicos in person, and I had dressed for the occasion: a pencil skirt and a tailored satin blouse. I had already sweated half-moons through the pale fabric.

"Damn it."

I stepped out of the car and walked around to the front to pop the hood. Smoke billowed out. I glanced down the highway and watched Lola stride along the breakdown lane, shading her eyes and pausing when eighteen-wheelers went hurtling past. We had only left Los Angeles forty minutes earlier, but already we were in the kind of geographical no-man's-land that defined so much of California: sparse, craggy hills sewn with scrub brush and chaparral, with a few small houses perched on the cliffs like sentries. The plants that survived here were the stalwart variety that could endure punishing sun and the salty gusts that came tearing in off the Pacific: oleander, poppies, California sage, wild rose.

El Matador Beach wasn't as popular as other beaches along this stretch of coast like Zuma, Leo Carrillo, Point Dume, or even Lechuza. El Matador had rocky outcroppings and monoliths that laid claim to the pristine stretch of sand, which meant that the waves were dangerous, unpredictable. Only last week there had been a story in the news about a family from Tehachapi who came out for school holidays. One of their children had gone in for a swim and never made it back to shore.

I shielded my eyes from the sun and waited for a break in traffic. It was too hot to stay with the car, so I crossed over to the other side of the four-lane highway, where a few stunted trees and a clump of pampas grass offered a slim margin of shade. Beyond the cliffs, the Pacific stretched out like a rumpled tarp. Waves of heat rose off the concrete.

Years ago, when my parents were still together, my family rented a house in Malibu for the summer. My father walked along the beach every morning before he started work. It cleared his head, he said, helped him tease out the complicated melodies he worked so hard to put on paper. My mother waited until he had started work before she went out for her own daily constitutional, always ending her walks with a swim. I watched her wrestle with the ocean from the kitchen window, amazed by the energy it took for her to stay afloat. Sometimes she stayed in the water for hours, bobbing and tossing like driftwood. Our house was busy with guests that summer, which meant that I could slip through the rooms undetected. Nobody noticed that I hadn't set foot in the ocean, not even once. There were so many things that could go wrong—there were two drownings that summer alone, not to mention the shark attacks in years previous.

The nasal wail of a truck horn jerked me out of my memories, and I spun around to see a rig bearing down on me. The driver was partially hidden behind the glare of the windshield, but I could see frantic hand movements waving me back, off the verge, into the bushes. I dove between two trees as the truck ate up all the road, waist-high wheels crushing the pavement where I had been standing only moments before.

I was still crouching among the trees ten minutes later when a tow truck eased itself up behind my car across the road. Lola descended from the cab and spotted me, then waved her arms and called my name. My heart pounded as I scanned the road for a gap in the traffic, then ran across to meet her.

"This is Cindy," Lola said, gesturing to the truck driver. The woman was small, compact, with bronze skin, and hair shot through with gray. The woman smiled at Lola and ducked her cap.

"*Gracias de nuevo por su ayuda*," Lola said. She turned to me and gave me a relieved grin, then explained, "Our families are from the same part of Mexico."

"*Mucho gusto*," I told Cindy. I had taken Spanish in high school, and Lola forced me to practice as much as possible. Thirty-six percent of Los Angeles spoke Spanish, she was always reminding me, and I was happy enough to learn, but in an emergency, I still leaned on her for help translating.

"She'll take us to a mechanic in Oxnard," Lola went on. Her irritation had faded; all was forgiven—at least for now. One of the things that I loved most about Lola was how she could draw anyone into conversation, from fellow lawyers to blue-collar workers, and her personality never changed no matter who she was speaking to. "She's graciously offered to drop us off at the Delmonicos' house afterward, and hopefully your car will be fixed by the time we're done."

The Delmonicos lived in a split-level ranch house with peeling white paint and a gappy fence. The lawn was patchy, but a fringe of marigolds added a touch of color to an otherwise bleak palette. The neighborhood was quiet, but that made sense; it was Wednesday afternoon and I guessed most of the neighbors were at work. After Cindy dropped us off, Lola double-checked the address.

"This is it," she said.

We were both quiet for a moment, assessing the house in front of us. It was a standard part of our routine, these five minutes: we would stay outside and try to read as much as possible into what we could see before we even entered the house. There were a great many details that people told you about themselves without even realizing it—how much money they spent, what they tried to hide—and it was useful to have a full picture of someone's situation in order to help them.

"Gutters are in good shape," Lola said. "Fence is falling apart, though."

"Lawn's in pretty good condition," I said.

"That car's at least ten years old, but it looks well maintained," Lola said. She turned and looked at me. "So, they're responsible people who live within their budget. Things have slipped through the cracks a bit in the last few months, but that makes sense, given the circumstances."

"We're already running late," I said. "Let's go talk to them."

The front door swung open before we reached it, and I shaded my eyes to see a woman in her late forties emerge, blinking in the sun. She wore khaki pants and a wrinkled Oxford shirt that looked like it had been slept in. Her dark hair was pulled back into a ponytail, and I could see the growth of gray roots under a dye job. The woman attempted a smile when she saw us.

"Rainey?" she called. "And you must be Lola—I'm Kathy."

"Hi, Kathy," I said. "I'm so sorry we're late, there was an accident on the highway."

"It's fine," Kathy said. "Come inside, get out of this heat."

She vanished into the recesses of the house before Lola could greet her. As soon as we stepped inside, I could feel the slow creep of stagnation, of decay. The entrance of the house was dim and cool, and the air was heavy

5

with the smell of something I couldn't quite identify: it wasn't one thing but rather a combination of odors—unwashed clothing, fruit on the edge of turning, dust.

"Through here," Kathy called.

Lola and I stepped into a darkened living room to find Kathy and a man with pale skin and dark hair wringing his hands.

"This is Michael," Kathy told us, "my husband."

"Nice to meet you," I said, and Lola murmured the same.

Once my eyes had adjusted to the dim interior, I saw that the walls had all been painted with a fantastic tableau: every surface of the room looked like a portion of the sky, from sunrise to sunset, with constellations painted onto the ceiling. Superimposed onto this background were all manner of haunting abstract creatures gamboling along the walls and up the corners, creeping through the sky and hanging from the ceiling.

"Wow," Lola said, scanning the room. "This is incredible. Did Chloe paint this?"

"She painted most of the house," Michael said. His voice was slow, measured. "We've closed the curtains because the June sun is so powerful. We didn't want it to fade the paint."

"We explained everything to Kathy when we spoke to her on the phone," Lola said, addressing Michael, "but I think it's probably best if we explain it to you, too. In case you have any questions." Her voice was soothing, and Michael nodded.

"First of all, allow me to express my condolences," Lola said. "I can only imagine how hard it must be to lose a child."

Michael stiffened and a cold look came over his face. "Chloe isn't dead," he said. "We haven't *lost* her. She's missing. There's a difference."

"Of course," Lola said. "I expressed myself poorly, and I apologize. We're going to do everything we can to locate your daughter."

Michael took a long, slow breath through his nose. I could read everything in the dynamic between himself and his wife: she was the one who had hired us, but he still had reservations. They had probably fought about it for the last few days, quibbling until things turned ugly. Hiring a private investigator was not a decision to be taken lightly: there were the costs, of course, but that was only one small part of it. A private investigator went prodding around in the dark corners of your life, looking for dirt. My team came with soft scalpels and other tools of excavation. We nearly always found what we were looking for, or at least, got close enough to see the outline. I had been doing this long enough to know that some people were better off with vague ideas of what might have happened to their loved ones than knowing the truth.

Michael glanced between me and Lola. "Tell me how this works," he said. "The police have no idea where she went, and they have the legal system on their side. What makes you think you'll be able to find our daughter when they failed?"

Lola glanced at me, and I nodded.

"We specialize in small cases," I said. "We don't have deadlines and quotas to fill, so we can look for your daughter until you tell us to stop. There's one other advantage we have over the police—we don't arrest people."

I watched Michael's face for signs of understanding. His brow furrowed, and he glanced at his wife.

"People tell us things that they might not share with police," Lola added.

"So?" Michael folded his arms across his chest.

Lola and I looked at each other, and I decided to be more explicit. "If your daughter was involved in anything illegal—if that's the reason she went missing—her friends might be reluctant to talk to the police. There's a chance they would share something with us they might not tell a cop."

"She wasn't like that," Michael snapped. Something in his face had closed down, and I sensed that we weren't going to get through. "Chloe was a good girl—she was only nineteen. Went to work, came home, and had dinner. That's it. Someone took her."

7

Lola nodded and took a deep breath. Kathy looked desperate to salvage the conversation. She gestured to the couches, then put a hand on her husband's arm.

"Let's take a seat," she said. "We'll tell you about Chloe."

Lola and I sat down. After a moment, Michael lowered himself into a chair next to Kathy.

"What can you tell us about your daughter?" Lola asked.

"She's a great artist," Kathy said. "I know every parent says that about their kid, but it's true. Look at this room."

"I can see how talented she is," Lola agreed.

"She's been drawing since she was four, but not just squiggles and dots," Kathy said, warming to her subject. "Really good stuff. She got a scholarship to Otis when she was only sixteen."

"She wants to do it professionally?" Lola asked.

Kathy and Michael gave each other shy smiles. It was the first time since we had entered the room that Michael had let down his defenses, and I relaxed a bit.

"Chloe's already been working for a year," Kathy said. "As an artist, I mean. She dropped out of school, even though we tried to talk her out of it. She said she was making so much money that it didn't make sense to spend all her time doing homework."

"That's very impressive," I said. "It's really hard to make a living from the arts, and at such a young age . . ."

"She's a good kid," Michael repeated, his voice gruff.

"Here," Kathy said, reaching under the coffee table. She produced a thick photo album and set it on the table before us.

I opened the cover and slowly turned the pages, pausing to notice Chloe's progression from a kid with a goofy smile into a solemn teenager. She grew in height and slimmed down, and suddenly she was a willowy young woman with long dark hair. Lola and I glanced up at each other at the same time. I could see that she was thinking the same thing that had crossed my mind.

8

"What is it?" Kathy asked. She sounded anxious.

"She's . . . Well, she's beautiful," I said. "She could easily be a model."

"Really stunning," Lola added, then quickly interjected, "Not that it matters for our investigation, of course."

"Thanks," Kathy said. "She is beautiful."

The last few pages of the album were sparse. There seemed to be a jump from weeks and months between photographs to a space of years. In the last few pictures, Chloe looked withdrawn, defensive, and almost too thin. I closed the book and looked up at Chloe's parents, who seemed uncomfortable. A silence had descended on the room, and it was a silence that I had experienced before with new clients, when they were trying to assess whether they could trust us.

Lola nodded. "You said on the phone that she went missing last week," she said. "Can you tell us what happened that day? Walk us through everything you remember, even if you don't think it's important."

"Everything," I chimed in. "Did she have a boyfriend? Was she fighting with her roommates? No detail is too small."

"She didn't have roommates," Michael said. His voice had turned sharp again. "Not anymore. She lived with us."

"Okay," Lola said. Her voice was still even, but I could hear the edge in it. I knew Lola better than anyone, and I could tell that her patience was starting to wear thin. Dealing with a reluctant client made our jobs next to impossible. "Friends? Boyfriend?"

"No boyfriend," Kathy said. "She had lots of friends."

"Any problems with those friends?"

"Not that I know of," Kathy said. She shot a few nervous looks at Michael, then looked down into her lap.

"And you're sure there was no boyfriend?" Lola prompted. "Maybe someone you didn't know about?"

"We had a very open relationship," Michael said. His voice was tense, and I saw his hands flexing. "She told us everything."

"Mr. and Mrs. Delmonico," Lola said. "We're willing to look for your daughter, but we can't do it unless we have all the information. Believe me, it's a waste of your money. We'll start looking in the wrong direction."

"We understand that," Kathy said.

"So why don't you tell me what you're hiding?" Lola asked.

The couple exchanged a glance. Kathy's body visibly tensed, and she folded her arms across her chest. She looked fearful.

"You're wrong," Kathy said. "We're not hiding anything."

Lola shook her head and stood up. "I'm sorry," she said. "I don't think we can represent you. I hope you find your daughter."

In the past I had sat through agonizing meetings with potential clients as they deliberated about whether or not they should hire me. The relationship we had with our clients was a lot like dating: there had to be trust, you had to be on the same page, and the partnership only worked if there was clear communication. If you sensed hesitation or—worse—that your client was hiding something, you had to walk away.

I followed Lola through the quiet house, to the front entrance. We didn't speak as we opened the front door and walked outside, back into the sunlight. The light was nearly blinding after the contrast of the dim house, and I held a hand up to shield my eyes.

Lola took out her phone and shaded the screen with her hands. "I'll call a cab," she said. "Let's hope the mechanic's done with your car."

We had almost reached the street when I heard the door open behind us.

"Wait," Michael called. "Please wait."

Lola and I turned to see him standing on the threshold, his hands in his pockets. He spread his arms in a gesture of supplication, then glanced around to see if there was anyone within earshot. After a moment's hesitation, he picked his way down the path toward us.

"I'm sorry," he said. "We're not usually like this. It's horrible. We've become different people in the last week."

"It's fine, really," I said. "No need to apologize."

Now that we were out in the sun, I could see how exhausted Michael was. I had never seen him before today, so I didn't have a basis for comparison, but he wore the kind of dazed look familiar among people with missing family members.

"You were right," he said to Lola. "There's something we haven't mentioned. It's the reason why the police stopped looking. We thought you might not be interested if we told you."

Lola waited.

"Chloe was using drugs." Michael's voice was quiet. "I know that she experimented a bit."

"What drugs?" Lola asked. She squinted against the sun.

He closed his eyes and pinched the bridge of his nose. "Last year it was cocaine. We confronted her about it, but she denied it, and ever since she moved out of the house, we couldn't control her. One of her friends said she was using pills for a while, but again, when we confronted her about it, she said it was nothing more than supplements."

"Alcohol?" Lola prompted.

"No, never," Michael said. "She hated drinking. Seemed to have an allergic reaction to it. Plus, she said it made her feel stupid."

"Really?" Lola asked. "Never?"

"As far as I know, never," he said. "Not that it's anything to be proud of. She was using drugs every day by the time she disappeared."

"You said things took a turn," Lola said. "What happened?"

Michael closed his eyes. He didn't say anything for a very long moment, and I could see that he was trembling.

"Something happened with her roommate," he said. "In Los Angeles. They had a fight or something, I don't know. Chloe moved back in with us. She was still working in Los Angeles, still doing her art, but she commuted."

"When was this?"

"About a month ago," Michael said. "For the first few weeks, things were great. She had dinner with us, made conversation. And then she started disappearing. She took Kathy's car one night and drove off the road. I don't know how she survived that crash."

A crease appeared between Lola's eyebrows. "A crash? Was she high?"

"I don't know," Michael said. "Probably. It was on the highway, early in the morning. Just past Point Mugu. She walked along the highway for an hour before calling a taxi, because she didn't want the police to know about the accident. I can't believe she survived."

I flashed back to a vision of my car smoking on the side of the road, the truck barreling down on me. The image of a young girl walking away from smoking wreckage at night was a hard thing to think about.

"She started staying out at all hours," Michael said. "And like we said, she had all this money. We had no idea where it came from. I thought . . . I thought . . ." He put a hand to his mouth and sucked back a few breaths. "I know she was doing something illegal. I don't know what. Really, I don't know—I would tell you if I did."

"How much money?" I asked.

He glanced at me, then looked back at the street. "Thousands of dollars. When she crashed the car, she left her coat and bag in the backseat. The bag was full of money—I'd never seen money like that. We claimed the car from the impound lot the next morning, and that's when we found it."

Lola thought for a moment. "What happened after the car crash? Did you report it to the police?"

"The car was a write-off," Michael said. "The only way our insurance would cover it is if we reported the car stolen and had Chloe arrested. There's no way we'd do that. We've gone down to one car between the two of us, which is difficult. We manage."

Lola nodded and took out her notebook, then scribbled something down. When she was done, she looked up at Michael again.

"Let's go back over some of the things we asked you inside," she said. "Please be honest with me. Can you do that?"

Michael took a deep, shaky breath. "Yes."

"Was Chloe seeing someone? A boyfriend or girlfriend?"

"Yes," Michael said. "It was a while ago, though. I think they had broken up."

"Do you have a name or description?" Lola held her pen between two fingers, waiting.

"He was rich," Michael said. "A man. I saw him drop her off at the house once, very early in the morning. The neighborhood was still dark, and I woke up because I heard something in the street. I looked out the window—it was a black SUV, one of those luxury models."

"License plate?" Lola asked.

"I couldn't see." Michael rubbed his chin, hard, then pointed at the curb. "They were parked *right there*. If it had been daylight, I might have seen more. I saw a man in the driver's seat, and Chloe leaned in and kissed him. That was it. That was the only time."

Lola continued writing down notes. "This man—could you make out any features?"

"Nothing. I've tried so hard to remember, but I could just see a forearm, the edge of his face."

"Hair color?"

"Dark, I think—but again, I couldn't see much. I could just see part of his face. Enough to say it was a man."

"Right." Lola tapped her notebook with the pen. "When was that?"

"A month ago."

"The same time she moved back in with you?" Lola looked up to confirm, and Michael blinked.

"Yes," he said. "That's right."

"What makes you think they broke up?"

"We had a fight about it," Michael said, a bit reluctantly. "I said we wanted to meet him, to know who she was spending all this time with. I thought he might be supplying her with drugs and money. She got really angry and said that she had broken up with him. They were always on-again, off-again, though."

"Do you still think he was the one supplying her with drugs?"

Michael's face closed down at the question. He shrank into himself, his shoulders folded inward, and for a moment I pictured a parade float limping along at half-mast as it bumped into buildings. The image was horrible, and I immediately banished it.

"Yes," Michael whispered.

"Any idea what drugs?"

"At first I thought it was meth," Michael said. His voice came out in a hoarse whisper. "I've never touched the stuff, but I had a friend who lost his son to drugs. I know the signs. She was paranoid and hyper, and she had this intense focus. I know it sounds horrible to say, but her art seemed to flourish when she was high. That's when she painted the living room. Her bedroom."

Lola made a note of this, nodding.

"The anger, though—it was horrible," Michael went on. "She became incredibly violent. She broke things, threw things—and she did this." Michael pulled up his shirt and revealed a thick surgical bandage across his abdomen. Michael's hands trembled as he turned to show us, and I inhaled sharply at the sight. Puckered skin showed at the edge of the tape, and there was something so vulnerable in the revelation. I could understand why Michael had been so defensive before, so quick to lash out: he had been ashamed. More than that, though, he was protecting his daughter.

"I'll spare you the wound, but I had to go to the hospital. Eighteen stitches. The hospital wanted to call the police, because they could tell someone had attacked me, but I wouldn't tell them what happened." He tucked his shirt back into his pants.

Lola slipped her notebook back into her bag and gave Michael a look of deep compassion. "The police," she said. "They don't know about any of this?"

Michael shook his head.

"What exactly did you tell them?" she asked.

"We called them last week," he said. "We waited twenty-four hours because we thought she might have been out with friends. She had left all her stuff behind, though—money, driver's license. We called her old roommate in Los Angeles, and he had no idea where she was. So we called the cops. Since Chloe is nineteen, though, all they can do is put out a missing persons report. She's just another number in a database."

"It's good that you called us," Lola said.

"You have to find her," Michael said. He looked scared, and he started trembling again.

"We have experience with missing persons cases, and while I don't want to give you false hope, we have a number of resources that will give us an advantage."

"Like what?" Michael asked. He sounded cautious, but hopeful.

Lola and I glanced at each other, and I cleared my throat. "My mother was an artist," I said. "I still have a lot of connections in the art world."

"Oh, god." Michael sank his face into his hands and started trembling. The door opened behind him, and Kathy appeared in the shadows.

"I guess you'd better see her room," she said. "Then you'll know how bad it was."

Chloe's room was on the second floor. We followed Kathy and Michael through the entrance of the house and up a set of carpeted stairs lined with windows, which looked out onto the dying garden behind the house. The walls of the staircase had been painted in a similar fashion to the living room downstairs, colors blooming along a spectrum of blues and purples.

At the top of the stairs was a short hallway, which ended in a closed door.

"This is it," Kathy said. "Chloe's bedroom."

After a moment's hesitation, Kathy opened the door and stepped aside so that we could see the room.

The effect of entering Chloe's bedroom was almost like stepping sideways through a portal into a world with no gravity: everything, from the floorboards to the ceiling, had been painted as a kind of skyscape. Here, like in the room downstairs, were nightmarish visions painted amongst the clouds: enormous faces with three eyes, tiny humanistic figures tumbling weightless through the ether, blocky cliffs melting into a beach. I recognized the sandstone monoliths from the coast along the highway, and the skill with which the details had been captured took my breath away. All the furniture—bed, dresser, nightstand—stood in the center of the room.

I was so captured by the beauty of the artscape that it took me a moment to notice all the damage: at intervals along the walls, at about shoulder height, holes had been punched through the drywall. Lines snaked out from the holes like cobwebs on cracked glass.

Lola and I stood at the edge of the room, taking everything in.

"She did it in two days," Michael said.

I turned to look at him. "Did what?"

"She painted the whole room in two days," he said. His voice was almost reverent. "We were out of town at the time and came back to find this. It's incredible, isn't it? Two days."

Lola nodded in agreement. "It's incredible."

"It was just a few weeks ago," he went on. "After she moved back home. We thought she was going through a creative spell, and then she did . . . Well, you can see." He gestured to the holes. "It was horrible. We said that she needed to get help, or else she had to move out."

Lola moved into the room, watching where she stepped. She turned around to face Michael. "Do you think that's why she disappeared? Because you asked her to leave?"

"No, no," Michael said. "It occurred to me, of course, but she left all her things behind."

"She didn't take anything with her," Kathy echoed. "Her passport, her wallet, her keys—she left everything."

"I told them about the drugs," Michael told her.

Kathy's shoulders slumped, and she looked out the window before nodding.

"Michael's told us some of what happened before Chloe disappeared," I said to Kathy. "But is there anything else you can remember? Even if you don't think it's important."

Kathy closed her eyes. "We had a fight," she said. "When she punched all the holes in the walls of her bedroom. She had already crashed my car, and I didn't know what to do anymore. I told her she would have to move out. She said that was fine, she would stay with her boyfriend. She said that he had a house down in Los Angeles—it belonged to his father, but his dad didn't use it anymore. A little cottage with roses in the garden. Stained glass windows and plenty of space. He knew lots of artists, people without money, and could take care of her."

The walls of the room stretched and contracted, and then everything seemed to snap back into place all at once. I felt my vision go black around the edges the way it sometimes did when I was having a panic attack. My heart was in my throat, and everything went all fuzzy—the noises around me were nothing more than a static blur.

"Rainey," Lola said. Her arm was around my shoulders. "Rainey, are you okay?"

"I need to step outside."

I stumbled past Michael, closing my eyes against the crazy room without gravity. I was going to be sick. I paused against the doorjamb for a moment before running down the hall and then down the stairs, taking them two at a time.

"Rainey!"

Lola was right behind me as I ran out the front door and leaned against the house, forcing myself to take deep breaths. When I felt the darkness recede and I knew that I wasn't in danger of throwing up, I lowered myself down to the ground and hugged my knees. I opened my eyes and saw Lola standing a few feet away, watching me with concern.

"I need you to write it down," I said. "Everything she said. The windows, the roses."

Lola nodded and took a small notebook out of her bag. She scribbled in it for a few minutes before tucking it away.

Michael and Kathy appeared in the doorway behind me. They both looked concerned.

"Rainey's feeling a bit sick," Lola said. "She gets migraines, and the heat makes it worse."

"Oh no," Kathy said. "Come inside, please. We'll get you some water."

Lola helped me to my feet, and we went back inside. I sat down as Kathy fussed over me, holding a hand to my forehead and filling a glass with water. There was a look in her eyes that I recognized, even though it had been a very long time since I had been on the receiving end: it was maternal warmth. Kathy's features smoothed and she seemed to take on a new confidence as she rubbed my back and I allowed myself to lean into her—just for a moment, only a moment—knowing all the while that it probably crossed a boundary that needed to stay intact in order for me to work for her.

When I started to feel a bit better, I stood up and thanked both Kathy and Michael.

"Can you give us the name of Chloe's roommate?" Lola asked. "We'll probably go talk to him first."

"Sure," Kathy said. She took out her phone and looked through the contacts, then went to a pad of paper and wrote down the information.

"We'll be in touch in the next few days," Lola said, accepting the paper from Kathy. "I'll draw up your paperwork and mail it to you for signatures. Call us if you have any questions or if there's anything you think we should know."

As soon as we had emerged from the house, Lola turned to me. "Are you okay? Do you want to sit down for a few minutes and have some water?"

"No," I said, squeezing her hand. "I just want to get out of here. Can you call a cab to take us back to the mechanic?"

Lola's eyes rested on my face for another moment, but I waved her concern away.

"It could be a coincidence," she said. "The boyfriend's cottage."

"It's not," I said. "The stained glass, the roses. It's exactly the same. We just have to prove that he took Chloe."

Finally, Lola nodded and took out her phone. "I'll call them right now."

While Lola spoke to a dispatcher and arranged a taxi, I wandered down the street and glanced up at the houses neighboring the Delmonicos' home. For the most part the houses adhered to the same modest form and color scheme: boxy double-storied homes in shades of peach and sand, coral and gray. Oxnard was a small coastal city, away from Los Angeles. People moved here to start families, to know that their children would be safe wandering the streets and coming home late. To have a child go missing despite the effort they had taken to make her safe must have been an unthinkable loss.

Like the Delmonicos, I knew what it was like to lose a family member. I knew what it was like to see your life come screeching to a halt and then stagnate for years as you wondered what had happened, if there was something you could have done. It had been a long time since I thought about my mother, since I wondered where she was, but driving past Malibu and seeing the untamed coastline had brought it all crashing back. There was something that I had refrained from saying to Chloe's parents, which was this: even if you found that missing part of your family, things almost never went back to normal. Sometimes you wished you hadn't gone looking for them at all.

"All sorted," Lola said, appearing beside me. "They'll be here in five minutes."

I could still see the concern on her face, and I laughed, then pulled her into a hug.

"I'm fine," I said. "Really."

Lola was quiet for a long moment, scanning the street in both directions. Beads of sweat appeared on the back of her neck, but she didn't seem to notice or mind.

"Do you think we should ask them about Ricky?" she asked.

"No," I said. "Michael didn't get a good look at the man in the car. We can't know for certain."

"He could have come around at other times," Lola pointed out. "It might be worthwhile to know if they recognize him."

I saw the taxi appear at the end of the street and raised my arm to summon it. "I don't think it's a good idea," I said. "Not yet. We don't have enough information, and if we give them a half-baked theory, they might go straight to the police. I think we should wait."

I was only twenty-six, but I had already lived two lives: the first part, neatly parceled away and almost forgotten, had consisted of summers in Malibu and trips overseas, the darkly hushed wings of concert halls and echoing backstage corridors. Both of my parents were artists—my father was a composer, while my mother painted and made sculptures that sold to private collectors who tucked them away like spoils of war in their second homes or vacation cottages.

Old family photographs show miles of beaches framed by cliffs, the sand marred by a single set of footprints. The summer we went sailing around the Adriatic, touching land only once for a dinner in Split. A foggy castle in Scotland, where I celebrated my ninth birthday, a cake borne aloft by two members of the staff. Thin wool jumpers and firelight, twilight games of croquet; a gilded life.

How long would it take for someone to notice that you were missing?

By the time I was twenty, though, I already thought of my life in terms of Before and After. Before was everything that happened in the years leading up to my fifteenth birthday—I was still playing violin, my father and I were still on speaking terms, my mother hadn't left us yet. After was when the police wrapped up their months-long investigation into her disappearance and concluded that there was nothing left to find. She had left everything in her bedroom, just as normal: keys, wallet, passport all in their correct places. The back door was left open, but other than that, it could have been any other summer afternoon. After was half the rooms in our house closed off, dormant in her absence. My father could never bring himself to sell that house because, even years later, he had convinced himself that she might come back.

How long would it take, Rainey?

There was a darkness in my family. I had seen snatches of it even before my mother disappeared—it showed up in quiet moments on lazy afternoons, when the wind pitched itself against the walls of the house and we locked ourselves in separate quadrants, existing side by side yet doing everything we could to avoid each other. It showed up in small acts of neglect and forgetfulness, like how my mother stopped attending my father's concerts, and then how he stopped asking her to come altogether. What an outsider would fail to see, had they looked in on our glittering, perfect life, was how we were each drowning in our own way. It took me years to realize how we had all existed as strangers and called ourselves a family. There were times when I went days without seeing either one of my parents, even though I was still in high school, even though we were all living under the same roof.

Would you come looking for me?

A year after my mother left, my best friend disappeared. I didn't talk about Alice, not anymore; it was too hard. When high school ended and I decided to forgo university, to stay in Los Angeles and spend my days trying to drink myself into oblivion, one of the only things that kept me alive was the chance, however small, that Alice might surface again. That we might find her. One year unfolded into the next, though, and she remained missing.

She had disappeared toward the end of August. Before she vanished, Alice and I had spent most of the summer together. We slept at each other's houses, borrowed each other's clothes, raided each other's fridges. She was the one who had held me when I cried about losing my mother. To lose her as well was a loss so great that I couldn't even begin to wrap my head around it.

Lola was one of the only people I had ever told about Alice. Everyone at my high school knew, of course; a brief notice had been sent out to all the staff and students at Edendale Academy apprising them of the situation (*our thoughts and prayers are with the Alder family*) but when I lost contact with all those people, I realized it was easier to stop telling people what had happened.

Part of the reason was that Alice had warned me that she was about to disappear, and I hadn't listened. I hadn't paid attention then, but over the next few years, I would parse out all the messages she had given me, searching each one for clues.

How long would it take for you to notice I was missing? she asked me, two nights before she disappeared.

Why do you ask these silly questions?

I want to know, she pressed, leaning against me. *How long would you look before you gave up?*

It was almost noon by the time we headed back to the mechanic to retrieve my car. I let my thoughts drift as we drove away from the Delmonicos' house, watching the suburban landscape slip by the window like a zoetrope.

"Rainey," Lola asked, pulling me out of my thoughts. "You okay?"

"Of course," I said. "Yes, I'm fine. Just distracted."

Lola knew almost everything about me, but I had never told her about that summer my family spent in Malibu. I couldn't remember that summer of salty clothes and rooms that smelled of seaweed without thinking of my mother bobbing in the waves, a dark cork tossed around in the water.

Every time I thought of her—the way she would come in the back door, toweling off her damp hair before smiling at me—I remembered a private wish that I had nursed that summer, a fantasy that sustained and sickened me in equal measure.

As much as I had feared for her safety, watching the waves to make sure she got back to shore, there was a part of me that prayed for her to disappear. I wanted her to get swept away by one of the undertows forecast on signs along the beach—SWIMMERS BEWARE—caught in a riptide so quickly that there wouldn't be the chance for me to shout, to go run for help. The fantasy never extended to the days afterward, when the emergency vehicles gave up their search for her body. It was unrealistic to think my father and I could coexist together in our big echoing house.

Later, of course, I got my wish, but not in the way that I had expected. My mother disappeared from our house one afternoon, on a June day much like any other. It was years after that summer in Malibu, and by then I had almost forgotten how much I had longed for her to drown. In the months after her disappearance the police couldn't find her, nor could any of the private investigators that my father hired to comb Los Angeles. Certain rooms of the house closed over her absence like scars. We tried to move on.

Ocean tides will eventually bring a body back to shore. Drowning is one of the most painful ways to die, but that horror extends to the family, as well: by the time a victim is found, their features have been bloated and decomposed beyond recognition, waterlogged and claimed in pieces by animals that live below the surface.

When I found my mother again, years after she disappeared, I remembered straightaway why, as a child, I had wished for her to disappear. She hadn't been stripped and scoured by the years away from our family; instead, she looked like she had been reborn. I was the weight that had pulled her under the surface for all those years. I was the thing she had to shed in order to live.

TWO

—⬡—

It was early afternoon by the time we hit the edge of Santa Monica. When the tangled knot of the roller coaster on the pier came into view, Lola turned to me.

"You wanna grab lunch before we head back to the office?"

"Can't," I said. I merged left to head into the tunnel that would keep me on the freeway. "I'll drop you off, then go straight to Echo Park. I might be able to catch him."

Lola drummed her fingertips on her armrest and glanced out the window. Convertibles and luxury SUVs streamed past, going well above the speed limit. When Lola didn't say anything for a minute, then two, I glanced over at her.

"What?" I asked.

"Nothing."

"Lo."

"What's your plan, exactly?" she asked. Her voice was careful. "Are you going to follow Ricky around all afternoon and hope he leads us to Chloe?"

I scratched my neck, irritated. "I just want to see what he's up to."

"Rainey," Lola said, shaking her head. "We have to do this the normal way. Talk to her roommate, former classmates, friends. If we make it personal, it's going to get messy."

"I haven't checked in on him for a while," I pointed out. "He has no reason to suspect that we might be onto him. If he's got Chloe hidden away somewhere, now's the time to strike."

For the last few years, Ricky had been keeping a low profile. I'd been watching him for nine years, and I knew almost everything about him—where he lived, where he worked, how he spent his mornings and evenings—but as far as I knew, he'd been keeping his nose clean. Sometimes months or even a year would pass before he did anything that held even a whiff of illegal activity. The Delmonicos didn't know this, of course, but I'd had good reason to believe that Ricky might have been involved in their daughter's disappearance, even before we had spoken that afternoon. If he was the one who had taken Chloe, though—and I had good reason to think he was—then the whole saga might finally be over. It would be enough to send him away for good.

Ricky was the kind of criminal who occasionally got arrested for small things—petty larceny, public intoxication, driving on a suspended license—but managed to stay on the police radar without raising any real red flags. There was a time when we ran in the same circles, even though Ricky was fifteen years older than me; in addition to committing minor felonies, he'd also come dangerously close to becoming a full-blown pedophile. I had heard from mutual friends that Ricky had molested high school girls when they were blacked out, but there was no solid proof, and without proof it was only maddening conjecture.

However, that wasn't why I was interested in Ricky. For the last nine years, I had been keeping an eye on him, following him and writing down observations about his routine, because nine years ago, Alice went missing after a party at Ricky's house. We were still in high school then, both seventeen years old, and we were both in a bad place in our lives. That was why I didn't think twice about going to Ricky's party, even though I didn't know him and he was already in his thirties. Alice and I both blacked out that night after mixing alcohol and a variety of drugs. When I woke up the next morning, Alice was gone.

"Rainey?" Lola was looking at me.

"Sorry, Lo, did you say something?"

"I hate it when you zone out while driving," she said. "It's like you shut down completely."

"I'm on autopilot," I said, reaching over to pinch her arm. "I love my car too much to crash. What were you saying?"

"You want to take lead on Chloe's roommate?" she asked.

"I'll do it tomorrow," I said. "I'm going to Echo Park first."

She furrowed her brow. "Fine," she said. "Just be careful, okay? And make sure to let us know if you get in any danger."

"Right-o, boss."

As far as I knew, Ricky had no idea that I had been trailing him for years. We moved in completely different orbits now, with very little overlap. I hoped that I was wrong about Ricky's connection to Chloe, of course; I wouldn't wish Ricky on anyone. The only reason I suspected Ricky might be involved in Chloe's disappearance was that I had spoken to one of Ricky's exes. She fed me tips when she could, even though she was putting herself at risk to do so; Ricky's wrath was focused and destructive.

When Chloe's face appeared on the four o'clock news, splashed across the cover of every newspaper in Los Angeles, she called me.

"I've seen her," she said. Her voice was strained. "Rainey, I saw her with Ricky. It was right before she disappeared."

I had only briefly hesitated before reaching out to the Delmonicos and telling them that we would cover their case pro bono. I said nothing about Ricky or my connection to him, though, partly because I couldn't guarantee that Ricky had their daughter. I didn't want to get their hopes up, either; there was no guarantee that I would be able to find Chloe.

—◦◦◦—

After dropping Lola off at our office in Culver City, I headed back out again. For the last year—ever since his ex-wife had kicked him out of their house—Ricky had been living in his mother's garage in Sherman Oaks. From what I had observed over that time, most mornings followed roughly the same pattern: Ricky woke at nine, spent the next hour smoking pot and half-heartedly lifting weights with the garage door open. Some of his poorly edited workout sessions ended up on YouTube. After a quick rinse in the shower, he schlepped his way over to his favorite café in Echo Park, where he spent the next three or four hours discussing philosophy and Big Ideas with other underemployed derelicts sporting patchy facial hair and stained clothing.

I was headed to the café now. There was a chance I had already missed Ricky—he normally left there by three—but I was relieved to see his car was parked in front when I drove past at three thirty.

Ricky drove a beat-up green Subaru. The car had a boat rack and bumper stickers boasting of camping, hiking, rugby, and trail running, but I knew this was a front: as far as I could tell, the most exercise he had gotten in the last year, other than his garage workouts, had been riding his bicycle around the neighborhood after a DUI had briefly curtailed his driving privileges. The car was one of many ways that Ricky advertised as someone much more capable and rugged than he actually was.

Ricky's preferred café, Article 19, seemed to attract mostly deadbeats and failed revolutionaries. The café was housed in a former crematorium and one of its claims to fame was that they made their rosemary focaccia in the same ovens that had once roasted bodies. The brick façade had been partially painted over with anarchist insignia, and the arched windows were papered with flyers touting political protests and something advertised as unvaccinated baby food. The chairs out front were nothing more than overturned milk crates clustered around tables made of plywood.

Ricky emerged from the café, chuckling to himself. The sight of him made my skin crawl, both from fear and a sense of loathing. While a stranger might pass Ricky and dismiss him as a once-athletic man whose vices had transformed him into something resembling a squashed Twinkie, I couldn't look at him without seeing his predilection for underage girls.

Ricky was a big man—tall and broad—with thick arms and the distended gut of a career alcoholic. His skin was taut, and poor circulation gave him a clammy appearance. Ricky was in his early forties, but his yellow hair had gone thin and brittle, aging him beyond his years. His bloated physique might have suggested poor health and sluggishness, but I knew that Ricky used his heft to his advantage: on more than one occasion I had seen him physically intimidate someone by standing over them and raising his arms a few inches from his torso.

Ricky scratched his stomach and said something to one of the men sitting at the outdoor table. The man reached into his pocket and produced a lighter. Ricky plugged a cigarette into his mouth and lit it, then leaned against the brick wall and inhaled. He was dressed like a college student—cargo shorts, a gray hoodie, oversized sunglasses—a look underscored by the fact that he wore socks but no shoes.

I peered through my windshield and kept an eye on him, but didn't want to risk being seen.

After finishing his cigarette Ricky tossed it in the gutter, then stretched his arms above his head, revealing a slice of white belly. He stood like that for a few moments before reaching beneath the table and retrieving his shoes. He slipped them on and waved goodbye to his straggle-haired compatriot before heaving himself back in his car. He gunned the engine and coasted down the street. I gave him ten seconds before I followed.

I trailed Ricky through Echo Park, passing bodegas and candy-colored houses with metal grates over their windows. Dogs lunged behind gates, barking at everything that passed. It was a beautiful day, and college-aged men and women strolled along the sidewalk, drinking iced coffee and smoking cigarettes.

Ricky turned up Douglas Street and we were suddenly in Angeleno Heights. This area was one of the oldest neighborhoods in Los Angeles, populated by stately Queen Anne, Victorian, and Craftsman-style mansions. There was something somnolent and lovely about the neighborhood.

The street had views of Downtown Los Angeles and the Echo Park reservoir, but otherwise this felt like a slice of antiquated Americana from a different century. I had visited one of these properties a few years ago because a friend was filming a movie in a house once owned by a real estate magnate from the 1800s. The place had four staircases.

Ricky parked at an angle in front of an address at the end of the block. The house was a mint-green Victorian beauty, three stories tall, with turrets and curved railings. It looked like an elaborate wedding cake, something plucked out of a Winsor McCay drawing and plunked down in the middle of Los Angeles. A wooden plaque hung suspended from chains above the front door, and on the plaque was a skull with a vine climbing out of it. Ornate gilt letters spelled out BONESEED. I couldn't imagine what business Ricky would have with whoever lived inside, and I almost felt like I should warn the occupant ahead of time—*Ricky is dangerous. He doesn't belong here.* I parked at a distance and waited for him to exit his car.

A few years ago, one of Ricky's favorite bars had been a place in Venice called The Alley. Venice was only a ten-minute drive from our office, and sometimes after work I would park near the bar and scan the street, looking for Ricky's car. He was there most nights, rolling up right at five o'clock, as though he had set a small goal for himself—*I will not drink before five o'clock, and therefore I am not an alcoholic.* Sometimes I slipped into the bar and watched him holding court at a corner table, hands shoved in his pockets, rocking back and forth on his heels and peering down at whoever was talking.

I didn't drink anymore—I quit after a few years of abusing alcohol—but The Alley was the kind of place I had once loved. It was dim enough that faces were reduced to shadowy contours, which lent the suggestion of anonymity. I didn't feel like an alcoholic when I went to these places because I could slip through the crowd, unnoticed: each night felt new. The Alley had its own clutch of regulars, and I got to know all their faces after a few months of watching Ricky lurch through the doors and order his standard drink, a Miller High Life. Sometimes I stayed long enough to watch him purge himself of his intake, from one end or the other, in the dank alley that ran alongside the bar.

Sometimes Ricky tried to pick up girls on these nights. He had a type—they all looked like Alice, with their slim waists, big eyes, and long hair—and I could tell that most of them were backpackers. His luck depended on how much they'd had to drink.

At some point Ricky got himself banned from The Alley, which I only found out after I went two weeks without seeing him there. I waited until a couple hours passed before I sidled up to the bartender and put on my best wounded look.

"I met this guy online, and he said this was his bar," I told the man, pulling up a picture of Ricky on my phone. "Have you seen him tonight?"

The bartender gave an unpleasant laugh and shook his head. "Yeah, he used to be a regular," he said. "Not anymore, though."

I tried to look confused. "You think he was blowing me off?"

"Fuck if I know. You want my advice? Keep your distance."

"But he seems really nice," I said, twisting a strand of hair around my finger.

"Yeah? You like guys who pick fights and can't finish them?" He slammed open the dishwasher and pulled out a tray of glassware. "I lost track of the amount of times Ricky started shouting at someone and then tried to hide behind the bar when they fought back. He's a fucking coward. I finally banned him because he called the police—from our phone—and asked them to come and arrest someone who was trying to beat him up. The fucking gall of that guy."

"Well, thanks anyway," I said, turning to leave.

"Seriously," he said, a warning note in his voice. "I've seen him take advantage of drunk girls more times than I can count. If I see it happen, I break it up, but I'm not always around, you know? Who else is going to watch after those girls?"

I left the bar that night feeling sick, telling myself once again that it was an illness, this obsession of mine. I managed to stay away from Ricky for three months before the bartender's words came echoing back to me—*I'm not always around. Who else is going to watch out for those girls?*—and then I was back at it. Ricky made things easy for me; his routine was standard in the way of the chronically underemployed—he sought out familiar places, places where he was recognized and safe. Article 19, for example, and a couple of bars in Sherman Oaks, near his mother's house.

For the last year I had been busy with other things, though, and only kept half an eye on him. This was the first time I had ever seen Ricky in this beautiful Victorian neighborhood, but it didn't bode well.

Ricky climbed out of his car and went sloping up the path toward the house with his long, uneven gait. I got out of my car, closing the door softly, then walked down the sidewalk to get a closer look at what was about to happen.

I watched as Ricky dug in his pocket and produced his cell phone, then started banging on the door.

"Travis!" he yelled. "Travis, open the fucking door."

Ricky pounded again. I felt a surge of hatred toward him then, a general revulsion roused by his cocky posture, by the slapdash way he dressed and conducted himself, by his rough voice.

"Travis!"

As soon as the door swung open, Ricky thrust the phone forward.

"This is for the courts, you fucker," he said. "I'm recording this."

It wasn't a bad idea. I took out my own phone and started recording the interaction. I could only see the snatch of a white face, a hand holding the edge of the door. Travis remained out of sight, and his response was too low for me to catch. Ricky stretched himself up to his full height and raised his arms a few inches to make himself look bigger. He swayed from side to side, menacing in his stature. The two men exchanged a few more words, all too quiet for me to hear, and then Travis slammed the door in Ricky's face.

"Where's my money!" Ricky roared. "Where's my fucking money!"

I dropped to the ground and hid behind a car, sensing that Ricky might spin around and leave at any moment. Sure enough, after a few more minutes of banging on the door without a response, Ricky finally gave up and headed back to his car.

This time, I didn't follow him. I had an idea of where he was headed, though—more often than not Ricky's afternoons were spent soaking up a large quantity of booze at his mother's house before he stumbled down the street to a nearby sports bar.

When I was sure that he was gone, I got in my car and drove away, casting one last look at the beautiful green Victorian. The façade gave nothing away—no curtains moved to indicate someone was watching the street, and once Ricky was gone, the neighborhood returned to its afternoon idyll.

My next stop was Mid City, where Ricky's ex-wife lived. Noa's house was halfway down a street lined with palm trees. The houses here were modest but well maintained, the lawns manicured green rectangles flanked by short driveways. Most of the houses were open to the street: no fences here, no towering hedges to shield the yards from view. The biggest concession to security was a few cameras over doorways.

I coasted to a stop half a block down from Noa's house, then leaned forward and narrowed my eyes, watching for movement inside.

When Alice had first disappeared, I went straight to the police and told them everything I knew: Ricky was much older; we were in high school; there was a chance we had been drugged.

The officer on duty had picked at her nails and sighed before raising her eyes to meet mine. "Did anyone force you to go to this party?" she asked.

"No," I said, after a beat. "But I'm only seventeen."

"You're not legal drinking age," she said. "So why were you at a party with alcohol?"

I flushed, ashamed. "That's not the point."

"I see girls like you every day," she said. "They get blackout drunk and do things they regret, then they come crying to the cops to fix everything. Let me give you some advice, sweetheart, and I'm really looking out for you: don't put yourself in that kind of danger."

"My friend is missing," I repeated, near tears.

She heaved a sigh and glanced over at her colleagues. "I'll take a report," she said. "But let me tell you something else: I've got three stabbings and a home invasion robbery to deal with. That's just this morning. Your friend getting sick from alcohol? Not my biggest priority."

The cops went by Ricky's house hours later, but there was no sign of Alice. I heard all about it from Spencer, who'd been the one to invite me and Alice to the party. Spencer was seventeen, too, but already seemed much older, more experienced. She could hold her liquor, was already an old hand at throwing back shots.

"Some idiot called the police," she told me later that week.

"Alice is missing," I told her, incredulous. "Don't you even care?"

She scoffed. "Why should I care? It's not like anything happened to her. She probably just turned her phone off."

It wasn't an obsession at first—I just started dropping by Ricky's house on days when I was aimless, looking for something to do. There were a lot of parties, I noted with some bitterness; Ricky clearly had learned nothing from the police visit. There were a lot of girls who looked underage, too, sitting on lawn chairs and drinking from Solo cups. I half convinced myself I would see Alice on one of these nights, but there was never any sign of her.

I could never quite shake the habit of tracking Ricky. Sometimes it felt like a game, or a sport, the way my adrenaline would spike when I saw him standing on his front lawn, smoking. I kept waiting for him to notice me, but if he did, there was no recognition. Other times it felt like an illness, almost an addiction. I knew I should forget Ricky and move on, accept that Alice was never coming back. Sometimes I would go months without driving past Ricky's house, then tell myself that I had gotten over the whole thing.

The longest I went without seeing Ricky was two years. I stopped by his house in North Hollywood one day and it was empty, with a For Rent sign hung up in the window. The loss was something I felt in the pit of my stomach: we no longer had any friends in common, because Spencer and I had stopped speaking years before. I had no idea where to find him or where to even begin looking. It felt like losing Alice all over again.

With Ricky gone—out of North Hollywood, or maybe Los Angeles altogether—I had to focus on other things. By that point in my life, I had already put distance between myself and my childhood, and I was trying to forge my own path by starting my private investigation firm. Being a licensed investigator gave me a lot of resources, including access to several online databases available only to registered PIs and police. One of the first searches I did once I registered was for Ricky, which is how I found out that he was still in Los Angeles. He was living in Mid City—that part didn't shock me—but he wasn't living alone. He had a wife, and she had given birth to their son, Taylor, six months earlier.

Noa emerged from the little blue house, tying her dark hair back into a ponytail. She was petite and slender, with large eyes and dark features. Most of what I knew about her came from my databases, but I had supplemented that with a few articles from the Entertainment section of the newspaper: she had been a lauded playwright in England before moving to Los Angeles to work in movies, which was where she met Ricky.

I sat in the shade across from Noa's house, watching her pick up stray toys from the lawn and tug some dying leaves from a lemon tree. She shaded her eyes and surveyed the garden, then wiped some sweat from her forehead with the back of her hand. There was a casual sensuality to the way that she moved, unselfconscious of being watched. She had been a dancer when she was young, and she still embodied the characteristics of someone who had studied movement. I had never actually seen Noa next to Ricky, but I knew from my research that there was a difference of a foot in their heights.

For the first year they spent in Los Angeles, everything seemed perfect on the outside, and I found myself hating Noa just as much as Ricky: she must be complicit in all the bad things that he gets up to, I convinced myself, or else she was an idiot. Noa became a kind of obsession for me, and I resented that she could live so happily with someone who—to me—was clearly a monster. Something within their marriage finally broke, though, the year before, which was when Noa threw Ricky out.

Noa sighed and scanned the street, turning to go back inside, then stopped. She had seen me. Her eyes narrowed, and she put her hands on her hips.

She was already halfway across the street by the time I opened my car door.

"Oy!" she snapped. "What the *fuck*?"

"Sorry, I'm sorry—" I tried to step out, but she blocked me, then leaned into the open car.

"What are you *doing* here?" Noa might have looked delicate, but she could curse a blue streak, and her anger was something to be reckoned with.

"Noa, just listen—"

Noa held up a hand to stop me. "Shut it," she said. "Do you have any idea what you look like out here? You're not as subtle as you think you are."

"We can agree to disagree—"

"Here's a tip," she said, blowing some hair out of her face. "Get a different car. You stick out like a sore thumb. Who drives a Datsun? Try a sedan. If you'd done your bloody research, you'd know it's the most common car in Los Angeles."

"Again, I think you're wrong—"

"Don't you ever check your phone?" She squinted at me.

"What?"

"I texted you," she said, glancing down the street. Her face was close enough that I could see the gold flecks in her irises. "Ricky's been watching the house, idiot. Do you ever check your text messages? Where were you this morning?"

I pulled out my phone and saw a string of texts from Noa.

11:42—Change of plans. Don't come. I'll meet you at the office.
11:45—Call me when you get this.
12:15—Rainey?
12:22—Seriously, he's watching the house. Not safe.

"Shit," I said, running a hand through my hair. "I'm sorry, Noa."

"Yep." She raised her eyebrows at me. "Lucky you, he took off around twelve thirty."

"I know," I said. "I just saw him in Echo Park."

"Article 19." She rolled her eyes. "So that's why you weren't answering your phone?"

"No, we were in a dead zone. Up in Oxnard. Bad service out there."

Her forehead creased. "Oxnard," she said. "Did you . . . did you go see the Delmonicos?"

"Yes," I said.

"Shit. That poor girl."

My friendship with Noa was something that I never would have imagined two years ago. I had spent so much time hating Ricky and resenting Noa for being with him that it never occurred to me that she might be his victim, too. I had worked in the film industry for years—one of our closest family friends composed music for films, and I was his assistant for a while—which meant it was only a matter of time before I crossed paths with Noa.

The first time that Noa and I spoke was at a fundraiser hosted by a film studio where I had worked in my early twenties. A mutual friend had grabbed my arm and brought me over to introduce me to Noa, and by the time I realized I was about to be face-to-face with a woman I had been casually stalking for a few months, I didn't have time to get away.

"This is Rainey Hall," my friend said. "Her family has worked in showbiz forever. Her grandmother was in films back in the twenties . . ."

But I couldn't hear the rest of what she was saying, because Noa had reached out a hand and took mine. I found that all the hatred I had been nursing for months was making it hard to breathe, and I stumbled away without managing so much as a simple greeting. Noa followed me and put a hand on my shoulder.

"Are you okay?" she asked. "You look white as a sheet. Maybe we should step outside . . ."

All I could do was stare at her. I saw something in her face shift then, and she looked uneasy.

"Hey," she said. "Do we know each other?"

"No, we don't." I tried to walk away, but she followed me again.

"Hey. *Hey*. Don't you walk away from me."

She grabbed my arm, and I whirled.

"Don't touch me, don't you dare touch me—"

"Why are you looking at me like we know each other?"

"I just told you—"

"Tell me," she said. She took both of my wrists in her hands and looked up at me. "Tell me."

"How well do you know your husband?"

The blood drained from her face, and she took a step backward. "Are you sleeping with him?"

"No—absolutely not—nothing like that," I said.

She smoothed out her dress and glanced around, then gestured toward a bench outside. "I think we should talk."

I didn't tell her about Alice, not then—that came later—but we spent the rest of the night talking. It turned out Ricky had a wandering eye, and he couldn't stay away from underage girls. Only a few weeks before, he had made a drunken pass at one of Noa's friend's daughters. It had been the last straw.

———

"We have to go," Noa said now, glancing across the street again. "Ricky could drop by at any moment. I'll just grab my bag. Hold on."

"Don't you have Taylor today? I thought that's why we were meeting at your house instead of my office."

Taylor was Noa's son. She still had split custody with Ricky, even though most of the time, he canceled on her last minute. It always left her scrambling to find a babysitter, and she'd had to abruptly call off work more times than she could count.

"No, my mum's got him," Noa said. "This is important."

She ran across the street and disappeared into the house. Her anxiety had gotten to me, and I found myself tapping my steering wheel, hoping that Ricky didn't make an appearance. As far as I knew, he wasn't aware of my relationship with Noa, but if he found out, everything could turn very nasty. Our relationship had gotten off to a rocky start, but she was a lot smarter than I had given her credit for, and she'd already made plans to leave Ricky.

Ricky had made it almost impossible for Noa to divorce him. He stalled on signing the paperwork, pitched fits in public, and threw up roadblocks at every step of the way. Noa lost most of her money in the process, but she got to keep the house. She had reluctantly agreed to split custody of Taylor, but the whole thing was a farce. When Ricky did make an infrequent appearance to see his son, he was late, or drunk, sometimes high. Noa and I had already forged a tenuous connection when she asked me to help her get full custody of Taylor. She also wanted a restraining order against Ricky.

"I can't pay you much," she'd said. "I'll give you everything I have, but it's not much."

"Don't worry about the money," I had reassured her. Left City occasionally did pro bono work, and Noa wouldn't be the first single mother we had helped out of a domestic abuse situation.

Noa had held up her hand to stop me. "I'm not asking for charity," she had said. "I have something you want. We can help each other out."

"What's that?" I'd asked.

She gave me a grim smile. "I'll give you Ricky," she'd said.

After a few minutes Noa emerged from the house, carrying a small leather purse and a pair of sunglasses. She locked the front door and scanned the street, then crossed over and slipped into my car.

"My office?" I asked.

"No," she said. "There's something I want to show you. Have you been to the Kloos Museum?"

"Off Beechwood Canyon?" I hadn't been there in years, but I knew the house quite well. My father had been friends with the woman who had owned it before the private residence became one of the most controversial museums in Los Angeles.

"That's the one," Noa said, slipping on her sunglasses.

THREE

‑‑‑‑⦅∞⦆‑‑‑‑

Noa didn't say anything until we had hit Wilshire Boulevard. Her shoulders relaxed and she leaned back against her seat, then turned and smiled at me.

"Fuckhead," she said. "He's such a shit."

"So Ricky's been dropping by the house again?"

"Yep. I saw him on Sunday with a notepad and a pair of binoculars. Moron thinks he's so smooth. I've had a security company drop by and look at installing some cameras."

"When did this start?"

"A few weeks ago. Not every day, but enough to keep me on my toes." She grimaced.

"Why didn't you tell me?" I blew some hair out of my eyes, annoyed, then drummed my fingers on the armrest. "That's why you hired us, isn't it?"

Noa gave me an expansive shrug. "I don't need a babysitter. No offense. And I'm not going to let him waste my time by tying my schedule up in knots."

"Do you think he knows?" I asked, glancing at her. "That we've been meeting up?"

She sighed and glanced out the window. This part of Los Angeles was all blocky buildings and parking lots, streaming lanes of traffic. I had an enduring fondness for the city, knew how complicated and beautiful it could be, but this kind of wasteland hollowed me out.

"I don't know," she said finally. "He's a moron, really; incredibly dumb. Every once in a while, though, he'll pick up on something. That's why I didn't want to meet at the house. I don't want to give him the *satisfaction*."

She punctuated the last sentence with a raised fist. I felt a surge of affection for Noa just then—she was only five-four, a petite woman with slender limbs, but she was tough. She turned her head and saw me smiling, then punched my shoulder.

"Ow! What?"

"What are you smiling at, you dope?"

I shook my head. "Don't take this the wrong way, but I can't believe you ended up with Ricky," I said. "You're so cool, and he's . . . he's such a loser."

She gave me an ironic smile. "You never made a bad romantic decision before?"

"Let's not go there." I grimaced, then glanced at her. "Yes. Of course I have. Let's leave it there."

"Fair enough."

"Hey, quick question," I said, remembering Ricky's visit to see Travis that morning. "Does the name Boneseed mean anything to you?"

She furrowed her brow. "Don't think so. No, it doesn't. What is it?"

"I just followed Ricky there," I said. "I wanted to see what he was up to. I know he's not going to lead me straight to Chloe, but I just wanted to see if his routine had changed. He drove over to this neighborhood of Victorian houses and got into a fight with someone."

Noa shook her head. "So what else is new? Believe me, if I hear anything, I'll tell you."

As soon as the ink on Noa's contract with Left City was dry, she started delivering information on Ricky. At first, it was just little things: Ricky was drinking too much and then driving under the influence, he was getting into drunken fights that sometimes led to violence, he sold a homegrown kind of pot without a license. None of it was large enough for us to present it in a package to the police, though—my team decided it was better to get something really big and keep Noa as a source until we knew that we could take Ricky down. If we went in for the small stuff, we risked Noa's access to information.

There had been other girls before Noa told us about Chloe. We had vetted all of them, made sure that they were of age, and kept an eye on things to make sure Ricky didn't hurt them. Other than that, there was nothing—legally—that we could do to interfere, because as far as we could tell, they were consenting adults. The whole thing felt dirty, though.

From what I could see, Ricky had never successfully held down a traditional day job. He had always been financially solvent, though, even during long periods of unemployment. That was a puzzle I hadn't managed to crack. For the last few years, he had run his own herbal supplements company called Hooks & Crooks, where he sold a variety of health pills and powders. A few years ago, he had even started calling himself Dr. Goff, although he had never been to medical school. At some point he had obtained a questionable mail-order philosophy doctorate from an institute in the Cayman Islands, which apparently gave him license to sign all his correspondences with the title of doctor.

Lola had always been cautious about diving headfirst into a relationship with Noa: we had worked with victims of domestic abuse before, and we knew how difficult it was for a victim to extricate themselves from that kind of relationship. Wasn't there a chance that Noa might change her mind, take Ricky back? There's no way, I had argued. Ricky had done everything he could to burn their relationship to the ground.

When Noa kicked him out of the house, Ricky sent out long email chains to all their mutual friends and acquaintances, lying about all the men that Noa had slept with and all the ways in which she was a poor mother. The email hadn't just gone out to friends, though: Ricky had cc'd staff from their children's school, Noa's colleagues, the head of her studio, and, inexplicably, a staffer at the mayor's office. The emails were long and deluded, full of inconsistencies, threats, and pleas for sympathy. They were horrifying in the way that late-stage untreated mental illness can sometimes be. Noa was never included on the emails, but she always received them regardless; the person who notified her changed every time. They were always horrified on Noa's behalf. Noa forwarded me each of these missives, and my colleagues and I had read them in disbelief.

We pulled up at a stoplight and I glanced at Noa.

"Any more of those deranged emails from Ricky?"

"Oh yeah," she said, with a dark chuckle. "I almost forgot. I've started applying for preschools, and Ricky sent this to the school. Have a look."

She passed me her phone so I could see the email.

To all reading this letter,

You may kno me as exhusband of a SLUT named Noa Cohen (former + still she did not change her name once wed). Noa with whom i have 1 son, with Noa cheating on me all the while,

This led to a lot of pain.

Both Noa + her man-hating mother made grievous lies against me being the kind which ruin reputations.

Meanwhile Noa sleeps w/ all male staff—(fathers too from the school more than once, also her boss)

Noa had NO reason to cheat NONE I am an excellent paternal figure + rolle model. For example i.e. see Martin Luther King Jr. also a father, prossucuted unfairly + only now understood to be free thinker ahead of his time.

Cordially Dr. Ricky Goff.

Noa watched my face for a moment before breaking into a wild cackle. "It's funny, Rainey," she said. "You can laugh. He's batshit."

"I don't think it's funny," I said.

"If you don't laugh, you cry."

There is a kind of solidarity that exists among victims of a common bully. I had spent years tracking Ricky and analyzing his movements, wondering how he could have gotten away with taking my friend, to the point where it sometimes made me crazy. I had tried to explain Ricky to a handful of people, like Blake, our other colleague, and Lola, but I could see from their dim incomprehension that I was alone in this endeavor. Until you had experienced a very specific kind of terror, you couldn't expect others to flinch in quite the same way.

That was why Noa and I had connected almost immediately: she knew inherently what it was like to feel vulnerable to a dangerous monster, someone intent on burning down everything she had worked so hard to build. Ricky might have seemed harmless because he was so stupid, but his stupidity was what made him relentless.

I had made my own poor romantic decisions in the past, so I didn't want to hammer her for sticking with him. I only asked her a few times what she had seen in him, and she had struggled to articulate it.

"Not all monsters start as monsters," she told me. "You may not want to believe it, but inside Ricky there are fragments of a good person, and that's what he showed me. Someone broken, someone who wanted to be good but kept fucking it up. I thought I could be the one to save him."

The road to the Kloos Museum was narrow and shady. Sunlight filtered down into the canyon through the trees lining the road—redwood, pine, and California oak. Every twenty feet or so the road bent back on itself to accommodate the nonsensical property lines that carved up the mountainside, and at intervals along the way I could see snatches of the palatial estates beyond. This part of Los Angeles was ultra-rich and exclusive in a way that other parts of the city were not: based on the remoteness of the location and the lack of parking, the neighborhood was mostly restricted to residents. Back in the 1920s, the first film barons had spent fortunes to build palaces up in this canyon, complete with golf courses, airstrips, and private cinemas. All the old gods were dead and forgotten now, their legacies packaged up and sold off. Most of the original properties had been carved up into smaller parcels decades ago, which their bankrupt heirs had sold off for millions of dollars.

"Why do you want to visit the museum?" I asked Noa.

She shook her head. "I'll tell you once we get there."

It had been a long time since I had visited the Kloos Museum. Noa couldn't have known this, but I had spent my childhood visiting the Shingle Estate, and I already knew the property inside and out. Esther Kloos had still been alive then, still living in the small bedroom where she had grown up. She was a slip of a thing, less than five feet tall, with a wispy fringe of white hair and enormous blue eyes. Esther had been one of the last vestiges of Old Hollywood, that golden era of Los Angeles when movies stars were regarded as deities, an untouchable breed separate from the rest of the human race. My grandmother had been one of them, an actress alongside women like Joan Fontaine and Barbara Stanwyck. I had never met her but my life had somehow been defined by her, because everything that my father did was carefully counterbalanced against his own childhood.

I reached the gates of the Kloos Museum and coasted down the drive toward the parking lot. The museum revealed itself gradually behind the stately oak trees that framed the yard. The Spanish revival house with its red terra-cotta roof tiles and wrought-iron balcony railings sent chills down my spine every time I saw it. The property felt frozen in time.

"Wow," Noa said, turning her head to look at the property. "Oh my god, it's so beautiful. Look at it! I feel like we're in a Billy Wilder movie!"

"Isn't it incredible?" I felt something like pride as we turned past a grove of citrus trees. I had climbed in these trees as a kid, skinning my knees against the rough bark.

"I've been wanting to come here for years," Noa said, craning her head to look around us. "I read about this place when I was still living in London. There was a photoshoot for *Vanity Fair*—I mean, it's one of the last old great houses from the twenties. And when they turned it into a museum, I thought, *Great, I'll go see it.* The last few years, though—I feel like I haven't had time to take a breath."

"This should be good, then," I said, parking my car. "I'm so glad you suggested it."

"You said you've already been here?"

"My dad was friends with Esther," I said. "The woman who owned it."

"Wo-o-ow," Noa breathed. "Lucky you."

"Maybe," I said, shrugging. "I didn't have a lot of friends my own age back then."

The house had been built by Esther Kloos's father, Jack Shingle. At the time, Jack had been one of the biggest stars in the world, one of the Famous Four, along with Buster Keaton, Charlie Chaplin, and Harold Lloyd.

While Charlie and Harold had managed to adapt and endure even after the advent of sound, Buster and Jack had fallen back into the shadows, unable to keep up with the times. Buster had died destitute, virtually forgotten, while Jack had retreated into the mountainside sanctuary that he had built with his movie fortune.

As Noa and I walked toward the entrance of the museum, I watched her take in all the details of the property: the gnarled olive trees clustered around a long, flat fountain; the statues peering out from between stands of cypress; the tennis court, long left to molder under the relentless sunshine. The Kloos property was a time capsule. I could almost imagine piling into a car with Douglas Fairbanks and Mary Pickford to head down to Hollywood Boulevard to attend their latest movie premiere.

"You must know about the controversy this place caused," Noa said, turning and raising her eyebrows at me. "I heard there have been death threats against members of the board."

"Really? Death threats?"

"Sure," Noa said, then shrugged. "People were talking about it at work. I'm sure it was a bit exaggerated, but when you drive up here and see all these gorgeous old houses with their miles of fences and hedge, you can't help thinking how much they'd hate for the public to come and infiltrate their little world."

I had still been working in the film industry when the museum had opened, six years earlier. Since Jack Shingle was a Hollywood icon and his house had been shrouded in an air of mystique for decades, the idea of a museum had been the topic of many conversations. I had heard snatches of it from various people. There had been a murder in the house, back in the seventies, which had contributed to the property's mystique. Oddly enough the details surrounding the murder had become convoluted and vague in their retelling, and while some Hollywood ghost tours drove past the edges of the Shingle Estate and spun out some version of events, the true story had become buried and vague next to the mansion's storied lore.

The ticket counter was held in what had once been a six-car garage. Above the garage were the former servants' quarters, where the butlers, chauffeurs, maids, and cooks had slept. Now the garages were one long airy room with white floors, white walls and a bank of floor-to-ceiling windows that looked out over Los Angeles. The long room was empty, save for us and the young woman behind the ticket counter.

"Two, please," I said, walking up to her.

The woman glanced up at me and smiled. Her dark hair was styled in a pixie cut, and her eyes were accentuated with winged eyeliner. She grabbed two museum programs and a map of the property, then handed them over along with our tickets.

"Forty, thanks," she said. "Unless you're a member?"

"No, I'm not." I handed Noa her ticket and program.

"Would you like to sign up? There are lots of members-only perks, like tours of the property and events every month."

"Oh yeah?"

"Black-tie festivities four times a year," the young woman said. "We've also started a true crime event every Halloween, with a fancy-dress ball afterward. And you can arrange private tours of the Shingle House, where you'll see rooms that aren't available to the general public."

"I will absolutely think about it," I told the young woman.

"We also have a special exhibit in the conservatory," the woman continued, pointing to a map on the counter. "It's just past the Living Library exhibit. In this room patrons are encouraged to interact with the art."

I was only half listening to her spiel, and it took me a moment to parse her meaning. "I'm sorry, interact?"

She smiled. "You can interpret that however you want."

"Is it . . . It's a room where you can touch the paintings? I'm not sure I understand."

She gave me a mysterious smile and shook her head. "It's not paintings," she said. "It's something else, but I'm not allowed to say. We like people to discover the room on their own."

I turned to Noa. "Do you know anything about this?" I asked.

Noa shrugged. "My colleagues were talking about it yesterday," she said. "But they wouldn't tell me what it was. Said it would ruin the surprise."

I opened the pamphlet. PARTICIPATE, read a bold headline. There was a brief history of the Shingle Estate and a summary about how the neighbors had tried to stop the museum from going ahead. I turned the page and saw a photograph of a man in a purple suit giving the camera a knowing look.

"Is this the artist?"

"That's Simon Balto," the docent said. "He's a guest curator this season. The museum did a big collaboration with him to shake things up."

Simon was somewhere in his forties, I would guess, with a single white stripe running along the left side of his dark hair.

"And the interactive exhibit was his idea?" I asked.

"Of course," the docent said, smiling and rolling her eyes. "Simon's a . . . Well, he's a character. He's the one behind the Living Library, as well."

"Just to be clear, when you say interactive . . ."

She glanced around before leaning in and giving me a conspiratorial look. "Well, we're not supposed to say more than that," she said. "Simon really wants people to be free to interpret it as much as they want. Most people just touch the exhibit and call it a day, but some of them write their names. One guy even took a shit in the corner. Sorry, I shouldn't swear. Simon was over the moon when it happened."

Noa stared at her. "He took a *shit*?"

The woman nodded, wide-eyed.

"Is it . . . still there?" Noa asked. "The shit."

The docent burst into laughter and shook her head. "Simon wanted to make a little plaque and put the turd on display, but the board stepped in. The entire exhibit's been decontaminated since then."

"Good to know."

"One more thing," she said, taking the map from my hands. "You're welcome to walk around the gardens. Restricted areas are marked off in gray. I probably don't need to tell you not to swim in the pool . . . oh! You might notice that the pool house is under renovation. We're going to have a special opening next month, and a top-secret exhibit is going to be announced then."

I thanked her, and Noa and I left the converted garage, then made our way toward the main house.

"True crime?" Noa asked, raising an eyebrow. "What's that about, d'you reckon?"

"There was a murder back in the seventies," I said. "You haven't heard?"

"I'm not a big fan of true crime," Noa admitted.

We entered the museum and stood admiring the spacious foyer, which was now the entrance hall of the museum. The museum renovations had included a restoration and waxing of the hardwood floors, which had been imported all the way from Venice. There was an oblong bloodstain the size of a dinner plate that they hadn't been able to get out, no matter how much they scoured the floors. The museum had covered the area with a rug.

I pointed to the spot where it had happened. "It was right there," I said. "In 1978. Esther shot her husband point blank one evening after dinner. It was two years after they got married."

"*No. Shit,*" Noa whispered. "Which caliber gun?"

I stared at her for a moment, stunned, then laughed. "Oh my god, Noa," I said. "Are you sure you're not a true crime fan?"

"A few years ago that might have horrified me," she said, her expression grim. "But now I can't help thinking, *I bet the fucker deserved it.*"

"Probably," I said. "I guess you'll have to come back to one of their true crime nights and find out."

We walked through the foyer, down a short hallway, and entered a long, low-ceilinged room that stretched along the entire eastern side of the house. This had been one of two dining rooms, designed to benefit from the morning sunlight, but I had never seen anyone eat in this room. The first time my father had brought me here—when I was nine—I had wandered into this room and found that it was full of props and old movie costumes.

Now the walls were adorned with modern graffiti that had been removed from the walls of old buildings slated for destruction. Brick walls and wooden beams had been arranged around the room, each showcasing a different type of tag. I had only been to the museum on the big opening night, and I hadn't seen the extent of the changes made to the house. Seeing it now was more than a little jarring.

"Thanks for coming," Noa said again. She glanced around the room as though to confirm that we were alone. "There's something I've been wanting to tell you, but . . . well, it's complicated. It's about Ricky."

"Okay." I waited.

"It's about Ricky's family, actually," Noa went on. "I told you that he had never known his father. That he was raised by his mother and stepfather."

"Right," I said. "You mentioned that his father was left off the birth certificate."

"Exactly," Noa said. Once more she glanced around the room. I was surprised to see that her hands were shaking—Noa wasn't an anxious person, at least not from what I had seen. "I'm sorry. Talking about Ricky always makes me nervous. *God*, I hate feeling this way. I thought I was past this."

"It's okay," I said, putting a soothing hand on her arm. "Really, Noa, we've got time. Don't rush."

It took a great deal of courage to ask professional investigators—and strangers, at that—to come in and rifle through your life, looking for dirt. Victims of abuse and stalking needed an additional layer of courage: they had already endured psychological warfare at the hands of someone who was supposed to care for them.

Noa broke away from me and exited the room. I followed at a distance as she moved through a long hallway that led into the former library, a spacious room with views out toward the San Gabriel Mountains. I had heard about the exhibit housed in this room, about all the controversy it had generated, but seeing it up close was a shock.

"The Living Library" was a display of human skin that was adorned with tattoos. After the death of the owners, the skin had been removed (with the owner's permission, naturally) and then stretched out over parts of a sculpture and put on display. Anyone who saw the exhibit without prior knowledge might have been able to view it dispassionately, at least at first—the displays themselves were not grotesque, but lovely in a strange way. The plaster figures were arrayed in different poses around the room: some were sitting to read a book, while others were engaged in what looked like an argument; one stood gazing out the window. Stretched across various parts of their bodies were those pieces of skin—some faded to matte, others bright and fresh, depending on how long the body had worn the tattoos before the owners died.

"I've read about this," Noa said, pausing before a sculpture of a young girl before a mirror. Her tattoo was wings that covered both shoulder blades. A small plaque next to each sculpture described how the tattoo's owner had died.

Marcy, twenty-eight, leukemia.

Noa was looking out the window. I followed her gaze toward the pool house. Sunlight glinted off the windows, obscuring the interior. The pool itself was a pristine rectangle of blue cut into the manicured lawn: roped off, now, of course. I could remember childhood swims there, so many years ago. I had even brought Alice; she was the only friend I had ever introduced to Esther. Back then the lawn had been tidy, but the garden was rambling—Esther had reduced the number of staff to a skeleton crew, and the roses and fruit trees were left to their own devices.

The pool cleaner had still come once a month, even though Esther never swam.

"Do you know what happened to Esther?" Noa turned to look at me. "After she shot her husband—did she go to jail?"

"She was convicted, but only with justifiable homicide. The sentence was a slap on the wrist—six months of house arrest." I kept my gaze on the pool.

"Only six months? That's incredible, for the time period. She must have had good connections."

"He was abusive. He had been abusing her for years. She called the cops on herself right after she shot him and told them exactly what had happened."

Esther had never again set foot outside the Shingle property after the trial. For thirty years the only people she saw were her father's old friends—Bette Davis, Lillian Gish, Barbara Stanwyck, and others. They would come to the Shingle mansion and reminisce about old times, while away the hours sitting in the library. And as the years passed those friends began to die, and for a while Esther only saw the household staff. The butler lived in the old staff quarters, as did the gardener. The cook came in three times a day to fix her a meal. Esther began to seclude herself even more, though, and there were long days when she saw no one.

And then one day, my father came to the house. His mother had worked with Esther's father during his short period of directing movies in the 1940s. Esther had known my father as a boy, before she got married. Once, they had spent an evening playing croquet, and when Esther hit her ball into the pool, he waded in and retrieved it.

I was six the first time my father took me to the Shingle mansion to meet Esther. The property was almost shabby, worn-in and tired in the way of old money without outside interference. Esther had become cautious about letting strangers into her house, but she remembered my father, remembered him as a young boy, and we started making regular visits to see her.

For years I only thought of Esther as an eccentric old woman who lived away from the rest of the world, caught up in her silent world of memories and movie props. She was always kind to me, perhaps a bit childlike at times. Her father had kept the world at a distance, and as a result, Esther had grown up with a sweet kind of ignorance about what Los Angeles had become. I didn't find out that she had killed her husband until I was thirteen years old, which was the year I started school at Edendale Academy.

Since both of my parents worked full-time, Esther was a convenient alternative to a traditional babysitter. If my father had any reservations about leaving me unsupervised with a woman who had killed her husband and openly acknowledged it, he never shared those doubts with me. In any case, I never felt unsafe with Esther, not once. It was also a nice way for me to get a glimpse of my father's childhood and where I had come from. It was hard to separate the memory of those years from what the home had become since the conversion to a museum.

Noa turned to me, and it looked like she was about to say something, but just then, there were footsteps and voices at the end of the room.

"It's down here, I think," a woman was saying, and I turned to see a trio of young people who might have been art students, the way that they were dressed. Two young women and a man with green hair.

"Don't embarrass me, Charlotte," the man said, then giggled.

"The point is to make a scene," the second girl replied. "You're going to love it, Hugo."

I remembered that the interactive exhibit was at the end of this hallway, beyond the heavy pair of doors. Noa and I watched the students as they moved through the library without even glancing at the tattoo exhibit. The young man opened the conservatory doors and then the three of them disappeared inside.

Noa glanced at me, and now that we were alone, I wondered if she would tell me what was on her mind. Instead, she cocked her head toward the conservatory.

"Should we have a look?" she asked.

"Sure, I don't mind."

The conservatory had once housed African violets and enormous ferns brought back from South America. Now, though, the entire room had been stripped and painted white. The room was bare of furniture or decoration, and at first, I wondered if we were in the wrong room, if the interactive exhibit was elsewhere. The only thing there was a young woman in a smock seated before an easel. A thick braid hung down her back, nearly waist-length. She was diligently painting, ignoring the three art students who stood over her shoulder, watching.

I felt uneasy. The whole thing felt meta and performative, and I was aware that no matter what we did, we were probably going to fulfill some expectation of the man who had engineered this exhibit.

The art students looked nervous but oddly excited. The young man pushed one of the women forward, toward the artist at the easel.

"*Don't*, Hugo!"

"It was *your* idea," Hugo replied.

"Just touch her," the other woman suggested.

Hugo stepped forward and grabbed the artist's shoulders, then started massaging them. He looked nervous and yet thrilled at his own audacity, and the pair of young women burst into laughter.

"*I* could use a massage," one of Hugo's friends remarked. She suddenly stepped forward and took a pen out of her pocket, then scribbled something on the canvas.

Noa looked stunned—her mouth dropped open, and she clasped her hands—but the artist at the canvas didn't react. She kept painting, unperturbed.

The second female art student stepped forward and poked the artist. There was no reaction. She poked her again, and then pinched her.

"Charlotte," Hugo warned.

"*What?* It says that the exhibit is interactive," she said.

"She's right," the other student chimed in. "Watch this."

She took a pair of scissors out of her bag and then advanced on the artist. After hesitating for a moment, she grabbed the end of the woman's braid and snipped off a tiny section.

"Hey!" I shouted, then moved toward them.

The three art students looked as though they had been caught in the act, scared, but the painter at her easel might as well have been alone. She still had not broken her rhythm of painting.

"What are you doing?" I exclaimed. "Back off!"

The art student with the scissors folded her arms across her chest and scowled. "It's an *interactive* exhibit," she said. "We're *allowed.*"

"You're allowed? Just because someone gives you permission, does that entitle you to harm someone else?"

"She didn't *harm* anything," Hugo said, stepping forward.

"No?"

"Look at her," he said, pointing to the seated painter. "She's fine."

"How do you know?"

The young woman with the scissors laughed. "You're obviously not an artist," she said. "The purpose of art is to challenge people. To get people out of their boxes. It's not always safe."

"Come on, Rainey," Noa said quietly. "Let's just go."

"Yeah, *Rainey*," Hugo chimed in. "Maybe you should just go."

"I don't think we should leave them alone in here," I said, glancing at the painter at her easel. She still hadn't shown any sign that she was aware of our presence. The whole thing felt rotten, haunted.

"I need to get out of here," Noa said. Her voice was a low, panicked murmur, and I remembered that my first duty was to her, to my client. This was a museum, after all; surely there were safety precautions in place to make sure things didn't get out of hand.

"Okay," I said finally. "Okay."

I followed Noa back through the Living Library and the foyer, then outside, back into the sunshine. Her eyes fluttered, and her breathing was shallow. She looked like she was on the verge of a panic attack. I was alarmed; in all the months that we had known each other, I had never seen Noa like this.

"Let's sit down," I said, guiding Noa toward a bench in the shade. It took a few minutes, but she finally seemed to get her breath back.

"Are you okay?" I asked.

"It's sick," she said. "I know it's art, but that whole thing was sick."

"I agree," I said.

"It's manipulative, that's what it is. No matter what our reactions are, whether we act out or feel disgusted or scared, they win."

"Who wins?"

She waved a hand. "I don't know. The guy who set this up. The museum."

I nodded, hesitated. "You mentioned there was a reason you wanted to come here," I said. "Can I ask why?"

She was quiet for a long time. "They're about to open the pool house again," she said finally. "They've got a big event planned for next month."

"Yes, the woman at the front desk mentioned something about that."

"There's a big donor," she went on. "He's been kept anonymous, but they're going to reveal who he is at the opening. They're naming the wing after him."

"I see."

Noa turned to me. "The donor is Ricky's dad," she said finally. "The one they left off his birth certificate. He was . . . well, he is really famous. He's a musician, and he was married when Ricky's mom got pregnant. He's been paying her off this whole time."

It took me a moment to connect what she was telling me.

"That's why I asked you to come here," she continued.

"The dad?" I asked. "Can you tell me who he is?"

"I didn't want to lie to you. You have to understand that. I'm really scared of the whole family, you see. There's all this money . . . But when I found out about *this*, about the museum . . . it's just too much. He's parading around like he's a philanthropist, and in the background, he's funneling money into his son's bank account. That's how Ricky can afford to stay unemployed. He's getting money from his biological father."

I waited.

"It's Laszlo Zo," Noa said. "From Dogtooth. The main singer?"

I became aware of a faint ticking sound, softer than the sound of nails on glass, something methodical and persistent; it must have been there all along, but I had only just noticed it then. It was a *tick-tick-tick-tick-psssst*, and all of a sudden, I couldn't hear anything else.

"Do you hear that?" I asked Noa. Then, not waiting for her response, I stood up and glanced around, looking for the source of the noise.

"Hear what . . . ?"

I scanned the yard, glancing past a pair of workers who were massaging the roots of a sick tree. Beyond them and out by the pool house were two women in black carrying a long box into the recesses of the building. A trio of women stood next to the swimming pool and peered into its depths. I imagined my father as a boy of eight, rolling up the hems of his pant legs to retrieve a croquet ball for a timid young woman dressed in blue silk.

Laszlo Zo. It was a name you couldn't escape anywhere in the world: as an international rock star from the 1970s, his moniker was recognizable even to those who had no familiarity with his music.

The ticking continued, and then I spotted it.

"It's the sprinklers," I said. "It's so loud. I can't believe I didn't notice them."

"Sprinklers . . . ?"

I rubbed my temples. "I'm sorry, I didn't mean to change the topic," I said. "It's just—Ricky's father. Are you absolutely sure? Laszlo Zo? He's one of the most famous musicians in the world. You said Ricky lies a lot."

"I thought he *was* lying when he told me," Noa said. Her voice had taken on a low, feverish quality. "It was after we had broken up for the last time. I thought he was just trying to get the upper hand. But it made sense—his father had always been this shadowy figure in the background. There were all these anonymous cash gifts when Ricky was growing up, and he went to this really expensive private school that Serena would have never been able to afford. She's just a receptionist at a law firm. The wonder is that Serena managed to keep the whole thing secret for so long. I've never met a bigger narcissist in my life."

"So, Serena and Laszlo . . ."

"She was a groupie. Back in the day, when Dogtooth was touring all over. She followed them. She was *obsessed*. You think fans now are bad, Jesus." Noa rubbed a hand across her face. "I saw them together. A few months ago. Laszlo was at Serena's house. I'd come over to pick up Taylor, and there he was."

All of a sudden, I felt exhausted. Noa turned to me with a pleading look on her face.

"I'm sorry I didn't tell you about this before," she said. "I've been scared of everything for the last few years, and I had to be sure I could trust you."

"I'm not angry," I reassured her. "I understand better than you think."

"If Laszlo is giving Ricky money, I can't fight him," Noa said. "He can pay for lawyers; he can get this whole custody case thrown out . . ."

"No, it's a good thing," I said. "There's a reason why Zo has kept this relationship secret for the last forty-odd years. Having a love child is one thing. It's an entirely different thing, though, when your offspring is a sociopath who goes around ruining people's lives."

We both sat there without speaking for a long time. To an outside observer we might have appeared like two old friends with nothing more to say, just enjoying the peace of a quiet afternoon. We were still sitting there when the trio of art students left the museum, laughing bawdily and snapping pictures of each other. One of the women brandished something above her head, looking triumphant. I narrowed my eyes to see what it was, and when I realized what I was looking at, my blood ran cold. She was holding the braid of the artist in the PARTICIPATE exhibit, and judging by the length of what she held, she had taken the whole thing.

FOUR

One of the only photos I still have of Alice was taken in my bedroom a week before she disappeared. She's lying on my floor, her legs up against the wall, shading her eyes against the sunlight streaming in through my window. You can't see her eyes, but she's smiling, her long blond hair fanned out on the floor behind her. It was an afternoon in the middle of August, when the last of the fires had finally died down.

I kept the photo even though it was the last known photo of Alice, and the police had asked me to hand over anything that could help them in their investigation. There were two reasons I didn't surrender it, even though I wanted desperately for them to find my friend: the first reason is that nearly everything Alice was wearing in the photograph was stolen, from her earrings down to the faded Henley regatta polo shirt riding up over her stomach. The second reason was that I had always blamed myself for letting Alice disappear, and I wanted to make sure I remembered what had happened to her.

During our last summer together we climbed onto my roof at night and watched as the wildfires moved closer to the city, claiming first the hills outside Sunland and then moving south, toward Altadena. Alice and I had driven down to Altadena a month before, at the beginning of July. The ruins of an old Victorian hotel sat on top of Echo Mountain, a little way outside of town. A hundred years before, women in starched pinafores and men in dark suits had taken trains to the highest ridge, where even now you could see pieces of the old railroad. From down in the valley below, the white hotel must have looked like something floating in the clouds, visible for miles around. The whole resort had burned down decades before, and now the only thing that remained were steps leading up into the sky and the foundation of the old tennis court.

"What would you save?" Alice asked me, late one night when we couldn't sleep. We had skipped dinner and foraged instead for snacks in the cupboards, tins of sardines and stale rosemary crackers from a dinner party weeks before. I liked to watch Alice eat because she wasn't self-conscious about it: she lifted each fish out with two fingers and dropped them into her mouth.

"What do you mean?" I asked.

"When the fires reach Los Angeles," Alice said. "What would you save?"

"I don't want to think about that," I told her. "Not yet. Can't we talk about something else?"

Alice was my best friend, but sometimes I wondered why she had chosen me. Over the last two years, we had become almost inseparable, but there were marked differences in our characters: Alice was sunny, sweet, striking me as almost naïve, while I was moodier and prone to cynicism. During our last summer I finally started to see how she was damaged, and how what I saw as cheerful ignorance was actually a studied façade.

"I would save you." Alice leaned her head against my shoulder and sighed. "I'm scared, Rainey. Sometimes I feel like you're the only one I have left."

The wildfires had threatened LA for most of July, and they showed no sign of abating. At first, they were a footnote on the news, bracketed between bigger local news: a merger between Hollywood studios, a celebrity divorce, a surprising conclusion to a string of murders in the Silverlake neighborhood. The fires magnified things that were already emblematic of summers in Los Angeles: heat and smoky skies, apocalyptic prophecies, and bad traffic. As the fires worsened, though, normal traffic became an exodus—out, away from the city, away from the fires. Alice and I stayed behind.

"You don't have to think about that yet," I told her. I wrapped my arms around her and kissed the top of her head. "I'd never let anything happen to you."

The fires raged for six weeks before dwindling down to soot and ash, but the smoke lingered for another week before finally clearing away to reveal blue sky. I've blocked out a lot of the summer Alice disappeared, but there are certain things I still remember.

The first thing I remember is how I couldn't stop coughing, because the air was so smoky. I felt like I couldn't draw a breath. I remember the dead coyotes found around the lips of swimming pools, their legs splayed as though they had died running. There were other animals, too, the dead deer and the birds with singed feathers found at the bases of trees, the raccoons and mountain lions that had come crawling out of the hills as they burned.

It was the summer of chlorine, of days where we spent listless hours in my pool to stave off the heat from the fires. At night you caught glimpses of flames in the mountains, far away but still close enough to scare. It was the summer of insomnia. I slept with my windows open even though the smoke got in, because everything about my empty house gave me claustrophobia. I couldn't stand the feeling of being locked in. Caged.

It's easy to forget now, looking back, but Alice and I were still in high school when all of this happened. We were both alone that summer, left mostly to our own devices because our parents were gone, but that had nothing to do with the fires.

Alice's mother was in the hospital after overdosing on benzos (prescription and black market both) and mine had left a month before. My father was working abroad, and hers had passed away two years prior. We had no one to call us to account and there were entire days when we didn't see anyone except the delivery drivers who came to my door with Thai food and pizza. Summers were always lonely for me, and yet I was never really alone—twice a week a woman named Elizabeth came to clean the house, and sometimes we had short conversations about her children and her husband. There was a pool cleaner and a gardener, too, but they were contractors for an agency and I never learned their names because they worked on a rotating roster.

While my life that summer was populated with a temporary cast of characters, Alice had Monica. Monica had been hired to look after Alice and her brother, Cameron, when they were young, and then stayed on as a kind of household majordomo to do everything from restocking the pantry to hiring someone to look after the rambling garden.

After Wendy overdosed, Alice started sleeping at my house all the time, and when we couldn't sleep, we drove down Mulholland to go to the all-night convenience store for cigarettes. There was a haunting beauty to the endless sunsets, the sky saturated with a smoky blur from the fires that lit up in shades of vivid orange, offsetting the city's terror with a kind of dumb beauty. It was the summer when I started finding small ways of hurting myself.

Even though Alice and I were both sitting on our own kind of trauma, there was a lingering innocence to the way that we conducted ourselves. We didn't go to many parties or stay out all night doing drugs, waking up on a beach with strangers. We kept to ourselves. It was a privileged kind of exile, easy enough to spot in retrospect; of course, neither of us could appreciate our situation at the time. Back then we both felt abandoned, unwanted.

What would you save, Rainey?

The feeling of abandonment was amplified by the vacant houses all along my street. Many of my neighbors already left each year for holidays abroad, but with the fire warnings and smoke in the sky, anyone who could leave the city did so. For Alice and me, that last summer was a kind of purgatory without distraction. We had no school routine or outside interference to draw our thoughts away from the truths we would rather not face: my mother had left and was not coming back, and we both knew without saying it that Alice's mother was going to die.

Whenever I try to go back and pinpoint the part of summer when things took a turn for the worse, it starts with Spencer. Before that summer I wouldn't have called Spencer a friend, and if we ran into each other outside of school, I doubt we would have acknowledged each other. Alice was the one who first reached out to her in a gesture of friendship. They crossed paths one afternoon in the middle of July at the hospital when Alice was visiting her mother. Spencer claimed that she had been visiting a friend, but later we found out that wasn't true: ever since a previous stint in rehab, her father had made her see a doctor once a week to get tested for drugs.

Later that day, when Spencer visited my house for the first time, she tied her hair up into a loose knot and then strolled from room to room. She picked up items and set them down again, ran her fingers along the countertops, and opened windows. She dropped into a chair and smiled at me. A wolf smile.

"Don't you get so *bored* in this great empty house of yours?"

The prevailing image I have of Spencer—the one which comes to mind now, when I remember her, as much as I try not to—is of her sitting on a window ledge, one foot on the sill, about to step over the edge. She was stunning, with freckles and long, light brown hair, sharp cheekbones, and long legs. She could have been a model, or an actress, but instead Spencer was an artist, which fit her lineage: her great-grandmother, Edith Frances, had been one of the most famous female artists of the last century. There was a carelessness about the way Spencer did everything, an attitude that suggested she held nothing sacred, and that philosophy carried over into her art as well. There was no denying that Spencer had real talent, though: as early as sophomore year she had been scouted by representatives from art schools in New York. Spencer's work reminded me of Edvard Munch, especially the way his subjects were reduced to blurry caricatures. Spencer's paintings featured the same haunting imagery, but most of the faces she created were mere whorls.

Our school, Edendale Academy, was one of the most exclusive private schools in the city, and all of our classmates came from backgrounds of privilege, but even so, there was something about Spencer that made her stand out. Still, I can't remember seeing her with a single friend, not until she joined us. There was a fierce independence about her, something that made me ache to know her. She possessed an understated cool that empha-sized her every gesture: she arrived at school each morning in her topless vintage Jeep—a car she had restored herself—with her hair pinned up in chopsticks, a vintage leather jacket slung over one shoulder.

The first time Spencer went to rehab was in sophomore year of high school, but of course, we hadn't known that then. Even though Spencer and I had shared most of our classes for the two years before we started hanging out, we had never mixed socially, and I had no idea of the private hell that she was going through. For the most part everyone seemed to believe the fiction that she had taken a leave of absence in order to pursue her art.

She was gifted academically but always seemed to be in trouble—with teachers, with the administration, whether it was over grades or her attitude problems. Still, Spencer's grandmother had founded the school, and with her dad on the school board, she never got kicked out. There were at least three occasions when Spencer missed a week of school because she had art lessons, a private fellowship, or the chance to study with a professional mentor. Or that was what we were told. Later, when I visited Spencer in the hospital, I felt stupid for allowing myself to believe the lie when there were obvious indications that Spencer had not been well for a long time.

One day the three of us spent the whole afternoon swimming at my place. Spencer emerged from the water and wrung out her hair with both hands, then glanced up at my neighbor's house.

"Who lives there?" she asked.

"An opera singer."

"Is she home?"

"She left because of the fires," I said, then added, "All the smoke."

"Bad for the lungs," Spencer agreed. She sighed and sat at the lip of the pool, resting her chin on one knee. She reminded me of a Maxfield Parrish painting then, dream castles and rocks in sunlight, women in profile kneeling by the water. She was quiet for a long moment, thoughtful, and then glanced up at me and smiled.

"So how well do you know that neighbor of yours?"

That summer Spencer taught us how to scale security fences and pick locks when necessary, or else climb through windows. We practiced walking on the balls of our feet so we wouldn't make a sound, because on one occasion we had been sloppy in our reconnaissance and found that a family had returned early from their summer vacation. We had walked into a master bedroom and found the homeowner sprawled out across the mattress, deep asleep.

Spencer was also the one who introduced us to alcohol. A simple statement, that, but if my life were laid out as a topographic map, Spencer's introduction into my life would appear as a rift, a gouge, a deep canyon between two parts. I wanted to blame her for a long time—and indeed, I did—but the fact that I took to drinking so easily indicates the disposition was already there. Any scientist examining the same map of my life could read the saddles and peaks, the tight contour lines of all the trauma that had come before. We didn't drink, and then we did. Alice sipped, while I took harsh slugs. I can still picture it now, those dark nights of Spencer walking through a dark kitchen, her fingers trailing along the bottles of drink. The clinks as they knocked against each other.

If any security footage exists from that time—blurry stills of three girls dressed in hooded sweatshirts, walking through expansive gardens and peering into windows—it hasn't surfaced yet. Most of the things we took that summer were small, anyhow, not enough to warrant a police investigation. At first, we only took things that nobody would miss—a small vase from one house, a pair of cheap earrings from another. Souvenirs, really, to remind us of where we had been. Later Spencer started stealing things of real value—jewelry, pieces of art—but in the beginning, everything seemed innocent enough.

For a long time, I told myself that I had only gone along with them because I was protecting Alice, because I knew that she was vulnerable and wanted to make sure that she didn't get hurt going along with Spencer. Now, though, I'm not as eager to let myself off the hook so easily: despite my mistrust of Spencer, she was right—I *was* bored in my big empty house. Spencer was many things, but she was never boring.

Those evenings always started the same way: Spencer's car idling in my drive while I pulled on a pair of dark jeans and tied my hair back. Spencer always picked me up last, and we always took her car, the vintage Jeep that hummed through the dark streets like something uncaged. Those nights were often unpredictable, but some aspects did not change: Spencer drove, and Alice rode in the passenger seat. I sat in the back. Some nights we went to as many as three different houses, moving with a kind of tactical efficiency that might have seemed choreographed.

Oddly enough, the biggest houses almost always had at least one door that was unlocked: once you got past the security gate, that was it, you were in. We would slip past the gates and up the long drive, past the empty guard cottages that were mostly for show. Sometimes the houses had alarms, and in those situations, we would leave right away. Spencer always seemed to know when it was safe to open a door or if it was better to climb in through a window. She knew which security cameras were genuine and which ones were just to scare away burglars.

As the weeks passed Spencer grew bolder, filling her pockets with things of obvious value. Alice was more modest, rifling through closets and scooping up vintage T-shirts. The most I took was stationery and pens, tiny rebellions to remember those nocturnal ramblings. Persephone and her pomegranate seeds, thinking herself immortal even as she sowed the seeds of her own destruction.

That I didn't question why Spencer—someone who had everything, or at least the appearance thereof—would feel the need to break into houses and steal things says just as much about my character as it does about hers. It never occurred to me that on all those nights of walking down moonlit hallways and traipsing through dark gardens, we were looking for something.

The very last house we visited that summer was in Holmby Hills, but I didn't know where we were going until we had already arrived. I was in the backseat of Spencer's car, sans seatbelt, my legs stretched out on the seat beside me. I liked to close my eyes and let the night air wash over me. Riding in the back of a car with no conversation reminded me of being a kid, of all the times my parents had taken me out on day trips.

That night I didn't sit up and start paying attention until we had stopped in front of a security gate. That should have been the first sign that something was different: Spencer knew the code to get in. Neither Alice nor Spencer seemed fazed by the security camera that tracked our progress as we followed a long, snaking driveway through a corridor of trees and finally pulled up to the back of a sleek modern mansion, all white walls and glass.

"Wait," I said, when Spencer opened her door. "Hold on."

"Oh god, what?" Spencer gave an irritated sigh.

"This doesn't feel right." I felt anxious, frightened, and like someone might be watching us. "Let's just go."

"I told you," Spencer said, with exaggerated patience. "I've checked it out. They're not home. They're overseas. We're fine."

"Alice, please don't go in there."

"Stay in the car, Rainey," Alice suggested. Her voice was light. "We'll only be a few minutes. You don't have to come."

"Why don't you make yourself useful and find us something to eat?" Spencer asked. "I'm fucking starving."

"She doesn't have to come," Alice said. "Really, Rainey, stay in the car if you want."

But of course, I didn't stay. I followed Spencer and Alice through the dark hallways of that house, peering into each room in turn. In all the photographs from that summer, Spencer and Alice look like siblings, with their long hair and golden skin, whereby contrast I was the dark sibling, my pale features and dark hair, my wide eyes, and solemn features. I had always felt separate but never more so than in that moment.

We slipped into the house through the door leading onto the patio. I walked through the downstairs kitchen and started piling together items for a picnic—smoked oysters and sundried tomatoes, crackers—while Spencer and Alice disappeared upstairs. One of our rules was that we didn't turn on lights or even use a flashlight, because while a homeowner might not be paranoid about locking their house, nothing looks more suspicious to a neighbor than seeing a flashlight move through a dark property.

It was four days after the mayor had gone on the news to say that the last of the fires threatening eastern Los Angeles had been extinguished; we no longer had any reason to fear. The smoke that had lingered in the sky for weeks began to dissipate, and all over the city people began to leave their windows open to air out the smell. My father was about to return to Los Angeles. I was thinking about school, which was starting up in a few weeks.

If I had known who the house belonged to, I never would have gone. It was too risky, too stupid. The property was covered in security cameras, but the man who owned the house wasn't the kind of person who reported to the police.

I could hear footsteps upstairs as Spencer and Alice moved about in the darkness. There was an exchange of words, an undercurrent of tension. I moved through the pantry and found a bottle of whiskey, unscrewed the top, and took careful sips as I moved barefoot down the hallway, exploring.

In the end, I found what we were looking for in a small study overlooking the swimming pool. At this point I could no longer hear my friends; either they had stopped fighting or else the sound of their voices was simply muffled by the distance between us. I took another swig of whiskey and then turned around and saw it.

The painting was of a woman standing at the mouth of a tunnel. I was already drunk but I knew that there was something horrible about the image in front of me, about the perspective and the blurry edges and the way that I couldn't tell if the woman was emerging from the tunnel or getting sucked back into it. One hand was to her face, and her eyes were closed. The woman's mouth was open, just slightly, and years later—when I tried to find evidence of the painting online and couldn't—I would torture myself by trying to remember whether the look on the woman's face was agony or ecstasy.

She had pale skin and seemed to exist on a plane separate from everything else in the world of the painting. Forced perspective. She wore a flowing white dress, high necked with long sleeves, and though it looked elegant, the way she stood made her seem unmoored. She looked like a bride—a bride trying to escape from her own dark wedding.

I peered at the bottom of the painting, where I could see a plaque that was almost obscured from view. *M.E. Stands Before the Mind of God.*

I heard footsteps above me, and then another snatch of angry voices.

"Rainey!" Spencer shouted. "Rainey, where are you?"

Her voice was muted by the distance. A part of me knew I should go find them, but I couldn't tear my eyes away from the painting. There was something horrible at play here, a feeling mutated by the alcohol coursing through my system. My mother was an artist, and for as long as I could remember our house had been filled with paintings, drawings, sometimes little more than a half-finished sketch on the back of a piece of scrap paper. As much as I had avoided art in the year after my mother disappeared, I could still recognize certain elements—the intersection of light and shadow, thematic elements that only became obvious on a fourth or fifth viewing. There was madness at play in this painting. It was brilliant—horrible, really, but brilliant all the same—and I couldn't work out why someone would tuck it in this small room, where no one could see it.

I didn't hear Spencer come into the room behind me.

"*Rainey*," she snapped, and I jumped at the sound of my name. I turned around to see her and flinched when I saw how angry she was, but as she walked toward me, something about her changed.

"Jesus, I'm coming," I said. "Chill out."

She floated over to the painting and stopped next to me, then turned and gave me a look I couldn't quite decipher.

"Where did you go?" she asked, and her voice was softer. She touched my arm. "We couldn't find you anywhere."

I moved toward the door, but Spencer lingered on, looking at the painting. She stood there for another minute before reaching forward and lifting the painting off the shelf where it stood.

I hesitated, only for a moment, then touched Spencer's arm. "What are you *doing*?" I hissed, keeping my voice low. "You can't take that with us. Someone will notice it missing—"

She tucked the painting under one arm and then strode out of the room, past me.

"We have to get out of here," she said. "Come on, Rainey."

Alice waited for us outside. She said nothing as Spencer got back into her car, then turned the key in the ignition.

"Come on," Spencer snapped, and we climbed into the car after her. The painting sat in the backseat, beside me. I glanced at it as I buckled my seatbelt.

"You can't take it," I repeated. "Someone will notice. It's not just jewelry or clothing. It's too valuable."

"Don't worry," Spencer said, turning around to look at me. "He's never home in the summer. That's when he tours."

"Who?"

"Laszlo Zo. This is his house."

Nothing else was said as we left the property, as Spencer eased the car back onto the main street and I finally saw that we were in Holmby Hills. Nobody spoke as we crossed the city and Spencer dropped me off in front of my house. Alice watched with dark eyes as I climbed from the car and walked to my front gate, pausing only once to look back at my friends.

The theft of a painting from a vast estate in one of the wealthiest Los Angeles suburbs would have been the most indelible part of that summer. In time—when my anger faded, when I stopped being so selfish—I might have been haunted by that night—the restlessness, the greed, the casual entitlement. Instead, something happened three days later that wiped out all thoughts of that house with its big empty gardens and the hollow windows that looked out over nighttime Los Angeles.

What happened is this: we went to a party in North Hollywood, in a house with cheap vinyl siding. The front lawn was an expanse of crabgrass and packed dirt. Certain details stick out even now—foaming swaths of morning glory, baked dog shit but no dog. We never would have gone to this party without Spencer: she knew the man who lived there, and told us he was cool.

The next morning I woke up on the couch in the front room and couldn't remember where I was. I heard the garbage truck trundling down the street, and then the quiet bumble of a fish tank from somewhere else in the house. I hadn't had that much to drink but had passed out so deeply that I wondered if I had been drugged. I stumbled to my feet, overcome by nausea, then tiptoed through the dim house, looking for my friends.

In every room there lay the sleeping forms of men and women I had seen the night before. They didn't look asleep, though, they looked dead. I searched every room, and even after I found Spencer, Alice was nowhere to be found.

"You need to fucking chill," Spencer snapped. I had woken her up and she was in rough shape. "She probably went home early."

"She wouldn't leave without me," I said, trying to mask the panic in my voice.

"Sure about that?"

—❦—

"We just want to find her," the police told me five days later, when Alice was still missing. Cameron had flown home from the East Coast and had kicked the police force into action. "We're not looking at other crimes right now. Give us all the information you can."

The last thing I remember from that summer was what happened after the fires. When the smoke disappeared and the air cleared up again, everything went back to normal as though none of it had ever happened.

Even nine years later I can't help telling myself that if the fires hadn't happened, we wouldn't have started breaking into houses, that we wouldn't have thrown away our lives and Alice might still be here. Maybe we would have both grown up and changed into people who didn't feel the need to burn our lives to the ground in order to make sense of all the chaos that surrounded us. There isn't a single version of my imaginary life where I imagine Alice and I would still be friends, but in each of these fragmented dream worlds, at least she's safe.

FIVE

For the last six months I had been living in the guesthouse of a rambling Spanish-style 1930s home near Griffith Park. It was a beautiful old mansion but falling apart in places—the swimming pool was empty, and each night rats climbed over the avocado trees near the tennis court. The place had a deeply romantic atmosphere, though, and living there made me feel like I had escaped modern Los Angeles. It was tucked down a quiet dead-end lane lined with eucalyptus and pepper trees.

The arrangement was temporary. The house belonged to a woman in her eighties, a patron of the Los Angeles Philharmonic who had been moved into hospice care because she was at the end of a lengthy cancer battle. Her adult children lived in New Mexico and the fate of the house was uncertain, so while they deliberated over a decision, everyone agreed to appoint temporary house sitters to maintain the property and protect it from trespassers.

One of my longtime family friends, Marcus Loew, was a composer who frequently worked with the LA Phil. When he suggested that I might like to move into the guesthouse for a few months, I leaped at the opportunity. The main house was spoken for—an oboist named Sadie had already moved in—but the property was too big for one person, and Sadie was happy for the company.

On Thursday morning, the day after the meeting with Noa at the museum, I woke up to sunlight streaming in through my window. The guesthouse was small, with just a bedroom and a tiny bathroom. The windows looked out over the pool, with a view of the main house beyond. I could hear cheerful humming outside my window. I stretched and climbed out of bed, then padded over to the door to see Sadie crouching by the mint patch, snipping off leaves. I knocked on the glass, then waved.

"Hey!" she called.

"Morning," I said, yawning. I opened the door and walked outside in my bare feet.

Sadie was in her early thirties, with a tangled mess of pale red curls. She wore big round glasses and blinked when she listened to you. She smiled more than anyone I knew, and being around her was a tonic.

"I hope I didn't keep you awake last night," she said, then gave me a guilty look.

"How's that?"

"I stayed up late practicing. You didn't hear?"

"Didn't hear a thing."

Before I moved in, Sadie had warned me that she practiced music around the clock, and a few potential roommates had declined the living situation as a result. I didn't mind music as a constant backdrop, though; it was what I'd grown up with. My father was an autodidact who seemed to have a base familiarity with every instrument he came across, and I had long ago learned to tune music out. Sadie knew that I had once played violin, too, at a professional level, but was stunned that I had given it up.

"Completely?" she had asked when we discussed living arrangements. "You don't even take it out every once in a while, to keep the instrument in playing condition?"

"I don't own a violin anymore," I replied, then laughed at her shock. My past was not something I readily discussed, and even though I had been a prodigious violin player as a young teenager, it had never been something that fully belonged to me. I had always felt like I was doing it for my parents, and when our family began to crack around the time I turned fifteen, I was altogether too happy to let music go.

"What are you practicing?" I asked Sadie now, bending to snap off a piece of mint.

"'Gabriel's Oboe,'" she said, then rolled her eyes and laughed. "I love Morricone but I'm ready for something new."

"I love Yo-Yo Ma's covers," I said. "You ever listen to those?"

"Oh yeah," she said. "The master. You working today?"

"About to head into the office. We're working on a new case, and I'm still getting my bearings. Just going to grab some coffee first."

Sadie was good—she never pried, and she knew I couldn't tell her very much about my job due to privacy issues. She brushed her hair out of her face and smiled.

When I first interviewed for the room, I had been honest with Sadie about my line of work and said that although it was unlikely to happen again, an angry client had once broken into my last apartment and attacked me. She had been surprisingly nonchalant about the whole thing, maybe in part because the woman who owned the house had been diligent about security and installed triple locks on all the doors.

"See you this evening, then."

The house on Loma Linda Lane was perfect in many regards, but its biggest detraction was the distance from my office in Culver City. In bad traffic it could take more than an hour for me to drive the twelve miles to get to work. To save myself the hassle, I almost always worked from home in the morning and then drove in somewhere around ten o'clock, when the bulk of morning traffic had died down. Today, though, I didn't want to wait, because I was impatient to fill my colleagues in on everything I had discovered with Noa at the museum.

I had started Left City Investigations several years before, almost by accident. I'd been working for Marcus at the time—I was his assistant for two years—and on the side, I had done everything I could think of to track down my mother. I combed through missing persons databases online, read message boards, and talked to the detectives who had helped our family when she first disappeared. By the time I finally found her and learned that she had left of her own accord, I had built up a rough kit of resources and found that I liked chasing leads more than working in film production.

Discord and secrets were part of my birthright: my paternal grandmother had been a starlet in the Golden Age of Hollywood, back when movie stars still made enough money to fill swimming pools with champagne. She had been an abusive alcoholic, too, but I didn't learn that bit until a documentary film crew came to our house and started asking my father questions. In the end they made their documentary without his help because that was a part of his life he would never discuss, not even with me.

The secrets didn't end there. There are a number of reasons I could single out as causes for my drinking and self-destructive years, and most of those reasons seem to overlap with the reasons why my father and I ultimately stopped speaking to each other. One snag in our otherwise perfect family was the fact that I walked away from a promising career as a violinist. Music was everything to my father, and turning one's back on it was anathema to him. He didn't seem to understand that I put on a mask every time I stepped onstage, that I felt myself seeping through the floorboards when the music ended and the applause washed over me.

The main reason I never completely self-destructed was Marcus, a man who had come to stand in as a kind of surrogate father for me in the last few years. Marcus Loew was a friend of my father's originally because they were both composers. Marcus, too, came from an Old Hollywood lineage, though if his resulted in any kind of hereditary damage, I have yet to see the signs. A few years ago, Marcus and his wife took me in and forced me to get well when I no longer cared about myself. It's not much of a stretch to say that I owe them everything I have right now.

Losing my mother twice had left me with lingering trauma, but Left City was one of the best things that had ever happened to me, and it was definitely the thing that I was most proud of. I had tried to do it on my own, at first, but got lucky when Lola fell in my lap: she was a friend of the Loew family. Lola was a young lawyer who was already disenchanted with all the legal sharkery she had witnessed. I had been cautious about hiring her at first because I still didn't know if the firm was going to last, but she had managed to talk me into it.

"We'll be partners," she'd said. "Don't think of me as an employee. We'll divide everything equally."

For a few months it was just the two of us, and it seemed to be working out just fine. Finding Blake, then, was another happy accident: I was scanning the amateur sleuth message boards for leads and I kept seeing something about a young woman who had managed to single-handedly bring down a sinister cult by exposing financial fraud. I sent her a message that afternoon, and a week later she came in for an interview with me and Lola. Six months later we moved into our offices in Culver City, and the rest was history.

I listened to the radio as I drove, occasionally tuning out when my thoughts drifted. I was inching along through stop-and-go traffic when something on the radio brought me back to attention, and I was so distracted I nearly slammed into the car ahead of me.

". . . because we were just talking about the museum the other day, weren't we?" one of the deejays was saying. He cleared his throat. "It's in this old Hollywood mansion. All the neighbors were up in arms about it. They do all these crazy exhibits . . ."

"Oh yeah," his colleague agreed. I recognized her voice from listening to the station for years, but I couldn't recall her name. "At this point I feel like the museum is *trying* to piss the neighbors off. A lawsuit would be good publicity, right?"

"Riiiiiight," the first deejay said, laughing.

"Guys, if you're just tuning in, you're listening to Conan and Stills," the woman said. "We're talking about the Kloos Museum. If you haven't heard of it, it's a modern art museum in a wealthy part of Los Angeles—"

"Coldwater Canyon," the man cut in.

"Thanks, Con," Stills replied. "Anyway, there was a story in the news this morning about an artist—what was his name?"

"Rhodes," Conan said.

"Rhodes," Stills repeated. "He just bit someone. The whole thing was caught on video. He was out of his mind on drugs, and he attacked some dude in the street."

"And he used to be really famous, is what I was trying to say," Conan added. "He had a show at the Kloos Museum."

"There's almost *too* much art these days," Stills complained. "It's all free. Everyone's creative, so if you want to do it professionally, you almost have to set your life on fire. Right? You need to get a reaction. You have to do something special. And you can't be completely sane to do that."

"Wild stuff," Conan said. "Kids, don't do drugs."

Their conversation ended abruptly as a song by The Who started playing. I had reached Culver City, and as I drove past the quaint buildings that made up the Downtown district, my car filled with the sound of John Entwistle chanting the song's chorus. I had always liked Culver City, which felt like a rustic movie set of small-town America. There was a lot of film history in this neighborhood, too, stretching all the way back to 1918. *Gone with the Wind* was filmed here, as well as the original *A Star Is Born*. It was almost impossible to drive down the main street without imagining the munchkins from *The Wizard of Oz* spilling out of the Culver Hotel, where they stayed during the filming.

The name Rhodes was unfamiliar to me, but that didn't necessarily mean anything. There was a time when I could have named all the up-and-coming artists around Southern California, because those were the people who attended parties at my childhood home. Both of my parents were supportive of new artists, and our house was filled with pieces that my parents had bought to help someone pay their bills. Now, though, I stayed away from art the same way I avoided classical music. It was a part of my past.

My mother would have appreciated the interactive exhibit at the Kloos Museum. She had always liked art that challenged societal norms and made people uncomfortable. Maybe that's why I was such a disappointment to her: I liked rules, I liked structure. A disappointment to my father as well because I had always gravitated toward rock and grunge over classical music.

I snapped off the radio and pulled into my parking spot outside the Left City office. We were in a converted bungalow which had once housed the wardrobe department for a now-defunct studio from the forties. There were six other bungalows on our little street, and they had all been used for various elements of film production. We didn't do much to advertise the agency, preferring to take referrals and let clients come to us through recommendations, but one concession was the gold lettering on the frosted window, which read LEFT CITY CONSULTANTS.

After I turned off my car, I rolled down my window and took out my phone to search for "Rhodes, artist." It took Google a moment to spit up a list of results. ARTIST ARRESTED FOR ASSAULT, read the top headline. I clicked on the link, which led to the *Los Angeles Times*.

If you lived in Los Angeles four years ago and were familiar with the art scene, there's a chance that you already know the name Rhodes.

*Once considered the most promising young artist of the decade, Rhodes
won the prestigious Gilman scholarship when he was only nineteen
years old. The artist seemed destined for stardom when he held a gallery showing at the prestigious Kloos Museum. Yesterday, however,
the artist was arrested in the middle of Abbot Kinney Boulevard
when he wandered out of a café and bit a stranger on the sidewalk.*

I skimmed through the rest of the article, which listed various awards and
exhibitions that Rhodes had won. The article included images of his artwork,
too—he favored jarring neon images in archaic pastoral settings, the beauty
enhanced through juxtaposition. The writer mentioned that Rhodes had
suddenly dropped out of sight two years before and had even been thought
dead by some in the art world. While this recent sighting had been alarming,
some people had been reassured to know that he was still alive.

*The artist was arrested and taken into custody early yesterday after-
noon. While the police have not yet made an official statement about
the incident, sources close to the artist have indicated a recent struggle
with drugs and alcohol.*

At the end of the article was a solicitation for any information about
Rhodes or the reason for his disappearance from the spotlight. I put my
phone away and grabbed my things, then walked to my office.

My colleagues were in the middle of a conversation when I walked in.
Lola glanced up and smiled at me, raising an eyebrow in surprise.

"Morning," she said. "You're early."

I wore a variation of the same outfit to work every day: a light blouse
and a pencil skirt over hose. Lola, however, put in real effort, and was the
most stylish out of the three of us. She had inherited a lot of old silver
jewelry from her Mexican grandmother, which she layered to great effect
over bright floral pieces she found at vintage stores around Los Angeles.

Today she was wearing a light-blue linen dress embroidered with magenta flowers. A hammered silver necklace inlaid with turquoise stones hung from her neck. Lola was tall—six foot two—and curvy, and knew how to dress to accentuate her body type.

"Traffic wasn't too bad," I said, walking over to my desk and dropping my bag off.

"Hey." Blake nodded at me.

"Morning."

Blake and I had the most in common with each other: we were both from wealthy, unhappy backgrounds. Blake had grown up in Montecito, with every privilege that money could offer, but with all its attendant miseries, too. Her parents made names for themselves as prominent African Americans rising in the Los Angeles political scene. Blake had trained to be a classical musician since she was very small. When she started high school, though, a rebellious streak came out, and she started sneaking out on weekends to drink with her friends.

A devastating car accident after a party had nearly ended Blake's life when she was seventeen. She had survived, but the accident had damaged her spine and left her in a wheelchair. It was at this point that Blake told her parents that she was done playing the cello—true to her word, she hadn't touched it since—and wanted to play the drums instead.

While Blake hadn't completely cut ties with her family, she kept them at a stiff distance. They didn't approve of anything she did: not Left City, not her punk-rock boyfriend, and definitely not the fact that on weekends, Blake played the drums for a heavy metal band called Shade Riot.

"I've caught Blake up on everything we discussed with Michael and Kathy," Lola said, taking a sip of her coffee. "I mentioned the thing about the house with the roses and stained glass, too. Do you want to catch her up on Ricky?"

"Ahhh, the good doctor." Blake grinned, then burst out laughing. For some reason she found everything about Ricky amusing, but nothing more so than the fact that he took every opportunity to introduce himself as Dr. Goff.

I sat down and laced my fingers together, then pointed at her. "First things first—what do you know about Dogtooth?"

"The band from the seventies?"

"Yep."

She looked at the ceiling thoughtfully. "One of Britain's most influential rock bands, revolutionary in some critics' eyes for introducing death metal rips to a wider audience; their first three albums were groundbreaking and yet palatable on a large scale, achieving the rare feat of bridging the gap between critical and mainstream success—"

Lola cut her off by clearing her throat. "Rainey, be more specific. We'll be here all day."

"Laszlo Zo in particular," I said.

"Judas. Broke the band up and sold out. He was, like, the John Lennon of Dogtooth. Half the talent, but just as much genius for controversy and bad publicity. Then again, it seems like he's tried to redeem himself in the last twenty years with all that philanthropy bullshit."

"Hugely wealthy?"

"Oh yeah. Didn't you watch TV fifteen years ago? Zo would hype anything from washing machines to rollerblades. I mean, every time Britain coughs up one of those 'all-stars for charity' medleys, he's there, front and center."

"What does this have to do with Ricky?" Lola asked.

I took a deep breath. "Noa has reason to believe that Laszlo Zo is Ricky's father."

There was a long silence. Then, "Bullshit," Lola said. "Come on. I thought Ricky was a compulsive liar."

"He is," I agreed. "But this isn't coming from Ricky. Noa told me herself at the museum yesterday. They're opening a new wing with money that Zo is donating. I think she's telling the truth."

"She might be telling the truth, but that doesn't mean it's *true*," Lola pointed out. "I mean, poor woman. She's been put through hell by a self-loathing narcissist. She probably doesn't know what to believe anymore. Ricky's a pathological liar, and it's very convenient that just as Noa is going for a restraining order, he pops up and announces his dad is one of the most famous musicians in the world."

"Noa saw Laszlo Zo talking to Ricky's mom at their house."

"Ricky lives with his mom, yeah?" Blake was trying not to smile.

"Serena Goff," I confirmed. "They live in Sherman Oaks."

Lola shook her head and frowned. "I think that's a pretty big leap," she said. "Noa saw Zo and Serena talking, and she assumes that Zo is Ricky's father? I don't see how she made that connection."

"Ricky never knew who his father was because Serena raised him as a single mother. She knew who the father was, but she would never tell Ricky about him. The only thing he knew was that his father was some really rich, powerful man. Noa assumed that Ricky had been lying about that bit, and then she saw Zo at Serena's house."

Blake was typing something at her keyboard. She squinted at the computer screen. "Show me Ricky?"

I opened my phone to find my folder on Ricky. I had photos that I had taken during a recent stake-out of his house, but also photos from the last nine years that Noa had given me. Ricky had undergone a horrifying transformation over the last six years, and skimming through the photos in quick succession was like watching a wax figure left out in the sun. Elasticity of skin disappeared, and all his features sagged downward.

Still, in his younger photos there was a lightness, a sense of joy. I showed Blake one of the younger photos, and she shrugged.

"You have to admit, there's a resemblance."

She held the phone next to a photo of Laszlo Zo from a concert thirty years before.

"I see it," Lola finally acknowledged, peering over Blake's shoulder. She frowned, and I could tell she was mulling something over.

"What is it?" I asked.

"Let's say that Laszlo's had a number of affairs over the years," she said. "I gather that birth control wasn't necessarily *prevalent* back when they were touring, so there's a chance that he fathered any number of illegitimate children. Why do you think he'd pay Serena a visit? Instead of just paying her small amounts to keep quiet?"

"Well, *I* think it's sweet," Blake suggested, and we all burst out laughing.

"But really," Lo pressed. "Why Ricky?"

"Because Ricky is a loser. Zo has built a brand on being a retired rocker turned philanthropist, and it's easy to pay Serena and Ricky to keep quiet," I suggested. I had been asking myself the same question since Noa had revealed it to me.

"How does this help us?" Lola asked. "What are we going to do with this new information?"

Blake and Lola were familiar with my connection to Ricky. I had told them about my theory that he was responsible for Alice's disappearance, whether he had kidnapped her or harmed her in some other way. Blake and Lola were able to see things from an unbiased perspective, unclouded with emotion, and I thought that they might be able to help figure out what had happened to my friend. So far, none of us had developed any real leads over the years, but neither of them seemed to begrudge my unflagging interest in Ricky or his movements. When we had made a connection with Noa and started looking at Ricky all over again, I had reminded them about the parallels between Alice and Chloe.

"I spent all day yesterday thinking about it," I said. "I think we should approach Zo and tell him we know about Ricky. Zo might cut ties with him, at least long enough for Noa to get custody and a restraining order. That's what we're after, in the end."

The room fell quiet as we thought about this. The sounds of street noise came trickling in through the open window, the snatch of a conversation, car brakes screeching. Blake rolled her wheelchair over to the window and slid it shut.

"Let's talk about our options," I said. "Option one is leaving Zo out of the whole thing. Noa still wants the restraining order against Ricky, along with full custody of their son. We proceed as normal, apply for the restraining order and hope that it sways the judge with the custody hearing."

Our hearing date was set for the end of the month, in three weeks' time.

"Mm-hmm," Lola said.

"The problem with that is, if Zo is really Ricky's father, and he's bankrolling the whole thing, Ricky can afford a much better lawyer," I said. "Another reason why Ricky might be telling the truth about Zo is that even when he's been unemployed, he always seems to have a source of cash."

"What's the worst that could happen?" Blake asked. "If we approach Zo and mention Ricky, I mean."

"Zo might sue us," Lola pointed out. "These superstars have lawyers on standby for extortion cases."

"I hope you're ready for a challenge," I said.

"I'll write something up." Lola sighed. "A small statement of facts, what he's been doing to Noa, that we're applying for a restraining order. How should we get it to him—courier?"

"Fine with me," I agreed.

"I think we should give it to him in person," Blake said. "Zo is one of the wealthiest celebrities on the planet. A standard courier wouldn't be able to get it to him, not in time for the restraining order to go to court. Zo just has to avoid us for a few months. That's child's play for someone like him."

"Good point," Lola agreed. "Do you have a better idea?"

Blake was typing something on her computer. She squinted at the screen.

"Well, Zo lives in Holmby Hills," she said. "When he's in LA, at least. It's an enormous compound with a big security fence and even a little guardhouse at the front."

I felt my face flush and I looked down at my hands so that Blake and Lola wouldn't notice. Lola was my best friend, and she knew everything about my past, all the unsavory details. She knew that I had struggled with alcohol for years after the disappearance of my mother, that I had stopped playing music—in part—because I felt an odd disconnect that resembled floating in a hyperbaric chamber, a disorienting feeling that was worse than anything. She knew about all the minor thefts I had committed during that summer with Spencer and Alice. What she didn't know, however, was that I had seen the inside of Zo's house.

"From what I can see on his social media, he's in America," Blake continued, skimming the information. "Hold on—he's going to be at the Orphans' Ball!"

"What's this?" Lola stood up and walked over to Blake's computer. She skimmed the screen and quietly read aloud. "The Emmett Auden Foundation . . . Pasadena . . . Shit, looks fancy."

"I've heard about the Emmett Auden Foundation," Blake said. "It's a charity thing, right?"

"It's a foundation for underprivileged and orphaned kids," I said.

"Right, right, that rings a bell," Blake said, nodding.

"And the Orphans' Ball is their big black-tie gala for celebrities," I said. "They sell seats and auction things off. It's like the Met Gala but in Los Angeles. All the money goes back into the foundation."

"How do you know all this?" Lola glanced at me.

"Marcus goes."

"Emmett Auden," Blake said, frowning. "He was an architect, right?"

"Right," I confirmed. "He was one of LA's biggest architects in the twenties and thirties. He designed a bunch of crazy mansions for movie stars. Some of them had speakeasies built into them. Bowling alleys, observatories, stuff like that. Trapdoors."

"Why does Marcus go to the Orphans' Ball?" Lola asked. Lola had known the Loew family before we knew each other; I had met her through Marcus's son, Diego. I had introduced Blake to Marcus on a few occasions, in part because they were both musicians.

"He's pretty high up on the Hollywood food chain," I said. "He's composed music for a lot of big movies."

"Wait," Blake said. I could feel her gaze on me. "So Marcus and Laszlo Zo are both going to be at this event? I know how close you are to Marcus . . ."

I immediately regretted having spoken. "I can't ask him to take me."

"Why not?" Lola asked. "The worst thing that could happen is he says no. If you and Zo both attend a super-exclusive event, you'll have a chance to get close to him. His guard will be down. It's perfect."

"Right. And what should I tell Marcus when I ask?"

"The truth," Lola said with a shrug. "Or a limited version, at least. Don't mention the allegations about Zo because we don't want to spread that information if it's false. Tell him that you need to speak to Zo and you probably won't get another chance."

"I'll think about it," I said. "I need some time."

"You don't have time to think," Lola said. "The gala is in two days."

"Okay," I said finally. "I'll do it. I'll ask Marcus. I don't know what he'll say, though. He might decline."

"Least you can do is ask," Lola said. "Hey, are you still happy to go talk to Chloe's roommate?"

"Of course," I said. "Give me the address. I'll head over right now."

SIX

It was Friday afternoon. The Orphans' Ball was the following evening, which meant I only had a tiny window of time to talk to Marcus and convince him to take me to the event. It wasn't a conversation I wanted to have over the phone, though, so I decided to call and ask him if I could meet up with him.

"Rainey." Marcus was always someone I could count on to pick up within two or three rings.

"Hey, Marcus," I said. "I was hoping we could talk about something."

"Oh?"

"It's nothing bad," I quickly added. "Just something I would rather discuss in person. Can I come and meet you?"

There was a pause. "I'm at the Farm," he said. "I'll be here late, working. You're welcome to come out."

The Farm was the Lime Farm, a twenty-acre filming location on the outskirts of La Crescenta-Montrose. The Farm had once been just that—a sprawling lime orchard and almond farm—but back in the 1920s, some enterprising studio moguls had bought up the space and built a bunch of sound stages and fake streets with conventional-looking buildings that could suit a variety of purposes: a brick firehouse, apartment blocks, suburban houses, churches, town halls. Jack Shingle, Esther Kloos's father, had even filmed a few slapstick reels there.

The farm itself had been razed to the ground, trees torn out by the roots, but contemporary visitors to the main office were greeted by framed black-and-white photos of smiling starlets wandering down rows of almond trees, their arms outstretched. The Farm was one of the only remaining physical back lots, and it was thanks to a few people who had rallied against the advent of modern technology steamrolling traditional filmmaking methods.

"I don't want to disturb your work," I said to Marcus after a moment's hesitation.

"You won't," Marcus replied. "It'll be good. I can show you around. You can get a first look at the new film I'm working on."

"Surely that's not allowed."

"For mere mortals, no," he said. "But you used to be my assistant, so I'm sure they'll allow you on the lot. I'll let the guard know you're coming—park behind Studio Nine."

Before I went to see Marcus, though, I wanted to talk to Chloe's roommate. I had the address her parents had given me, so I drove straight over there.

Chloe's old apartment was in the MacArthur Park neighborhood. I hadn't been there since I was a kid, but when I was growing up, it had been known as a rough area. Years ago, when I was just out of high school, some of my friends had gone to a party in Koreatown. The party had broken up late, and after they stumbled out of a bar, they decided to go for a walk by MacArthur Lake. The neighborhood was almost entirely empty, but as they strolled along the waterfront, a young woman with black eyes approached them and held up a knife.

"Give me your shoes," she said.

When they protested, a second woman with wild hair shuffled out of the trees and held up a broken bottle. The pair made my friends strip down to their underwear, tossing their wallets and jewelry onto the pile.

"Now get lost," the first woman said. "Fuck off."

My friends ran. When they stumbled to a nearby bar and called the police, the dispatcher hadn't sounded surprised. *What did you expect*, she told them. *It's MacArthur Park. It's late at night. You're lucky you weren't killed.*

I parked a few blocks away from Chloe's address and decided to walk so I could take in some details of the neighborhood. Even from just a brief glance, I could tell it had evolved and shifted from the earlier perception I'd had about the place: instead of pawnshops hidden behind dented grills, ice cream parlors and expensive coffee shops populated the streets leading down to the lake. When I got close enough to see the water, I caught sight of young families pushing strollers and kneeling to play with toddlers.

Chloe's address was an old pre-war brick apartment building. It squatted between two modern glass towers, a stalwart holdover that had managed to endure while everything around it crumbled under the dual forces of time and new money. There was something appealing about the place with its grim parapets and dormer windows; I had always preferred places with history to shiny new complexes stripped of warmth. I wondered how many of the original tenants were still alive.

The front gate had been propped open with a dolly, and as I approached, I saw two men hauling a box into the complex. I waited until they had moved inside before slipping in after them and consulting a map of the building. The complex was ten degrees cooler than the outside, and the shadowy sounds of voices came echoing down the halls as I climbed up to the third floor.

I found Chloe's door, then knocked and waited. After a few moments, a man's voice called, "Yes, I'm coming!" and then the door swung open and a man stood there blinking at me. He was young and thin, with a floppy tumble of hair falling into his eyes. He couldn't have been much more than twenty, and I guessed that he was probably a student. His demeanor was rumpled and unwashed, but even so I could tell he came from a solid home: he looked healthy, and he had good teeth.

"Hi—yes? Can I help you?" He laced his fingers together.

"I'm looking for Chloe Delmonico," I said. "Are you her roommate?"

"I was," he said, then scratched his head. "Who are you?"

"My name is Rainey Hall," I said and pulled out my driver's license to show him. He squinted at it.

"Are you a cop?" he asked.

"I'm a private investigator," I said. "I'm looking for Chloe. Her parents hired me. Do you know where she is?"

"Um, like, the police came looking for her, so," he said. "No. I haven't seen her."

"When was the last time you saw her?"

"Two months ago," he said.

I frowned—this contradicted what Kathy and Michael had told me. They had mentioned that Chloe moved back home the previous month.

"Can I ask your name?"

"Ahmad," he said.

"Right," I said. "Do you mind if I ask you a few questions, Ahmad?"

Ahmad brushed his hair out of his eyes. I wondered if I had woken him up.

"That's fine," he said. "I guess you should come inside."

I followed Ahmad down a dim hallway into a living room that looked out over MacArthur Park. The living room was occupied in one corner by an electric keyboard and a podcasting setup. A pair of mismatched couches sat on opposite sides of a coffee table covered with sheet music. Posters for classical concerts were framed on the wall. The room felt very clean, though filled with personal details.

Ahmad scooped up the papers off the coffee table and gestured for me to sit.

"Are you a musician?" I asked, pointing to the keyboard.

"I'm at the College of Music," he said, then yawned and stretched. "I had a late concert last night. Slept in. Sorry."

"It's fine," I reassured him. I took out a notepad and pencil. "How did you meet Chloe?"

Ahmad looked down at his hands for a moment, then picked at his fingernails. His hands were long and tapered. "My last roommate was an artist," he said. "We'd lived together for a few years, and then she moved out. They met at Otis."

"Okay. How long did Chloe live here?"

Ahmad looked up at the ceiling and thought. "A year? She moved out a couple months ago, though."

He sounded confident about that date. I wondered if Michael and Kathy had their information wrong, or if Chloe had stayed with someone else before coming back to live with them.

"Do you know where Chloe went after she lived with you?"

Ahmad thought. "Yes," he said, frowning. "Well, not the address. But she said she was going to live with a friend."

"Do you know who the friend was?" My heart rate accelerated, waiting to hear Ricky's name.

"Some girl. She came here once. Blond. Kind of spacey."

"You get a name?"

"Probably, but I don't remember. Sorry." He shrugged. "Oh! Chloe said not to tell her parents she was moving out. They were a bit clingy. She asked me to say that she was still living here."

I wrote this down. Ahmad looked at the notepad with open curiosity. "Is she in trouble?"

"I don't know," I said honestly. "Not with me. And not with the cops, as far as I know. I'm just trying to find her. Have you seen her since she moved out?"

"Sure, we're friends," he said.

"When was the last time you saw her?"

Ahmad took a deep breath and thought again. "She was here like two weeks ago," he said. "To grab some things. Water her plants. Oh, shit—I was supposed to do that. Excuse me."

He stood up and walked into the kitchen, which adjoined the living room. He grabbed a pitcher from a cupboard and filled it with water from the sink, then disappeared from view. I could hear the trickle of water being poured into plants. I moved into the kitchen doorway and saw that Chloe had painted this room, too, but the artwork was more restrained than what I had seen at her parents' house: the walls here had been painted to look like a forest, the dark leaves framing slender boughs and branches. Poisonous-looking mushrooms sprouted from the baseboards.

Ahmad saw me and started. On the kitchen windowsill were a variety of potted plants. Some of them looked wilted. Ahmad gave me a guilty look.

"I'm a bad plant dad," he said. "Please don't judge me."

I held up my hands in a sign of surrender. "I'm not here to judge," I said. "You're looking after her plants?"

"Sure," he said. He cradled the pitcher of water to his chest. "She asked me to. She said she couldn't take them with her. Plus, she always planned to move back, once she'd gotten her life sorted out."

"Sorted out how?"

Ahmad gave me an expansive shrug. "I just heard snatches from her, here and there. Seemed like she had a lot going on."

I walked over to the plants on the windowsill.

"I like plants, but I don't know how to keep them alive," he admitted. "And some of these are rare. I'll never forgive myself if I let them die."

I looked at the array of foliage. The leaves ranged in shape, size, and color: some were a deep, glossy green, while others were white and red. I reached out to touch one, but Ahmad grabbed my arm before I could reach it.

"You don't want to touch that one—it's covered in these horrible spines, and you'll never get rid of the splinters. Trust me."

"Thanks for the warning," I said, withdrawing my hand. I looked at the pot then, and noticed the label that was printed on it. It was a skull with a flowering vine coming out the side.

"Wait," I said. "I know that from somewhere. Do you know where she got these?"

Ahmad frowned. "A nursery in Echo Park," he said. "I don't remember the name, though."

I tried to remember the sign that I had seen on the Victorian house Ricky had visited.

"Boneseed?" I suggested.

"That could be it." He shrugged. "It was a while ago."

I looked at the plants again, then thought of something else.

"Do you have a podcast?" I asked.

"What?" His brow furrowed.

"I saw your setup in the living room," I said. "The headphones and recording equipment."

"It's just a hobby," he said, blushing. "Something I do with my sister."

"What's it about?"

"Film scores," he said, then ran a hand through his hair. "Soundtracks. We're both music nerds."

"You talk about movie music?"

"We analyze scores," he said. He seemed cautiously proud. "We talk about movie history, and sometimes we interview people."

"Have you heard of Marcus Loew?"

Ahmad rolled his eyes and smiled. "Of course. He's one of the best. I like his father, too."

"I know him quite well," I said. "Would you like me to introduce you? Maybe he'd be willing to do a spot on your show. I can't promise, of course . . ."

Ahmad looked rapturous. "That would be amazing," he said. "But how . . . how do you know him?"

"He's an old family friend," I said, then smiled at him. "I used to work for him."

Ahmad seemed to open up a bit more. I glanced around the room and tried to glean what I could about Chloe without being intrusive.

I turned to Ahmad. "Do you know where she is?"

"No," he said. "I told the police everything I know. Really."

"I'm not the police," I reminded him. "You're not going to get in trouble for anything you tell me."

He watched me, guarded.

"I know she was using drugs," I said gently. "Her parents told me."

His shoulders relaxed slightly. "Okay," he said. "I didn't know . . . I'm surprised they knew. I don't mess around with that stuff. I told her she couldn't do them here—I would make her move out."

"I heard it was pretty bad," I said. "Do you know what drugs she was using?"

Ahmad rubbed his chin and shook his head. "Pills," he said. "That's all I know. I saw her with a bag of little purple pills."

"Did you see her when she was high?"

He nodded slowly. "It really scared me. She was completely out of it. She was standing in the corner of the living room—just *standing* there. But she couldn't hear me. She couldn't talk. I was going to call the police, but her friend told me not to."

"Friend?"

"The blond girl," he said. "The one she went to live with."

"Did you tell the police about this friend? It seems like an obvious place to start looking, if she went to live with this girl."

"I mentioned it," he said. "I don't know if they did anything with the information, though."

I took out a photo of Ricky and showed it to him. "Have you seen this man?"

Ahmad scrutinized the photo, then shook his head. "No," he said. "But then again, we didn't cross paths much. That's why the arrangement worked."

I turned my attention to a plant with glossy leaves striped with pale green. The leaves had started to wilt, even though the soil was thoroughly drenched.

"What happened here?" I asked Ahmad.

"Honestly, I don't know," he confessed. "I've been watering it just as much as the other plants. They're all so finicky."

The plant had the same logo imprinted on the pot.

"Do you mind if I take this one?" I asked. "If she was getting all her plants from the same place, maybe she was friends with the nursery owner. They might know something."

"It's fine," Ahmad said. "Do whatever you need."

"Thanks," I said. "Thanks for talking to me, too."

"Don't think I was much help." He shrugged.

"You never know."

We walked back through the apartment, and when I was at the door, I turned.

"Give me your number," I said. "I'm going to see Marcus later. I'll ask him if he can do that interview with you."

The look of surprised joy on his face reminded me that sometimes my job was worth it.

I got back in my car and sent Marcus a text to let him know that I was heading his way. There was traffic around Downtown Los Angeles, so it took me an hour and a half to get to the Farm. It had been a long time since I had visited the neighborhood, but somehow not much had changed; La Crescenta-Montrose was a sleepy, rugged area tucked into the nook of the San Gabriel mountain range. Stone churches sat alongside family-owned bakeries, which yielded to the gentle creep of the suburbs. There was still a touch of the wilderness about the place, which I found reassuring. Marcus had told me about the history of this region, which had been occupied by the Tongva people for thousands of years. American settlers started creeping in after the Civil War to start fruit farms and tuberculosis clinics, both of which benefited from the healing mountain air.

The Farm, too, seemed mostly unchanged since I had last visited: the same stalwart buckeye trees lined the curving front drive, which was hidden behind a sweeping arch that spelled out the lot's official name. A middle-aged guard in a rumpled uniform climbed out of the guardhouse and shuffled toward me with a clipboard.

"Afternoon," he said. "Help you?"

"Hi," I said. "I'm here to see Marcus Loew."

"Name?"

"Rainey Hall."

He consulted the clipboard and nodded. "Drive straight until you see the main office, then take a left and follow the soundstages until the end. He's in Studio Nine."

I listened and nodded as the man spoke, even though I already knew the layout of the lot and could have driven there in my sleep. He retreated inside the guardhouse and opened the gate, and the lot gradually revealed itself as I drove through.

I was six years old the first time I visited the Lime Farm. It was back when my parents were still together, a time that even now I look back on with a certain nostalgia. Things were happier then, or at least they were happy for me.

While my father predominantly wrote music for ballets and philharmonic performances, he occasionally consented to film jobs. I always remember these periods with a kind of lightness, because the studios were so accommodating to our family, and no matter how much my father claimed to want nothing to do with Hollywood, he seemed at home at the studio.

The Lime Farm wasn't a back lot in the traditional sense, because it wasn't physically connected to a studio, but it served the same purpose. While the original big studios had once owned acres of land adjacent to their corporate offices—land that served as the backdrop for thousands of scenes in hundreds of movies—the back lot as a concept was mostly outdated. As land became scarcer and more expensive in Los Angeles, studios sold off their back lots and switched instead to green screen technology. I had been devastated to learn as an adult that where Tara once stood in *Gone with the Wind* was now a parking lot in Culver City, only a few blocks from the Left City offices. Likewise, Mayberry, from the *Andy Griffith Show*, had been carted off and paved over only a few decades after the show went off air.

The Farm was comfortably familiar: there were the modern soundstages, inside of which were filmed sequences which needed digital alteration. Beyond the soundstages, though, was a miniature world of city streets, suburban dwellings, outdoor amphitheaters, and simulated outdoor environments, which were used as the backdrop for any number of sequences. It had been a dreamy place to play as a kid—there were lots of streets with real houses along them, convincingly staged to look like an actual neighborhood—because if filming wasn't happening, my friends and I were allowed to explore to our hearts content.

Studio Nine was one of the original buildings from when the area was still a farm. This had been one of the biggest buildings on the lot, the citrus-sorting facility, and I felt an odd stirring of nostalgia every time I saw the white building with its balloon roof and green trim. I parked out front, then walked to the main entrance and let myself in.

Marcus's office was at the back of the building. I knocked on the door, then waited until Marcus called "Come in!" before I stepped inside.

Marcus sat behind an enormous wooden desk, and across from him sat Isabel, his assistant. Isabel was Cuban American, with glossy dark hair tied in a messy knot at the base of her neck. She looked up and gave me a tired smile when I came in.

"Hey, Rai," she said.

"Isa, hi," I said, leaning down to give her a hug.

"Took you long enough," Marcus intoned, scribbling something in his notebook.

"Hi, Rainey, how are you, good to see you, Rainey, thanks for driving all this way," I said, coming around his desk to give him a hug. Even sitting down, he was nearly as tall as me; he was the only person I knew who towered over Lola. He had wispy white hair and thoughtful brown eyes hidden behind small round glasses.

"Thanks for coming," he said, closing his notebook.

"What are you guys working on?" I asked, glancing at Isabel. "Wait, am I allowed to ask?"

"You're allowed," Marcus said. "You can probably guess, anyway."

Isabel held a script in her lap.

"Wait, is it the Louis B. Meyer biopic?" I got excited. "It is, isn't it?"

"Shhh. No." Marcus nodded.

"I can't wait to see it! Has it been cast yet? When are you guys filming?"

"It's in preproduction," Marcus said. "They asked me to produce it because my family's Old Hollywood, but I said no. I value my sleep too much."

There had been rumors of a Louis B. Meyer biopic for years, but there had been so many people jumping in with their opinions that it had taken ages to get started. I was a big fan of classic MGM movies, and I had been excited about it for a long time.

"How's everything else going?" I asked.

"Don't ask," Isabel said, then laughed and rolled her eyes.

Isabel and I only saw each other a few times a year, usually at events that Marcus attended. I was enormously fond of her, not least of all because I had trained her to replace me as Marcus's assistant. At the time I had gone through dozens of resumes, and all of the candidates were overwhelmingly qualified—Yale and Harvard graduates, aspiring screenwriters who had attended the Iowa Workshop, even some published novelists. Isabel's collegiate pedigree was just as impressive—she had an undergraduate degree from Mills, and a post-doc from Williams—but she didn't have any experience in the film industry. Instead, she had spent the last eight years working for a pharmaceutical company whose main claim to fame was a revolutionary approach to Alzheimer's treatment.

When I asked her why she wanted to transition to film, she was surprisingly honest.

"I can't watch humans get treated like lab rats anymore," she said.

"What do you mean?"

"All the testing and trials that my company conducts," she said. "We have to go through years of beta testing before a drug gets approved. The only ones who go through it are poor people, and once the drug works, they can't afford it anymore."

"But they agree to those trials, right?"

Isabel looked like she was trying to suppress a thought. "I studied biochemistry because I wanted to help people," she said. "I wasn't helping anyone. It just made me see how health is commodified in this country. The bodies of poor people belong to the highest bidder."

Isabel had emigrated from Cuba when she was a baby and grew up in Florida within a predominantly Latino community. Her grandfather had been a celebrated poet in Cuba, then a revolutionary. She was a voracious reader herself, studied German in Berlin for a year, and she couldn't care less about working with famous people. The real reason I hired her, though, wasn't down to her background or even how well equipped she was for the position. When I left the office at the end of the day of interviews, I saw that Isabel was still in the parking lot. She had taken off her jacket and was frowning down at her cell phone, talking to one of the interns. The intern hadn't been able to start her car and Isabel had stayed with her for the last half hour, trying to problem solve solutions and then ultimately calling a tow truck. I hired her on the spot. The intern told me later that ten other people had passed by without even asking what was wrong.

The rest was history. Isabel was honest and outspoken, but kind, and she had dealt with enough fragile egos in the pharmaceutical industry that nothing at the film studio fazed her. She had an incredible memory for faces and names and was happy to devote most of her week to working with Marcus.

"Have you heard about the Orphans' Ball?" Isabel asked me. "It's tomorrow night. Marcus is meant to go but he keeps trying to find a way out of it . . ."

My heart started pounding. I wasn't going to bring up my request in front of Isabel, but her comment reminded me that time was running out.

Marcus heaved a sigh. "I'm going, I'm going," he said. "I'll stay through the appetizers and leave before the auction."

"I heard they have something big for the auction this year," Isabel replied.

"They say that every year," he said.

"No, really," Isabel said, her eyes lighting up. She glanced at me. "Have you ever gone?"

"No, it's for the ultra-elite," I said.

"I've always been curious about what happens there," she said. "I used to hear some crazy stories about rich people, back when I worked in pharmaceuticals. The shareholders' annual events were meant to be nuts."

"You don't want to know," Marcus assured her. "In reality, rich people are the most boring people you'll ever encounter. They have no taste, but they act like they're the arbiters of culture. They buy things they don't value because someone told them they should. They buy rare items not because they're valuable but because they're rare—they want something nobody else can have."

"Well, anyway," Isabel said, waving his comments away. "I've told Marcus I expect all the gossip on Monday."

Marcus was watching her with amusement. He rubbed his hands together, then nodded at me. "I think we can break here," he said. "I'm going to show Rainey around."

"I'll be here," Isabel said, giving us a wave.

We climbed into a golf cart to drive through the lot. As we drove past the main soundstages, the back lot began to reveal itself in the form of different neighborhoods: New York City streets yielded to suburban houses, which collapsed into artificial farmland. None of it was real, of course; when the lot was empty these streets were dead silent. It looked so convincing that I always had to remind myself that everything had been built for the express purpose of filming movies and television.

"This is top secret," Marcus said. "But since you were my assistant, I think it's fair game."

"What are you showing me?"

"It's a surprise." He gave me a knowing look. "It's just a production prop, but I figured you'd enjoy it. Are you bringing anyone to the premiere in a few weeks?" Marcus asked, looking at me. "I don't think you ever told me."

Marcus had been working on the music for a movie called *Hogarth*, all about Virginia Woolf and her husband, Leonard. It was an independent picture with a few big names, and the screeners had solicited some very promising feedback. I always attended Marcus's premieres out of solidarity.

"Probably Lo and Blake," I said. Marcus knew my colleagues well.

"The studio's putting together a little package with all the invites," Marcus said. "I'll have Isabel bring you one."

"No need to put her to extra trouble," I said.

"She lives near you, anyway," he said. "I'm sure it won't be a problem."

We reached a modern-looking building at the edge of the set, and Marcus parked between a Lexus and a beat-up Toyota. The building was new, or at least it was new to me. It felt modern and devoid of the charm of the rest of the lot. Marcus scanned a key card at the entrance and stood aside to let me enter. The gray carpet and pale furniture could have been mistaken for a doctor's office or a suite of real estate offices.

"It's down the back," Marcus said. "Follow me."

Our footsteps echoed in the long hallway as we approached the back of the building. The Lime Farm was designed to look like a city, with all the municipal and suburban features one might find in a neighborhood of Los Angeles, but when filming wasn't in progress, the whole place felt like a ghost town. This was one of those times.

Marcus reached a set of double doors and opened them with a flourish, then waved me inside.

The room was as long and spacious as an airplane hangar. The space was plunged in darkness, with spots illuminated in pools of light. It took me a moment to realize what I was looking at. Tiny buildings, narrow streets. It was a scale model that took up half the floor, with long pathways between different sections, to allow, I imagined, the path of a camera dolly.

Marcus was watching me.

"It's a model," I said. "But a model of what?"

"The MGM back lot," Marcus said. "The studio itself and a bunch of different filming lots for some of the most famous movies."

"Oh my god," I said, moving closer. "This is amazing."

Spread out below was the set of the movie *Meet Me in St. Louis*. The beautiful suburban street where the Smith family had lived was built waist high, with its stately Victorian homes constructed in great detail. There was the ice wagon trundling down the street, and a trolley parked at the intersection. I felt a deep sense of nostalgia thinking of a teenaged Judy Garland leaning against her porch railing and singing about the boy next door.

I heard distant voices and glanced up to see two figures standing at the edge of the room, deep in conversation. The space was large and echoey enough that I didn't notice them until we moved closer to the model. Two men, one tall and one short, but I couldn't make out any features yet. Marcus noticed them at the same time I did, and frowned.

"Didn't realize anyone else was here," he said.

It looked like the men were in the middle of a quiet argument. The taller man was thin and agitated, illustrating whatever he was trying to say with his hands. The shorter man looked older, maybe in his forties, and he was listening without interjecting. Even from this distance I could tell a marked difference in their demeanors, just by the way they conversed.

"Bradley?" Marcus called.

Both men startled and turned in our direction. Marcus walked toward them, laughing.

"I'm sorry," he rumbled. "I didn't mean to frighten you. I thought I had the place to myself."

The shorter, older man laughed and came to meet Marcus halfway. "Not a problem!" he said. "I told the guards I was leaving a few hours ago, but realized I needed to get a few things done."

The taller man lingered in the shadows, his arms folded across his body. He made no move to approach, but Bradley turned and beckoned him forward.

"Lucas," he said. "Come on, I think we're probably done here. Let's give Marcus the space."

Lucas detached himself from the edge of the room and came stalking toward us. As he got closer I could make out some of his features: he looked to be somewhere in his twenties, with curly black hair. His clothing looked expensive, a tailored suit with a silk pocket square.

Bradley, by contrast, looked comfortably rumpled. His hair stood on end, and he wore a T-shirt and jeans over an old pair of Converse All Stars. He was unshaven and looked tired. When he got close enough that I could make out his face, he smiled at me and extended his hand.

"I'm Bradley," he said. He had kind eyes and an easy smile. He was also a few inches shorter than me. "Hi. I don't think we've met."

"Rainey," I said. "Rainey Hall. Nice to meet you."

Lucas pressed his lips together and made a noise of irritation, then glanced at his watch. "I thought you said we were going," he said to Bradley.

"Nonsense! Lucas, you know Marcus. Marcus, I think you've met my assistant—Lucas Mankerfield? And this is Rainey."

Lucas's eyes flitted over my outfit, but he said nothing.

"Rainey, I think I know you from somewhere," Bradley said, turning back to me. "Have we met?"

"I've been to the Farm before," I said. "But it's been a long time."

"Hmm," he said, cocking his head to the side. "I'm not here that often. Do you work in the industry? Maybe we've met somewhere else."

"I used to work for Marcus," I said. "But that was a few years ago. I haven't worked in film since then."

I had seen that curious look before, and it always made me uncomfortable. There were any number of reasons why someone in the industry might recognize me, and that recognition often lent a probing tension to whatever conversation we might have. When I was young, even before high school, someone who recognized me usually did so because I played violin, or else because of who my parents were.

More recently, however, people recognized me as a has-been virtuoso or because my name had been publicly dragged through the mud when an investigation went sideways and a client tried to frame me for a crime that I had been investigating. Thanks to the quick solve and a lot of paperwork on Lola's behalf, most of those headlines had been scrubbed from the internet, or at least pushed so far down into the search results that it wasn't the first thing people saw when they looked for my name. It had been a quick news story that blew up overnight and then fizzled almost as quickly. There were so many things to be distracted by that nobody seemed to remember yesterday's bad news headline unless they were already acquainted with you. I wasn't famous enough for people to remember that I had once been—wrongfully—wanted by the police.

Marcus never outed me, either for my musical past or my famous family, and for that I was always grateful.

"You're a violinist," Bradley said quietly. "You used to be a violinist. I saw you perform once. It was in London."

I glanced at Marcus.

"I'm sorry, I don't mean to make you uncomfortable," Bradley said.

"It's okay," I said quickly. "It's been a long time since I played, that's all."

He nodded. "Of course. Well, we're about to head off, unless you needed something else?"

"I just wanted to show Rainey the scale model," Marcus said.

Lucas looked affronted. "This is top secret," he said. "She's not working on the film, is she? She should really sign an NDA—you should have cleared this ahead of time, Marcus."

I was immediately affronted and jumped to Marcus's defense. "Who do you think you are?" I asked. "You can't talk to Marcus like that. He's worked in the movies longer than you've been alive."

Lucas reared back and looked down his nostrils at me. "Who the *hell* do you think *you* are?" he sneered. "Bradley, tell them to leave. Now!"

"Lucas," Bradley said, putting a conciliatory hand on Lucas's arm. "Maybe you should wait outside. I'll just be a minute."

"You can't be serious," Lucas replied.

"I think you should apologize to Marcus, too," Bradley warned.

Lucas widened his eyes at Bradley, then spun on his heel and went stalking off without a word.

"I'm sorry, Marcus." Bradley sighed. "I'll have a word with him."

"Not necessary," Marcus said.

"No, it's not okay," Bradley said. "He probably doesn't know who you are. Regardless, though—he shouldn't speak to anyone that way. Lucas is overworked, and that's probably my fault. He runs my entire life, you know, I would be completely lost without him."

"Don't let us keep you," Marcus said. "I'll see you tomorrow."

After Bradley disappeared after Lucas, I turned to Marcus.

"What an asshole," I said.

"Lucas? I wouldn't let him worry you. He's power hungry and probably a bit too greedy for his own good. Those people burn out quickly."

"Who's Bradley—is he a director?"

"He's one of the creative executives around here," Marcus said. "You might know his family, though—the Audens."

"As in Emmett Auden?"

"That's right," Marcus said. "Bradley's in charge of the Auden Foundation. Bradley also works in the film industry, so he's stretched quite thin."

The mention of the Auden Foundation reminded me why I had called Marcus in the first place.

"I need to ask you a favor," I said.

Marcus raised an eyebrow.

"It's about the event this weekend," I said. "The Orphans' Ball."

"Yes, Rainey?" He was looking at me over the top of his glasses and I could already sense all the reasons why this wouldn't work.

"Are you still going?" I asked.

"I'm contractually obligated . . ."

"And is Jac going with you?"

"You know she hates those things," he said. "But I'm sure she'll put on a good face."

"Well, if she decides she doesn't want to go, and you need a plus one—"

"If you're going to ask me, just ask," he cut me off. "But I want to know why, since you've always avoided those events."

I hadn't felt the need to lie to Marcus in a very long time, and I wasn't going to break that streak now. Still, I could think of a dozen reasons why he might not want me to come if he knew what I planned to do.

"I heard that Laszlo Zo is going to be there," I started.

"I didn't know you were a fan of Dogtooth."

"That's Blake," I said. "I'm Led Zeppelin all the way."

"So? What's the attraction of Zo, then?"

I was suddenly nervous, but I had to be completely honest with Marcus or else I ran the risk of humiliating him at an event.

"I'm starting to think this was a bad idea," I admitted.

"Rainey."

"Zo's involved with a client," I said. "I can't go into too much detail right now, but I need to talk to him, and he's not going to like what I have to say."

Marcus let out a sharp breath, then glanced toward the door.

"Are you serving him with papers?" he asked quietly.

"Not at this point, no," I said. "But he might threaten me with a lawsuit."

"So, you're asking to come to a big Hollywood event with a lot of important people, and you're going to make a scene."

"That's about the size of it," I said, then added, "You can say no."

"I'm well aware." Even though I had known him my entire life, I found him just as inscrutable as always. Then: "I met Zo a very long time ago. This was back in London when we were both just starting out. He got involved with one of the girls at the recording studio, made her lots of promises, and then got tired of her. I think she left the music industry altogether."

I waited.

"It's black tie, you know," he said. "They won't let you in unless you follow the dress code."

I bit back a smile. "Thanks, Marcus."

"Come by my house on Saturday evening and we'll head over together."

"One more thing," I said, reaching into my pocket. I had just remembered my promise to Ahmad, Chloe's roommate. "I don't know if you'll have time for this, but I met someone who does a podcast about movie music. Would you be willing to give him a call?"

I handed him the slip of paper with Ahmad's contact information.

"I'll give it to Isabel," Marcus said. "I hate to say it, but Bradley's right. The entire town is run by the people with the schedules and contact information. You'd never expect it, but they're the ones with the real power."

<hr />

My street was quiet when I arrived home a little after seven P.M. The sun lingered at the bottom of the sky, illuminating the rooftops of the houses nearby. A flock of green parrots chattered in one of the palm trees at the edge of the yard, and for no particular reason, I felt melancholy. I walked up the path to the main house and let myself in.

"Sadie?" I called out.

I listened for a minute, but the house was silent. I walked down the hall and into the kitchen, then put on a pot of coffee and set my bag on the table. For the last few years, I had managed to keep myself busy with so much work that I didn't have to think about things that made me uncomfortable. It was in quiet moments like this, though, when those feelings managed to settle on my shoulders.

Ever since Noa had mentioned Chloe's name to me—ever since Alice's disappearance had taken root in my life once more—I had been confronted with feelings that I had tried very hard to ignore. It was impossible to pretend that my life hadn't crumbled in high school, with both my mother's departure and then Alice's disappearance. I wasn't the only one who had been affected by the loss of Alice, though.

I hadn't looked up Cameron Alder, Alice's brother, for a while. He had already left Los Angeles for college by the time Alice disappeared, but he came back for a few months to help with the search efforts. We had been united during that time, closer than we had ever been, but eventually the search went cold and he had taken a job abroad. Letting him go from my life had been almost too easy: it started with missing each other's phone calls and then dropped from text messages to the occasional email wishing each other a happy birthday. Then a year went by with no contact, and I was so busy I didn't even notice Cameron's absence from my life. By the time I realized that he had changed his number and moved abroad, we had already become strangers to each other. Even as Alice stayed present in my life, eternally seventeen, I released my grip on Cameron so I could pretend to move on with my life.

Before I could second-guess what I was doing, I took out my computer and looked up the contact information I had for Cameron. The phone number was out of date; it was a Los Angeles number that had been canceled when he moved to Paris. I typed his name into Google and waited a moment for the results to load. The top result was a website for an architecture firm in Paris. On the "meet the team" page was an image of Cameron wearing a suit and smiling. *Cameron grew up in Los Angeles and studied architecture at Yale*, read the caption. My pulse quickened as I clicked on the email address included next to his name.

I hope you've been doing well, I wrote. *Just wanted to reach out to you and let you know that I haven't forgotten Alice. I still think about both of you.* I included my email address and phone number.

After a moment's hesitation, I sent the email and then closed my computer.

SEVEN

※

I woke up the next morning with a sense of trepidation about the Orphans' Ball that evening. I hadn't been to a black-tie event in years: even after I stopped performing violin, stopped playing music altogether, Marcus had invited me to attend galas on a regular basis. With the exception of one or two occasions, I almost always declined. There was something about these events that always struck me as false, insulated from the real world. As the years passed and I still did not go back to music, I felt less and less desire to return to that world of light and magic, sleight of hand and artful deception.

After lying in bed for a few minutes I sat up and stretched, then padded into the kitchen of the main house to make coffee. Sunlight angled into the kitchen and illuminated the pale green tiles on the wall. It already promised to be a beautiful day outside, and I could hear the faintest sounds of traffic as cars moved up the road toward Griffith Park.

I hadn't allowed myself to dwell on the evening ahead, but now, waiting for my coffee to percolate, I began to feel the first vague stirrings of dread. Ever since we had stolen the painting from Laszlo Zo's house, I had done my best to avoid news about him. Now I was going to have to confront him directly.

I had gotten rid of most of my childhood belongings when I moved out of my father's house, but there were a few things I kept, including a box of fancy clothing I had worn in a previous life. The box sat in a dark corner of my closet, and I hadn't opened it since moving in six months before. After bringing the coffee back to my room, I set the box on my bed, then took a deep breath and lifted off the lid. The dress on the top of the box was pale blue satin with an empire waist. The last time I had worn it was to a garden party when I was eighteen. I ran my fingers down the fabric and felt a wave of sadness at the memory of how much had changed since then.

All the items had been cleaned and neatly folded before I put them away, some of them years before. There were black velvet dresses that I had worn to performances in Europe, pale linen slips for more casual outdoor events. I paused when I reached the bottom of the box and my fingers brushed against cool fabric. I pulled the dress out and held it in front of me, trying to remember the last time I had worn it.

It was a floor-length gown of mint-green silk. I remembered boats on the water, strings of white lights illuminating the shore. Marina Del Rey. One of the last parties that we had attended as a family, I remembered, before my mother walked out on us. I closed my eyes and took a deep breath, trying to recall the night in question. *My mother had been there. My mother had been there.*

For a long time I had avoided anything that reminded me of my mother. For the first few years it was too painful to have that connection, to think of her. When I started to get over the pain and turned toward anger, I stopped using those nostalgic items out of spite.

I laid the dress on the bed before me and considered it. It was silly, really, to discard something I loved just because I had worn it to an occasion with my mother. *Fuck you, Matilda*, I thought, and felt a little thrill at the rebellious thought. Maybe it was time for me to stop letting my past dictate the way that I still lived my life.

When I wore the dress at fifteen it had been a loose, flowy fit, but now the fabric hugged my curves. I had grown into myself since then, filled out and learned to stand properly. I left the green dress out on my bed, then put the rest of the things away. There was something I needed to do before I met up with Marcus. I grabbed my keys and headed outside.

⁂

The neighborhood around the elegant green Victorian was quiet when I pulled up out front. I sat there for a moment and wondered how I was going to convince the owner to let me past the front door.

I stepped out of my car and surveyed the street: all the houses on this block were historic, well-preserved Victorians in sherbet tones: apricot, lime, rose, lavender. The mansion next to the mint-green house was a stately two-story confection painted oyster white, with a widow's walk and a turret. I glanced at the upstairs window and saw someone peering down at me—just the flash of a hand, a face—and then the curtains were snapped shut.

I opened the back door of my car and took out Chloe's plant. The leaves were drooping, and the single flower had withered to a crumpled nub. I locked my car and walked up the path toward the green house.

The front yard was full of desert plants: statuesque fence-post cacti towered above me, creating a slim grove. Agave plants lined the walkway, each one the size of a boulder. Their blue-green leaves were spooky and otherworldly, a haunting kind of beauty. I hesitated, then walked up the steps leading to the front door. The plaque on the door was almost ominous, now that I was close enough to see the gothic letters spelling out Boneseed.

The doorbell was an ornate brass creation. I pressed the button and heard a deep, resounding bell inside the house.

After a moment, an intercom next to the front door crackled. "Yes." The voice was male and unfriendly. I didn't see a button that I should press to respond. I glanced around for a moment, and then I heard another sigh from the intercom.

"Yes, hello, *what?*"

"Can you . . . hear me?" I said.

115

"I can hear you," he said. "Obviously."

"I didn't see a microphone—"

"Just talk normally. What do you want?"

"I wanted to buy some plants," I said. I felt like someone was watching me, but there was no sign of anyone looking out of a window. I looked up and saw a camera pointing down at me. The black eye shone down, impersonal. It gave me the creeps.

"Appointment only." The voice through the intercom was off-putting and aggressive.

"Okay," I said, slightly annoyed. "Well, can I make an appointment?"

"Who are you, and what do you want?"

The whole situation felt very strange. A few years ago, I would have assumed he was selling weed, but now that pot was legalized in California, it seemed like an unnecessary degree of security. I held Chloe's potted plant up to the camera for a moment and waited.

"My friend bought this here," I said. "It's dying."

There was a long silence on the other end. Then, "Who's your friend?"

"Chloe Delmonico."

After a very long pause, I heard movement on the other side of the door. A latch was lifted, and then there were the *chink-slurrr* sounds of locks being undone. The door opened a crack, and a pair of eyes glittered at me from the darkness. The door finally opened enough for me to see a tall, thin man with a sweep of dark hair styled in a rockabilly wave. Tattoos adorned his ropy thin arms. He was very pale, with dark eyes and long eyelashes. This, I gathered, was Travis, the man that Ricky had been yelling at.

Travis held out his hands for the plant. I handed it to him and he turned it from side to side, analyzing the leaves and tutting a few times.

"What did you do to it?"

"*I* didn't do *anything* to it," I said, affronted. "I told you; the plant belongs to a friend."

"All right," Travis sighed. "Come in."

I hesitated for a moment, and he turned around and snapped, "Come in, come in! You're affecting the humidity quotient."

I hurried in after him and was immediately enveloped in a kind of tropical warmth. The interior of the house had been completely transformed into a lush jungle: I felt like I was in an Edgar Rice Burroughs story come to life. We were standing in an old-fashioned entryway, next to which was a parlor with high ceilings. To the front of the entry, a thin hallway stretched toward the back of the house, and a narrow staircase led to the top of the house. Even the wooden furniture looked to be about a hundred years old, and we might well have stepped back a century. Every surface of the house—the side table, the railings, the coat hooks—were all covered in potted plants. I turned in a slow circle, taking everything in. The air felt so green and healthy that I felt like I could heal from just standing there, breathing it all in.

Travis lifted the leaves of Chloe's plant and then smelled the soil. He looked concerned, almost fatherly.

"What happened to you?" he murmured. "Oh, for the love of Christ."

I found the interaction oddly touching. I had a lot of questions—how did he know Ricky, what were they arguing about, what kind of business was this—but I didn't want to spook him.

"Well," Travis said, finally, "some people shouldn't own plants. Obviously. Some of these are too advanced for the dilettante. You can see for yourself."

"Can you save it?"

Travis scoffed. "Can I save it? That's what I do. Of course I can save it. She'll never see it again, though."

"Chloe will be bummed," I said.

"Don't know her."

"Surely you know Chloe," I said. I took out my phone and dug through my files until I found one of the pictures that her parents had given me. An innocuous photo, recent, but nothing that would necessarily set off warning alarms in Travis.

He peered at my phone. "No," he said. "I don't . . . Wait, hold on. Is she some kind of artist?"

"That's right." I tried not to get excited.

"Yeah, yeah," he said. "One of my other clients brought her around. She got really excited and bought a bunch of plants. She's the one who killed my plant?"

"I'm sure she didn't mean to," I said.

"I don't just give away plants to anyone," he said. "This is a very exclusive business. I vet people. These are my babies—it's like pet adoption, you know?"

"Why is it so exclusive?"

He shot me a look. "How much did Chloe tell you?"

I shrugged. "Not much."

"Everything in here is poisonous," he said. "I sell poisonous plants."

His approach to the world was strangely endearing. I could almost forget that we were surrounded by death, a thousand different ways to die by slow poison.

"Sure," I said. "You spend so much time growing these plants, you want to make sure they survive."

Travis nodded at me, cautious. "She really seemed interested," he said. "She came back a few times on her own. She said money wasn't an issue."

I tried to look impressed and remembered that Chloe was supposed to be my friend in the scenario I had invented. "She came back a few times? I didn't know she was that interested in plants."

Travis straightened and gave me a look of appraisal. "Tell you what," he said. "I'll let you pick something else, and we'll do a clean swap. Deal?"

"Deal!"

Travis gestured around the room. "Anything take your fancy?"

I moved toward a spindly plant composed of green spines. "What's this?"

"Pencil cactus," he said. "Part of the spurge family. A devilish little nemesis, that: it can grow to six feet tall, and it's full of poison sap."

"Really?"

"Sure. If it gets in your eyes, it can blind you."

I shivered and took a step back.

"Of course, that's hardly the worst member of the spurge family," Travis said in a cheerful voice. He was warming to the subject. "You've got the castor bean and the manchineel, also known as the death apple. Just one bite can kill you. The sap can burn your skin right off."

I moved away from the plant so quickly that I wasn't looking where I was going. I felt something bump against the back of my leg, and I nearly tripped. Travis's eyes went wide, and he clapped his hands to his head.

"Jesus, be careful!" he said.

I spun around, expecting to find a cactus or plant with thorny spines. Instead, I was face-to-face with a cluster of beautiful, delicate green stems, topped off with lacy white umbels.

"You're lucky that's only water hemlock," he said. "But you should wash your hands, just to be safe."

"I didn't touch anything," I assured him.

He scoffed. "That's one of the deadliest plants in America," he said. "You don't want to take your chances."

I followed him down a long, narrow corridor toward the back of the house. We emerged into a narrow kitchen with high ceilings. The walls were painted pale green, and ferns drowsed in baskets. A sweet pea vine climbed a trellis and yearned toward the sunlight. Another pot contained lily of the valley, with its tiny little flowers shaped like bells. The smell had always reminded me of my mother's perfume.

I washed my hands and accepted a towel from Travis. "Can I ask you something?"

He glanced at his watch. "What?"

"Why deadly plants? Why not sell regular houseplants?"

He gave me a skeptical look. "What's a regular houseplant?"

"I don't know . . . succulents?" I gestured to the flowers and ferns. "Why don't you keep those out front?"

Travis laughed. "You're joking, right? Sweet peas are deadly, in certain doses. They can paralyze you."

"That's if you eat them, right?" I was starting to get annoyed. "I'm not an idiot."

"Lily of the valley causes heart attacks," he continued, as though he hadn't heard me. His voice was dreamy.

"You didn't answer my question," I said. I was starting to feel a little creeped out by the place, but my curiosity was stronger than my fear.

"Most houseplants are poisonous," he said, turning to me. "Think about it—these are wild things, brought in from the jungle. They were picked because they're pretty, and because they can survive the heat of a house all year round. Most people have no idea how dangerous they are."

"Fair enough."

"I've got a client coming in ten minutes," he said. "You gotta get moving. Pick something and get out."

"Well, what's your favorite plant?" I was flustered and didn't know what to choose. I had forgotten why I was really there—to gather information about Ricky—and had allowed myself to get wrapped up in the fantasy.

A little smile played over Travis's face. "Coyotillo shrub," he said. "But you're not allowed to have it. You seem like a liability."

"Never heard of it."

"It paralyzes you," he said. "But slowly, over days or weeks. It starts in the feet, and then moves its way up the legs. You can't move, can't run—but it doesn't stop there. Your lungs stop working, and then your tongue. You can't breathe. Can't speak. It's horrible."

"No thanks."

"Yeah. Thought so. How about a nice sundew?"

I followed Travis into a greenhouse at the back of the house. The room was so damp that water dripped off the walls and collected in pots around the room. Plants filled the space, their leaves reaching toward the floor-to-ceiling windows. Enormous pitcher plants hung like organs from green stalks.

"I know these," I said, touching one of the plants. I realized my mistake and jerked my hand back, but Travis just laughed.

"You're cool," he said. "These aren't poisonous. They've got a different secret."

"Not sure if I want to know," I said.

"The plants in this room are carnivores," Travis said, gesturing around him. "The smallest eat things like ants and flies. The biggest ones hold a quart of digestive fluid."

I shuddered involuntarily.

"They can eat things as big as rats," Travis said, lovingly stroking one of the plants. "Darwin loved them—he fed them all sorts of things."

"What's that?"

I pointed to a flower that looked like a dark calla lily. Its blossom was a smooth magenta sheath.

"Voodoo lily," Travis said. "A bit smelly. She eats flies."

"Done. Sold."

"Cool." Travis picked up the lily and I followed him back out front. Chloe's plant rested on a sideboard near the front. I had to try one last time.

"So," I said. "How well did you know Chloe?"

"Who?"

"My friend," I said. "The one who killed the plant?"

"Oh," he said. "No, not at all. She was just a customer."

"When was the last time she was here?"

"I already told you," he said. "Couple weeks ago?"

"You haven't seen her since?"

He was still looking down at my plant, and he didn't respond right away. Something in him stiffened, though, and I felt a kind of creeping dread. I had pushed it too quickly. Travis glanced up at me.

"What do you mean?"

"Oh, nothing," I said, trying to make my voice light. "I was just wondering if she was a regular customer. You know. How exclusive this place is."

He peered at my face, narrowing his eyes. "You're lying."

I had blown it. Travis tensed up, cagey and paranoid. I could see him glancing around, skittish and defensive, and I knew that I only had minutes before he kicked me out.

"She's missing," I said. "Her parents are worried about her. I'm just trying to find out where she is."

"I don't know. I just sell plants. You need to leave."

"You're not a suspect," I said. "But you might know something. Who was she with the last time you saw her?"

"Leave," he said. "I'm done talking."

"Please," I said. "Just one more question. What can you tell me about Ricky Goff?"

The look of fear that passed over Travis's face was so sudden and all-consuming that I felt it in every part of my body. Travis had a face that communicated emotion, which was part of what made him a good salesman: you could tell that he cared about his plants. The look of horror I saw there was absolute. His mouth dropped open and his eyes looked beyond me, as though Ricky were standing there.

"Leave," he said, regaining his senses. He pushed me toward the door, and I stumbled on a fold in the rug. "Get the fuck out of my house!"

We were in the foyer then, and he yanked open the door and pushed me out onto the stoop, then slammed the door in my face. The change was shocking: I was back in the Los Angeles desert air, dry as a bone, with the dazzling sun beating down on me. Whatever peace I had experienced for the last fifteen minutes had dissipated entirely, and I found that I was trembling. The neighborhood was still quiet, still peaceful and drowsy, but now there was a kind of eerie warning undertone: *You are not safe here. This is not a safe place. You have been warned.*

EIGHT

After leaving the house I was so rattled I almost forgot the Orphans' Ball was that evening. I was about to call Lola and fill her in on my conversation with Travis when a text pinged through from Marcus.

Last minute work emergency for Jac. You'll just miss her.

At first I assumed that he had texted me by mistake, because I had no idea what he was talking about. I was still sitting in my car outside Boneseed, adrenaline surging, and then I remembered that I was going to see Marcus in a few hours' time.

Jacqueline, Marcus's wife, was like a surrogate mother to me. When my own mother had left my family without so much as a note explaining why, Jac stepped in and helped steer me and my father back on track: she had attended events, made us food, gone grocery shopping, done loads of laundry. She had also helped sort out a lot of paperwork—my mother had been in charge of our family finances—and essentially saved me and my father from drowning in our respective griefs.

I took a deep breath to ground myself, then composed a text to Marcus: *All good. I'm sure I'll see her soon.*

The Loew household was in Pasadena, only a five-minute drive from Banter House. I had spent my childhood visiting the Loew house—first because my father worked with Marcus, then because I got close to Marcus's kids, Paloma and Diego. I had even lived with them for a time when I was working with Marcus.

As soon as I pulled up outside the Loew house, Marcus came lumbering down the steps. He wore a rumpled tuxedo, and his hair stood up in wisps. He grunted a greeting at me through the window and nodded toward his car.

"Leave your car here. I'll drive."

Banter was in one of the oldest neighborhoods of Pasadena, one block over from the famous South Orange Grove Boulevard. The houses here were what people pictured when they heard Jan and Dean songs back in the sixties, dreaming about moving out to the orange groves and learning how to surf. It was easy enough to see why that fantasy still existed, even now, because visiting this part of Los Angeles made me feel like I had stepped back eighty years. You could almost imagine actresses leaning back in their lawn chairs and gossiping in those broad mid-Atlantic accents about the studio system.

I didn't feel anxious about the Orphans' Ball until we got to the Ross Grove Landmark District, where groups of walking tours prowled the sidewalks with their maps and cameras. We had almost reached Banter, and any minute now we would turn the corner and see the fabled conical rooftops and shingled walls of the house where Emmett Auden and his family had lived. Laszlo Zo would be there, and at some point, I was going to have to confront him.

Marcus glanced at me as he turned down the street to Banter House.

"It's not too late, you know," he said quietly. "If you've changed your mind."

I looked out the window, at the perfect green lawns sloping toward the street, at the gardens that never suffered from drought or heat or Japanese beetles. This street was a time warp, insulated in a way that only money could provide.

"I need to do this," I said.

And then Banter was before us. Banter House had always existed in the background of my visits to Pasadena, but I had never actually been inside. Like many of the old Craftsman houses in Pasadena, the house was open to the street, not hidden behind a massive wall or hedge. It was a beautiful sprawling house with a curving driveway and mountains of teacup roses swarming over the portico. I had always longed to see the inside but had never had the chance.

Marcus joined a long line of cars waiting for the valet in front of the house, and I glanced out the window of the car, trying to imagine what might be inside.

"Have you been here before?" I asked Marcus.

"Once," Marcus said. "Recently. Bradley and his family moved into the house last year when his father died. He hosted a dinner for everyone who worked on the film."

"What do you think of him?" I asked.

Marcus thought for a moment. "I've known him for a long time, in a distant context," he said. "He's worked in film production for years. He's always been sweet, maybe even a bit naïve. He's not your typical executive—he's always struck me as the kind of person who preferred to be at home, with his family. Besides, he's always had issues with his father."

"Really?" My ears perked up. I always felt an additional degree of kinship for someone when I found out they struggled with their family.

"Sure," Marcus said. "Bradley's always been into art, and his father wanted him to focus on business. He told me himself. I guess he stepped up when his dad died, though. Now he runs the Auden Foundation, with his wife's help."

We had reached the front of the line, and a beaming valet opened the door for me. "Welcome, miss, welcome!"

Event photographers were staged outside, snapping photos of guests as they arrived. A backdrop with the Auden Foundation logo had been set up beside the heavy front double doors, and people paused before entering the house so they could get their photo taken. Marcus and I exchanged a quick look before heading straight inside, past the photo stand, despite one of the photographers calling after us.

The interior of the house unfolded like a piece of origami. It was so beautiful that I actually gasped, then stood at the threshold, taking everything in. The front door was made of wood and stained glass, and light filtered through to make beautiful patterns on the floor. The stairs leading out of the front room were like the wooden slats of Japanese lanterns, each piece interlocking and yet seemingly part of the same piece of wood. The room was long, with a low ceiling intersected by wooden beams that seemed to glow as though they were lit from within.

I tried to take everything in as we moved through the foyer and entered the living room. There were exclamations from behind us and the sound of photographers snapping away; I figured that someone really famous must have arrived. I glanced around the room, trying to suss out whether or not Laszlo Zo was already there, but there was no sign of him. I recognized a few actors and musicians amongst the crowd, but nobody I was acquainted with.

Marcus touched my elbow. "I'll go grab drinks," he said. "Let me know if you see him."

Zo was six-five, which worked in my favor, because he was a head taller than everyone else. I recognized some people that I had known from the art world, years ago. At the edge of the dining room were a pair of French doors that led out into the garden. I crossed the room and stepped out through the doors, then scanned the garden to see if Zo was outside.

The garden was a manicured space framed with tall hedges. The grass was a neat, even green, the kind of unnatural color that only occurred when plants were coaxed, bullied, and prodded into submission. At the edge of the grass, by one of the tall box hedges, a little Black boy in a suit was crying. A man kneeled on the grass next to him, speaking in a low, coaxing voice. The man was somewhere in his thirties, in a slim-fitting tuxedo that looked expertly tailored. His dark blond hair was swept back from his face, and light glinted off his round tortoiseshell glasses.

I watched from a distance, concerned about why the little boy might be crying.

"No, he *won't*!" the boy cried, stamping his foot.

"Sure he will," the man replied. "I happen to know a great deal about rabbits. You just have to wait here quietly for a moment. Then ask him to come out."

"I already *tried* that," the boy whined. His voice was pitched, and I could see he was on the verge of a meltdown. He was about five years old.

"He's scared right now," the man soothed. "He knows he did something wrong, and he wants to come back to you. Just say, 'It's okay, Clover. I won't be mad.'"

The boy wiped his tears away with the back of his hand. "I'm not mad, Clover. Please, Clover."

Both the man and the boy turned their attention to the hedge.

"Come on, Clover," the man coaxed. He leaned down and eased a hand under the hedge. "Come on, boy. We're not going to hurt you."

I watched, fascinated and invested in the outcome. I had completely forgotten about finding Laszlo Zo.

The little boy leaned against the man, putting both hands on his shoulders. The man rooted around under the hedge for another minute, then exclaimed "Ha!"

He pulled a fat black rabbit out from under the hedge. The rabbit kicked and struggled, but the man held the animal against his chest and rubbed its back, making soothing noises. Gradually the rabbit calmed down enough that the man could hand it over to the little boy, who was ecstatic with relief.

The man stood and brushed the grass off his knees, then turned and saw that I was watching him. He gave me a perplexed smile and nodded at me before turning his attention back to the boy. I flushed, embarrassed at having been caught watching a private spectacle, then turned back inside to continue the hunt for Zo.

More people had arrived at Banter, and the rooms were full of laughing guests. The buzz of conversation floated around me, and I felt almost claustrophobic at the amount of activity. I moved through each room—the kitchen, the dining room, the library—before concluding that Zo hadn't arrived yet. I decided to go find Marcus.

Marcus was standing at the edge of the bar in the living room, and to my surprise, he was talking to the man I'd seen in the garden. The man was nodding as Marcus spoke with animation, one hand tucked in his pocket. In the other hand was a slim notebook.

Marcus looked up when he saw me approach.

"This is Rainey Hall," Marcus said. "Rainey, watch what you say about this one. Hailey's a journalist."

The man looked up and smiled in recognition, then extended a hand. "Max Hailey."

He was a good six inches taller than me and had a firm handshake. A tiny leaf stuck out from his hair, but I felt like it would be too intimate and familiar to point it out.

"The rabbit whisperer," I said.

Hailey laughed. "Hardly."

"Was that your son?"

A crease appeared between his brows, but just as quickly disappeared. "Oh, no, I should be so lucky. That's William Auden. Billy. Sweet boy."

"Oh—he's one of the Audens!"

"Yes, Bradley's son," Hailey said. "Not that I know the family. I was just outside when the rabbit ran away, that's all."

I longed to reach over and pull the leaf out of his hair, but I refrained.

"What are you doing here tonight?" I asked. "Are you covering the event?"

"We'll see," he said, giving me a wry smile. "I was invited to write about it, but my paper doesn't usually cover the social events of Los Angeles. My sector usually covers the misdeeds of the wealthy. They invite us to this event every year, but I don't always come. My editor asked me to attend this year."

"Which paper do you write for?" I asked.

"The *LA Lens*," he said.

"Oh, right, yes, I know it. You write about unsolved murders—right?" Blake sometimes used it for research, because the articles were very thorough. She liked to send the crazier stories to me and Lola.

"Yes, we do." He was watching me.

"Rainey, I need to speak to a few people before they slip away," Marcus said, glancing at me. "Can I leave you here for a moment?"

"Sure," I said, then gave Hailey a guilty smile. "You don't have to babysit me, if you need to leave."

"Not at all," Hailey said. "I came by myself, anyway."

"How do you know Marcus?" I asked.

"I was researching a story a few years ago," Hailey said. "His father had connections to the story."

I raised an eyebrow. "An old story, then."

"Very," Hailey agreed. There was a curious glint in his eye that I couldn't quite decipher.

"Did you get what you needed from Marcus? For the story?"

"We didn't run it," Hailey said. "In the end it went off in a different direction, and it wasn't worth going to publication."

There was a wave of commotion near the front door and excited whispers as people moved in that direction. Hailey and I turned to see what was causing the excitement. Bradley Auden had just arrived, freshly shaved, hair brushed back, and dressed in an expensive-looking and well-tailored tuxedo. He looked a little overwhelmed at all the attention, but he smiled and shook hands as he made his way through the crowd. To my surprise, when he caught my eye, he smiled and waved.

Hailey raised an eyebrow. "You're acquainted with the guest of honor," he said. "I'm impressed!"

"We only met yesterday," I said.

Bradley caught sight of Hailey and faltered. He deliberated for a moment and then advanced toward us, his hand outstretched.

"Max Hailey," he said. "I'm Bradley Auden."

They shook hands.

"Thank you so much for coming tonight," Bradley said. "I'm sure there are other stories more deserving of your time."

Hailey gave him a wry smile. "We'll see."

I wondered if Hailey would mention William's rabbit, but he said nothing. I was impressed and thought it was a mark of integrity that he refrained from saying something that might ingratiate him to someone so powerful.

"Good to see you again, Rainey," Bradley said. "Please let me know if there's anything I can get for you."

He gave us a small bow and then vanished into the crowd.

"What will your article be about?" I asked Hailey.

"I doubt we'll run anything," Hailey said. He clasped his hands behind his back. "We're not a social paper, and unless there's some form of wrong-doing, there's no reason to run a story."

"You think they're trying to prove something by inviting you," I guessed.

"Exactly."

"What do you think of him?" I asked.

"Bradley? It's a fair question. I know he didn't get along with his dad, but that could be a swing in his favor. It's always impressive when someone turns down a massive amount of money in order to work in philanthropy. He and his sister are the only heirs to the Auden fortune—sorry, excuse me, I'm leaving Bradley's children out of the equation. But they're eight and four. Bradley turned down the money before they were born, before he married Violet."

"You seem well versed on the family," I said.

"I have my sources." He sighed. "And we did look into them several years ago because I thought there might be a story."

I was keeping half an eye on the door, wondering when Laszlo Zo was going to turn up. My anxiety had ebbed a little bit, and I was surprised when I realized it was partly from talking to Hailey. There was something comfortably reassuring about his presence. We both turned as there was another flurry of excitement at the door, and I saw a flash of dark hair and a purple suit.

"Ah, the big event," Hailey murmured. "Do you know Simon Balto?"

I saw the streak of white hair and recognized Simon's face from the flyer at the Kloos Museum. He was taller than I had imagined, thin and almost a caricature of bizarre proportions. Simon was grinning, flashing his white teeth, bending to speak to a woman with diamond earrings.

"We've never met," I said. "But I know a little bit about him. A few days ago, I saw that exhibit he curated at the Kloos Museum, the interactive one."

"*Participate*," Hailey said, nodding. "That's right. Do you know much about the art world?" Hailey was watching my face with a friendly, curious look.

I cleared my throat and looked away. "Less and less these days," I said.

"What line of work are you in?" he asked. "Do you work in film? You came with Marcus, so . . ."

"I used to," I said. "Marcus is an old family friend. I'm a private investigator."

He gave a thoughtful nod. "Are you working tonight?"

"I'm never really off the clock," I said. "I can't seem to turn my brain off."

"I know the feeling."

"What do you know about Simon Balto?" I asked, hoping to change the subject.

Hailey sighed. "He's the curator at BALTO, which speaks for itself. He makes a lot of controversial statements. He's always in the news for something shocking that he says. The man's a narcissist, he'd do anything for attention. His gallery is very exclusive—you can't just walk in off the street and buy a painting. He works with the richest people in the city. The country, in fact. No names that make the news—the wealthiest people in the city aren't out there bragging about it and showing off their diamonds. Real wealth hides."

There was a time when I would have had a finger on the pulse of the art world, would have been familiar with every curator and every major gallery, but that world had fallen off my radar. Still, I had heard the name BALTO from somewhere. It lingered there, at the edge of my memory, just out of reach.

"Do you know BALTO?" Hailey asked.

"I don't think so," I said. "I don't really keep up with art news."

"Well, one of their former artists was just in the news for bad behavior," Hailey confided. "He got high and assaulted someone."

"Hold on—Rhodes?"

"That's right!" Hailey looked surprised and almost delighted. "What do you know about Rhodes?"

"Only what was in the news," I said. "That he was on drugs, that he wandered out of some dark alleyway and bit someone."

"It's pretty shocking," Hailey agreed.

"Bad publicity for BALTO," I said.

"You might think so, but I disagree," Hailey said thoughtfully. "That's Simon's brand, after all. Shock and awe. It's all about clout and front-page news."

I felt a chill recalling the story about Rhodes in the news.

"So how is BALTO connected to the Orphans' Ball?"

"Apparently Simon brought in a top-secret painting that was recently discovered," Hailey said. "He's donated it to the auction."

"A top-secret painting?" I raised my eyebrows.

"I've heard it's an Edith Frances, but that's just a rumor."

At the mention of Edith Frances, my heart skipped a beat. Edith's name always made me think of Spencer. I wondered where she was at that moment, and if she knew about the newly discovered painting. Suddenly there was a flurry of activity near the front door as a group of very sleek, well-dressed people entered the house.

I scanned the crowd again and then my heart dropped. Laszlo Zo stood at the back of the room, nodding and listening to the person standing next to him. He was wearing a black tuxedo, as the dress code called for, but the sleeves were rolled up to reveal tattoos and leather bands around his wrists. He wore large sunglasses and a rose tucked into his lapel. A ratty scarf was knotted around his throat.

I felt my pulse quicken.

"Sorry," I said to Hailey. "Will you excuse me for a moment?"

"Of course."

My limbs went heavy as I moved through the crowd, toward Laszlo Zo. There was no room for thought, no time to overthink what I was going to say. It was now or never; I had to approach him and speak to him, or I might lose the chance forever. I was ten feet away from him, five feet; he looked up and started to smile as I approached. I opened my mouth to speak—

The music cut off and microphone feedback filled the room. Everyone turned toward the sound, and the lights dimmed for a moment, then came up to illuminate a makeshift stage at the front of the living room. Simon Balto stood there, smiling and squinting into the crowd. He held a microphone.

"Sorry about that," he said. "I just wanted to say hello and welcome everyone to the Orphans' Ball. Let's give a round of applause to our hosts, Bradley and Violet Auden."

The entire room filled with the sound of enthusiastic applause. Laszlo Zo moved closer to the stage, and the crowd closed in behind him.

"Thank you so much for that," Simon continued. He gave the room another blinding grin. "If you've just arrived, make sure to grab a drink from the bar, because we're going to kick off our auction in just a few minutes. As you already know, all the proceeds from the auction will go to the Auden Foundation, which was founded by Emmett Auden to assist children in need. Today the foundation is headed by Emmett's grandson, Bradley, and his wife, Violet."

Loud applause filled the room. Simon beckoned to someone in the crowd, and after a pause, Bradley joined him onstage, looking abashed and pleased by the applause. Bradley shielded his eyes for a moment to peer through the crowd. He was almost a foot shorter than Simon.

"Where's Violet?" Bradley said. "Violet! Come on, come on, don't leave me alone up here."

I turned to look at Hailey, who was watching the stage intently. A woman made her way through the crowd and joined the men onstage. She was stunning, a beautiful Black woman in a silver dress. She was probably a foot taller than her husband and seemed somewhat aloof. Her hair was cropped in a short, sleek cut that accentuated her sharp cheekbones. I glanced at Hailey, and he smiled back at me.

Simon handed the microphone to Bradley, who accepted it with some reluctance.

"I'll be very brief," Bradley said, smiling out at the audience. "I had nothing to do with tonight. My grandfather's legacy is one of the smaller reasons you all came, but the bigger reason is Violet—my wife."

Another round of hearty applause. Violet acknowledged it with a tight smile.

"Violet married down when she married me," Bradley said. "She's the star of the show. Violet, please say a few words about the foundation and what you've managed to achieve this year."

"Thank you, Bradley," she said, accepting the microphone. She had a rich British accent that carried beautifully throughout the room. "I'll keep this short, because I want the attention to stay on the work that we're doing with our foundation. Most of you are already familiar with Emmett Auden's charitable works—after the death of his daughter, Cecilia, he chose to devote his life to sick children. We carry on his legacy today by working with local children's hospitals and establishing arts programs for orphans and foster children. Thank you. Simon?"

Simon took the microphone back and grinned out at the audience. "Some of you may have heard the rumors surrounding tonight's auction," he said. "Normally I don't like it when a surprise gets out early, but in this case, I can understand all the hype."

There was murmuring in the audience, and I glanced at where Zo stood near the stage.

"Lacy, would you come up here?" Simon said, glancing into the crowd. "Come on up, sweetheart. Here you go."

A young woman with curly blond hair appeared at the edge of the room. Beside her was something tall—the shape of an easel—covered with a sheet. The girl beamed out at the audience and pushed the sheeted object on wheels toward the stage.

"Most of you know the legacy of Emmett Auden," Simon said, glancing into the crowd. "He was an enigmatic man who built strange and beautiful houses for the most important people in Los Angeles. I'm not here to tell you about Auden, though—I want to tell you about Edith Frances, a woman who was just as important, for different reasons."

The crowd was silent, waiting.

"When Emmett first saw Edith's paintings he knew he was looking at real genius," Simon said. "So he commissioned her to start painting the insides of his houses. Murals, lifelike figures, tableaux of Los Angeles. Some of you have been lucky enough to see these masterpieces, but tonight, you have the opportunity to own a piece of history. Because tonight, we have the absolute *privilege* of presenting—for the first time—Edith's recently discovered lost painting!"

The room was dead silent as he moved to the sheeted easel. With a flourish, he whipped the sheet away to reveal a painting. Then, as one, the crowd burst into thunderous applause. The sound was almost deafening, and the excitement was palpable.

The painting was immediately recognizable as one of Edith Frances's—it was a cityscape, perhaps Los Angeles in the early part of the twentieth century, but there was a flat, dreamlike quality about it. It looked like a city on Mars, with its neutral tones and earthly palette. It was incredible to me now that I could have grown up around so much beauty and talent and never given it a second thought. I had taken it for granted because it had always been there: the way that my own family tree was twisted Hollywood royalty, how Spencer's grandmother had been a trailblazing luminary. Bradley had grown up just as we had, but from everything that I could see, he had somehow escaped the damage that had nearly killed us.

I took advantage of the crowd's enthusiasm to push toward Laszlo Zo.

"We'll start the bidding off at a hundred thousand," Simon said, and instantly twenty paddles went into the air.

I had lost sight of Marcus and Hailey, and the crowd surged forward, crushing me. I had always hated crowds, feeling panicky even at the distance between stage and audience, back when I was a performer. I wriggled my way past the people who were pushing me forward, getting an elbow in my stomach, trying to breathe, trying to breathe—I could hear Simon's voice over the din of chatter, and then there was another announcement from onstage.

"Going once . . . going twice . . . ladies and gentlemen, we have a *winner!*"

This was followed by thunderous applause.

"A man who needs no introduction," Simon continued. "Equally famous for his philanthropy as he is for his music . . ."

"And his misdeeds," Zo called out from the crowd.

The room filled with laughter.

"Congratulations, Mr. Zo!" Simon crowed. "You've won the auction!"

I slipped through the room and felt the applause wash over me. It was now or never, I realized; this was my only opportunity to approach Zo. He stood at the edge of the room, and there was a crowd of people jostling toward him to make their introductions and congratulate him. He was greeting each one with a warm smile.

Before I could second-guess myself or question my approach, I moved forward and touched his elbow. Zo turned and smiled down at me, and I could see my face reflected in his sunglasses. I returned the smile and leaned toward him as he bowed his head.

"Have we met?" he asked, tipping my chin up with one of his long fingers. The unexpected touch made me recoil, but I forced myself to plaster on a smile so I didn't frighten him off.

"I know your son," I said. "Ricky, your son Ricky."

I had almost forgotten that my team had decided to give Laszlo Zo a printed statement about what we knew. The statement that Lola had drafted was folded in my purse, but reaching for it seemed like it might disrupt the moment.

Someone jostled me from behind and there were cameras going off and I couldn't even be sure that he had heard me. Zo didn't react but continued smiling down at me in a vague way. I pressed in again, and as someone pushed past, I nearly stumbled into Zo's arms.

"We know everything," I said. "I know all the reasons why you might want to keep this quiet. How long do you think Ricky can keep his mouth shut?"

There was so much adrenaline pumping through my veins that I felt like I was levitating as I pushed through the crowd, away from Zo, through the room and away from the flashing lights, toward air. Panic settled over my body in a way that hadn't happened in a very long time. I couldn't breathe. I needed to find Marcus and tell him I was leaving, but more urgently, I needed to get away from the crowd. I was so intent on getting away from the room and all the chaos that I didn't realize who was standing outside, on the porch, until I was nearly on top of her.

She had her back to the door, head down, fumbling in her bag. She was the bony kind of thin I had seen in the news about meth and cocaine users.

Her arms were long and ropy, and she had a nervous energy, but she didn't look frail. There was a fluidity about her movements, the way she tossed her hair or bent to adjust the hem of her dress. She was wearing torn dark silk, something that looked like it might have cost ten thousand dollars.

"I'm so sorry," I said, bumping against her back.

She held up a hand to wave the comment away but didn't turn around. The hand was covered in rings, and a small tattoo adorned her wrist. I knew that tattoo; I had seen it before. The woman's blond hair was tucked into a loose knot secured with a silver hairpin. It was Spencer.

I backpedaled across the deck so quickly I must have looked like a Tex Avery character.

I needed to find Marcus, I needed to get out of there—

Before I could enter the house and go looking for him, though, someone leaving the house burst past me. He knocked against my shoulder and as I turned to look at his face and register who he was—Simon Balto—he had the nerve to give me a withering look and continue walking without a hint of apology.

I stood there for a moment, shocked, then walked back inside to find Marcus. Before I could gather my thoughts, though, I heard shouting.

"I told you—no, I *told* you!" Simon's voice was ugly.

"Get your hands off me." I could hear the slur in Spencer's voice. She was drunk or high, possibly both.

"Come on. I can't discuss with you when you're like this."

There was a slap, and then Spencer screamed something I couldn't quite understand. Without weighing the consequences, I rushed back outside and saw Simon holding both of Spencer's hands. She was fighting him, tooth and nail.

"Hey—*hey!* What are you doing?" I cried.

Simon immediately released Spencer, then whirled to face me. He took a moment to recover, smooth down his hair and suit, then he plastered on an irritated smile and held up his hands.

"Can I help you with something?"

I was momentarily speechless. I glanced at Spencer, hoping that she would give me some kind of signal about what she needed. As soon as I saw her face, however, I realized she was beyond any kind of rational capabilities. She was completely hammered—her mouth drooped open, and her pupils were so large her eyes looked black.

"Did you hit her?" I asked.

"No," he snapped. "*She* hit *me.*"

"You can't just . . . *grab* her," I said. "Look at her, she's completely wasted."

"And I was *asking* her to leave."

"Did you call her a cab? Make sure she's going to get home okay?" I could hear the angry pitch in my voice and tried to make myself calm down. "Spencer?"

Simon and I both turned to see Bradley Auden standing on the porch behind me. His bow tie was undone, and his brow furrowed as he took in the scene before him. The easygoing host that I had seen earlier was gone; in his place was a concerned father. He gestured at Spencer, then looked at Simon. "Is she okay?"

"She's high," Simon said. "I told her she needed to leave."

Bradley's eyes went dark, and his mouth was set in a thin line. When he spoke, his voice was cold. "What the hell, Simon?" he said. "Jesus Christ, she's a kid. Did you call her a cab? Or maybe you suggested she just drive herself home?"

Simon ran a hand through his hair and kicked at something. He looked guilty. Spencer was somehow still standing upright, but it was clear by the look on her face that she had mentally checked out a long time ago.

Bradley turned to me. "I hate to ask you this, but if you're about to leave, would you mind giving her a ride home?"

"Of course," I said. "I don't know where she lives, though."

"Have you tried asking her?" Simon's tone was disdainful.

"Sure," I said, keeping my voice even. Little jolts of anxiety traveled down my spine, and my stomach was in knots. Simon frightened me, though I couldn't say why, exactly; it was partly to do with his status and also his ability to drop his polite façade and reveal the ugliness underneath. I focused on Spencer and tried to ignore Simon. "Spencer? Spencer, can you hear me?"

There was no response.

"Spencer, I'm going to take you home," I said. My voice sounded false to my own ears, and I was acutely aware of how many times I had been on the receiving end of this kind of care. I had lost count of how many times Jac or Marcus had found me slumped over drunk and put me to bed, wiping my forehead and putting a bucket next to my pillow. Being on the other side of it made me feel like I had been thrust into an adult role I wasn't ready for. "Can you tell me where you live?"

She swayed for a moment, then turned around and vomited over the railing.

"I know where her stepmom lives," Bradley said. "But we can't take her home like this."

Spencer had grown up a few blocks from Banter House, in a gorgeous old house that had been built for Edith Frances, and as far as I knew, her stepmother was still living there.

There were footsteps on the porch behind us, and we all turned to see Violet Auden, Bradley's wife. Her eyes went wide for a moment when she saw the four of us, but she glanced around and made a quick assessment of the situation.

"Does she need to go to hospital?" she asked.

"She drank too much," Simon said.

"She's on drugs," I cut in, but Violet ignored me. She didn't even glance in my direction.

"If she doesn't need a doctor, would you get her off my porch, please?" Violet folded her arms across her chest.

I turned and gripped the railing on the porch so Violet wouldn't see my face and read the pure loathing. None of these people knew me—they couldn't know that I had been in Spencer's position before—but it was hard not to take Violet's callous dismissal personally.

"I'm going to take her home," Bradley said.

"Don't be ridiculous, Bradley," she said. "You've just had the car cleaned. Simon can take her."

She didn't even wait for a response but turned on her heel and disappeared back into the house. Someone behind me cleared his throat, and I turned around to see Marcus standing there.

"What's going on?" he rumbled.

Spencer was slumped on the porch, passed out. When Marcus saw her, he crossed the distance between them in three neat steps and then knelt.

"Can you hear me? Miss?"

Spencer's head lolled.

"Rainey, get the car," Marcus said. "We need to get this girl to a hospital."

"It's okay, Marcus," Bradley said. He looked gray around the gills. "I'm a friend of the family. I'm going to take her. I'll keep her stepmother updated, if need be."

Marcus looked up at Bradley and nodded. "Call me if you need to," he said.

Bradley wasn't a tall man, he wasn't much bigger than Spencer, but he knelt and picked her up in his arms and carried her off the porch like she weighed nothing at all. I watched him disappear into the darkness, and even after Marcus had called my name twice—*Rainey*—*Rainey, it's time to go*—I couldn't help staring after Bradley and wondering if I should have gone with them.

NINE

—∞—

The next morning, I woke up with a feeling almost like a hangover. I groaned and rolled over in bed, pressing my pillow over my head to extinguish the rays of sunshine streaming in through the window. I knew why I felt this way, of course: it was the combination of confronting Zo and also the fact that for the first time in years, I had been face-to-face with Spencer. Spencer's stabs at rehab clearly hadn't worked, or maybe something had triggered her into using again, but either way she looked like she was in a bad place.

My phone pinged, and I picked it up.

Is this Rainey?

The text was from a Los Angeles number, the contact wasn't in my phone. I hesitated before writing back.

Who is this?

Saw your email and wanted to reach out but have been busy til now. Then, *It's Cameron Alder.*

My heart started pounding at the sight of the name. Cameron was a ghost, someone from my past, and even though I had emailed him less than twenty-four hours before, seeing his name again was a shock. People who haven't lived through years of trauma and then recovery can't realize how cleanly your life splits in two, how the past feels like a place you can no longer visit.

Cameron, hi, I wrote back. *Yes, it's Rainey. Where are you?*

I'm actually in LA, came the response. *Just temporarily.*

Before I could think about what I was doing, I clicked on Cameron's number and pressed Call. The phone rang three times before there was a click on the other end, then an intake of breath and a pause.

"Rainey?"

I felt butterflies in my stomach. "Cameron?"

Cameron laughed. "Oh my god," he said. "Wow. Wow. Hi."

"Hi," I said, and for a moment I was overcome with emotion. "God, it's been forever. How are you?"

"I'm . . . yeah, I'm good," he said. "Life has been good. I can't complain."

"Do you live in LA? I'm sorry I haven't been in touch. I thought you lived abroad . . ."

"I do," he said, murmuring assent. "I still live in Paris—did I ever tell you that? I work for a firm that restores old buildings."

I had always found Cameron's voice comforting and was reassured that nothing had changed since the last time we'd spoken. Hearing his voice, though, I felt a deep sense of nostalgia.

"So, what are you doing in Los Angeles?" I asked.

He sighed. "I'm here about Alice."

"Oh?" My heart skipped a beat. "What do you mean?"

"This is going to sound strange," he said, then paused. "She was at my house a few days ago."

I was so stunned I couldn't even begin to form a response. "Sorry, what?"

He sighed again. "Look, there's a lot we need to talk about," he said. "I hate to leave you with that, but I'm in the middle of something right now. When can we talk? I really need to see you."

"Can you come over tonight?"

"I can't," he said, sounding regretful. "What about tomorrow? What are you doing tomorrow?"

"I'll be at work," I said. "I run a private investigation firm in Culver City. It's called Left City Consultants."

"Right, right, I actually heard something about that through the grapevine," Cameron said. "I'd love to hear more about that."

I was surprised. "You've heard about me?"

He laughed. "I haven't forgotten about you, Rainey Hall," he said. "I'll see you tomorrow, okay? I'm looking forward to it."

—⚬—

The Left City offices kept mostly normal business hours, though of course those hours didn't reflect all the work we did outside of the office. Still, we tried to keep at least one person in the office during the week in case we had new clients, many of whom were wary of speaking on the phone about the sensitive details of their cases. Since our team dynamic was one where we liked to bounce ideas off each other, often we all found ourselves in the office at the same time.

On Monday morning I woke up later than I intended. I slid out of bed and quickly washed my face, brushed my teeth, and finger-combed my hair. After getting dressed I drove down the street to my favorite café, where I picked up coffee for the team before heading to the Left City offices.

I was so distracted by my thoughts about Cameron and what he might have to say that I didn't notice a thin young man standing outside my office. He was wearing a school uniform and chewing gum, his backpack slung over his shoulder.

"'Scuse me, is this Left City?" He pointed at the door behind him.

"Yes," I said.

"You must be Rainey Hall."

"Yes," I said, and before I could get out anything else, he handed me a manila envelope.

"Have a nice day."

The young man had disappeared before I could open the envelope. When I pulled out the papers inside and saw what they were, I quickly looked around to see where he had gone, but it was pointless; he was just the messenger, and it wasn't worth chasing after him.

As I reached the office door, I could hear Lola's calm, measured voice, and then laughter. Then came the response, a low male rumble. I opened the office door and stepped inside. Lola was the first person I saw, because her desk faced the door. She was leaning against her desk and smiling. When she saw me, she grinned and pointed a finger pistol at me.

"Fashionably late," she said.

"But with coffee," Blake piped up, as I set the tray of coffee in front of her.

And then I turned and saw him sitting in the corner, one leg crossed over the other. He was smiling up at me, hands folded in his lap, and it took me a moment to realize that I was looking at Cameron Alder.

"Hello, Rainey," he said, standing.

"Oh my god, Cameron," I said, crossing the room. Cameron was taller than me, a comforting height, and his broad shoulders had filled out in the years since I had seen him. He had the same green eyes, the same thick wavy brown hair, but he was older, wiser. He pulled me into a hug, and I inhaled his familiar smell, black pepper and soap. It was disconcerting to see him after all this time. The last time I had seen him, Cameron was still young, only nineteen years old, and now he was a man. He wore suit pants and a crisp white shirt, but it was a hot day, and his sleeves were rolled up.

He stood back and held my shoulders, then looked at me and shook his head. "It's so good to see you," he said. "I'm sorry it's been so long."

"Likewise," I said, momentarily at a loss for words. "Wow. I see you've already met my colleagues?"

"They've been entertaining me with stories about some of your less savory customers," he said, smiling at Lola.

"Don't worry, we've filled him in on everything that you've been doing, too," Lola said, and then she saw the look on my face and frowned. "All good things, Rai, don't worry."

"No, no, it's not that."

"What's up?"

I held up the thick manila envelope. "I've just been served."

It took Lola a moment to react. "You mean now? You've just been served, now?"

"On the way into the office," I said. "It was a courier, but the papers are from Laszlo Zo."

I handed her the paperwork.

Cameron looked confused. "Laszlo Zo? From . . . Dogtooth?"

"The very same."

He raised his hands up in a gesture of supplication. "I won't even ask."

Lola was skimming through the packet of papers that the young man had given me. "I think it's a good sign, actually," she said. "There's a reason why movie stars don't sue tabloids when they print stories about the stars having three-legged mutant babies from outer space."

I rubbed my forehead and closed my eyes. "Where are you going with this?"

"If he sued, it would mean there was some kind of truth to the story," she said. "Or else they were scared about what else the story might uncover."

"You're saying this is a good thing?" I asked.

"Well, it's a headache for me," Lola conceded. "But I think it probably means that we're headed in the right direction. Laszlo Zo is a rock star. He's slept with hundreds of women, I would imagine, and I think anyone with a decent imagination could approach him and say they have a paternity suit on their hands. Do you think he's going to sue every single one of them? No, probably not. Let's keep going forward with what we're doing."

"You can handle this?"

"I always do . . ."

I turned to walk to my desk, then stopped. "Thanks," I said.

"You're welcome . . ."

Blake pointed at Cameron. "Don't repeat any of this, or we'll have to kill you."

He gave her a wide-eyed look and shook his head. "No, no, of course not."

Lo approached the coffee tray and selected her drink, then offered the tray to Blake. I removed mine, then brought the last cup over to Cameron.

"I had no idea what to get you," I said. "I don't even know if you drink coffee, so I just got you a latte. I hope that's okay."

"I love lattes, thank you," he said, accepting the coffee.

I hadn't been nervous to see Cameron, to talk about Alice, but now that I was sitting across from him, I realized that I had been holding my breath all morning.

"Well," Cameron said, slapping his knee. He gave me a nervous smile, then glanced at Blake and Lola. "I'm not just here to catch up. It's great that you run your own PI firm, because I was hoping I could hire you."

It took me a beat for his request to sink in. "Oh—of course! Hire us for what?"

Cameron rubbed his chin and gave me a bashful smile. "To find Alice," he said, and then his face went serious. "Only if you feel comfortable with it, of course! I don't know if you want to go back there, maybe you've moved on . . ."

"She hasn't," Lola chimed in, and I smacked her leg.

"We'd be happy to," I said, then glanced at Blake and Lola. "Right?"

They both nodded their assent.

"No doubt," Blake said, as Lola added, "Of course."

"Okay, Cameron," I said, taking out a pad of paper and pen. "The floor is yours. Where do you want to start?"

"I guess I should start by telling you why I came back to Los Angeles," he said. He rubbed his jaw and looked thoughtful. "I'm not sure if you know this—I don't see why you would—but I still own the house where Alice and I grew up. I've been renting it out for the last nine years, but I'm between tenants at the moment. Last week someone showed up at the house and tried to use our old security codes to get in. The realtor changes the codes every time a new tenant moves in, of course, and the system got triggered. When the police arrived, they found a young woman claiming to be Alice. My sister."

Lola and Blake looked at me. I felt chills go down my arms.

"What did she tell the police, exactly?" I asked.

"She said her name was Alice Alder and that the house belonged to her family," he said. "She had a driver's license, which was expired, but it was authentic. She was older than the photo, obviously, but the cop said it still looked like her."

I felt my hands start to shake. "Do you have any security footage?" I asked.

Cameron sighed and ran a hand through his hair. He drummed his fingers on his knee. "We have cameras around the property," he said. "But they're freestanding devices which need to be charged on a regular basis, and since the house has been empty for six months, they weren't charged."

"Maybe one of the neighbors has cameras," Blake suggested.

"Not a bad thought," Cameron said, nodding. "The only thing is, I don't know any of the neighbors, not anymore."

"What happened after Alice identified herself to the police?" I asked.

"The cops called the security company and said they were satisfied that she was the owner of the house," he said.

"And then Alice vanished?"

"Correct."

I wrote all this down. "And what are the police doing about this?"

"Nothing," he said. "It wasn't a break-in, and as far as they could see, no crime had been committed."

"When did you hear about all of this?" Blake asked.

"The security company called me the next day," Cameron explained. "They waited because of the time difference between Los Angeles and Paris."

"Did the police know Alice was once a missing person?"

"That case went cold years ago," he said. "I spoke to a detective at the Hollywood police station and explained everything to her. Since Alice is twenty-six, now, she's an adult and therefore capable of making her own decisions. According to the police, anyway. We would have to open a new case and make a petition for why she's still missing."

Lola cleared her throat. "And you don't want to go down that route?"

"I don't want to waste another nine years trying to find her," Cameron said, drumming his fingers on his knee. "I have no idea where she's been, but if she's in some kind of trouble, I want to find her as soon as possible."

Lola wrote something down, then cleared her throat.

"Cameron," she said, her voice gentle. "We have experience with missing persons cases, and this is something that we can look into, but I need to prepare you for the reality of the situation. Even if we're successful—even if we track down the person who was at your house the other night—you're not going to get your sister back."

"You don't think you can find her?" Cameron asked. He looked crestfallen.

I spoke up. "We just want you to be prepared for how different Alice might be," I said. "It's been nine years—people change a lot in that time. And we still don't know why she went missing, but whatever happened to her, it can't be good. She might have gone through a lot of trauma. Trauma changes people."

He sighed and leaned back against the couch. "I guess I'm prepared for that," he said. "Maybe she doesn't even want to see me. I just need to give it one last shot, and then maybe I'll be able to move on with my life. And if she needs help—she probably does—I can't rest knowing that she's out there."

"Have you been looking for her this whole time?" Blake asked gently.

"I've gone through three different private investigators," Cameron admitted. "The first one took advantage of me, because I was just a kid, and I inherited all my parents' money. I was an easy mark. The second was quite good. They produced a few promising leads, but then they moved to New York, and the case lapsed. My latest PI would look into her every few months, but he just retired. The cops stopped looking for her after a few months, because I think they just assumed that she had run away."

"Did your PIs find anything valuable?" Lola asked.

"A few things," Cameron said. "I kept a box with all that information. I'm happy to share it with you. It's in Paris, but I can have someone express post it out here."

"But nothing to indicate where Alice might be?" Lola pressed.

"There were a few leads, but they never led anywhere," Cameron replied.

"I'll take a look," I said. "You never know what you might find."

Lola tapped her notepad. "Can you think back on anything unusual or out of character that happened around the time that she went missing?"

Cameron hesitated. "I used to think that I knew Alice," he said. "It was just the two of us for a really long time. My dad died when we were young, and then we lost our mother to drugs."

"What's the age difference between you and Alice?" Blake asked.

"I'm three years older."

"That's tough," Blake said. "I mean, if you were the older kid and your parents were never around, you were basically a parent yourself."

"You're right," Cameron said, slowly nodding. "Wow, I guess nobody's ever put it that way."

"Rainey?" Lola was watching me. "Are you okay?"

"Yeah," I said, my voice tight. "I haven't faced the full weight of this stuff in a while. It's easier to let myself forget about it."

"Yeah, of course it is," Blake chimed in.

Both of my friends looked concerned. Lola's hands had drifted up to cover her mouth, and a crease appeared between her brows. Blake picked at her fingernails, which was one of her telltale signs that she was stressed or worried about something.

"What happened to Alice isn't your fault," Cameron added, looking at me. "I've told you before: nobody thinks you're responsible."

The weight in my chest returned, and I glanced down at my notebook. I had never reassessed my culpability regarding what had happened to Alice, at least, not since I had become an adult. It had always lingered there in the back of my mind—*this is your fault, this happened because of you*—because I had been at the party when Alice went missing.

"You don't have to take point on this," Lola said. "Someone else can do it."

"No, it's fine," I said. "I want to do this."

Lola turned back to Cameron. "Normally we need to have a group discussion about whether or not we're the right match for a case," she said. "But since you're an old friend of Rainey's, and she's okay with it, I think we can go ahead and sign you as a client."

Blake nodded.

"Just a few questions," Lola said. "How long are you planning to stay in Los Angeles?"

"I can't stay indefinitely," Cameron said. "My office has been really understanding, and they're letting me work remotely. I can probably stay for about a month before they start asking questions."

"We can continue the investigation after that, but it might help to have you here to ask questions," Lola said.

"Of course."

"Have you talked to Spencer at all?" I asked Cameron.

"Recently? No, no, we haven't been in touch. She doesn't know that I'm back in Los Angeles."

"When was the last time you talked to her?"

"We lost contact a few years after Alice disappeared. I think some of the PIs reached out to her, but as far as I know, she wasn't much help. I don't think she knew anything."

"Who's Spencer?" Blake asked.

I took a deep breath and glanced at Cameron. He gestured with his hand to indicate that I should go ahead.

"She was my friend in high school," I said.

"She went to Edendale Academy?" Blake asked.

"She went to Eddy," I confirmed. "Actually, her grandmother was Edith Frances, the painter who worked with Emmett Auden."

Blake's eyes went wide. "No kidding?"

"I think I told you that Edith was one of the founding members of Eddy—right?"

"You might have mentioned it."

I laced my fingers together. "Spencer was really troubled. Drugs, dropping out of school, stealing things. I'm sure she would have been expelled if her grandmother wasn't one of the founders. Oh, and her dad was also on the board."

My team waited for me to go on.

"I saw her at the party last night," I said.

Lola looked stunned. She opened her mouth once or twice, trying to formulate a response, then shook her head. "Really?"

"We didn't talk," I said quickly. "She was . . . I don't know if she drank too much or if she was high, but either way I don't think she knew I was there."

Cameron shook his head, looking sad.

"Anyway, Alice and I were friends with her in high school. It's probably not fair, but I always felt like we started making bad decisions once she came into our lives."

There was a lull in the office, and I suddenly felt like I had shared too much. Thankfully, Lola came to my rescue.

"Anything else?" she asked, glancing between me and Blake.

"No, nothing," I said. "I have a lot to think about."

Lola grabbed a standard client form from her desk and handed it to Cameron. "Fill this out and email it back to us in the next few days," she said. "I'll draw up an official contract and send it over to you."

"Great," Cameron said, standing up to leave. He looked relieved, hopeful. "It was good to see you, Rainey. And nice to meet both of you. Oh!" He reached into his pocket and produced his wallet, then withdrew a business card. "The officer who talked to Alice is named Casey Lennon. She's at the Hollywood branch of the LAPD, but all her contact info is on this card."

He slung his bag over his shoulder, gave me a smile, and left. Once he was gone, Lola turned to me. "I can take point on this one."

"No, I should do it," I said.

"What about Noa?" she reminded me. "You're her contact, and she trusts you."

I sighed and ran a hand through my hair. "I don't see why I can't do both," I said.

"You just got served," Lola said, her voice gentle. "That's going to be a lot of paperwork and hours."

"We knew that was a possibility," I pointed out. "And for the moment there's nothing for me to do until we present our evidence at her restraining order hearing."

"And Chloe?" Lola pointed out. She turned to look at Blake. "Where do we stand on Chloe—have you managed to find anything?"

"Not yet," Blake admitted. "I've tried all the usual avenues, all the normal searches and checks on our databases. I've got a few more tricks up my sleeve, but I'm a bit stumped at the moment."

"See," I said, looking at Lola. "This is why we should try to find Alice. I think there might be a connection between them. If we find Alice, we'll find Chloe."

"That's a stretch," Lola said. "You're making a huge leap."

"Well, once we find Alice maybe we can talk to her about Ricky," I said, and I was enormously pleased to see Blake nodding along with me. "Ricky was with Chloe a few days before she disappeared. Right?"

Lola was struggling to come up with a counterargument.

"You're going to run yourself into the ground if you work too hard," she said finally. Her voice was soft, caring, almost maternal. Her eyebrows drew together and a crease appeared in her forehead. I remembered all the times that she had been there to pick me up after I had pushed myself too hard. Still, I couldn't let this go.

"I think Rainey's right," Blake offered. "We're running out of options with Chloe. Alice might know something about Ricky—something that could lead to an arrest, at least. If he *was* involved with Chloe's disappearance."

"Okay," Lola conceded. "You might be right."

"It makes sense for me to take the lead with Alice," I said. "She was my best friend. I know her better than anyone—or at least I did before she went missing. If we find her, she's going to need someone she can trust."

Lola looked at Blake. "Back me up here."

"I think Rainey has a point, actually," Blake said, then shrugged. "You and I both have a lot of paperwork to get through; she might as well be the one hitting the street and talking to people."

Lola raised her hands in a gesture of defeat. "Fine," she said, then pointed to me. "But you're not going to do this all on your own; we'll work on the case, too. Do you have a picture of Alice, so we know what she looks like?"

"All the pictures are nine years old, obviously," I said, taking out my phone. I found the photos that I had taken of Alice that last summer, shots of her in my kitchen and standing by the pool. "But yeah, that's a good idea. I have some photos that I uploaded from that summer. I'll send them to you."

Lola drummed her fingers on her desk. "Where do we stand with Ricky? What else do you need to do on that front?"

"We've got Noa's restraining order petition in about three weeks," I said.

"And what about Ricky?" Lola asked.

"I think we've got enough information on him for the moment," I said, then suddenly remembered I hadn't filled in Blake and Lola on my visit to

Boneseed. Between the Orphans' Ball and the excitement of the weekend, it had gotten lost in the shuffle. "There's something else I need to tell you guys about."

I quickly filled them in on the visit to Boneseed and mentioned finding the plants at Chloe's place.

"Okay," Lola said. "Good. Where do you want to start looking for Alice? Do you want to wait until Cameron gets us the box of stuff from the previous investigators?"

"No," I said. "I don't want to wait. I'm going to talk to the neighbors and see if they noticed anything."

TEN

———∽∾———

The Alder family home was in the neighborhood known as Hollywood-land, near Beechwood Canyon and Griffith Park. This part of Los Angeles had always felt more like part of a small town because it was quaint and somewhat insulated. The streets were lush, lined with trees and flowering bushes. On one side was the canyon and the reservoir, hilly mountainside and chaparral, while Griffith Park sat on the other side. The homes up here were whimsical but not grotesque in size. Still, the real estate was wildly expensive, and I imagined that Cameron would make a fortune if he decided to sell his house.

I needed a moment to ground myself before I got out of my car and walked down the street toward Alice's house. I hadn't been up here for almost nine years, right around the time that Alice went missing. Back in high school we had spent most of our time at my place, because even before Alice's mother overdosed and ended up in the hospital, there was something spooky about her house. It was too big, for one thing, too spacious for Alice's family. That feeling only intensified as first Alice's father died, followed shortly by her mother. By the time Alice disappeared the place felt like a tomb.

It was difficult to see much of the property from the street: the house itself was hidden behind a fence and a winding driveway. Cameron had mentioned the house had not been rented for the last six months, since their longtime tenants had moved out. Still, the yard and property had been so well maintained that the place felt occupied. I walked up to the front door, then took out the keys that Cameron had given me. I took a deep breath and let myself in.

The beauty of the home was evident as soon as I stepped through the front door. The door opened into a small cupola with stairs leading down into the two-story entry, which was fronted by tall windows that looked out over Los Angeles and the nearby Hollywood reservoir. It nearly took my breath away, the view and the familiar smell of the house, which transported me back to high school. I took a moment to compose myself before slipping off my shoes and descending the staircase into the house.

The house had been built in the seventies for a music mogul and his wife, and there was a comfortable retro feel about it. The layout of the rooms was an open floor plan where one room folded into the next, and steps led down into a sunken living room from which you could see Los Angeles crumpled into a topographical map leading down to the ocean.

The house was cleaner than it had been the last time I visited, but still, it was unmistakably the Alder home. Nothing about the interior had changed: there was the same golden furniture, the same orange-and-brown rhomboid wallpaper, the brown tiles edged by shag carpeting. I walked through the house slowly, taking in all the details and looking for any clues that might lead me to Alice. It was hard to stand there and not think of all the people who had once shared this same view, people who had since passed away: the music producer and his wife, Alice's father, and then her mother.

But not Alice, a small voice in my head reminded me. *Not yet.*

I walked back outside. The hedges near the front were neatly trimmed, and a jacaranda tree cast wide shadows over the path leading around to the back of the house. I slipped through a side gate and then walked around the back to the pool, which was hidden beneath the pool cover. It was a hot day, and I was struck by how I was at that moment privy to one of the most beautiful views in the city, but there was no one to share it with. I found the notion deeply melancholy. As I turned to walk back to the house, I glanced at the next-door neighbor's house. I shaded my eyes and scanned the rooftop and fence, then spotted what I was looking for. *Bingo.* A security camera pointed down at the Alder residence.

I walked out the front of Alice's house and over to the house next door, hoping they would be home. There were two cars out front, but that didn't necessarily mean anything. Holding my breath, I knocked on the front door. There was a long silence, and then I heard movement. I could hear voices behind the door. It sounded like they were close to the door.

"I'm not going," a woman's voice hissed. "You go!"

"I'm *busy.*" This was a man's voice.

"Oh, Dave, please. You're eating an ice cream cone. Where did you even *get* a cone? Did you buy cones when we were at Gelson's?"

There was a long pause.

"I *prefer* my ice cream on a *cone,*" came the reply.

"Open the door," the woman snapped.

There was a long silence. I hesitated, then reached out and knocked again.

"She's still here! Just get the stupid door!"

"She can probably hear us," the man said. His voice was furtive. "I'll bet she can hear us."

"She can't hear us." The woman didn't sound convinced. "Let's just ignore her. Maybe she'll go away."

"I can hear you," I called.

There was a long silence, then, "Fuck!"

The door swung open, and a woman with long blond hair stood there, arms folded across her chest. She wore an all-black ensemble, a silky dress over black tights, with a thin scarf wrapped around her neck. Her style was New York glamorous, and she gave me a look of defiance as she took me in. I glanced behind her to see a short, balding, middle-aged man licking an ice cream cone. He wore a black sweater and shorts and waved when I looked at him.

"We don't need anything," the woman said. "You must have the wrong house."

"Ask her about the internet," the man suggested.

"Oh. Right." She peered at me. "We can't get our internet working. Do you know anything about that?"

I was at a loss, but I tried to think quickly.

"Are you using a computer?" I asked.

The man named Dave nodded with enthusiasm. A trail of ice cream dripped over his fingers, and he licked it off.

"What happens when you try to connect?" I asked.

"There's nothing to connect to!" the woman exclaimed. "There's just a big list of networks. I have no idea which one is attached to the house."

"Do you want to show me your router?" I offered.

"We can do that," Dave said.

"Wait, wait," the woman replied. "How do we know we can trust her?"

"I should introduce myself," I said. I pulled out my ID and showed it to them. "I'm Rainey Hall. I'm a private investigator who was hired by Cameron Alder. He owns the house next door."

They squinted at me for a moment, not seeming to understand. I pointed at the Alder house.

"Your neighbor," I prompted.

"We haven't met any of the neighbors," Dave said.

"Well, he's not technically your neighbor," I said. "He lives in Paris and rents the house out to tenants."

"Paris is overrated," the woman said. "I prefer Toulouse. Have you been to Toulouse?"

"No, never," I said.

"*Toulouse* is overrated," Dave cut in. "What about Avignon? Have you been there?"

I glanced between them. "Did you still want help with the internet?"

Dave finished his ice cream cone and wiped his hands on his shorts. "Come with me," he said. "I'll show you the router."

I followed him through the foyer and into a spacious living room. From what I could see of the house so far, it was entirely empty of furniture. A pile of boxes sat in the middle of the room, and the air hung heavy with the smell of lemon wood polish.

"We don't really live here," the woman explained. "Not full-time, anyway. We've come out from New York. I'm Irene, by the way. We can't get a handle on Los Angeles—I don't know if I love it or hate it."

"That's a common reaction," I said.

"You haven't been past Hollywood," Dave said, poking Irene.

"Don't poke me! I *hate* it when you poke me!" Irene whirled around and jabbed her finger into Dave's soft belly. He let out a soft *whoof!* and clutched his stomach. Then, to my surprise, they both burst out laughing.

I didn't know how to react. They made such an odd pair that I couldn't figure out what their connection was.

Dave pointed to a makeshift desk with a jumble of wires and a network router. "That's it," he said. "We had someone come out and hook up the electricity and internet, but now we can't figure out how to get online. If you could help, we'd be really grateful."

"Very grateful," Irene agreed.

I sat down at the desk and looked at the router. All the lights were green, indicating that it was connected. I turned it around and saw a sticker on the back. And there it was, clear as day: a username and password.

I almost laughed at how easy it was, but I knew that I should draw out the conversation a bit to build rapport. Besides, I needed their security footage, and there was a chance they might kick me out as soon as I helped them get online.

"Do you mind showing me your computer?" I asked.

Dave opened his laptop and typed in his password. "There you go."

"So, what are you doing in Los Angeles?" I asked, stalling for time.

"My mother died," Irene said. "She owned this place. Moved out here about twenty years ago. I've been here a couple times, but not for ages. Not sure if we're going to keep it."

Dave peered over my shoulder as I opened the internet settings. "You said you're a private investigator?" he said.

"That's right."

"What are you investigating?" he asked.

"There was an attempted break-in at the Alder house a few days ago," I said, deciding to be vague.

"Next door? A break-in?" Irene's eyes went wide with fear, and her hand drifted up to her throat.

"I don't think you need to worry about anything," I said, but she cut me off.

"Oh, god, are there problems in the neighborhood? What are the police doing about it? Should we call them?"

"No, no, there's no need for concern," I said. "My client knows this person; he just needs evidence. Unfortunately, his own cameras weren't working that night, which is why I came to talk to you. I was hoping to have a look at your security footage."

They both peered at me, then glanced at each other.

"Do we have security footage, Dave?" Irene asked.

Dave shrugged. "Mike could have set it up with everything else," he said. "Maybe your mom had the cameras installed."

"Did she have a computer?"

Irene rubbed her chin and thought. "I think it's in her office," she said. "It's a big mess, but you can have a look, if you want."

"Let me see if I can get you hooked up to the Wi-Fi, first," I said. I opened the laptop's computer settings and clicked around for a few seconds. "You know what . . . sometimes the password is written on the back of the Wi-Fi module . . ." I turned the tower around and feigned delight. "Your mom must have been organized—let's try this!"

I typed in the username and password. When the laptop connected to the internet, Dave let out a whoop of joy.

"Oh, let us pay you, please!"

"No, no, it was easy," I said.

"Fifty bucks?"

"Forget the money," I said. "It was nothing at all. On the other hand, if you'd let me have a quick look at your security tapes—just for the last few days, of course . . ."

"It's probably just a bunch of cats fucking," Irene said. "But sure, come on back."

I followed her through the house, down a long hallway and past a series of empty bedrooms. This house had its own brand of melancholy, similar to the Alder home, a story of loss and dying generations.

"Here," Irene said. We emerged into a small office overlooking a rambling garden. Ivy climbed up the windows, lending an aquatic feel to the room. Stacks of paper and boxes cluttered the floor, and a desk covered in boxes sat against the wall. An old computer and monitor sat next to a printer. The computer hummed, plugged in.

"You sure you don't mind?" I asked. I was always surprised at how much people relaxed around me once I showed them my credentials.

"You said you're looking for someone breaking into houses, right?" Irene shuddered. "Stop them before they get to mine."

She left. I sat down at the computer and clicked on the mouse to wake it up. The screen blinked awake with a little pop. The desktop was a cluttered mess of icons and tabs, folders, and documents. I felt a sense of urgency, the need to get in and out as soon as possible, before the couple changed their minds.

I decided to save time by calling Blake.

"Hey, Rainey," she said, picking up after a few rings.

"I'm at the neighbor's place and they've agreed to let me see their security footage," I said. "I'm sitting in front of an ancient computer, and I don't have the first idea about where to start looking."

Blake paused. "What's the name of the security company?"

"They just moved in; they don't know anything."

"Okay," she said. "Windows computer?"

"Yes."

"Go to the Start menu and pull up the search bar," she said. "Then type *security* and see what comes up."

I did as she asked.

"Any luck?"

"There we go," I said. "I see a Domicile icon."

My team had enough experience with private security companies that I recognized the name. It was one that I had used in the past, and it was Blake's preferred security company.

"Good one," Blake said. "Do you have time to view the files, or do you want to email them to me?"

"That's a better option."

I logged into my email, then glanced over my shoulder, wondering when Irene or Dave would remember I was there and change their minds about letting me see the security footage.

"Any luck?" Blake asked.

"They're buffering," I said. "It's an old computer."

"No point asking if you have a USB drive, I suppose."

"Alas, no."

I held my breath for the next five minutes, waiting for the files to upload. When I finally got a confirmation receipt, I exhaled.

"I'll see you back at the office," I told Blake, then hung up.

I went back into the living room and found Dave sprawled on the floor, reading a magazine. Irene was hunched over at the computer, feverishly scrolling and clicking. Dave glanced up and waved.

"Find what you need?"

"Yes," I said.

Irene finally looked up. "Did you identify the robber?" she asked.

"For the moment I think we're in the clear," I said. Lola had taught me phrases to deflect questions without lying or giving too much away. "You've both been very helpful, thank you. I'll get out of your way now."

My next stop was to talk to the officer who had spoken to Alice on the night in question. I didn't know if she would be at the police station that afternoon, but since I wasn't too far away, I decided to drop by and try my luck.

Hollywood was a neighborhood I avoided as much as possible. It was an odd place, a dusty cluster of office blocks sequestered between the two busy thoroughfares of Sunset Boulevard and Hollywood Boulevard. Whatever glamour had existed back in the early days of Los Angeles was long gone: the tram cars and pepper trees that Nathaniel West had written about had been ripped up by their roots, and everything covered in a layer of asphalt. There was little shade to be had, save for the dim alleyways where drug deals went down, and the streets pulsed with heat. Vast parking lots had taken the place of the modest hotels and ranches that once stretched along Sunset.

I always felt sorry for the tourists who flocked here hoping to see movie stars. What they found instead were exhausted Charlie Chaplin impersonators and people in mildewed superhero costumes strutting around in front of Grauman's Chinese Theatre. There was no respite to be found anywhere in Hollywood, no quiet parks or gardens; there were only vastly overpriced franchise restaurants and liquor stores.

There were still little snatches of old Hollywood to be seen amongst the modern wreckage, though, including the walk of fame. The large pink stars emblazoned with the names of celebrities popped up in the oddest of places, winding their way down stretches of pavement outside quiet shops no longer frequented by tourists. I had never been to the Hollywood branch of the Los Angeles Police Department, and I almost laughed when I saw there were dusty celebrity stars leading up to the station itself.

As I walked into the station I heard screaming, and it only took a moment for me to realize that the source of the ruckus was a pretty young woman in green fishnet tights and a silver dress. She sat on the floor, kicking her heels in protest, while a young man in a Superman costume did his best to ignore her.

"Why can't we just leave her!" the woman screamed. "It's her own fault for getting arrested! I want to go home! I want waffles! I want waffles! You promised me breakfast!"

In another city this scene might have seemed out of place, but since this was Los Angeles, it didn't matter that it was four P.M. I gave the woman a wide berth as I walked up to the reception desk, where a bored-looking Black woman sat reading a Chuck Palahniuk book.

"Help you?" she asked, without looking up.

"Hi," I said. "I was hoping to speak to Casey Lennon."

The woman sighed and folded down her page, then glanced at something on her computer.

"She expecting you?"

"No."

Her eyes flicked up to meet mine. "What is this regarding?"

"She responded to a security alarm last Tuesday," I said. "I'm here to follow up on that."

The woman stood up and walked toward the back of the station without saying anything. I waited for a few minutes and then the door to the back area opened, and the woman reappeared and waved me through. I followed her, relieved to be out of range of the screaming woman who wanted breakfast.

A female officer stood at the end of the hall, watching me. She was young—early thirties, I would guess—with dark hair pulled away from her face. She was on the slender side with bronze skin, but something about the way that she stood suggested athleticism, a lean, muscular mass. Her arms were folded over her chest.

"I'm Officer Lennon," she said. "Can I help you with something?"

I took out my ID and showed it to her. "Rainey Hall," I said. "I'm a private investigator. You spoke to my client a few days ago about a break-in at his property."

"Where was this?"

"Above the Hollywood reservoir," I said. "Alice Alder. She had an expired driver's license?"

Officer Lennon immediately nodded. "Right, I remember," she said. "How can I help?"

"Is there somewhere private we can talk?"

She hesitated, then indicated that I should follow her. We emerged into a small interview room with grills over the windows. Dim light filtered in through opaque glass. Officer Lennon hit the light switch, and a fluorescent bulb blinked three times before fizzing to life.

We both sat down.

"I'm not sure how much Cameron told you," I said. "But his sister has been missing for nine years. If you spoke to her the other night at his house, it raises a lot of questions."

Officer Lennon nodded. "He mentioned something about that, yes," she said. "I explained he would have to open a new missing persons case, but since she's an adult, he would need to prove that she's in danger."

"How can he prove that she's in danger if he doesn't know where she is? She could be missing against her will."

To my surprise, Officer Lennon bit back a smile. "I agree that the logic is faulty."

I knew Officer Lennon wasn't the enemy, but situations like this often left me frustrated. It was one of the reasons I had opened my investigation firm in the first place, to look for people who might have otherwise slipped through the cracks because the police didn't have the time or the inclination to look for them.

"Your client's sister is lucky that he hired you," Officer Lennon pointed out. "Believe me, I wish we had the resources to look for everyone. We're stretched to a breaking point at the moment."

"She was my friend," I said. "Alice Alder, I mean. I spent years looking for her when she first went missing."

A shadow passed across Officer Lennon's face. "I'm sorry to hear that," she said.

"Can you tell me how she looked? When you saw her at the Alder residence, I mean."

She thought. "She looked healthy enough," she said. "A little thin if anything. A little anxious, too, but I attributed that to the fact that the police had been called."

I felt a sudden wave of envy and despair that this woman—a stranger, no less—had been within feet of Alice only a few nights ago, and the moment had meant nothing to her. It wasn't her fault, of course, but it seemed desperately unfair that this woman had happened across her by chance, when I had looked for Alice for such a long time without luck.

"And there was nothing to indicate where she might have gone?"

"Nothing, I'm sorry." She glanced at her watch. "Is there anything else I can help you with? I have to head out soon on patrol."

"One more thing," I said. "Chloe Delmonico."

Officer Lennon's face was impassive. She drummed her fingers on the desk, and a faint line appeared between her brows. "Oh, that missing woman," she said. "The girl who was on the news. What about her?"

"Her parents hired me to find their daughter. I know it's a long shot, but I was wondering if there was anything you could tell me about her. Have you heard anything?"

Her face closed off. It was subtle—just a tightening of the jaw, a slight downward glance—but I had studied people's faces enough to know the signs.

"Nothing."

"Are you looking for her?" I was slightly irritated at the quickness of her response. I felt like I was being dismissed.

"No, not me," she said. "From what I understand, that girl went missing somewhere up in Oxnard, right? That's where she lived?"

"Yes, but—"

"It's a different department. We have nothing to do with that." Her voice was sharp.

I hesitated, then nodded and pushed back from the table and stood. "Thanks for your time."

I had reached the door when Officer Lennon called out, "Wait—wait a moment."

I turned.

"I apologize for my tone," she said. "I know you're just doing your job. We're both trying to do the same thing, at the end of the day."

I was surprised by the apology. "Thanks. It means a lot."

"Have you been doing this long?"

"A few years," I said.

"I've been here eight," she said. "And by the time you get to where I stand, you'll be able to see how many of these cases don't get solved. How many people go missing. The difference between my job and yours, though, is I deal with families who can't afford to hire a private investigator."

I didn't think it would be judicious to mention that I was helping the Delmonicos without payment.

"And most of those missing girls who make the news are White," she added. "And beautiful. You see my point?"

"I understand," I said, nodding. "I won't take up any more of your time. Thanks again for your help, Officer Lennon."

"Call me Casey," she said. "I hope you find your friend."

"Will do," I said, surprised. "And thanks."

"Keep in touch," she said. "Let me know if you find anything."

I was walking to my car when my phone rang. I took it out of my pocket and saw it was Blake.

"Hey," I said. "Just finishing up at the police station."

"I finished going through the security footage from Alice's neighbor," she said. "I think it's good footage, but of course I need you to confirm that it's Alice. I have the photos you gave us, but I can't tell."

I felt a flood of relief and gratitude toward Blake. "Thanks so much, I owe you one," I said.

"You don't, actually," she said, laughing. "You did everything. I just watched the footage."

"Still."

"There's something else," she said. "I'm not sure Cameron knows. Alice wasn't alone at the house that night."

My heart started pounding. "What do you mean?"

"She arrived at the house by herself," Blake said. "And then it looks like she walked around the property, trying to find a way in. About twenty minutes after she arrived, someone else came. Another young woman."

"And?"

"They had a fight," Blake said. "I can't make out any sound, the cameras were too far away. I'm looking at it now. The other woman grabs Alice and tries to drag her away. The police must have come soon afterward, because they both turn to look at something on the street."

"She must have slipped away without the cops noticing," I said, my heart pounding. "The officer I spoke to only saw Alice."

My thoughts were racing. Something suddenly occurred to me.

"Can you take a photo and send it to me?" I asked.

"Sure thing. Doing it now."

I stood on the street where I had parked and felt an odd sense of disconnect as I watched people moving in and out of shops, walking along the sidewalk and talking to each other. It had been nine years since I had seen Alice, and I was moments away from seeing her again, now. A text from Blake pinged through and I opened it with a sense of nervous excitement.

"So, here's Alice," Blake said. "At least, I think it's her."

I looked at the photo and felt faint. It was Alice, all right, there was no doubt about that. Her hair was cropped into a messy bob, and her face had become leaner in the years of her absence, but all the other features were unmistakable. Officer Lennon had been right, too: even in the photo, I could see that she was nervous.

"Here's the other woman," Blake said. "I just sent it through. You should have it in a minute."

I felt numb when I saw the photo that Blake sent through. In some ways I already knew who the other person was; I probably could have told you that she would have showed up in this mess eventually. She had been there all along, from the moment of the disappearance until Cameron had finally given up and moved to Paris. And here she was again.

"Do you know who it is?" Blake asked, and all at once her voice sounded very far away.

"Yes," I said. "I know who it is."

In the photo, grabbing Alice's arm, her face twisted in a mask of fury, was Spencer.

ELEVEN

There were a lot of things from my past that I had allowed myself to forget, including the months that existed on either side of Alice's disappearance. Other than some photos of Alice, I had few souvenirs to remember that time. Before I stopped drinking, in those years when I acted like I was able to shut off memories and feelings that didn't suit me, I had returned to my childhood home, drunk on champagne, and rifled through my closet, looking for a cigarette lighter that had once belonged to my mother. It was there, sitting on the floor of my closet, that I found a leather satchel I hadn't seen since high school. Inside were disposable cameras, still wrapped in foil, a shirt with a name tag—my name spelled out below the words SAN RAFAEL DEL CAMPO. A few crumpled dollar bills, a handful of coins, and a battered deck of Bicycle cards.

Seeing the cards, bent and nearly worn clean of their wax, I remembered those months four years before when my two friends and I had sprawled out on the floor of my bedroom and played cards for hours. Spencer had learned to play in rehab, she told us, revealing the personal information in an off-the-cuff way. We hadn't even known that she had been to rehab, but beyond that quick statement, she didn't seem to want to discuss it. That summer she taught us poker, cribbage, oh hell, and rummy. Her favorite game, though, was hearts, which needed a fourth player.

Once, when we were at Alice's house, Spencer roped in Monica, Alice's nanny, who rarely had patience for games.

"Come on, Monie, please," Alice cajoled. "Just one game."

"Do you know how to play?" Spencer asked.

"Of course I know how to play hearts," Monica replied.

I could see immediately why Spencer liked the game. It was easy enough to pick up but could result in a quick loss if you weren't paying attention. Each player was dealt thirteen cards, which were played out in rounds. The object of the game was to avoid negative points, which were garnered through cards in the heart suit. The only other point card, the queen of spades, delivered thirteen negative points in one fell swoop.

Monica only lasted three rounds that day. After the third round, when Spencer was tallying the points in triumph, Monica threw down her cards in disgust.

"You're cheating!" she cried.

"I'm not," Spencer replied, her voice cool. "It's a standard move. It's called Shooting the Moon."

"You never explained that!" Monica protested.

"Why would I? You said you knew how to play." Spencer sat back and smiled.

Monica marched out of the room without saying another word.

"What happened?" Alice asked.

Spencer responded by spreading out all our hands. "See how I have all the hearts?" she asked.

"Yes," Alice said.

"And the queen of spades?"

"I thought those were bad," Alice said.

"They are," Spencer said, "unless you get every single heart. If you get all the hearts and the queen of spades, you don't get any points. All the other players get twenty-six negative points."

Alice scowled and crossed her arms. "Monica's right, you should have told us," she said.

Spencer shrugged. "She said she knew how to play. It's a standard move."

Alice folded her arms across her chest. "I don't want to play anymore," she said. "You fight dirty."

Spencer was struggling to hold in a smile, and in that moment, I hated her.

"Fine," she said after a pause. "I'll go home, then. No fun hanging out with sore losers."

We didn't have long to be mad at Spencer, though, because a few days after that card game, her father called with bad news. Spencer had relapsed; she was back in rehab. She would be there for a week, but she was desperately homesick, and he asked if we would be willing to pay her a visit. She had spoken so highly of us, he said; it would mean the world to her. "Please," he added. He would send a car; everything would be arranged.

The rehab center was in Ojai, two hours north of Los Angeles. Family-run vineyards stretched alongside golf courses and boutique hotels. A squat range of peach-colored mountains framed acres of farmland, an idyllic setting that seemed at odds with the purpose of our visit. San Rafael del Campo, the rehab clinic, was so beautiful that it could have easily been mistaken for another ritzy hotel. As we drove past the tall hedges that marked the boundary of the property, a kind of manufactured somnolence descended upon us: the thick smell of jasmine and cut grass, the buzzing of honeybees on the rows of lavender bushes leading up to the chapel.

The facility consisted of a series of low-slung buildings and covered outdoor walkways that extended through the rose gardens like spokes. The main building, which housed the old chapel, was the pure white of scoured bone. The rest of the complex was brick and Spanish tile, all of it dating back to the 1800s, when it had been a mission. We found Spencer waiting for us in the visitors' lounge, a sun-drenched room lined with windows overlooking the vegetable garden. She wore a uniform of soft beige linen:

slacks and a shift. I glanced around and saw that all the inpatients wore some variation of the same.

"The head shrink studied Hegel and decided that ego is the root of individual evil," she said, bowing her head in a gesture of ironic supplication. "We had to surrender all our own clothing. To heal."

It was hard not to give some kind of credence to whatever philosophy was behind the surrendered possessions: Spencer did look better. Stripped of makeup, of designer clothing, she looked like a fresh-faced girl of seventeen. Her hair was tucked behind her ears, and for once, it seemed like she was able to sit still. Alice and I were both nervous, unsure of how to act around her.

"We were worried about you, Spence," Alice said, in a low voice.

Spencer suddenly teared up. She quickly wiped her eyes with the back of her hand.

"I'm so embarrassed," she said quietly. "I thought . . . I had everything under control. It wasn't that bad, you know—I don't know why my dad made me come back."

"Oh, Spence, he *loves* you." Alice reached over and took Spencer's hand. "We all want you to get better."

Selfishly, my first reaction at hearing Spencer's dad's voice was fear—I thought that we had been caught, that they knew about our break-ins. Our little crime spree. And then, even worse, had been the relief I felt when I heard Spencer was in rehab.

That afternoon Spencer took us for a walk around the compound and showed us the rose garden, the vegetable patch, the tennis courts, and the alcoves where migrating swallows had nested for decades before migrating down to Argentina. There was an outdoor *lavandería* where unseen hands had once tended to the monks' laundry; now patients had to wash their own clothing. "Part of the healing process," Spencer explained, rolling her eyes. Clean cotton tunics stretched along the lines, flapping in the breeze.

The facility was good for Spencer, even if she wasn't willing to admit it. For the entire afternoon, I found myself asking how much of her personality had been just a *character*, a construction, because she seemed so much different in this setting. Stripped down to basics. Sober.

When we were back in the visitors' lounge, Spencer took out her deck of Bicycle cards. I watched her hands deftly cut the deck and shuffle—once, twice—before dealing out four stacks of thirteen cards.

Alice and I exchanged a nervous look.

"Spencer, I'm not sure this is a good idea," Alice said.

"Come on," Spencer replied. "I can't watch TV or use a computer. I don't even have access to a cell phone. It's the only thing I'm allowed to do in here."

She glanced around the room and then whistled.

"Cat! We need another player!"

A young nurse with dark hair sighed. "I'm on rounds," she said.

"Your rounds start in an hour," Spencer said. "This won't take that long."

The nurse glanced around and then checked her watch. "Fine," she said, then came over to join us. "I'm not betting today, though. You'll get me in trouble."

Spencer grinned. "I'll go easy today," she said. "No betting."

"Spencer has an unfair advantage," Cat added. "She has a special tutor."

"To teach you cards?" Alice asked.

"She's kidding," Spencer said, her voice abrupt.

"You and Tall Boy play for hours. I've seen you," Cat said. She wore a teasing smile. "He's cute, Spence. I think it's sweet."

"Who's Tall Boy?" Alice asked.

"A friend," Spencer said quickly.

"More than a friend, from what I've seen," Cat teased.

Spencer's face had closed off, and I tried to change the topic.

"Shall we play?" I asked.

Spencer beat us handily, round after round, and the game was soon over. I felt an odd relief as I watched her tally the points and smile to herself: she might have been struggling, but at least Spencer had retained some small part of herself, which the clinic and its neutered aesthetic couldn't strip away.

Afterward Spencer showed us her room, which was a clean space with wide windows. Behind her bed were a small collection of personal items, which had apparently been spared the clinic's Hegelian view on the destruction of the ego. When I saw what Spencer had placed in the center of her shelf, my blood went cold.

It was a small bronze bust, the size of a papaya. The sculpture was roughly hewn, almost unfinished in its appearance—neither distinctly male nor female, the face itself came floating to the surface of the head as though through a skin of water, dreamlike, stagnant. A sharp nose, eyes unformed and receding into the contours of the skull, cheeks melting into indistinct geometry. I recognized the bust immediately, and my heart sank. It was something that Spencer had scored in one of the houses we had raided just a few days before she had been sent off to rehab. She hadn't known it until I told her, but the bust was one of the most famous and controversial works of art to come out of Europe in the years between the wars, and there were many museums who had refused to display it.

"You have to get rid of this," I said, picking it up. I couldn't believe she would be so brazen.

"Don't be ridiculous," Spencer said. "Nobody cares what I have in my room."

"What if someone recognizes it?"

She scoffed and sat on the bed. "Who would recognize it? One of the nurses? Nobody cares about art in here."

I felt a surge of anger toward Spencer and her cavalier attitude. If she went down, it was likely the rest of us would go down with her. Up until then I hadn't really thought about the implications of our stint of breaking into houses—how selfish it was, how criminal—but, for the first time, it hit me. *This is wrong. We are going to get caught.*

I cradled the bust in both hands. I thought momentarily about running from the room, disposing of the bust somewhere Spencer couldn't track it down. I knew it wouldn't be that easy, though. Nothing with Spencer was ever easy.

The small bronze bust was a piece of art called *Lille, Après*, and it was probably my fault that Spencer had taken it. She might never have noticed it if I hadn't gone over and picked it up, felt its heft in my hands. The house we had broken into was an ugly round cement monstrosity with views of Los Angeles. The artwork around the house—paintings and sculptures both—was arranged as though it had been curated by a highly paid decorator: impersonal and pretentious.

When we walked through the office, I spotted the bust on a bookshelf. It was innocuous enough that it wouldn't necessarily stand out as something of value, even though it was worth at least two million dollars.

"Oh my god," I said, lifting it from the shelf.

Spencer's ears perked up. "What is that?"

"It's really fucked up," I said, turning the thing around in my hands. I knew the story behind its creation well, because my mother had told it to me with fascination. "The guy who made this killed his muse."

Herve Rossignol was a French sculptor in the late 1800s who became known as an abusive partner, as well as a bit of a lothario. At the time his promiscuity was celebrated, but viewed through a modern lens it was more than a little disturbing. The rate at which he used women and then discarded them would have to suggest that there was something criminal about him, a view further supported by the way his career ended.

Lille was a sixteen-year-old student when she met Rossignol, who was thirty-four at the time. In his circles the age gap wasn't enough to raise eyebrows, but when she left him after six months, it caused a huge scandal. Not one to be humiliated by a woman, Rossignol went to her house in a drunken rampage and strangled her to death. The horrifying part of the story was what happened afterward: he took her body home to his studio and spent the next three days creating the bust that later became so controversial.

When the crime was discovered, it became a massive scandal throughout the European art world. Rossignol wrote a letter confessing to the deed, which would have been too much for the police to ignore. Rossignol was never arrested, though, because immediately after sending the letter he killed himself by taking an overdose of morphine.

We had been to three houses at that point—first my neighbor's, and then two houses in the Hollywood Hills. Spencer was always in charge of the selection, and she was less than forthcoming about her process, if indeed she had one. There seemed to be an element of chaos to most of her decisions, and I doubted she had put any thought into the locations other than places that looked empty.

Now, standing in front of Spencer, I tried another tack. "Please," I said gently. "I'll get rid of it for you. We can take it when we go."

"What are you going to do, return it?" She laughed and picked at her fingernails. "Just leave it here. You're making a big deal out of nothing."

"You can't have it out in the open like this where anyone can see it. This affects all of us."

Spencer met my eyes, and I was shocked to see the look on her face. She looked scared.

"I'll get rid of it, okay?" she said. "I'd never do anything to get you in trouble."

———

Later, when we were waiting out front for the car to collect us, Spencer asked us not to say anything to her father. She tugged on her sleeves, nervous, glancing around to make sure we were alone.

"About what?" I asked. It came out more irritated than I meant; I was still angry at her.

"About any of it," she pleaded. I had never seen this side of her, and I didn't know how to respond. "The houses. The sculpture. He'll never let me out of here."

I folded my arms across my chest and scanned the road leading up to the center. Spencer put a hand on my arm.

"Please, Rainey," she said. "I know I can be a shit, but please. *Please.*"

"Fine," I said.

"And one more thing," she said. "He doesn't know that I have a boyfriend."

Alice and I exchanged confused looks.

"You have a boyfriend?" Alice asked.

"Tall Boy," Spencer said. "I mean, he's not really a boyfriend, he's just a friend. It's complicated. My dad's really old-fashioned, though, so keep it to yourself."

"Why even ask?" I said, irritated. "It's not like we can tell your dad about your boyfriend if we don't know who he is. What kind of name is that—Tall Boy?"

"It's a nickname," she shot back. "You know what a nickname is, yes, Rainey?"

"Fuck off, Spencer."

"Guys!" Alice tugged on her sleeves and looked anxiously between us. She cast a look over her shoulder and folded her arms across her chest. "Let it go, please."

"You don't know him, okay?" Spencer snapped. The car Spencer's father had sent appeared in the driveway, and Spencer grabbed my arm.

"I know things about you, too," she said. "We'll keep each other's secrets."

I shook off her hand, and Alice shot me a look. "We won't say anything, Spence," she said. "I promise."

"Thanks." Spencer relaxed, then shot us a grin. "I'll be out in a few days, anyway. I'll see you guys then."

TWELVE

Lola had left the office by the time I got back to Culver City, but Blake was still there. She gave me a look of sympathy when I walked through the door and dropped my things on the desk.

"So that's Spencer, huh?" she said.

"I feel disgusted." I sat down at my desk and dropped my head into my hands.

"Fair enough." She waited.

I sat up and ran a hand through my hair. I was suddenly very tired, and even though I had work that I should be doing, I didn't want to be there.

"Tell me about Spencer."

"How much have I told you already?" I asked, sitting up.

She frowned. "You were friends in high school," she said. "She was the granddaughter of Edith Frances."

"Yes."

"So did she inherit a lot of money?" Blake asked.

"No," I said. "Apparently she got nothing. That's what she told me, anyway, the last time I spoke with her."

"When was that?"

I thought for a long moment. "There was a party," I said slowly. "It was in Downtown LA. Four years ago, maybe?"

Blake took out a notepad and started writing things down. Although Blake was the most tech savvy out of all of us, she was also the member of the team who relied on analogue methods the most, not trusting the security of technology. She had been an expert hacker in high school and knew how easy it was to get lured into a false sense of security and wind up vulnerable.

"Whose party?"

"Friend of a friend." I closed my eyes and tried to remember. Six years had passed since Alice's disappearance, and Spencer and I weren't talking anymore. I had been caught by surprise to see her there. "She seemed happy to see me. Said that we should hang out. Her dad had died by that point . . . She made a comment about her stepmother keeping everything."

Blake nodded and framed her face with her thumb and index finger. "Did she have a source of income?"

"Yes," I said, trying to remember if Spencer had told me what she was doing. "She didn't tell me, but she was wearing an expensive dress. I got the sense it wasn't entirely legal, whatever it was."

Blake scribbled some more notes. "You think Alice was involved?"

I frowned, confused. "What do you mean?"

"With whatever Spencer was doing," she said.

"This was six years after Alice disappeared," I said.

Blake gave an expansive shrug. "Maybe they've been in contact the whole time."

I felt the comment like a gut punch. Dual feelings of shame and nausea came over me, and I turned my head so that Blake couldn't see the look on my face. She waited as I took a moment to compose myself.

"Yeah," I said finally. "I think you're probably right."

"Has it occurred to you in the past?"

"When Alice first disappeared," I said. "I thought Spencer knew something then. Ricky was her friend, after all. She was the one who brought us to the party. But when Alice stayed missing I told myself Spencer didn't know anything. She would have said something."

Blake tapped her notepad and nodded. She glanced back at her computer screen, where Spencer's face was frozen in a rictus of rage. "What do you think they're fighting about?"

"It didn't look like a fight," I said after a moment. "It looked like an attack."

Blake turned to look at me. "Spencer on Alice?"

"Yes."

"Okay. Why would Spencer attack Alice?"

I was drawing a blank. The day had been overwhelming and my cognitive thinking skills weren't at their sharpest. I was emotionally depleted.

"I don't know if I can do this right now," I said.

"Just a little bit longer," Blake said. "Tell me more about the relationship between the three of you. What was the power dynamic? What did you guys do together?"

"Spencer was in charge," I said, and I could hear the edge in my own voice. "We started getting into trouble once she joined us. That was the summer Alice disappeared. We committed a lot of small crimes."

"Like what?" Her voice was neutral.

I had given Blake vague details before, but I decided to be completely honest. There was no point in hiding it now.

"We broke into houses. Big houses."

She glanced up. "To steal things?"

"Not always. We stole things sometimes, but I think the whole point of it was just to break rules."

"And what kind of things did you steal?" Blake was watching me. There was no judgment in her tone.

I cleared my throat. "Really stupid things," I said. "I think I took some ChapStick from one place. Um, playing cards. A pen. Just little things. Spencer stole some art."

"I'm not going to judge you, Rainey," Blake said quietly. "We come from similar places. I know what rich kid rebellion looks like. We both found ways to hurt ourselves, remember? There's a difference between that and going out of your way to hurt someone else. Try to remember. What was the first house that you broke into?"

"It was my neighbor," I said slowly, remembering. "The opera singer. She was never home, but her lights were always on. It was strange. She . . . during the summer, she went home, back to Portugal. She had a house sitter, someone who came in and took care of the plants, cleaned, you know. And they always left the lights on at night."

"Intentionally?"

"It's so weird. I've never even thought about this," I said. "It's just one of those things you accept without questioning because it happened so long ago. I think it was probably to deter people from breaking in. There were so many break-ins that summer because of the fires. So many people left the city."

"I remember."

"And so, all these houses were empty, and people started looting them." I felt chills go down my arms, remembering all of this. Seeing it from a different perspective. "People on my street always left in the summers. I remember that. I stayed home, though."

Blake nodded. I closed my eyes and tried to remember the first time we walked through my neighbor's house. I had never been inside it, not once in all the time that we had lived next to this woman. I had heard her sing for years on end, exchanged a few greetings with her when we saw each other on the street, but that was Los Angeles: you could know someone for years and never see where they lived.

Blake nodded. "Okay, let's leave your neighbor's for a second," she said. "What was the next place that you broke into?"

"There was a string of them," I said. "They just blur together."

"Spencer was always there?"

I nodded, thinking. "Always."

"And when you took things, they were always small?"

"Sometimes," I said, rubbing my eyes. That summer came back to me then, with the hot slurry of guilt and fear, the knowledge that we were going to get caught, the feeling that it was all my fault. In some ways I felt like that part of my life had always lingered there, waiting to be discovered. I didn't know how to tell Blake about the escalating thefts without it coloring the way she saw me. "We took food, too. I'm not trying to downplay what I did . . . I know that it was wrong. All of it was wrong. Spencer stole jewelry, and Alice stole clothes."

"Sure," Blake said. "But let's just look at what you've told me. You and Alice were pretty naïve, innocent girls until Spencer came along, and then all of a sudden you were drinking alcohol and breaking into houses."

"That's the oversimplified version."

"And you never took anything of value, but later, you found out that Spencer did," Blake prompted me.

I closed my eyes and took a few deep breaths. "There was a bust," I said. "It was worth a lot of money."

A small furrow appeared on Blake's forehead. "How much?"

I could feel the tension just below my chest, a knot in my solar plexus. "Um. Millions. Millions, I think."

Blake flexed her fingers and then laced them together. "Okay," she said, her voice quiet. "That's a lot."

"Yes. And I have to tell you, Blake, it's probably my fault that she stole it."

Blake tilted her head to the side. "How's that?"

I recalled the way moonlight had played over the walls of the mansion where Spencer had stolen the bust. The windows made the house feel like it was all on display, like it was just sitting there for the taking. I had felt sick even at the time, thinking that the whole thing felt staged, like we were being watched.

"I recognized it," I said. "It's called *Lille, Après*—this bronze bust from Paris. It has a messed-up backstory."

I waited as Blake typed the words into the computer and then read the results in silence. She nodded, then whistled.

"This artist killed his muse and then sat with her body," she said. "Horrible. I can't believe it's so valuable. Then again . . ."

"Spencer liked art," I said. I felt sick, thinking of it. "She's an artist, of course she liked art. So she stole it."

"Okay," Blake said, writing this down.

"The painting," I said, remembering. "There was a painting. It was horrible, and brilliant. I can't get it out of my head. I don't know what happened to it."

"A painting," Blake echoed. "What painting?"

"It was called *M.E. Stands Before the Mind of God*," I said. I suddenly felt very cold. I had never told anyone about this.

"What was the painting?"

"A woman at the mouth of a tunnel. She was wearing a white dress. That's all I can remember."

"And do you know if it was ever reported stolen to the police?"

This was the part of the story when I was going to have to admit we stole it. I was going to have to tell Blake something that I had never admitted to anyone.

"I don't know," I said. "But there's something I need to tell you. About where we got the painting."

She looked up and the light glinted off her glasses.

"I don't know if you're going to believe me," I faltered. "It sounds so crazy."

"Try me."

I took a breath, hesitated. Then, in a quiet voice, "It was Laszlo Zo. We were at his house."

A crease appeared between Blake's eyebrows. "Laszlo Zo."

"Yes." My voice was faint.

"Sorry," she said, and she looked like she was trying to put the pieces together. "I didn't realize that you had a connection to him before this case with Noa. Does Noa know . . . ?"

"No," I said quickly. "Nobody knows, except Spencer and Alice. I'll tell Lola, I will. I just haven't yet."

Blake was writing all of this down. There was something soothing about the constant *scritch-scritch* of her pencil on paper. Her face was smooth, unconcerned, and I knew that she wasn't the type to judge.

"You said that Alice disappeared after a party at Ricky's house," she said. "Right?"

"That's right."

"Was that the first time you met Ricky?"

"Yes." My stomach turned thinking about it.

"And Spencer introduced you?"

"Yes."

"Had she ever mentioned him before that?"

I thought for a long moment, tried to remember the first time Spencer had told me about him.

"She called him Fits," I said slowly, remembering. "She never called him Ricky. She called him Fits. I always thought it was short for something—Fitzgerald, Fitzherbert."

Blake frowned. "What did it mean?"

"He *had* fits," I said. "He was diabetic. When he drank, or didn't take his medication, or did drugs—he'd have fits."

A look of comprehension dawned on Blake's face. "That's messed up," she said. "Did she call him that to his face?"

"Oh, yeah. 'Fitsy, meet my friends.'" I shook my head. "You'll never believe it, but later, she told me that they had hooked up. They dated for a while."

"But he was . . . wasn't he in his thirties?"

"Yeah." I gave a bitter laugh. "It was illegal."

Blake's lip curled up in disgust, and she gave a short, sharp breath.

"She started calling him Tall Boy instead of Fits," I said. "And that bust she stole? She gave it to him so her dad wouldn't find it."

Blake shook her head. "I don't even know where to start with all of this," she said.

"It's a lot."

"Since Spencer was on the tape with Alice," she said, pointing back at her computer, "it might be a good idea to talk to her. I don't know if she'd be willing, of course. Do you have a way to contact her?"

"No," I said. "I deleted her phone number years ago."

"No friends in common? Even though you went to school together?"

"Spencer doesn't have friends," I said, and then it dawned on me. Spencer didn't have friends, but she did know people. And there was someone I knew who might be able to tell me where she was.

THIRTEEN

⸺◦◦◦⸺

That afternoon, I drove over to Atwater Village. Fifteen years ago, when my mother was still a famous artist, there was an art curator she had entrusted with nearly all of her works. Calder Reyes had a big gallery in Atwater Village, a spacious area with skylights and cement floors. His gallery was down a quiet street overlooking a section of the Los Angeles River, which was nothing more than a dried-up canal at this point in the summer. Calder had been in residence in the neighborhood long before it was home to hip coffee shops and overpriced boutiques, a fact that he never failed to mention when I saw him.

I parked underneath a papaya tree and sat watching Calder's gallery for a few minutes, thinking about how I should approach this. The gallery was unpretentious from the outside, just a stretch of concrete leading up to the warehouse where all of Calder's art was stored. There was no signage, either; from the outside the space could have been mistaken for a storage facility. This was all intentional, of course: Calder catered to the type of people who had to be introduced to him, not just anyone off the street.

When my mother first disappeared, Calder had put the word out in the art community and had been surprisingly generous with his time. Even after I turned my back on the art world and stopped seeing all my mother's old friends, I maintained a casual relationship with Calder. When I was still friends with Spencer, Calder had seen some of her work and realized that she had real talent. There had been talk of a show once, but as far as I knew, her unsuccessful stints in rehab had put a kibosh on that.

Still, Calder was well-connected, and even if he wasn't in regular touch with Spencer, there was a good chance he knew how to track her down.

Before I could get out of my car, my phone rang. I glanced down to look at the screen. *Noa Cohen.*

"Noa, hi," I said, picking up the phone. "What's up?"

"Nothing to be alarmed about," she said, her voice cool. "You don't need to come over. I just wanted to let you know—Ricky's been sitting outside my house all morning."

I squeezed my eyes shut. "Okay," I said. "Is he doing anything?"

"He's *filming* me," she said. There was anger and disgust in her tone. "I just wanted to give you advance notice, in case I decide to go out there and start smashing his windshield with a baseball bat."

I barked a laugh, surprised. "Do you have a baseball bat?"

"Girl, I've got three."

I glanced at Calder's gallery and then looked at my watch. I wasn't doing anything urgent at the moment; this could wait.

"I can come over right now," I said.

"No," she warned. "I don't want that, Rainey, really. I just wanted to let you know he was here."

Outside my window, a sudden gust of wind shook loose a bundle of jacaranda blossoms from a tree by the sidewalk. The purple blossoms cascaded down and decorated the pavement. I flexed my fingers and took deep breaths so that I wasn't completely consumed by hatred for Ricky. We hadn't told Noa that we were going to approach Zo regarding Ricky, but there was a chance that Zo had told Ricky about the encounter, and this was the reason why Ricky had shown up outside Noa's house.

"I'm in Atwater Village," I said. "I'm about to go talk to someone, but I'll have my phone on me the entire time. You can call me if things take a turn. Okay?"

"Roger that."

"Noa," I said. "I can have Lola go over there right now. Really. She's just as tall as Ricky, and about twice as mean, if provoked."

Noa laughed. "Don't worry," she said. "Ricky's a coward. He just wants me to *think* he's going to do something. I'm not worried—you just asked me to keep you updated."

"Okay," I said, feeling some of my anxiety ebb.

"I'm hanging up now, Rainey," she said, her voice light. "I'll call you if I need to."

I was in a bad mood when I climbed out of my car and walked to Calder's gallery. I knocked on the door, but hearing no response, tried the handle and found that it was open. The space was cool and dim, and light filtered in from the windows high up on the walls. There were voices, and I realized that Calder must be with someone out back.

"Hello?" I called. "Calder? It's Rainey."

The cadence of the conversation continued, and I made my way toward the voices. The warehouse was filled with various pieces of art that were either for sale or half-finished, an array of sculptures and canvases propped against the wall. The front room was for customers, a display area, while Calder allowed artists to work in the large warehouse out back. I studied a beat-up garbage can that had fallen on its side and wondered whether it was art. Calder had admitted to me that he had once sold the remains of his takeaway lunch to an obnoxious client and claimed that it was the latest work of an up-and-coming artist.

"And the bitch believed me," he cackled. "I've got too much power, Rainey, I swear to god."

The voices out back fell silent as I moved through the gallery, and I was about to call out again when I heard Calder shout.

"For fuck's sake," he said. "I'm doing you a favor. Drop it."

The response was cool, measured, and hard to hear. I cleared my throat and emerged into the warehouse space, which was open to the back of the property. Calder was speaking to someone, his hands on his hips. He was wearing a long kimono of black silk, and I could see from his profile that he was wearing gold eyeliner.

"Calder?" I said.

Calder whirled; his face contorted with anger. He was tall, fat, and bald, and he never tried to hide what he was thinking. If he didn't like you, you would know it immediately, which some people found extremely off-putting. It took him a moment to register who I was, and when he finally calmed down, he smiled.

"Rainey, my darling. Hello. Kiss-kiss."

I moved toward Calder and finally saw who he was talking to. It was a man with dark blond hair. He was leaning against the wall and his arms were folded across his chest, but he looked surprisingly calm. He smiled at me, and then I realized where I knew him from.

"Max Hailey," I said.

"Hi, Rainey."

"Oh, great," Calder said. "Has this guy been bothering you, too? I was just telling him to leave."

"We met at a party," I said.

Hailey glanced between us. "How do you know each other?"

"*None* of your business," Calder snapped. "Please leave. I'm not going to ask you again."

Hailey raised his hands in a gesture of defeat and walked out of the gallery. I watched him go, then turned to Calder.

"What was that about?"

Calder bustled toward the back of the room and put a kettle on the stove to boil. Ever since I had known him, he had favored a Japanese aesthetic, long flowing robes in neutral tones. His robe swished with the movement of his body. "I'm making tea. I'm so upset, I might need to lie down. I can't . . . I just can't. Everyone wants a piece of me."

"Hailey wants a piece of you . . . ?"

"I've got green tea," he announced, rummaging through his cabinets. "It's matcha. When I was in Japan last month, I hired a little Japanese woman to come to my hotel every morning and tutor me in the art of whisking matcha. Do you know that you're not supposed to boil it? We must pay homage to the tea before we drink it."

He bowed his head in mock piety.

"What did Hailey want?" I asked again.

Calder threw tea-making implements onto the counter. "I've already had three cups and I'm completely jazzed," he said. "Still better than coffee, though, right?"

"Calder."

"I don't know. I don't know! He's a vulture. Works for some vulgar blog out of Hollywood. Celebrity gossip and all that. I told him I don't *deal* in gossip. It's beneath me."

Calder was the biggest gossip I knew, which is why I was there.

"He's writing about drug addicts, you know, preying on the weak," Calder said.

I raised an eyebrow.

"I don't know, so don't ask me." Calder threw his hands up in the air. "What am I, a gossip? A font of information? How should I know what happened to Rhodes? The whole thing is a disaster. It makes artists look bad when you think about it. Rhodes was *selfish*."

"So, Hailey's writing about drug addicts?" I leaned against the counter.

"You look *great*, darling, what have you done with yourself?" Calder touched my shoulder.

"I washed my hair this morning."

"Stop, why don't you come see me, it's been forever. Tea? Line of cocaine? How about some *voooodddkaaaa?*"

"You know I don't drink." I sighed.

"Of course, darling, I'm sorry. You would have made a great artist, you know, with the substance abuse issues."

"Cheers, Calder, thanks for that." I folded my arms. "Listen, I need a favor."

Calder bustled around the studio, suddenly all business. He glanced at me and then sighed. "You know I can't say no to that beautiful face of yours. What is it? Let's hear it."

"Spencer Collins."

Calder's face dropped. "Oh, god," he said. "Please don't tell me you're still hanging around with that girl."

"Why not?"

"Biggest disappointment of my career, I tell you," he said. "She could have been the next Peter Doig. People were *excited* about her, Rainey, I can't even tell you. She had talent, and god, it didn't hurt that she was beautiful."

As much as I had hated Spencer at times, I could never deny that she was talented. It was the kind of thing that you don't see until you're older, though, when you grow up and have perspective on your childhood and realize that not everything about your life was normal. Spencer's art was haunting and oddly perceptive for someone so young. Calder was right; she could have been big if she hadn't gotten in her own way.

"Is Spencer still painting?"

"What she's doing," Calder replied, walking toward me, "is drugs. Lots and lots of drugs. She scammed me a few years ago, promised me a big show and asked for money up front, and then once I got all these buyers interested, she ghosted me. Went to rehab or something, I don't know. I lost a fortune, told myself I'd never talk to her again. Then she comes back to LA a few years ago, talking about how she's changed, blah blah blah. Apparently, her dad died, and she was going through his things, found some really valuable paintings. I mean, the man had a massive art collection. She brought me an Ed Ruscha and asked me to sell it for her, but she needed money up front. It was a gorgeous piece, probably could have gone for half a mil, but I wasn't going to give her money up front. Not after what happened last time. Anyway, she got pissed and disappeared. Haven't heard from her since."

"Do you have Spencer's phone number?" I asked.

"No, no, I got rid of that years ago."

I felt defeated. "Do you have any idea where she lives?"

"Oh, it's this shithole. Her place is awful. Casa Nowhere. It smells like popcorn. This is why I avoid Hollywood. It's so filthy. Back in the old days when Greta Garbo and Ingrid Bergman attended their movie premieres, they never could have imagined what would happen to this place. It's filthy. I mean, someone was shooting up heroin outside Spencer's apartment. In broad daylight."

"You've been there?"

Calder squirmed, started to look uncomfortable. "Rainey, Rainey, why are we talking about Spencer? I told you, that's over for me. I don't want to talk about her anymore. Why are you grilling me?"

"I need her help with something," I said, not wanting to get specific.

"She can't help anyone, darling, not even herself."

I took a deep breath and wondered how to press Calder without scaring him off. If he didn't want to talk about something, he would change the topic a dozen times until you relaxed your grip.

"Rainey," he said, looking much more serious. "Please be careful. I don't want you to get involved with Spencer again."

"Oh, no," I said, waving the comment aside. "You don't need to worry about that, really. I'm not going to get involved with Spencer."

"No, no, listen to me," he said. "You need to be careful. She's involved with bad people."

"Who?"

"People have a way of disappearing."

"That's very dramatic."

"Have you ever heard of Eiko Mars? No? Exactly. Just like Spencer, she was this super talented artist who made enemies with the wrong people. One minute she was everywhere, everybody couldn't get enough of her, and now *poof.* Gone."

"What happened to her?"

"I don't know." Calder threw his hands in the air and walked away.

I took a deep breath and reminded myself not to press him. Nothing good could come from it—I had tried it in the past. He was a mollusk: you could poke as hard as you wanted, but ultimately, he would just withdraw into his shell and sulk. Still, there was one more question I had to ask him. I didn't want to seem needy, so I tried to make my voice nonchalant.

"My friend mentioned a rare piece of art," I said. "She saw it in a home years ago but hasn't been able to track it down since."

Calder cocked an ear.

"She's come into a lot of money recently and was thinking of making an offer," I went on.

"A wealthy friend, Rainey?" Calder purred. "When are you going to introduce me?"

"She's very modest," I went on. "She's a smart woman, too. Cultured. A good eye."

"Don't play hard to get, Rainey."

"She can't stop thinking about this painting," I said. "She said she's willing to pay any price."

"What's the painting?"

"It had some weird name," I said, feigning ignorance. "Something about the mind of god."

Calder shook his head. "That's it?"

"Someone standing before the mind of god. Not ringing any bells?"

"Give me the exact title. I'll look through my database."

I took out my phone and pretended to look through it. "I wrote it down somewhere," I said. "Hold on . . . hold on . . . ah! *M.E. Stands Before the Mind of God.*"

"Never heard of it," Calder said, and my heart sank. "If it's important I would know it. But let's have a look, I'll see if it's been displayed anywhere."

He went over to his computer and typed the title in. "Nothing," he said. "You sure that's the title?"

"It's just what she told me."

"Artist? Anything else?"

"I don't know the artist. Sorry."

He shrugged. "Must have been done by an amateur," he said. "I've got access to all the art databases in the world. There's nothing here."

———

I stepped outside and blinked at the sunshine, feeling defeated. Before I could forget anything Calder had told me, I took out my notebook and scribbled down key things: Eiko Mars, drug abuse, Rhodes, Hollywood, Casa Nowhere.

As I walked toward my car, I realized there was someone waiting next to it. Max Hailey.

He raised a hand in greeting.

"Uh-oh," I said.

Hailey laughed. "That bad?"

"Word on the street is that you're a vulture," I said, biting back a smile. I never took anything that Calder said at face value—people were always all good or all bad to him—and I couldn't help remembering Hailey kneeling in the grass at Banter to help Bradley's son find his rabbit.

"I'm an ethical vulture," he said, eyes twinkling. "Promise. What are you doing here, though? You buying art?"

"I know Calder from way back. What about you?"

He glanced up the street, then back at the gallery. "I'm writing a story about that artist, Rhodes," he said. "He was all over the news a few days ago, and then he just vanished. Into thin air."

I remembered that Hailey and I had briefly discussed Rhodes when we met at the Orphans' Ball.

I squinted at him. "That's really normal, though, isn't it? Whenever celebrities have bad publicity, their teams usher them out of sight. He's probably at rehab."

"No," Hailey said. "That's what I thought, too. His sister has no idea where he is, though. There's something weird going on."

I glanced down the street, then looked back at Hailey. "Do you think your line of work primes you to see conspiracies everywhere?"

"Absolutely!" he said, then burst out laughing. "My brain is a sad and lonely wasteland, but I'm not always wrong."

"What do you think happened to Rhodes?"

"I have some dark theories, but I shouldn't go into them," he said, smiling. "Not without more proof. I could be completely off base."

"Just from what happened last week?"

"No, I've been looking into him for a while. I was going to write a story before this thing happened last week."

"So why were you talking to Calder?"

"He used to represent Rhodes," Hailey said. "I asked him if he felt any duty of care toward his clients, especially those with a history of substance abuse issues."

"I can guess why Calder told you to fuck off." I was surprised by his candor.

"It was worth a shot." Hailey shrugged.

"This is for the *Lens*?"

He glanced down and then nodded. "My editor took some convincing. She hasn't completely signed off on it, actually. We're treading dangerous ground here."

"Why is that?"

He looked like he wanted to say something, then refrained. "Sorry," he said. "I've probably already said too much."

"You're a mysterious man, Max Hailey."

"Completely unintentional," he replied. I suddenly had the sense that he was appraising me. "I can tell you're interested. What do you know?"

"Nothing," I said, spreading my hands. "Believe me, I have very little to do with the art community these days."

"Look," Hailey said, and for a moment he looked uncomfortable. "I should probably mention something."

"That sounds alarming."

"Your name came up in my research."

I felt a familiar anxiety take hold. It was part of the reason why I had walked away from working in film production, because I never wanted to be famous again. I had experienced enough of that during my childhood, and I had always hated that people could research you and think they knew everything about you.

"I can probably guess," I said.

"Your mother was an artist," he said.

"Please don't remind me."

"Fair enough." He raised his hands. "I'm sorry I mentioned it. Do you still have anything to do with the art world?"

"As little as possible. Why do you ask?"

"I want to talk to Simon Balto," he said. "The only time I've been able to get in the same room with him was at the Orphans' Ball. He's completely shut me out."

"Have you tried going to his gallery?"

A little smile played around the corners of Hailey's mouth. "Yes. I went there first."

I felt stupid. "Of course you did."

"No, no, it was a good suggestion," he said, raising his hands in a gesture of supplication. "You need an appointment to get inside. They've been blocking me at every turn. I'd go to his house, but it's in a gated community."

"Why do you want to talk to him?"

"He made a lot of money from Rhodes," Hailey said. "Of course, he's probably not even in Los Angeles most of the time, now that he's trying to get that museum happening."

"Museum?" I frowned.

"Simon Balto has been pushing to get a museum built outside Palm Springs for years," Hailey said. "It's been tied up in red tape. Calder acted like he didn't know anything about it, which makes me think he's lying."

"What makes you think that?"

"Calder's an art dealer!" Hailey exclaimed. "It's a museum, two hours from here—it's going to be massive, if it ever goes ahead. Of course he knows about it."

"I haven't even heard about it," I said. "Then again, I try to stay away from that kind of news."

Hailey tapped his notebook with his pen. "How would you feel about trading information? We might be able to work together."

My heart started pounding. My family had always been wary of journalists; there had been a lot of negative stories throughout the years. "What makes you think I know anything?"

"You were born behind the wall," he said.

"The wall?"

"Sure, the one that keeps outsiders out," he said with a smile. "Do you know what I'm talking about?"

"I've never thought about it that way, but sure, I guess you're right."

He cocked his head and looked at me. "You didn't come here to buy art, did you?" he said. "You're a private investigator. You're here looking for something."

"Clever lad. Afraid I can't say, though."

"We could share information. I know some PIs; we trade information sometimes."

"The ethical vulture, right?"

"You got it." He grinned.

"I can't make any promises," I said. "I have to think about the ethical implications."

"Fair enough." He took out his wallet and produced a business card. "If you change your mind, you know where to find me."

FOURTEEN

———∞∞∞———

Calder hadn't meant to help me, but he had let some information slip about Spencer without realizing it. As soon as I got in my car, I took out my phone and got to work. It wasn't much information, but it was enough for me to take a stab at narrowing things down by process of elimination.

He had mentioned that the last time he saw her, she was living in a shitty apartment in Hollywood. *Casa Nowhere, smells like popcorn.* There were 1920s apartment complexes sprinkled all over Los Angeles, many of them with Spanish names, and knowing that it was in Hollywood narrowed things down considerably. I scanned through a list online and found three complexes with "Casa" in the name. Casa Azul, Casita Linda, Casa Nopales.

The first one was a luxury condo complex with three buildings around a pool. Definitely not in Spencer's price range, if she was as broke as Calder believed. The second looked like a wellness commune where all members were encouraged to participate in community living. The website had a lengthy waitlist and an application form. WE'RE A SOBER COMMUNITY! a banner bragged. LIFE IS A BLESSING, AND WE CHOOSE TO LIVE WITH OUR EYES WIDE OPEN. Definitely not Spencer.

The last apartment complex, Casa Nopales, didn't have a website or any information that I could see online. I didn't have anything else to do that morning, though, so I decided to drive over to Hollywood and take my chances.

The neighborhood surrounding Casa Nopales was oddly quiet, but there was a stagnant buzz in the air. I parked outside a taqueria and walked down the street until I found the address of the apartment complex in question. It was housed in a pink stucco building with wrought-iron window fixtures. The bottom floor was occupied by a rundown cinema advertising $5 tickets. It was closed for the afternoon, and a few peeling posters in the display cases were faded movies from the eighties. "Smells like popcorn," Calder had said. I was on the right track.

The entrance to the apartment complex was to the left of the theater. The glass door was scratched, and the metal was bent out of shape. I hesitated, thinking it might be locked, but when I tried the handle, I found that it easily opened. The door led through a dim exterior hallway into a cement courtyard with a dried-up fountain and a dying cactus garden. The interior of the complex was quiet; the sounds of traffic outside were muted to a dull white noise.

I glanced around the courtyard and wondered where I should start looking for Spencer. There were three apartment doors downstairs, and four upstairs, but none of them had names next to them, and I hadn't seen a list of buzzers with tenant names. A door on the other side of the courtyard had a plaque with MANAGER on it.

I debated my options: I didn't know which apartment was Spencer's, or if I was even in the right place. Besides, I hadn't spoken to Spencer in four years, not since the time I ran into her at a party. I couldn't just show up to her apartment; it might spook her. She would probably refuse to talk to me, and what's worse, I might endanger the entire investigation.

While I considered my options, I decided to sit down and wait. There were some old stone benches on one side of the courtyard, in the shade and out of sight of a few of the apartments. They were dusty and it looked like nobody had sat in them for a very long time.

An hour passed, and the only person to emerge from one of the apartments was a middle-aged man in a wife beater and boxers. He was smoking a cigarette and reading what looked like a movie script. He scratched his belly and leaned against the wall, then chuckled at something on the page. At one point he glanced up and stared at me, then disappeared into his apartment.

Another hour passed with no activity. I was about to leave and head back to the office when the front door of the apartment complex banged open, and Spencer stalked in.

She looked harried, disorganized. She was so thin I had to do a double-take before I recognized her. Her hair was pinned at the base of her neck in a loose bun, and strands fell down around her face. She held a big leather satchel over one arm, and I could see that the contents were bursting out of it. She glanced around, paranoid, then scuttled up the stairs to the second level. Moments later she vanished into one of the apartments and shut the door.

Spencer had hardly gone when the door to the manager's apartment flew open and a tall woman with dark curly hair burst out. She was obese, in a tight spandex dress with polka dots. Still, she moved with surprising speed as she charged up the stairs and began pounding on Spencer's door.

"Spencer! *Spencer!* I know you're in there, you little shit! *Open this door!*" The woman banged and kicked at the door until it flew open.

"Fuck off, Michelle!" Spencer cried.

"You're a month late on rent, you little witch—I'm calling the police unless you cough it up today! I'll evict you!"

"Yeah? What about when I tell them about your pervy husband? You're both freaks." Spencer tried to shut the door, but Michelle had wedged herself into the crack. I watched them struggle for a moment, sure that Michelle would manage to get inside, but Spencer must have hit her with something, because Michelle cried out and flew backward. Spencer slammed the door on her.

"You bitch! That's it—I'm calling the cops!"

Spencer threw the door open. "Go ahead," she snapped. She pushed past Michelle and ran down the stairs. "I'll tell them everything!"

Michelle watched Spencer exit the apartment complex, then she trudged downstairs and retreated into her office, slamming the door behind her.

I ran out of the complex and scanned the street in both directions. Spencer had already vanished. I walked to the end of the block and looked left and right, but there was still nothing. Feeling defeated, I walked over to an ATM, withdrew two hundred dollars, and folded it into my wallet. When I returned to the courtyard, Michelle was standing in front of her office, furiously typing something into her phone.

I approached her and cleared my throat. "Sorry to bother you, but is Spencer Collins here?"

Michelle turned, surprised to see me, and narrowed her eyes. She was probably six inches taller than me, with a smattering of freckles across her bronze face. Her aesthetic was oddly childish: in addition to a polka-dot dress, she had a headband with a bow. She wore cat-eye glasses.

"Why? Who are you?"

"I'm one of her clients. She did a painting for me. I was supposed to meet her here to pick it up."

"She's gone," Michelle snapped, then went back to her phone.

"Are you sure?" I asked, feigning irritation. "I've got the cash and everything. I just need to pick it up."

Michelle glanced up. "You came to give her cash?"

"Two hundred dollars."

I could see the cogs ticking in Michelle's mind. "She'll be back soon, I think," she said slowly. Then, "Of course, you could always leave the cash with me. I'll make sure she gets it."

I pretended not to understand. "Did she leave the painting with you?"

"No, no, but I have keys to her apartment. I could get the painting for you."

I gave her a wary look. "Oh, I don't know," I said. "Maybe I should just wait."

Michelle grimaced, then exhaled sharply and gestured impatiently toward me. "It's fine. Tell me where to get it."

I took the cash from my wallet. "She texted me a photo of the painting," I said. "If you let me in, I'll just grab it. I'm sure I can find it."

Michelle glanced at the money in my hands. I could almost see her weighing her options.

"You know what, don't worry," I said. "I'll just give her a call."

Michelle shifted her gaze around. "Fine," she said. "I'll let you in, but you're in and out. Got it?"

I held up my hands. "Got it."

Michelle snatched the money from me and led me upstairs, to Spencer's apartment. I held my breath, willing her not to change her mind. She took out her keys and opened the door, then nodded at me. "Five minutes. Don't make me come back and find you."

"Not a problem."

Spencer's apartment was shrouded in darkness, and I was immediately hit by a smell: it was unwashed hair and bare feet, rumpled piles of laundry, and faint mold. I flicked on the light and walked down the hall into the living area, then saw that Spencer had pinned sheets over her windows, which contributed to the darkness.

Now that I was standing in Spencer's space, I felt overwhelmed with uncertainty. For the past few days, I had convinced myself that once I found Spencer, finding Alice would be easy. I would confront Spencer and tell her everything I knew and demand she tell me where Alice was. Having seen Spencer a few moments ago, though, I knew that it wasn't going to be so easy. She was clearly in a bad way, either from drugs or mental illness. The best I could do now was some small measure of reconnaissance by going through Spencer's apartment.

The space felt so intimate that I felt an added degree of vulnerability just by being in it. There were things I recognized from our time together, elements of Spencer on display: her elegance and sense of fashion, her artwork, but there were other things—the filth, the lack of care—that worried me. Although I hadn't thought of Spencer much in the last few years, I had never considered her a stranger. Being in her space now, however, and seeing so much madness on display, I wondered if I had ever known her.

Art books were stacked on the table next to a filthy bong. The remnants of what looked like cocaine were dusted across the glass, and a few coins were scattered across the table. I walked to a bookcase and looked at the spines, then opened my bag and took out a pair of latex gloves. I had gotten into the habit of keeping a bag of them with me at all times for moments like this.

I entered Spencer's bedroom. The mattress was half-bare, partially covered in tangled sheets. I smelled dirty hair and something intimate, like the aftermath of sex, the funk of human bodies. *Think, Rainey.* I wanted to know what Spencer was hiding, what she knew about Alice, where they had been. I felt a surge of anger, then: *I deserve to know. I have the right to know. Fuck you, Spencer.*

Canvases were propped against the wall, art supplies strewn across the floor. There was something geomorphic about the room, different eras of Spencer's life stacked one on top of the other. If I had an endless amount of time and free reign, I would have gone over the room inch by inch, reading every gory detail into what I found.

Think.

The door to Spencer's closet hung ajar. On the back of the door was a black dress with a tulle skirt. It was the dress she wore to the Orphans' Ball. I moved across the room and touched the dress with my gloved fingertips. On the floor of Spencer's closet were shoes, a collection of bags. Hanging on the hook behind the dress was a beaded purse, the one that Spencer had worn with the dress.

I grabbed the bag and started going through it, but it was empty. *Damn it.* I scanned the room for anything else, anything that could give me a clue to where Spencer had been, what she had been doing at Alice's house. *Think.*

I was so engrossed I almost didn't hear the sound of the front door opening in the next room. By the time I realized I wasn't alone in the apartment, it was too late for me to find an exit. It had been more than five minutes. I almost emerged into the living room to apologize to Michelle when I heard voices. Male voices.

"Spencer? Spencer!" came a man's voice. He sounded angry. "Great, she's not here. This is disgusting. Oh, god—what's that smell? I can't believe she *lives* like this. Where is she?"

"Your guess is as good as mine," came the second voice. I recognized it. Pinched, annoyed. "She won't answer the phone. I've texted her, too, but fuck all."

My heart was pounding, I glanced around Spencer's room, looking for somewhere to hide. The closet was packed with clothing, bags, and accessories, and there was no furniture other than the bed. With no other option, I dropped to my knees and crawled under the bed.

"Call her again," came the first voice.

There was a tense silence, and then the other man responded. "Well, I tried. She's going to be pissed when she gets back here." I knew his voice from somewhere, it was on the tip of my tongue, but I couldn't place it. I closed my eyes and tried to imagine a face to go with the irritated tone, and then it came to me: it was Lucas, Bradley Auden's assistant.

"Do I look like I care?" This was from the first man. "I'm done. I'm not dealing with her anymore. Look at this place. She's a drug addict. We never should have gotten her involved."

There was a long silence.

Then, "Bradley's known her forever," Lucas said. "He seems to trust her."

"Bradley's an idiot. He has no idea what's going on." There was the sound of swearing, and then someone kicked something. "Fuck! I don't care about the rest, but we need that key. Call her again."

"She's not answering," Lucas snapped.

I heard footsteps and then the sound of furniture being overturned. My mouth was dry, and my pulse was so loud to my own ears I was sure that the men must be able to hear it. The space under the bed was crammed with dirty laundry and dust so thick on the floor it almost felt like skin, like fur. My eyes teared up and I started coughing. I clapped a hand over my mouth and exhaled all the air in my lungs through my nostrils. I couldn't breathe.

"Where did she put them? *Fuck!*" The voice was dripping with acid, but the scariest thing of all was how quiet it was. I associated anger with shouting and slamming doors, but this was almost worse: a snake's hiss, right before it strikes. There was something almost familiar about it, but I was too scared to think of where I might know it from. I heard wood snapping, and then cabinets banging open. It felt like it would go on forever. It was only a matter of time before they came into Spencer's room and started pulling it apart, looking for whatever they were trying to find. *What a stupid place to hide*, I thought, *under the bed. I'm an idiot. Only a child would hide here.*

I closed my eyes and tried to visualize everything I had seen of Spencer's apartment. There had to be a back door or a window I could escape out of. All I had to do was make a break for it, run through the hallway and hope that both men were distracted. I didn't know what they were doing there, but it didn't matter; it wasn't good. I had seen Lucas and thought that I could overpower him in a physical match, but I didn't know who the other man was.

All of a sudden, the commotion in the other room stopped.

"*Someone's coming*," Lucas hissed.

"It better be Spencer," his companion growled.

I heard the front door swing open, followed by a prolonged silence.

"What . . . what are you doing?" It was Michelle. I felt a surge of relief. "You're tearing up—what are you—oh my god! Who are you? I'm calling the police! You need to leave! Get the fuck out of here!"

"Relax," came the voice of the unknown man. "We're friends with Spencer. She invited us."

"I don't care *who* you are. You're destroying the apartment! Who are you?"

"Fine," the man replied. "We'll leave."

There was a physical scuffle and Michelle squawked in fear and indignation. I wondered if I should jump out, take them by surprise, come to her assistance. A moment later, though, it sounded like they had left the apartment; I could hear the clattering of footsteps on the stairs outside.

"Assholes!" Michelle called. "I'm calling the police!"

I heard the door close, and then there were heavy footsteps outside. I waited for a count of ten, then slid out from under the bed. I started coughing so heavily I was sure someone was bound to hear me. When I regained my breath, I ran through the apartment, looking for a window. All of Spencer's windows opened onto the courtyard and the back alley. I couldn't catch sight of anything.

I burst out of the apartment and ran down the stairs two at a time, then ran through the courtyard.

"Hey! *Hey!*"

I whirled to see Michelle standing by her office door. She held a phone in her hand and pointed at me.

"I'm calling the cops!" she yelled. "You hear me? I don't know who you people are, but you're not getting away with this!"

Once I was back at my car—after I had locked the doors and convinced myself that nobody was coming after me—it took a full five minutes before I was able to stop shaking. The interior of my car was hot as a clay oven, but I didn't feel safe rolling the windows down. Pinpricks of sweat broke out over my scalp. I roughly brushed myself off to get rid of the lingering dust from underneath Spencer's bed.

When I felt like I could breathe again, I started my car and coasted down the street, then rolled down the windows and let the air wash through the car. I got onto Melrose Avenue to head back to the office, but suddenly had another idea. I turned left toward Larchmont Village, then east to MacArthur Park. I had a question that I couldn't get out of my mind, and wanted to see if Chloe's roommate, Ahmad, might be able to shed some light on it.

I was about to buzz the doorbell at the entryway when I heard someone call my name, and turned to see Ahmad walking up to the apartment building with grocery bags slung over his shoulder.

"Sorry—it is Rainey, isn't it?" He wore a cautious smile.

"Hi, Ahmad," I said. "Yes, it is."

"I've been meaning to call you," he said. "I wanted to thank you!"

"For what?"

"You talked to Marcus Loew for me!" His smile was sunlight and champagne. "I can't thank you enough, really—it's so hard to book guests, but we've already set up an interview!"

"Oh, it was my pleasure," I said. "Marcus has a lot of time for people just getting their start."

"If there's any way I can repay you," Ahmad said, his voice serious, "tell me. Really."

"There might be something, actually," I said. I took out my phone and pulled up a photo of Spencer. It was one of the images I had saved from that summer with Alice. The three of us sat around my pool, squinting and smiling at the camera, which had been set up with a self-timer. I zoomed in on Spencer's face and handed it to Ahmad.

"Do you recognize her?"

He looked at the photo for a long time before shaking his head. "I don't think so," he said. "I'm sorry."

The phone screen died and I entered my password again so that he could take another look at the photo. The entire image appeared, and Ahmad frowned.

"Wait," he said.

"What?"

"I recognize her," he said, tilting his head to the side.

I zoomed in on Spencer's face again, and he shook his head.

"No, no," he said. "Not her. The other girl." He moved the photo's focus to look at Alice's face. "Yes, that's her. That girl was at my apartment. She was with Chloe when she got high."

I frowned. "You're sure?"

"Positive," he said, then looked up at me. "I can't remember her name, though. She helped Chloe move out, too."

My mind was spinning with the implications of all of this. "When was this?"

"Two months ago?"

"And she helped Chloe move her stuff out?"

"Sure," Ahmad said. "Chloe said she was moving in with her."

———

I was exhausted by the time I finally returned to the office. Blake and Lola had gone for the day, but there was something I wanted to check before I called it quits. I logged onto Blake's computer and pulled up the security footage I had sent her from Dave and Irene's security cameras.

As soon as I sat down to watch it, I felt a wave of fatigue crash over me. It was the kind of exhaustion I used to feel when I was strung out on nerves all the time, an anxiety hangover. My body had stopped producing adrenaline and I was wearing off the aftereffects. I knew that I should call my team, I needed to update them about what was going on, but I was concentrated on the task at hand and didn't want to lose focus. *Tomorrow*, I decided. *I'll call them tomorrow.*

I skimmed through the footage until I got to the day Alice showed up to the house. I had sent Blake a week's worth of footage, but I didn't need to view all of it. I knew that Blake had already gone through it a few times, and she was much better at picking up on small details, but I had the advantage of knowing the Alder house personally and thought I might see something she had missed.

I watched the entire day on fast-forward, stopping only when there were signs of activity. A pedestrian on the street walking a dog; two children jostling each other and swinging their backpacks. A nanny and a stroller. Finally, at seven o'clock, Alice appeared.

One of the cameras was pointed down the street, showing Alice arriving at the house on foot. If she had driven herself there, she had parked at a distance. The hairs on the back of my neck stood up when I saw my old friend, because even from the gait and the physical mannerisms I would have recognized her anywhere. Her long blond hair was pulled back into a messy bun, and she wore a light trench coat over a T-shirt and shorts.

"Alice," I whispered, leaning in to look at the screen. Something caught in my throat, and I sat back to watch her. I almost wanted to warn her, even though I knew that it was impossible. I wanted to tell her to run, to get inside the house and far away from Spencer and whatever trouble she had gotten herself into.

Alice disappeared from the view of one camera and appeared in a different frame. She walked around the house, dipping in and out of camera range, and in some angles, looking into the windows. She looked cagey, frightened. There was an intensity of focus in her actions that put me on edge. When she reappeared at the front of the house, I almost thought that she would find her way inside. She lingered there for a moment, and then Spencer appeared.

It was almost too hard to watch. There were tiny snatches of audio, but like Blake had said, the recording devices were too far away to hear anything of substance. Crackling leaves and radio interference clogged up the audio file. I watched Spencer grab Alice and try to drag her back toward the street. Alice fought back.

I paused the video and stood up. I walked around my office a few times. Taking deep breaths, I reminded myself that I needed to stay focused; that was the only way I would find my friend. There had to be something in the video clip that would help me find her.

I went back and watched it three more times before something jumped out at me. A small stain, just a minor dark spot that was almost indistinguishable from the grainy footage. One of Alice's sleeves was wet. It hadn't been wet when she arrived at the house.

I closed my eyes and thought for a moment, imagining what she had been doing at the house. Walking around and around, trying to find a way in; at least, that was what I had assumed. Maybe she was looking for something else, though. Before I could second-guess myself, I grabbed my things and locked up the office, then got in my car to head over to the Alder house.

The street was quiet when I arrived, and the lights in the neighboring houses were out. I parked in front of Alice's house, then took out my phone and sent Cameron a quick message—*Just stopping by your place to check something. Wanted to let you know in case I trip an alarm somewhere.* I could hear crickets in the garden as I made my way around the back of the house, and the wind rattled the branches above my head.

Cameron responded quickly. *All good. You find anything yet?*

Not yet, I replied. *Just double-checking something.*

I got the documents from the other PIs. You free to meet tomorrow?

Let's grab breakfast, I wrote back.

Alice's vacant house was additionally spooky at night. I didn't mind going out on my own, and was confident that I could defend myself in a pinch, but I felt uneasy. I almost felt like someone was watching me, and I half wondered if I should take off and come back in the daylight.

The pool stretched out in the moonlight, hidden by the taut white cover. *Why had Alice's sleeve been wet?*

Glancing around me to make sure that I was still alone, I knelt by the pool and stuck a hand into the water to check the temperature. I hesitated for a moment, then lifted the cover back to see what lay underneath. The Alder house was old enough that the pool had been built without an automatic retracting cover, and each time we wanted to swim we had to spend twenty minutes unrolling the plastic and making sure that it aligned with the big metal roller at the end of the pool. Rolling it back out to cover the pool was equally taxing, and there were many afternoons when we swam laps in the deep end, having only rolled back a small portion of the cover. It was dangerous to swim that way, we had been warned, but there was something shocking and a bit delightful about dipping into those shadowy depths, shooting up too quickly and scrabbling against the underside of the plastic tarp.

Something was bobbing against the pool cover now; I could just make out a shape about the size of a human head. I briefly contemplated the wisdom of what I was about to do: tampering with a potential crime scene instead of calling the police. Taking a deep breath, I grabbed the pool cover with both hands and removed it from the pool.

I was relieved when I scanned my flashlight over the water and saw that what I had feared might be a human head was, in fact, just the pool skimmer. The round plastic pump head was about the size of a skull, with a wide plastic lip attached to a filter. A hose underneath it snaked into plumbing inside the wall of the pool. Alice had made a game of throwing things into it, even though her mother told her not to: it would be nearly impossible to replace if broken, because the company that made it had gone out of business in the eighties. Wendy had once retrieved her missing wedding band from inside the diaphanous interior, a place where all lost objects seemed to end up. The filter was old but stalwart, and Alice and I had once bought ourselves lunch from coins found within its depths.

I had a thought and walked over to the opposite side of the pool, where I could grab the skimmer. I reached inside, all the way to my elbow, getting my shirt wet in the process. At first, I felt nothing but clotted leaves and slimy mesh. I shone my flashlight into the depths of the skimmer.

Something bright glinted within. I reached in once more and grasped a plastic bag that contained something hard.

I pulled the bag out and sat down, then turned my light on it. Inside the Ziploc bag was a key attached to a dull bronze fob. It looked like an old hotel key, the kind that people used in the thirties and forties. I didn't want to take the key out of the plastic bag, in case I damaged evidence, so instead squinted at the script and tried to make out what it said. The room number was clear enough—323—but I was having trouble with the name of the hotel.

I moved my flashlight over the surface and read it at an angle. I was finally able to make out the letters of the hotel, one by one.

The Hotel Stanislas.

FIFTEEN

⌐⌐⌐⌐

As soon as I got home, I fired off a quick text to Blake and Lola with a photo of the key. *Dropped by Alice's house and found this in the pool. Connected to her disappearance?*

Without waiting for a response from my team, I went online and started hunting around to see what I could find about the Hotel Stanislas.

The top Google result was a two-year-old article from the *Los Angeles Times*. Iconic Los Angeles Hotel Gets New Face, read the title. I clicked on the link and skimmed through the article, which showed glossy images of lofty hotel rooms and a chic lobby done up in shades of pale pink and green.

The Hotel Stanislas, once the temporary home of movie stars and titans of industry, fell into decline after a family feud in the mid-seventies, the article began. *For twenty years the hotel sat empty, victim to vagrants and petty criminals. Seven years ago, the Norgren Group bought the building and began a lengthy process of renovations, all of which had to be approved by the Los Angeles Historic Society. What you see when you enter the hotel is a testament to the power of determination and a vision toward respecting our city's past.*

The rest of the article contained quotes from the management team, a pithy quote from an aging actress who had stayed at the hotel's first iteration, and photos of the rooms, the bar, and the rooftop swimming pool.

I closed the article and continued searching to see what else I could find about the hotel's history.

Lola called me fifteen minutes later. I was so engrossed in what I was reading that I almost didn't hear my phone buzzing.

"Rainey," she said, sounding breathless. "You found a key? Oh my god, good work! What's the hotel?"

"It's called the Hotel Stanislas," I said. "It's in Downtown Los Angeles."

"Dodgy area, good start," Lola said.

"Not so fast," I countered. "This hotel is really ritzy. Rooms start at three hundred dollars a night."

Lola whistled. "I guess there are always waves of gentrification," she said. "What do you know about the hotel?"

"Well, the hotel itself is over a hundred years old," I said. "Looks like one of the oldest buildings in the area. I've been reading about it online— it used to be one of LA's top hotels, back in the thirties and forties, but it started to go downhill in the fifties."

"Any reason why?"

"There was a murder-suicide in one of the rooms in 1954," I said, reading from my computer screen. "A married businessman got his younger mistress pregnant. The murder was huge tabloid fodder at the time. That room was taken out of use, but then there were a few more deaths and murders in the hotel, and rumors of haunted corridors."

"What's a Los Angeles hotel without a few ghosts?" Lola asked.

"Exactly. The hotel ended up closing in the nineties, and it was empty for years before the new owners bought it and renovated it. It's only been open this time around for about two years."

I could hear Lola typing in the background. "Wow," she said. "You're right, it does look fancy. God, the old hotel was beautiful, though. Charlie Chaplin stayed there!"

"I can imagine how many underage women he brought back to his hotel room," I said.

"Oh, I know. Man, I would love to see what it looked like back in the thirties." Lola sighed. "Can you imagine all the fashion?"

"Oh, okay," I said, reading another article. "Here's another reason the hotel went downhill. A massive family feud, starting in the seventies. The original owner died and gave the hotel to his two adult children, who disagreed about how the hotel should be run."

Lola squawked with delight. "I love that," she said. "This sounds like a movie waiting to happen."

"Hold on, I'm just going to read this," I said. I set the phone down and put it on speaker. "I'll send you the link."

I skimmed through the article, which was on *Cue LA*. The brother had wanted to turn the hotel into an SRO residence, but the sister had wanted to turn it into a fancy hotel. The hotel was split into two halves, with each sibling inheriting one side. When it became clear that the brother was going to go ahead with his plan to rent out rooms to all manner of itinerants and anonymous delinquents with cash, the sister retaliated by walling off the entrance to the brother's half of the hotel. His half of the hotel had only been accessible through the lobby, and when the sister built a wall across the entrance, it effectively cut off all the access points to the brother's wing.

Building the infrastructure needed to get to the rooms in his part of the hotel would have been financially out of reach, so instead, the brother punished his sister by converting the Edwardian ballroom into a smutty theater which streamed pornographic films all through the night. The ballroom was the only part of the building accessible to the street. The rooms above were only accessible via the shared stairway, so they were all walled off and abandoned.

"He sounds like an asshole, but I kind of love this," Lola said. "Have you finished the article?"

"Halfway through," I said. "The Red Door. What a great name for a porn theater."

"It's like an evil version of *Gift of the Magi*," she said. "She cut him off, so he had to build this theater, but when he built the theater, he scared off all her fancy guests. The cops kept coming to arrest all the sex workers who hung out on the street."

"I wonder why nobody's restored the theater," I said. "If the Stanislas has a new developer, why don't they buy the theater and turn it back into a ballroom?"

There were some images that trespassers had taken over the years; the raggedy doorways and walls covered in tags made me indescribably sad. Los Angeles had a bad track record of respecting old buildings, and this was a perfect example.

I wondered how trespassers had gotten into the building if there were no stairs leading to the upper levels. I went to Google and looked up an image of the hotel and the adjacent theater. There was one possible point of entry I saw: above the bar of the Hotel Stanislas, there was a flat rooftop with possible access through one of the windows of the theater.

"Have you called the hotel to see if Alice has been there?" Lola asked.

"Not yet," I said. "I'm going to swing by tomorrow and check it out."

"Keep me posted."

The following morning, I drove to Santa Monica to meet Cameron for breakfast. He was staying at the Georgian Hotel, a beautiful art deco building with a turquoise exterior, and had suggested that we meet up at one of the hotel's restaurants overlooking the ocean.

I was buzzing with energy as I drove. Most of my job was paperwork and dead ends, a long sludge of trying and failing until I found what I was looking for. It was about persistence and dedication, about beating my head against the wall until I found the last remaining option. Moments of triumph were rare, and even though I hadn't yet turned up anything definitive on Alice's connection to the key, I was still intrigued.

I arrived at the restaurant ten minutes early and was surprised to see that Cameron was already seated at a table in the corner. A cardboard box sat next to him. He saw me coming and jumped out of his seat, then gave me a hug.

"Thanks for coming all this way," he said.

"It's only twenty minutes from the office," I said. "Plus, it's nice to see the ocean every now and again. When you live in Los Angeles, it's easy to go a month without seeing it."

"I remember," Cameron said. "We take so many things for granted."

We both took a seat, and a waitress came over with menus.

"Good morning," she said. "Can I start you off with some coffee? We've got a single-origin roast from Guatemala this morning. It's from a local coffee roaster in Culver City."

"Just an Americano, thanks," I said.

"I'll have the same," Cameron said.

The waitress went away, and I glanced down at the menu. I never went out for breakfast—I rarely even ate a proper meal in the morning—and everything on the menu was an obnoxiously fancy take on normal breakfast food. When I looked up, I realized Cameron was studying me. We both started laughing.

"I'm sorry," he said. "It's been a really long time. It feels so weird to be sitting across from you now."

"I know exactly what you mean," I said. "You're a proper adult now."

"I could say the same about you!"

"I feel like a fraud half the time."

He smiled at me, and his eyes twinkled. "It sounds like you're too hard on yourself."

"Well, that's probably true."

"You look great, Rainey."

I cleared my throat and felt myself blush. "How do you like Paris?"

"The city's great," he said. "I live in the city, but I work in La Défense. Do you know it?"

"That's outside the city, right?"

"Right." He nodded. "And when you work twelve-hour days, you don't have much time to explore Paris."

The waitress returned with our coffees. "Ready to order?"

"I'll have the muesli," Cameron said.

"That sounds fine," I said, handing the waitress the menu.

When she had left, Cameron patted the box next to him. "This is the evidence that my other private investigators found on Alice," he said. "I'm not sure if there's anything good in here. There was a time when I was going through it on a regular basis, but I realized that I was fixating on the past and not allowing myself to live my life . . ."

I watched him for a moment, waiting for him to continue, and he glanced up and met my eyes.

"Sorry," he said.

"What for?"

He blushed. "It was something an ex told me, actually. My last girlfriend."

"Oh?"

"She was a great girl, don't get me wrong," he said. "Woman. A great woman. We were together for about three years, and it looked like we might get married, but I still had a foot in Los Angeles. Because of Alice."

I knew all too well what it was like to feel stuck because you had lost someone. "You remember that my mother disappeared?" I asked.

"Of course," he said. "I had forgotten, I'm sorry. Did you ever find out what happened?"

"It turned out she had another family," I said. "She fell in love with someone else, and it would have been too complicated to divide up assets with my father and try to decide custody. It was easier to leave it all behind and start from scratch."

Cameron's eyebrows shot up and his mouth dropped open. His expression mirrored the appalled looks that people had given me for years, every time I explained why I no longer had a relationship with my mother. It was exhausting being on the other side of that look, which was one of the many reasons I no longer spoke about Matilda.

"It took me a long time to hate her," I said. "Because I was so determined to forgive her or to understand why she had left. Sometimes you don't ever get those answers."

"I'm sorry," he said, his voice quiet.

"Don't be," I said, then laughed. "Really! I don't hate her anymore. I actually don't care at all, which might sound unfeeling, but it's a lot better than hating someone. She didn't want a family—or at least, she didn't want *our* family. I think she has other kids now. I really don't care. That's my gift to her. I let her go."

Cameron was quiet, and I wondered if I had overshared.

"Are you saying that I should let Alice go?" he asked, raising an eyebrow.

"Not yet," I said. "Give us one more crack at it. If we don't find her this time, then yes. Go back to Paris and get your girl. Let's see what you have for me."

He lifted the box and set it on the table.

"You can take that with you," he said. "It hasn't done anything for me, and I don't know if you'll find anything of value in there."

I lifted a set of files printed with the name of a PI agency at the top. *William E. Scott Endeavors.* There was a detailed list of everything the PI had done, from tracking down old friends and staking out the Alder house to going through the county morgue. From a cursory look, it seemed like all the research had led to a series of dead ends.

Underneath the stack was a folder of photos. I felt a pang as I went through them and saw Alice as a child, grinning and running through a garden; Alice at a Halloween party, waving a golden wand. She had been Glinda from *The Wizard of Oz* for three years running, up until she was nine. I hadn't known her then, of course; we met in high school, but she had told me everything about her childhood. She had been one of the only people I could confide in about my broken family, too, and seeing these photos made me sense the loss of Alice all over again.

I closed my eyes and set the photos down.

"Are you okay?" Cameron asked, his voice gentle.

"I'm sorry," I said. "This is harder than I thought. I spent so long looking for Alice that I thought it wouldn't be an issue, but seeing this, now . . ."

Left City had a policy of limiting information to clients while an investigation was ongoing; we had learned from experience that certain clients might take it upon themselves to act on what we tell them, and it could send an investigation sideways. It was something we assessed on a case-by-case basis, and I decided to take a risk and share something I had found with Cameron. There was a chance he might know something, after all, and it might help us in our investigation.

"Remind me," I said. "When was the last time you saw Spencer?"

"Not since I left Los Angeles," he said.

"And you haven't been in contact with her since?" I asked.

"No," he said. "I don't mean to sound cavalier, but once I realized that she was involved in drugs and the whole party scene, I decided to keep my distance."

"I think Spencer might know where Alice is," I said.

Cameron's face went dark.

"I'm taking a risk by telling you this," I warned him. "Normally we don't share details of our investigations with clients until everything is done, but I need to know if there's anything you might remember."

He looked down at his hands and thought. "My mom told Alice to stay away from Spencer," he said. "I came back from college one summer. I think you guys were sophomores . . . ? Juniors? My mom said that Spencer was bad news. Even at seventeen."

"Okay. I didn't know that. Do you remember why?"

Cameron rubbed his hands together and frowned. "Spencer had an older boyfriend," he said slowly, frowning as he tried to recall the details.

"I can't believe I remember this. I just remember all the screaming matches that happened between them. 'That girl's a bad influence. I don't want you hanging out with her . . .'"

A sense of dread settled over me. Back when Alice had first disappeared, Cameron and I had shared everything we knew with each other. I had told him about the party at Ricky's house, and we had both spoken to the police about that night. I had mentioned the possibility that I had been drugged, and the cop we spoke to had actually rolled her eyes. I felt a wave of anger all over again remembering how they had treated me like I was responsible for it, even though I was a kid, just seventeen.

I hadn't seen Cameron in years, though, and there had been developments since then.

"Cameron," I said carefully. "Do you remember that party Alice and I went to in North Hollywood? The night she disappeared."

"Sure I do," he said. "I told my PIs about it, and they looked into that guy. I don't think they ever found anything."

"Yeah," I said, looking down at my hands. "I think Spencer was dating him when she was in high school."

"What the *fuck*," he whispered.

"He visited Spencer in rehab. She didn't tell me all of this until later, believe me." I decided not to tell Cameron about the stolen bust that Spencer had given to Ricky. "I would have reported it if I knew who he was. I didn't find out until later."

Cameron was flexing his hands. He looked like he was trying to calm himself down.

"Do you think she was involved in Alice's disappearance?"

I had to tread very carefully. There was a reason why we didn't share details of ongoing investigations with our clients—people got emotional, acted without thinking. I knew Cameron a long time ago, but now he was a virtual stranger. I didn't know how he would react, and I didn't want him to take matters into his own hands.

"We're looking into a lot of different possibilities," I said.

Cameron closed his eyes and took a few deep breaths. I watched the tension recede from his shoulders and jawline.

"Spencer always seemed like the type to keep her cards close to her chest," he said. "Did she ever tell you the full truth about anything?"

"No," I said finally. "I don't think she did."

———

After leaving Santa Monica I got on the I-10 to drive out to Hollywood. I didn't want to stop at my office first, but I knew that I should check in with my colleagues and let them know what I had discovered, so I called Blake as I drove.

"Hi, Rainey," she said.

"Lola there?" I asked.

"Right here."

"Can you put me on speaker?" I asked. "I want to catch you guys up on everything."

I heard a click and a clatter as Blake put the phone on her desk.

"Hi, Rai," I heard Lola say.

"I just met with Cameron and got his box of stuff," I said. "I don't think there's anything useful in there, but I'll bring it in later. I'm on my way to Hollywood."

"Well done on the key, by the way," Blake said. "Good stuff."

"Thanks," I said.

"There's one more thing I should mention," I said. "I met someone who's been researching Rhodes, and he's come up against the same obstacles that we've encountered."

"Oh yeah?" Lola asked. "Who?"

I paused. "His name is Max Hailey. He's a journalist," I said, then quickly added, "I didn't tell him anything, of course. He did suggest that we might be able to work together, though, you know, compare notes."

"Bad idea," Lola said.

"Well, that was my first instinct, too," I said. "But he's friends with Marcus—that is to say, Marcus is the one who introduced us. And if I don't reveal anything about our cases, I don't think it could hurt to have a conversation with him."

There was a long silence on the other end.

"Lo?" I prompted.

"What do you think you'd gain from talking to him?" she asked.

"I think it's always good to have contacts with different information."

Lola sighed. "Give me a chance to think about it," she said. "You'd need to be sure that we could trust him. And don't mention anything about our cases or clients, obviously."

"Got it."

"What are you up to now?" Blake asked.

"I'm going to talk to Officer Lennon in Hollywood and see what she thinks about the key," I said. "And then I'll go to the Hotel Stanislas and see what I can find."

⸻

Officer Lennon wasn't at the station when I got to Hollywood. The same receptionist was there, but she didn't seem to remember me or care that I had come back. The Chuck Palahniuk book was gone; now she was reading James Ellroy.

"Do you know when she'll be back?" I asked.

"No idea. She's on rounds."

"Can you call her?"

The woman sighed. "Is this urgent?"

"Kind of," I said.

She stared at me for a long moment, then picked up the phone and dialed. "Casey? I've got someone here who needs to see you. She said it's urgent." There was a pause. "I don't know. I'll tell her to wait."

She hung up and glanced at me. "She'll be back in two hours. Feel free to wait."

While I sat in the waiting room with nothing to do, I pulled out my phone and started going through my notes, specifically the ones I had written down when I spoke to Calder. *Eiko Mars*; *Ian Rhodes*. I wasn't familiar with the work of either artist, but I had heard their names at various times. I typed Eiko's name into my search bar and waited while the results loaded.

According to her biography, Eiko was only twenty-two, so her catalogue was limited, but she had been prolific for someone her age. I hadn't known what to expect from her art, but when the images appeared on my phone, I was stunned. The paintings were incisive, observant in a way that I wouldn't expect from someone so young. They reminded me of Jeffrey Smart's cartoonish nightmare landscapes, but these images were definitely Los Angeles: in one, a yawning parking lot threatened to dwarf the wilderness of Griffith Park, with asphalt stretching from one side of the horizon to the other. In one image, oil derricks tattooed a prairie, while in the background, factories churned out toxic smoke.

When I finished scanning each of her paintings, I looked up Rhodes. Rhodes's work was starkly different from Eiko's in terms of style, but there was a similar cynicism at play. His work reminded me of Andrew Wyeth, all tilting lines and unstable perspectives. I could see the suggestion of madness in each of the subjects, whether they were elderly or very young, a sense of despair I found unsettling. There was an unfocused gaze in the people he portrayed, the suggestion that they were mulling over something awful.

Three hours passed in this way. I was starting to wonder if I should keep waiting for Casey when she came strolling through the front doors and nodded at me.

"Follow me."

I followed her back into the same small interview room that we had spoken in last time. I removed the bagged hotel key from my satchel and placed it on the table in front of Casey.

She raised her eyebrows. "What's this?"

"I'm still looking into Alice Alder," I said. "I went by her house the other night and found that in the swimming pool."

Casey picked the key up and looked at it. "And what is it?"

"It's a hotel key."

"I can see that," she said. "Why is it important?"

"It was hidden inside her pool filter," I said. "I think she put it there the night that you came out to speak to her."

"So?"

I hadn't prepared for this reaction. "It could be important."

"Important how?"

"Why would she hide it?" I asked.

"Do you have proof that she did? Do you have video footage of her doing so?" I could see the faintest hint of a smile on Casey's face. "Do you see where I'm going with this?"

I sat back in my seat. All the conjectures and theories that I had dreamed up had evaporated in the space of ten seconds.

"Okay," I said, trying to keep the frustration out of my voice. I had imagined Casey standing up and summoning a group of police officers to go straight to the Stanislas and break down the doors. I knew that it was naïve and probably a little shortsighted—Lola had called me out on these things before—but I had been looking for Alice for so long that I just wanted the search to be over.

"What were you hoping would happen if you brought me the key?" Casey prompted, her voice kind.

"I thought it might indicate an exigent circumstance," I muttered. As soon as I had spoken, Casey's face lit up and she gave me a surprised smile.

"Okay," she said, then suppressed a laugh. "You're up on your police terminology."

"I'm a PI," I snapped, then immediately regretted my tone. "I'm sorry."

"It's fine," she said, leaning back in her chair. She still wore a delighted smile. "An exigent circumstance means we get to leap over the normal hurdles because someone is in critical danger."

"I know that," I said, irritated.

"From what you've told me, Alice has been gone a long time," she said gently. "It'll be hard to get an exigent circumstance here. You have to remember that police deal in hard facts. I need to see something more than theories. Show me footage of her hiding it. Prove there's blood or drug residue on the key."

"Don't you want to take it in for testing?" I offered meekly.

"We're stretched so thin as it is," she said. "I can't take on anything that isn't already attached to my caseload. Now, on the other hand," she added, "if you bring me something solid, something with proof, I can do something with that."

She was giving me a meaningful look. I took it as subtle encouragement, even if she wouldn't vocalize it. "Anything else?"

It was worth a shot to ask. "You still haven't heard anything on Chloe Delmonico, have you?"

"Nothing," she said. "But again, it's not my case. I suspect I'll hear it on the news before anything else."

"Okay," I said, standing up. I put the key back in my bag.

"Don't get discouraged," she said. "I can tell you have good instincts. You might be onto something. I just need more."

"Okay."

"Keep checking in," she said. She gave me a small smile. "Let me know what else you find. We might be able to help each other eventually."

SIXTEEN

———◦◦◦———

I wanted to take one last stab at trying to reach Spencer. That afternoon I went over to Casa Nopales to see if I could talk to her. When I walked into the apartment complex the landlord, Michelle, was spread out on a lawn chair, sunning herself. She was wearing pink polka-dot sunglasses and a sarong.

"Hi," I said.

She glanced over at me, then looked away.

"Is Spencer here?"

She sighed and adjusted her sarong but said nothing.

"I'm sorry about what happened last time," I said. "I have no idea who those guys were."

"I'm not Spencer's secretary," she said.

"Fair enough." I walked up the steps and knocked on the door. There was no response. I waited for a moment, then knocked again.

"She's not here," Michelle called. "But if you pay me, I can let you inside her apartment."

I deliberated for an agonizing moment. "How much?"

"My price has gone up," she said, lowering her sunglasses. "Three hundred."

I balked. "That seems like a lot."

"Well?" Michelle fanned herself with a magazine and then picked up her phone.

"Two fifty."

"Three."

My phone rang. I glanced down and saw Lola's name, then ignored the call and put it away. I hesitated for a long moment, then pulled out the cash. I had already gone to the ATM and was prepared. I walked down the stairs and handed Michelle the bills. She tucked the money into her sarong and picked the keys up off the ground.

"No rush this time," she said. "Take as long as you want."

Surprised but gratified, I headed up the stairs to Spencer's apartment. I unlocked it and stepped inside, but immediately could see that something was wrong. Light flooded into the hallway, and the place reeked of bleach. All the windows had been opened to air out the apartment, and as I made my way down toward the living room, I realized that every last thing had been removed from the apartment—furniture, personal belongings, even the carpet. It looked like Spencer had never been there.

I stood there for a moment, then walked back outside and looked down into the courtyard. From above, Michelle looked like a big, melted puddle of polka dots.

"Hey!" I called. "*Hey!*"

She didn't respond, but I saw a little smirk distort her features. I ran down the stairs and crossed the courtyard.

"What the hell? You charged me three hundred dollars to go in an empty apartment?"

Michelle shrugged, then burst out laughing. "I mean, I thought it seemed like a lot, but it was your money."

"Right," I said. "That clearly wasn't the deal. Give me my money back."

"Nah." She hadn't even taken her sunglasses off. I had a brief fantasy of tackling her, but it would have been like wrestling with a manatee. Besides, the idea of reaching into whatever crevice she had stored the money in was enough to dissuade me.

It wasn't the first time someone had lied or tried to manipulate me in the line of investigating a case. I shouldn't have been surprised; I had lost money in similar situations when I took a gamble on something that turned out to be nothing at all. Michelle's deceit had caught me off guard because of my own ego, though: I thought that I was smarter than her. It was my own fault for dismissing her as simple or stupid.

"You're dishonest," I said, because it was the only thing I could think of.

"I'm a businesswoman," she said, slipping a finger under the edge of her swimsuit to scratch herself.

My phone rang again. I took it out to see Lola's name again, then silenced it once more. A text came through. *Call me.*

"I'm feeling generous, though," Michelle continued. "I'll answer a few questions, if you have any."

I weighed my options. I already knew that I wasn't going to get my money back. Anyone who was dishonest enough to let people into her tenants' apartments wouldn't care about screwing a stranger over for a few hundred dollars. I didn't know if she had any valuable information to offer me, but at this point, it was the best I was going to get.

"Who cleared out her apartment?" I asked.

"I don't know."

"I thought you said you had information," I snapped.

"I do know, however," she said slowly, "that someone paid me a thousand dollars for the key to her apartment and said that I should keep my mouth shut."

My phone buzzed with a text from Lola. *Urgent.*

"I see you're good at keeping your word," I pointed out.

"They broke theirs first," she snapped. "I was happy enough to take their money and hand over the key, but those fuckers came in and disabled my entire security system. They found all my cameras, even the hidden ones. That system cost me five grand. I'm pissed."

"Wow," I said slowly. "You have no concept of loyalty, do you? You sell your information to whoever pays you enough."

Michelle gave an expansive shrug, then gave me a knowing look. "That's why you're here, isn't it? You paid me to go snooping around in Spencer's apartment. Don't get all hoity-toity on me now."

I looked at her with disgust. She was right, of course, but it didn't make me resent her any less.

"I'm not stupid, you know," Michelle went on. "I'm guessing Spencer probably owed you money, just like everyone else. Only those people got here first."

"What did they take?"

"You saw." She pointed vaguely toward Spencer's apartment. "Everything."

"Who were they?"

"Two men."

"Can you be more specific?" I asked, trying to keep the irritation from my voice. "Tall, short? Thin, fat? How old?"

"What is this, Guess Who? Two men. One had an annoying voice. The other was wearing a baseball hat and sunglasses. I don't know what else to say."

I took a deep breath to ground myself. "Fine," I said. "Thanks for your help. I'll just leave my card, in case you think of anything else."

I took my card out and handed it to her. I walked away and took out my phone to call Lola, when Michelle called after me.

"There's just one thing," she said, glancing at my business card.

I turned. "Yes?"

"I've got Spencer's bag," Michelle said slowly, turning the card over in her meaty hands. "I think it could be quite valuable."

"Why do you think that?"

She shrugged, nonchalant. "Before they came through and cleaned everything out, I went in there first," she said. "She was months behind on bills, and I thought I might find some cash in her apartment. I'm well within my rights!"

"And did you? Find any?"

"No," she said, but after a long enough pause that I knew she was lying. "So, this bag?"

"If you report me, I'll deny it," she said. "But seeing as how you're clearly operating by your own set of rules, I thought we could strike a deal."

I waited.

"It's not a knockoff," she said. "It's real Chanel. I was gonna sell it online, unless you're interested, of course."

I hesitated. "How much do you want?"

"Three thousand."

"Three thousand!" I exclaimed. "Is there anything inside the bag?"

"Oh, yes," she said. She lifted a leg and swatted away a horsefly. "It's full of lots of interesting trinkets. Some pieces of paper, a few phone numbers . . ."

I tried to downplay my interest. "How much for the contents?"

"It's a package deal. You have to take the bag, too."

"I don't think so." I wasn't even bluffing to get the price down. The whole affair with Michelle made me feel ill, and I wanted to be done with it. There was nothing else this woman could offer me.

"I guess I'll just throw those things away, then," she said, with a dramatic sigh.

I turned around and made out like I was leaving.

"Five hundred," she called.

"Two."

"Fat chance," she said. "I know those people were looking for something. Maybe this was it."

"The bag? You think you just happened to grab the one thing they were looking for?"

"I saw Spencer every single day for the last six months," Michelle said. "This was the same bag she always wore. I know she kept important things in there."

"Two fifty is my last offer," I said. "I've already given you three hundred."

She stretched luxuriously, buying time. She scratched herself again, and I wondered if she was allergic to her sunscreen. I waited in agony as she deliberated, then smelled her fingers and shrugged.

"Fine," she said. "Two fifty for the contents of the bag. Just the contents, not the bag itself!"

I followed her into her office, and she grabbed the bag off her desk.

"Money first," she said.

I produced the cash from my wallet and hesitated for a moment before I handed it to her. Michelle wouldn't know what information I might be able to glean from Spencer's lost property. Even if she thought she was pulling the wool over my eyes, I might get something unexpected from looking through Spencer's things.

"Knock yourself out," she said, then reached under her desk and produced an empty cardboard box. She dumped the contents of the bag into the box, then handed it to me. My initial excitement immediately faded when I realized that Michelle had cheated me, once again. The bag had been full of trash: chip wrappers, receipts, and empty gum packets. The receipts were mostly from a nearby gas station: cigarettes and gum, packets of jerky. There was a bill from a dry cleaner on Beverly Boulevard, an expired gift certificate to Anthropologie.

"That's it?" I exclaimed.

Michelle shrugged, then folded the money and tucked it into the bra of her swimsuit.

"I'm not a secret spy or detective. I don't know what I'm looking at," she said. "I just rent the apartments."

Once I was back on the street, I took out my phone and called Lola.

"Rainey."

"What?" I asked, with more irritation than I intended.

She took a beat. "Is now a good moment?"

"I guess." I was tetchy, in a bad mood. I didn't want to fill Lola in on everything that had happened with Michelle because it was just going to make me mad all over again. "What's up?"

"It's Ricky," Lola said, after a pause. "He just filed an application for a restraining order against Noa."

It took a moment for the words to sink in. "What . . . the . . . *fuck!*"

"Rainey . . ."

I closed my eyes and clenched my fists. It took everything in my power not to chuck my phone across the road. I counted to ten and then brought my phone back to my ear.

"This is bullshit," I said, my voice low and angry.

"I know. It's a tactic."

"On what . . . what *grounds?* He's the abuser—what about all those emails he sent? Where he accused Noa of being a slut and sleeping around? What about that—how can he—"

"Rainey, breathe," Lola said. She took a few loud inhales and exhales to demonstrate. "It's fine. I just wanted to let you know, because now we have to be more careful about following him around and filming him. He might use it against us."

I pictured Ricky standing outside Article 19, laughing and scratching his crotch. I wanted to punch him so badly I thought I might pass out.

"Okay," I said, trying to keep my voice level. "What does this mean for us?"

Lola sighed. "It's good that we already have a hearing on the books for Noa's application against Ricky," she said. "But it does tend to muddy the waters a bit."

I clenched my fists. "He doesn't have a case."

"Of course not," she said. "It's more common than you might think, Rai. Abusers act like victims when they're out in public. It's another form of abuse."

"I have to go," I said. "I can't think about this right now."

"Understood. I'll keep you posted."

I was famished, but I didn't want to stick around and eat something in Hollywood. I wanted to get out of there, wash my hands of Michelle, and now Ricky. Besides, it might be the perfect time for me to follow up on the mysterious hotel key I had found in Alice's pool. I tossed the box into the trunk of my car, then drove toward the 101-S to head into Downtown Los Angeles. I was in luck: it was early afternoon and traffic was nonexistent. In rush hour, this six-mile journey could take almost an hour.

The Hotel Stanislas was at the edge of the Toy District. Downtown was a part of the city that I only visited once or twice a year, and it was usually on client business. While attempts had been made over the last decade to rehabilitate the area and bring in wealthy tenants to spacious lofts with enticing rent, the grid of dingy streets that defined Downtown retained an element of seediness, crime, and neglect.

There were elements of beauty amidst the decay, like the central library and a few other historic buildings. Even on sunny days the neighborhood was mired in shadow, because on many streets the buildings were so close together that they shut out the sunlight.

The Toy District was home to a big, covered mall filled with hawkers' stalls. On the streets outside were more stalls and fruit carts, a variety of food trucks, and vendors selling knockoff makeup brands. I found parking in an overpriced car lot and walked back a few blocks to the address I had for the Hotel Stanislas. There was a beat-up food truck selling Mexican food just down the street. It smelled so good that I checked to make sure I had cash left after my dealings with Michelle, then stepped up to the battered window and ordered a $5 chicken burrito. Food trucks, particularly the ones selling authentic Mexican food, were one of the best meals you could get in Los Angeles. I had become a regular customer of one when I first moved out of my father's house, when I was flat broke. It was one of the only ways you could get a decent meal when you were short on money, and I knew from experience that the best food came from trucks that looked barely road safe: dented panels, faded lettering, and bald tires, with a surly chef in a stained apron.

I sat down on a low wall by the truck to eat and survey the street. My perch gave me a direct view of both the Hotel Stanislas and the vacant theater next door, which still bore a marquee reading THE RED DOOR. It was hard to believe it now, but this had once been a neighborhood that catered to very wealthy visitors, businessmen, and tycoons who were looking to make a move out west. I took out my phone and pulled up a photo of the original hotel, then compared it to what stood before me now. What had once been a single building with wings was now divided in two: the two halves had once shared the bottom atrium, but once it was sealed off, construction had separated the two pieces and made an alleyway between them.

The hotel was as dignified and elegant as the theater was run down, and it was almost impossible to believe that they had once been part of the same building. While the Stanislas looked like a beautiful old ship borne aloft by the shifting tides and gradual decay of the surrounding neighborhood, the theater looked almost intentionally shabby, with plyboard nailed over the doors out front.

I finished my burrito and cleaned my hands with a napkin, then crossed the street and walked through the glass doors of the Hotel Stanislas.

The lobby had been given a modern facelift, with a chic California vibe: the mint-green wallpaper hosted a selection of bold modern art pieces, and mustard-colored furniture was offset against glass and chrome end tables. Elements of the old hotel were still prominent, though: the pillars leading up to recessed ceilings had been lovingly restored, and vintage wingback chairs were posed next to potted palm trees. An enormous chandelier hung from the center of the ceiling.

In the wrong hands the juxtaposed set pieces could have created a nightmare effect, but the color palette was the right balance of bold and understated. It felt expensive, hip, and inviting. There was a buzzing energy about the place, and well-dressed guests glided through the lobby. Women in red lipstick and white shift dresses waited for the elevator, while a group of men in designer suits came out of the bar area, laughing.

I made my way over to the reception area, where three members of staff were having a conversation. Two young women in white shirts and slacks spoke to a man in a dark suit, who appeared to be the manager. As he spoke to the women, they suddenly all burst into laughter. When he noticed me standing there, he immediately rushed over to greet me.

"Good afternoon," he said, smiling. His teeth were brilliantly white but too small for his face. They looked like Chiclets. "How can I help you today?"

"I'm looking for someone," I said.

"Absolutely, absolutely," he said, rubbing his hands together. His name tag read JUAN. "What is this person's name, may I ask?"

"Alice Alder."

Juan glanced back at the two women and made a discreet shooing gesture with his hands. They melted away and disappeared into a back office.

"And is Miss Alder a guest with us?"

"I don't know, actually," I admitted. "I got some information that she might have been here."

A small crease appeared in his forehead, but his double-decker smile remained frozen. "I see," he said. "What information is that?"

"Would you mind checking to see if she's a guest?" I asked.

"Well, unfortunately, we cannot give out guest information." He enunciated every syllable of his words. "It is our privacy policy."

"That's fair." I considered my options. "She's been missing for a while, actually. Her family opened a missing persons case with the police."

Juan's smile grew even wider, and he bowed his head again. "We are always happy to assist the police with their queries. I just need to see a warrant."

The man's age was hard to determine, but I estimated that he was in his mid-thirties. His grooming was immaculate, and he obviously took great care in his appearance, even down to the smallest details, like manicured fingers. If I had to guess, I would say that he came from money and had always led a gentle, comfortable existence. He was almost handsome, but there was something slightly off about the intensity of his gaze, his desire to please, and the way his smile didn't extend to his eyes. Every time I made eye contact with him, he broke into another grin. I found it unnerving.

I placed the bag with the old hotel key on the counter in front of Juan. He frowned and picked it up, then started to take it out of the plastic bag.

"Please leave it in the bag," I said quickly.

"What's this?" He weighed the key in his hands.

I was taken aback. "I thought it was a key to your hotel."

"No, no, I am sorry," he said. He took a plastic credit card–style key out of his wallet and set it on the counter. "*This* is what our keys look like. We are in the twenty-first century. Everything is digitized! Much safer than old keys."

I made to take the old key back, but Juan held on to it.

"You know what," he said, holding the key up to the light. He broke into a surprised smile. "I know what this is. Ha! Wow!"

I felt an unexpected glimmer of hope. "What is it?"

"This is from the old hotel," he said. "Of course, I should have realized it right away. I have never seen the old keys, because, well—when we bought this place it was defunct, out of commission. We completely transformed it."

"Oh, you're one of the owners! I didn't realize—"

"No, no," Juan said, cutting me off with a wave and a little bow of his head. "I am the general manager. I have been with the company since we began renovations."

He held the key in his hand, turning it over and admiring it a few times. He ran his thumb along the fob and then held it to the light again.

"This is very old," he said. "Where did you find this?"

"How old do you think it might be?" I asked, dodging the question.

He narrowed his eyes and held the key in a better light. "Oh, this could be one of the very first keys made for the hotel," he said. "The hotel was built over a hundred years ago. Our first guest was in 1902."

I glanced around the lobby, at the tanned young women heading toward the cocktail lounge, at the well-dressed family entering through the double doors.

"Where did you find this key?" Juan asked again. "It could be very valuable, you know. It's an artifact from a bygone era."

"I read that the hotel closed in the mid-nineties," I said. I took the key back from him and noticed that he handed it to me with some reluctance.

"That is correct."

"Do you know if the hotel was empty during that entire time?" I asked. "Were people squatting in the rooms while it was vacant?"

His smile faltered, just for a moment. "That is a very interesting question," he said. "May I ask where your line of inquiry comes from?"

"I'm helping the family to locate Alice."

"You seem like a historian." The smile was back.

I returned the smile and waited. Juan clasped his hands together.

"Your question about the rooms," he said. "Alas, I do not know. If anyone was living here, the contractors would have chased them out. Construction began seven years ago. The old infrastructure was falling apart, and many of the old rooms were combined, so all the room numbers changed. Here, have a look at the room guide."

Juan produced a glossy brochure.

"Do you mind if I keep this?" I asked.

"Please." He pressed his hands into a gesture of supplication and bowed.

"Thank you." I slipped it into my bag. "I'm sorry, I just have a few more questions. Do you mind?"

"Not at all."

"I saw the theater next door," I said. "The Red Door. It looks pretty run down—is that a deterrent for guests?"

"The Red Door," he said, nodding. "The man who once owned that building sold it to a real estate developer about twenty years ago. Before they could tear it down, the city slapped a bunch of zoning restrictions on the neighborhood. There have been some attempts to revitalize the building, but there is a lot of bureaucracy and red tape."

"Have you seen the inside?"

"I have only been inside once, back during renovations," Juan said. "There was a big fire about four years ago that nearly destroyed our hotel."

"That's right," I said. "I think I read something about that. Do you know how it started?"

Juan shook his head. "It is an accident waiting to happen, if you ask me, but there is little we can do. It is in the city's hands now. Of course, if someone renovated it, it would be a major draw to this neighborhood."

"Thanks for your help," I said. "Do you mind if I have a look around the lobby?"

He took a deep bow. "Please, be my guest," he said, then swept his arms to the right. "The cocktail lounge is that way. Have a look around—maybe you will stay with us one day!"

Light filtered into the bar through narrow windows and illuminated the dark wooden floors and Persian rugs. The original wallpaper had been lovingly restored, and photographs from the hotel's heyday were arranged at eye level: businessmen and dark-eyed ingenues wrapped in furs. The bar itself was behind a large square burnished-copper counter that I recognized as being part of the original hotel; I had seen the photos. A young bartender with a neatly styled mustache made efficient work with a cocktail shaker. He poured a drink into a highball glass and twisted a curl of lemon peel as garnish. In the corner of the room, a trio of young women took pictures of themselves.

I approached the bar and took out a photo of Alice.

"Excuse me," I said to the bartender. "Have you seen this woman?"

He narrowed his eyes at the photo, then shook his head. "Sorry."

"Have you worked here long?"

"Since we opened."

I walked back into the lobby and took a look around. A beautiful couple with towels under their arms waited for the elevator, and I joined them. Once we were inside, the man pressed the button for the twelfth floor, next to which was a small brass plaque that read POOL. The elevator glided up to the top of the building in silence, and I followed the couple out onto the rooftop.

A glittering blue infinity pool stretched along the length of the rooftop, lined with potted palms and reclining wicker chairs. The pool area was empty except for the couple and a woman polishing glasses behind the bar. I approached her and showed her the same photo of Alice.

"Excuse me, I'm looking for this woman—have you seen her?"

"No, sorry."

"Thanks anyway."

I put my phone away and walked along the perimeter of the roof. The edge was protected with a high glass wall, and views of Downtown Los Angeles were visible from three sides. The fourth side—next to the old theater—was shielded with opaque glass. I tried to peer around the edge, but I couldn't see anything, so I headed back to the elevator and went down to the street.

The Red Door theater was such an eyesore that I wondered how the Stanislas could attract clientele with it right next door. The façade of the building was faded, sun-mottled, and damaged by decades of weather and neglect. Paint and stucco peeled away from the building, and the marquee was warped. A few disjointed letters clung to the signboard—T, W, and Q—though not in any coherent order.

The doors had been covered with plyboard, but the plyboard itself was bent and swollen with weather damage. A few years of spray paint had accumulated, and behind the curved wood I could see a glass door, which had been shattered into a spiderweb. I stepped up to the space in the wood and glanced through a small hole, into the entrance of the old theater. Stretching my arm, I shone my flashlight through. I could just see the beginning of the dim interior—a dusty carpet stained with water damage, animal droppings, and more graffiti.

"Can I help you?"

I turned to find a security guard standing on the sidewalk behind me. His hands were on his hips.

"I'm just having a look," I said.

"It's private property."

"Sorry," I said. "I like old theaters."

He nodded but made no sign of moving away.

"Why hasn't anyone restored it? It's a part of Los Angeles history."

The man glanced up at the disgraced old building with a look of reluctance.

"History?" he asked, and he shook his head. "They showed porn flicks here."

"Do you mind if I ask who you work for?"

"I'm private security."

"Do you represent the owners of the theater?"

He stared at me without responding. My phone started ringing, which startled me. I glanced down at the screen and saw Lola's name. I groaned internally because I couldn't handle any more bad news about Ricky. I deliberated about whether or not I should take the call or hit her back later. After a moment's pause, I picked up.

"Hi, Lo," I said. I walked away from the man and then glanced around to make sure he hadn't followed me. He had already disappeared. "I'm just leaving the Hotel Stanislas. What's up?"

"Rainey," Lola said. She sounded stressed, out of breath. I was immediately alarmed.

"What is it? Are you okay? Is it about Ricky?"

"It's Spencer," she said. "You haven't heard yet?"

"I haven't heard anything," I said, alarmed. "What do you mean? I just left her apartment. Her landlord said she moved out a few days ago."

"She's dead," Lola said. "Spencer's dead."

The words didn't register at first. I had reached the corner across from the car lot, and I pressed the button for the WALK sign. It was a hot day and there was no shade in this corner of Downtown, just long sidewalks marked by old gum and cracked pavement. A woman in hot shorts fanned herself with a brochure.

"What?"

"Spencer's dead," Lola repeated, her voice quiet. "It's on the news right now."

I exhaled sharply, and it came out like a groan.

"Oh, Rai," Lola said. "I'm sorry. I know you used to be friends."

"Oh my god," I whispered. The news felt like a gut punch, but at the same time I felt curiously numb. It didn't feel real, not yet. I felt tears in my eyes, but whether they were from shock or genuine sadness was impossible to tell. "What happened?"

"There was an article in the *Los Angeles Times*," Lola said. "Cause of death has not yet been determined, according to the article."

For a moment I was disoriented, wondering why Spencer's death would make the news. Was there something suspicious about it? Did someone know that it was part of a bigger story?

"They mentioned her grandmother," Lola went on. "Edith Frances."

Of course, I remembered. Spencer was the heir to the Frances legacy.

"Are you okay?" Lola asked.

"I'm fine," I said, but then I suddenly felt spooked. It was broad daylight, and I was in the middle of a busy street, but there was a chance that I could be in danger.

I hadn't told Lola or Blake about the voices that I had heard in Spencer's apartment. I hadn't told them that I had broken in, either, but if there was anything suspicious about Spencer's death, this might be the time to do it.

"Where are you?" I asked.

"I'm heading to Noa's house," she said. "We're going to talk about next steps regarding her restraining order petition. Especially with this latest development. I'm also going to clarify a few things so I can get all my paperwork ready for the meeting with Zo's lawyers."

"Did you tell Noa about the lawsuit?" I asked Lola.

"No, I thought we had decided not to," Lola said. "She also mentioned that there's something she wants to show me."

"Show you what?"

"No idea. She asked me to come over when I could."

"Okay," I said. "Wait out front. I'll meet you there."

SEVENTEEN

——⟨∞⟩——

Half an hour later, I pulled up down the block from Noa's house and parked. As I walked to her house, scanning the street for signs of Ricky, I noticed Lola's car parked out front. She must have been watching me, because she opened the door and stepped out as I approached.

"Hey, Rai," she said. Her face was creased with worry, and she pulled me into a hug. "Are you okay?"

"I'm fine," I said, even though I wasn't sure it was true.

She stood back and analyzed my face. "I know it must be a shock."

I didn't respond for a moment, thinking. "I don't know how to feel," I said. "Maybe you're right, maybe I'm still numb. I haven't had a relationship with Spencer for a long time, so it's not a deep blow. I guess I feel spooked by it, when I think about it."

"Right." Lola nodded.

"There wasn't any news about her cause of death?"

"Nothing so far," Lola said. "But I think that's pretty normal. Didn't you say she had problems with drugs for most of her life?"

"Yes," I said. "Yes, she did. I guess we'll find out soon enough. Lola, I need to tell you something."

She listened, watching my face.

"I know you're going to get mad," I said. "And I understand. You're allowed to. But if you could just save it for later . . ."

"What did you do?" Her voice was stern.

"I've been trying to find Spencer," I said, stalling for time.

"And?" Lola gesticulated. "Spit it out."

"I paid her landlord to let me see inside her apartment."

Lola narrowed her eyes, parsing my words. "What—how? When was this?"

"A few days ago, the first time," I began, but Lola cut me off.

"You did this more than once . . . !"

"Just listen," I said. "The first time was right after I talked to Calder. He said that Spencer was in a bad way. I found out where she lived, then drove over. I just wanted to have a conversation."

Lola groaned.

"She was there, but just for a few minutes," I said. I was having trouble meeting Lola's eye: while I was content to occasionally get my hands dirty as a means to an end, Lola was my moral counterweight. It was rare for her to even jaywalk. "The landlord let me into her apartment."

"Did you find anything when you were there?" Lola peered at me.

"Her apartment was disgusting," I said. "She was obviously struggling. I didn't find anything, but while I was there, two men broke in and ransacked the place, looking for something."

"Jesus, Rainey," Lola said, sinking her face into her hands. "You can be such a goddamn cowboy sometimes. I can't believe you haven't told me this."

"I'm sorry." I tried to look contrite. "I think I recognized one of the voices."

"And? Who was it?"

"Does the name Bradley Auden mean anything to you?" I asked.

She narrowed her eyes and thought for a moment, then shook her head. "I don't think so. Who is he?"

"He's the grandson of Emmett Auden," I said. "The architect."

"Right . . ."

"Bradley works with Marcus. He has an assistant, Lucas—kind of an asshole. I think he was the one who was in Spencer's apartment."

Lola's expression was hard to parse. Her gaze settled somewhere past my shoulder, and I could tell that she was mulling things over.

"Okay," she said. "We'll have to get into this later. We're here to do something else. Let's go see Noa."

Lola and I walked up the path. I could hear birdsong in the tree above us, and I was reminded that while we were in the trenches, toiling away at all the mess and decay in the city, millions of other people were living their lives, happily unaware of all the chaos that existed on a subterranean level. Once I would have been bitter at the thought, but now I found it reassuring.

Noa opened the door before we had a chance to knock. "Hi," she said, looking at me with surprise. "Good to see you, Rainey—Lola said you were out of the office today."

"I finished early," I said. I was surprised that she seemed to be in a good mood—I would think the news of Ricky's restraining order petition would have knocked her sideways. "I thought I'd join her here."

"Fine with me," she said, beaming. "Taylor's with a friend of mine, so we've got the house to ourselves. Come on in."

Lola and I slipped our shoes off and followed Noa into the living room. We exchanged a baffled look. Noa indicated that we should take a seat on the couch. The coffee table in the middle of the room was covered in a variety of plants. The plants had thick olive leaves and a different variety of unfurling white flowers.

"There it is," Noa said, sweeping her hand toward the plants. "That's what I found."

Lola looked confused. She turned and gave me a questioning look, then turned back to Noa.

"Did I miss something?" she asked. "I'm not sure I understand what I'm looking at."

"Is this morning glory?" I asked, going over to touch one of the plants.

"I think so," Noa said. "It's a deadly plant. I got it from Ricky's place. Why would Ricky have a bunch of deadly plants growing in his house?"

Lola and I exchanged another perplexed look.

"He's going to kill someone!" Noa exclaimed. "Maybe he's trying to kill me!"

Lola looked alarmed, but I was pretty sure Noa was kidding. She had a dark sense of humor.

"I'm only joking, Lola," Noa said, giving her a reassuring smile. "But you have no idea—my mind goes to some pretty dark places these days."

Lola looked like she was trying very hard to choose her words carefully. "How did you get these?"

"I just told you. I got them at Ricky's house."

"When?"

"Yesterday," Noa said.

"Were you dropping your kid off?"

"Exactly," Noa said. Her eyes gleamed. "I took him over to Ricky's mum's house in Sherman Oaks. Most of the time Ricky isn't there, even on the days he's supposed to have Taylor. When he does take Taylor, he usually just puts him on the floor of a café while he sits and talks to his mates."

"Noa," Lola said carefully. "I know that you're really angry with Ricky, and you have good right to be, but you can't do that anymore. He's trying to get a restraining order against you—breaking into his house is just fodder for the petition."

"Nobody was home!" Noa exclaimed. "I just hung around in my car til they were gone. Once Ricky drove off with Taylor, I let myself in—I have a key, in case of emergencies—and that's when I found all these plants."

"How do you know Serena's not the one with a green thumb?" Lola pointed out.

"Please," Noa said, making a face. "She can't grow anything, I've asked. Ricky was always obsessed with plants."

Lola steepled her fingers. "Don't take this the wrong way, but I'm not sure that this helps us," she said.

"Aha," Noa said, pointing a finger at Lola. "We can make the case that Ricky is negligent. These plants are everywhere. All over the house. I can't leave my son in a place with poisonous plants."

Lola looked at me, then shrugged. "Okay," she said. "We should probably take these off your hands, though. I don't want Ricky to find out that you broke into his house and stole things. That won't look good."

"I thought you might say that," Noa said, walking over to a desk. "But over the last few days, he's sent out at least a dozen emails. I just want this to be over, Lola. I want to get rid of him, once and for all. He's done dodgy shit in the past, and I thought I could find evidence of it at his house."

Lola took the stack of emails from Noa and scanned through them. "You mean that he's still sending out emails, even though he applied for a restraining order?"

"That's right." Noa's expression was grim.

"Have a look at some of these," Lola said, passing me a few sheets of paper.

My heart lurched when I started to read. These emails were just like all the others, a combination of erratic punctuation and randomly dispersed capital letters.

dearsir—

> *This is to advise that you have in your employ a destructive woman who has soght manytimes over to destroy my reputation,*
> *Her name is NOA COHEN. This letter I am writing to advise,*
> *Please know that she has tried to destroy my reputation and made grievous lies about my character it is an assignation.*
> *If a lawsuit is brought there will be damages and please know that you may be liable to pay. It occurs to me you may not know but I am a*

doctor and I know how bad it is for a man to be deprived of his child
(i have one). I am currently suing Noa to the full extent of the law,
*   also Noa cheated.*

Cordially Dr. Ricky Goff.

I glanced up and saw that Lola was silently murmuring under her breath and counting something on her fingers.

"What are you doing?" I asked.

"Oh," she said, looking up. "The way he writes—I was trying to work out if it was iambic pentameter."

"He should be arrested for his treatment of punctuation," I said. I nodded to Noa. "Who did he send this email to?"

"My boss," she said with disgust. Her mouth was a thin line, and her eyes were slits. "All of my bosses, actually. It's not enough to take out a restraining order—now he's trying to get me fired."

I skimmed over the list of contacts on the email I had just read. "There are at least twenty names here. You have that many bosses?"

"Look closer," Lola said. "You recognize any of those names?"

I looked again and nodded. "Sure, who are they?"

"He's emailing people at City Hall," Lola said.

I stared at her. "You can't be serious."

"The evidence is right in front of you," she said, then shrugged.

"What the fuck?"

"Rainey, remember that this man is completely out of his mind," Lola said. She continued flipping through the emails, shaking her head in disbelief. "They read like hostage notes. In this one, Ricky refers to himself as a prophet in three separate paragraphs, then talks about how martyrs are mourned only after they get sacrificed. He manages to threaten us at the same time as he begs for understanding. And—oh, bless—he sent this one to the White House."

Noa sank her head in her hands.

"Don't worry, Noa!" Lola said, coming over to squeeze her shoulder. "We're good at this stuff. Any half-decent judge will see through this the moment the docket crosses the table. And once we've got your restraining order, we'll sue Ricky for defamation."

"Yeah?" Noa looked up.

"Course. It's so obvious why he's doing this. Men with fragile egos are always concerned about their reputations being damaged. Anything that threatens their self-image must be destroyed. Ricky's mother works as a legal secretary, right?"

"She used to. She retired a few years ago."

"I'm guessing she taught her baby boy that the fastest way to shut someone up is to threaten a lawsuit. There's a type of person called a vexatious litigant. They'll sue at the drop of a hat. They'll sue the weatherman because it rained when it was supposed to be sunny. They'll sue you for looking at them the wrong way and find a way to bring in all these other things that have nothing to do with the original issue. Ricky needs to find a way to blame someone else for the rotting mess that his life has become, and because he can't stand to look in the mirror, someone else has to pay."

<hr />

We walked back to my car so that I could put the plants in the back. Lola leaned against the side of the car and glanced at the flowering vines.

"It's probably nothing," she said, gesturing toward the plants. "I guess it must help her feel like she's being productive, though. Better than nothing."

"You're right. And who knows? Maybe it will lead somewhere."

"You said you visited Spencer twice," Lola said, after a pause. "What happened when you went the second time?"

"I was there this morning," I said.

Lola's eyes went wide.

"Her apartment was empty," I said. "Someone had cleaned it out."

"Jesus," she whispered. "I think we should talk to the police, let them know that you were looking for her. It doesn't look good that you were snooping around her apartment the same morning she winds up dead."

"She didn't die in the apartment," I pointed out, cross. "And I didn't spend more than a minute inside. I just opened the door and saw that the entire place had been scrubbed. Completely empty."

"Who do you think it was?"

"Probably Lucas and the other guy," I said. "The people who were ransacking the place and looking for whatever Spencer stole from them. They mentioned a key, but I have a feeling they were looking for something bigger, too."

"I still think you should talk to the police."

"Well, thanks for the free legal advice."

I slammed my car door shut and put my hands on my hips. Lola saw my defensive posture and burst out laughing.

"God, don't be like that," she said. "I'm on your side. Come on, walk me back to my car."

She slung her arm around my shoulders, but I shimmied out of her embrace. "It's too hot," I whined.

"All right, all right."

We had almost reached Lola's car when I realized that a big black SUV was parked at an angle across the street. It hadn't been there when we left Noa's place; I would have noticed the terrible parking job. I squinted to see who was in the driver's seat, but before I could make out a face, the car door swung open, and Ricky stepped out.

"For fuck's sake," I muttered.

Ricky scratched his crotch and then folded his arms across his chest, trying to look menacing. The pose made his belly stick out, though, and he looked uncomfortable. He unfolded his arms and shoved his hands in his pockets.

The passenger door opened, and a compact older woman hopped out. Her golden hair was permed into a nimbus that floated around her head. It was the same shade of Easter-chick-yellow as Ricky's, and I wondered if she dyed it to emphasize their connection. She looked dignified, wearing a pink tweed skirt suit and pearls, but the sneer on her face was identical to the look I had seen on Ricky.

"Who *is* that?" Lola muttered.

"Serena Goff," I said. I was full of dread. "Ricky's mother."

"You," Serena seethed, one finger pointed in my direction. I waited for Ricky to approach, but to my surprise, he hung back while Serena advanced. "I know who you are. You need to leave my son alone!"

I placed a hand on my chest. "Excuse me?"

"Don't say anything, Rainey," Lola warned.

"That's right, I know who you are," Serena continued, not bothering to glance at Lola. She kept her eyes fixed on my face. "I know all about you. Do you know who you're representing? Do you *know* who your client is? I'm talking about Noa. Well? What do you have to say for yourself?"

"I can answer that for *my* client," Lola said, stepping in. "If you've got a legal matter to discuss, have your lawyer get in touch. Otherwise, we've got nothing to say to you."

I knew that I should walk away from Serena and go back to my car. I also knew that nothing good could come from this interaction: Serena was crazy, her son was a bully and a narcissist, and they both ached for a fight. The worst thing I could do was take the bait.

"It's okay, Lo," I said, putting a hand on her arm. I turned back to Serena. "Does your son speak for himself, or do you do the talking for him?"

Serena sneered up at me. She was tiny, but she had gravitas. I tried to imagine the once elegant woman she had been before hatred and entitlement had distorted her features into a perpetual look of disgust.

"Your client has poisoned my relationship with my grandson," she said. "She forces my son to pay her alimony and then she turns my grandson against me."

"Your son doesn't *pay* alimony," I replied. It was pointless to argue that Taylor was still a baby; it was impossible to turn him against anyone. "I've seen Noa's bank statements. As far as I understand, your son is unemployed and has made no effort to find a job. I imagine it must be difficult, though, when you get fired every three months. I've always wondered how someone so lazy can manage to pull off entitlement, but now, looking at you, I think I understand everything."

Throughout all of this, Ricky stood by the car, his hands in his pockets. His chin jutted out in an expression of condescension, and he squinted when I glanced over at him. When Serena approached me again, I took out my camera and started filming her.

"You're filming me right now, aren't you?" She started pacing up and down the street like a caged, mad thing. "You stupid, stupid girl. Stupid, silly woman. What's the obsession with filming? You're obsessed. Obsessed with Ricky, obsessed with harassing him. Obsessed with filming. Leave my son alone! We're going to get the police involved. We are going to ruin you. We are going to take everything you have. You will be in court for years. We will tie you up in so many legal battles that you won't have time to tie your shoes."

I didn't mean to laugh, but I was so surprised I couldn't help it. "Sue me for *what?*"

"That's it," Lola said, grabbing my arm and pulling me away, down the street toward our cars. I half expected Serena to follow us, but when I turned to glance over my shoulder she had climbed back in Ricky's car.

"Idiots," I said softly.

"You can see where he gets it from, at least."

As soon as I got home, I took a quick shower just to rid myself of the sensation of our confrontation with Ricky and Serena. The pair of them were vile, and even being in the same breathing space made me feel ill.

After I dried off and got dressed, I went to find Hailey's contact information. I had kept the card in my wallet ever since meeting him, and I felt a little thrill every time I saw it. There was something about Hailey that made me want to know more. I found his calm manner reassuring, and I felt a little giddy relief at the idea of calling him.

He picked up after two rings. "Hello?"

"Hailey? It's Rainey Hall."

A beat. "Rainey, hi," he said. "How's it going?"

"I think we might be able to help each other," I said. "I want to talk."

"Okay," he said, sounding surprised. "Yes. You free this evening?"

"Sure."

"Great. Come to my place. It's in Laurel Canyon. I'll send you the address."

EIGHTEEN

⁘

I had always found Laurel Canyon to be one of the parts of Los Angeles that was hardest to explain to people who didn't know the city. Laurel Canyon Boulevard was unpredictable and narrow, leading to clogged traffic that used the route as a main thoroughfare. The road led directly from Los Angeles into the San Fernando Valley, with incredible views on either side of the mountain.

Unlike other parts of Los Angeles, Laurel Canyon had maintained a lot of its kooky personality throughout the decades, and it was an odd patchwork quilt of overlapping tastes and sensibilities, ranging from seventies swing pads to gothic mansions built in the early days of Hollywood. I didn't know Hailey well, but I never would have guessed that he lived in Laurel Canyon—for one thing, I imagined the median rental price was way beyond the means of a journalist.

When I finally pulled up to the address Hailey had given me, I had to check the number three times before I was convinced I had the right place. The house was a little fairytale cottage, all sloping roofs and round windows in cob walls. Geraniums sat beneath a front window, and a rough-hewn wooden gate led off into a side garden. It looked like something a person might've stumbled across in a Bavarian Forest a hundred years ago, when they deviated from the path. I climbed out of my car and laughed in surprise and delight.

I knocked on the door, and a moment later it swung open to reveal Hailey, standing there smiling at me.

"Thanks for coming," he said. He wore a pale blue linen shirt and jeans. "Come on in."

"Your house . . . ! Hailey, it's so beautiful—I'm so jealous!"

"Don't be," he said, raising an eyebrow. "I love it, don't get me wrong, but the upkeep is a nightmare."

I had a dozen questions, but I didn't want to pry. I followed him into the living room, which had wooden floors and a low ceiling. Flowers gently bobbed against the stained glass windows, and I felt a sense of calm I hadn't experienced in a long time.

"It was my grandmother's house," he said, waving a hand. "I lived here for part of my childhood."

"You're lucky," I said.

He nodded, then shrugged. "Do you want some coffee? Unless it's too late for you, of course, I can get you something else."

"Coffee is good."

We walked into the kitchen, which was quaint and old-fashioned. A pale blue Smeg fridge occupied a corner of the room, and the tile counters looked like they hadn't been changed since the place was built. The room was immaculate and well-appointed.

"It's so . . ."

"What?" Hailey cocked his head.

"Clean." I breathed in. "And it smells good."

He laughed. "Well, thanks," he said. "How do you take your coffee?"

"Black is fine."

Hailey poured the coffee and then we returned to the living room. He opened up his computer and put on his glasses, then skimmed the screen. "So," he said, "what do you want to talk about?"

I drummed my fingers on the table and wondered where I should start. If Hailey was looking into artists who were using drugs, there was a chance he knew something about Spencer. Spencer could lead to Alice, and hope-fully that would lead me to finding Chloe Delmonico.

"Did you hear about Spencer Collins?" I asked.

Hailey nodded. "I did."

"No cause of death mentioned," I said.

"I saw that." Hailey's voice sounded guarded, and he was watching me carefully.

"We used to be friends," I said. "We knew each other in high school."

He pressed his lips together and nodded once. "I'm sorry for your loss," he said.

"We lost touch a while ago."

Hailey waited for a moment, then glanced down at his notes. "Is that what you wanted to talk about?"

"Partly," I said. "When I saw you at Calder's gallery, you mentioned that you were looking into missing artists. Spencer was an artist."

"I see."

"Have you found anything else about Rhodes?"

"I've had a few leads," Hailey said.

"Right. Where has he been for the last few years, and who's been hiding him?" I asked. "In your opinion, of course."

Hailey looked at my face for a moment, then laughed and leaned back in his chair. "Down to brass tacks. I admire that. Maybe we should discuss our intentions first."

"Intentions?"

"I suggested a dialogue," Hailey said gently, spreading his hands on the table. "An exchange of information."

"I'm not sure I have anything you want," I said.

He smiled and inclined his head to the side. "I disagree."

"What do you want?"

He flexed his fingers. "Why don't you tell me why you're really here?"

"Confidential."

Hailey gave an expansive shrug. "Seems like we're at an impasse."

"Okay." I exhaled, frustrated. "A client's life has been adversely affected. Better?"

"Rainey, please." He shut his computer and took off his glasses. "If you need to go home and think about what you're willing to discuss, I understand. Maybe we should reschedule."

I took a deep breath and held it. "I'm looking into a missing artist. I think there's a connection between Spencer and another friend of mine who went missing in high school. I'm trying to see the bigger picture."

Hailey leaned back and steepled his fingers. "How do you think I can help you?"

"Tell me what you know about Rhodes. Maybe I can use the information to hunt down my missing artist."

He pointed at me. "Chloe Delmonico."

I held myself as still as possible and hoped I gave nothing away. Hailey gave me a mischievous look.

"Aw, come on," he said. "There aren't *too* many missing artists at the moment. Unless you're looking into Eiko Mars. She's an orphan, and her aunt and uncle probably don't have enough money to hire a private investigator. That leaves Chloe Delmonico. Her parents live in Oxnard, and I'm guessing they have spare funds."

"You're kind of an asshole. Has anyone ever mentioned that?" I was furious with myself for being so stupid. Lola was going to ream me.

Hailey burst out laughing. "I'm sorry, I'm sorry," he said. "I won't say anything—promise. I got into journalism because I care about making the world a tiny bit better. I'm not going to run off and print something about a missing teen."

"I should go."

"Wait. Please." He gave me a contrite look. "I won't publish anything you tell me, unless you decide otherwise," he said. "And in return for that, you won't share this confidential information with anyone."

"I can't agree to that," I said. "I have to be able to discuss this with my team."

He hesitated and looked like he was about to decline my conditions.

"I tell them everything," I said. "It's just three of us. We share all our cases, and I would be lying if I promised not to tell them."

He took a long moment to respond, then he stood up and extended his hand. We shook.

"Rhodes was on drugs—you know that bit. There's something they haven't printed in the news, though. I think this drug is something new. I've heard rumors about it. It sounds horrifying—beyond anything else I've heard of."

I was curious but tried to remain neutral. "How do you know this?"

"I have a lot of sources," Hailey said. "This drug is really exclusive. You can't buy it on the streets. It's not being sold anywhere, at least from what I can see. Someone is giving it away for free."

The hairs on the back of my neck stood up. "Why would they do that?"

Hailey gave me a loose shrug. "That," he said, "is what I can't work out. There seems to be a link, though, between artists who used the drug and then went missing."

"Wow," I breathed. "That's really creepy."

"Yes. Yes, it is." Hailey was watching me. "Are you sure that Chloe is still alive?"

My heart lurched. "No," I said. "Of course not. But I'm going to keep looking for her regardless. I need to find out what happened, if that's all I can offer her family."

He gave me a small smile. "I can tell you care about what you do."

I stood up and stretched my arms above my head; I was starting to feel restless. It happened sometimes, that feeling like I couldn't sit still, and it usually occurred after a bunch of information fell into my lap. I wanted to go out and pursue leads, to do something with all this data.

"Hailey," I asked, "why did you go see Calder last week?"

Hailey hesitated before he spoke. "Is he a friend of yours?"

"Not exactly," I said. "Don't get me wrong—I like Calder in small doses, and I'm sure he feels the same way about me. As much as I like his company, though, I don't really trust him. He can't keep his mouth shut."

Hailey laughed. "He seemed to like you well enough."

"Well, my mom was famous," I said. "My whole family was famous, actually, and that's what matters to Calder. The moment I lose that clout, though, is the moment when Calder forgets we ever knew each other."

Hailey rubbed his chin and thought. "Okay," he said. "I've made a list of artists who were promising, but then they just vanished overnight. I'm not talking about people who went crazy or got sent to rehab or moved back to Montana. I'm talking about disappearing acts."

"Rhodes," I said.

He pointed at me. "Exactly. There are a few other names, but Calder wouldn't confirm anything."

"How do you know Rhodes isn't in rehab?" I asked. "That's what happens when famous people have a public meltdown in Los Angeles. Their publicity teams shuffle them offstage and make them disappear for a few months. Come October, he'll make a grand reappearance and have a gallery show."

"I don't think so."

"Why not?"

"I think he's dead," Hailey said.

We fell silent, and I could hear the muffled ticking of a clock in some other room. It struck me then how quiet this part of Los Angeles was, away from all the bustle and chaos of the other parts of the city.

"That's a dark thought," I said. My limbs felt heavy, the way that they sometimes did when I was overcome with panic.

"It is," Hailey said. "Sometimes I want to be wrong. It happens more than you'd think. I catch wind of a story or get a crazy idea, and I keep trying to prove myself wrong. I chase leads. I interview people. And when the truth remains, despite my best efforts, that's when I go to press. With my editor's blessing, of course."

I took out my notepad and flipped to the page where I had written down bits of my conversation with Calder.

"Have you tried to find Rhodes's family?" I asked.

Hailey nodded, his face grim. "Rhodes has a sister, but it looks like his parents are dead. I tried reaching out to her, but she wouldn't return my phone calls, and when I went out to speak to her, she got cagey. She said she didn't know where he was, they didn't have a relationship. That's it."

"And Eiko?"

He tapped away at his computer. "Eiko has been really hard to track down. Both of her parents are dead, too, but I can't find any other family. There's a clear link between Rhodes and Eiko, though, which makes me think I should keep pushing."

"More than the fact that they both went missing?" I frowned and thought for a moment. "They were both orphans, so they didn't have parents to look for them."

"They both had gallery shows at BALTO," Hailey said. "That in itself isn't pivotal; BALTO has shown lots of artists. But from the intel that I could gather, it seems like Simon took a special interest in both of them."

"Special interest? How did you come up with that?"

"I went through his archives, all his public mentions, any time he was listed in the society column," Hailey said. He flipped through his notes on the table. "They were pictured out and about for a while. The new hot thing. Then they both just seemed to disappear."

"I wonder how many other artists have gone missing in the same way," I said. "Ones we haven't heard about."

It was an ominous thought. We sat in silence for a moment.

"You mentioned that Simon was trying to build a museum," I said. "Out near Palm Springs?"

"That's right."

"Why hasn't the museum gone ahead yet?"

Hailey ran a hand through his hair. "From what I could find, it seems like an environmental issue," he said. "There have been a few stories about the stalemate in development, and they usually circle around this guy." He turned his computer around and showed me a photo of a chubby, middle-aged man in a cowboy hat. "Dan Everson. He's a conservative Republican, but I can almost forgive him for that because he's pushed some good environmental initiatives. The crux of his argument is that he doesn't want the museum to go ahead because it could change the desert for the worse."

I walked over to the window and looked out at the garden. "Do you mind if I tell my team that you think Rhodes is dead?"

Hailey watched me for a long time without responding. He took a deep breath and leaned back in his chair, then slowly exhaled. "Okay," he said.

"I'll just have Blake keep digging into both of those artists," I said. "We can keep communicating. I think it's a good idea for us to help each other."

"That's fine."

"I told you that I was looking for a friend," I said. "Alice Alder. She disappeared nine years ago."

Hailey thought for a moment, then nodded. "You mentioned that when I ran into you at Calder's gallery."

"I think she's caught up in this," I said. "She went missing when we were in high school. I saw her on some security footage; that's the only reason I know she's still alive."

"Why do you think she's caught up in this?"

I needed to tread very carefully here. "There's a sketchy guy," I said. "I can't tell you his name—not yet. I need to make sure I'm not violating client privilege by doing so. I've been looking at him for years, trying to find a way in. He was with Alice the night that she disappeared, and I think he might have been responsible for Chloe's disappearance, too."

Hailey's face fell. "How can I help you catch him?"

"I'm not sure yet," I said, then gave him a grim smile. "But I'll definitely tell you when I know."

I was driving home when I started to feel the beginning of a panic attack. They always started the same way for me: I would feel my heart rate plunge and nearly stop altogether, and then it would accelerate at a frightening pace. I pulled over on the side of Ventura Boulevard and turned my car off, then started hyperventilating. It took five minutes of slow breaths with my eyes closed for things to start to even out. I stepped out of my car and walked up and down the sidewalk, taking small, conscious steps.

When I got back in my car, I burst into tears. Crying was out of character for me. I had learned sometime during childhood to distance myself from my more difficult emotions. I flashed back on Spencer's face, back when we were still in high school. Spencer, before she had gone off the deep end, before she had gotten involved in this whole convoluted mess. I felt wretched, and the guilt came upon me all at once. I could have done more for her, I reasoned, even though we had lost touch in the last few years. I had struggled with my own alcohol issues in the years after high school, and I knew how hard it could be to pull yourself out of that hole. It was worse when you didn't have someone looking after you.

I turned on my car and continued on Ventura Boulevard toward Laurel Canyon Drive, then got on the 134-E. I wasn't going home, not anymore; there was somewhere else I needed to go first.

Spencer's house was three blocks away from Banter House and a ten-minute drive from where Marcus lived. Even with all the times I had visited Pasadena in the last few years, though, I hadn't seen Spencer's house since high school. Spencer had grown up in a house that had been built for Edith Frances back in the 1920s, a sprawling Tudor Revival mansion surrounded by vast gardens of winding paths lined with rosebushes. The front of the house was visible from the street, all dark wood and sunlight sparkling off mullioned windows.

I had been full of purpose when I left Hailey's neighborhood, but now, standing in the street, I had no idea what I was going to say to Spencer's family. Before I could second-guess my mission, I walked up to the front door and knocked.

After a few minutes, I heard the lock unlatch, and the door opened a crack. Someone inside was appraising me, but I could only see a single eye. Then the door opened all the way, and standing in front of me was Melinda Collins, Spencer's stepmother.

"Rainey . . . ? Is that Rainey?" Melinda was a petite Filipino woman, regal in her stature and manner of speech. Her voice was gently accented, with a slight British tilt. Melinda looked wan, with the roots showing underneath her dark hair. Still, she was well-dressed in a sweater set and pearls.

"Melinda, hi," I said. I had met Melinda a handful of times, but it had been back in high school, and I wasn't sure if she would remember me.

"I don't know if you've heard," Melinda continued. Her voice sounded drawn, monotonous with either exhaustion or grief. "Spencer was found dead early this morning."

I took a deep breath and squeezed my eyes shut. I could feel the beginning of tears again. "That's why I'm here. Melinda, I'm so sorry."

Melinda took a ragged breath, then reached out and squeezed my hand. "Thanks, Rainey. Thanks."

Spencer had always hated Melinda, and in some ways, it was understandable: Melinda had met Spencer's father when Spencer was thirteen, and after dating for only a few months the two had gotten married. Melinda had been born and raised in the Philippines but immigrated to Singapore for university, which was where she met George. She had been in her fifties at the time, with two daughters of her own. The transition to married life with Spencer hadn't been smooth. Still, although I had known Melinda to be a firm and serious woman, she had always been kind to me.

"Melinda, what happened? Can you tell me?"

She looked wary, then glanced past me. "Did you see anyone when you came to the house?" she asked.

"No, what do you mean?"

"There was a car parked out front earlier," she said. "A big SUV. I think someone was watching the house."

I was immediately alarmed, and my mind went straight to Ricky. "Did you call the police?"

"Psh! Police! I'm not going to be intimidated. Let them sit there!" The color rose in her face, and her mouth was a tight line. "I'm not scared."

I felt a touch of admiration for Melinda.

"Let's go for a walk around the garden," she said. "I need the fresh air."

Melinda was a few inches shorter than me, but she took long strides. I had to hurry to keep up with her as she walked around the side of the house, into the rose garden.

"Were you in touch with Spencer?" she asked, turning to look at me.

"No," I said. "No, not really. We haven't been friends for years."

She appraised me for a moment, then nodded. "Thank you for your honesty," she said. "I've become paranoid over the last few years, because of all the people who go in and out of Spencer's life. Bad news, all of them."

I wanted to know more, but I was also conscious of Melinda's grief. I didn't want to push her if I didn't have to.

"Melinda, I'm not sure if you know this," I said. "I can't see why you would—it's been so long since we've been in contact. I'm a private investigator."

"Oh! No, I didn't know that." A flicker of a smile appeared on Melinda's face. "I'm glad you turned out okay, Rainey. I watched Spencer go through so much trauma."

"I know," I said. "I'm sorry things didn't turn out better for her. Melinda—do you mind if I ask what happened?"

She hesitated, then reached out to touch a golden rose. "We found her in the bedroom upstairs. It looks like it might have been a drug overdose . . . We called the ambulance, of course, but they said they wouldn't be able to revive her."

"Wait, she died at your house? She was living with you?"

"She had moved back in two days before because she was scared of someone. She wouldn't tell me who."

My heart started pounding. "She didn't tell you anything?"

"Nothing."

"And have you talked to the police about what she said?"

"Yes," Melinda said. Her voice was strained. "When I called 911, I told them I thought she had overdosed on drugs. They sent a pair of police officers out with the ambulance. I told them everything that Spencer had said, and they told me . . . they said that addicts are often paranoid, convinced that someone is out to get them."

"And you haven't heard from them since?"

"No," she said. Tears welled up in her eyes, and she brushed them away with the back of her hand.

"I see."

"We wouldn't hear from her for months at a time, and then suddenly she would show up, asking for money. It was horrible, Rainey. Horrible. We tried everything to get her off drugs, to make her get better, but nothing worked. After George died, I begged Spencer to come home and let me take care of her, but she said some really horrible things about how I was . . . well. That doesn't matter now."

"I didn't realize that you still had a relationship," I said. "I wasn't in touch with Spencer for a long time, but the last time I saw her, she didn't mention it."

"I tried, Rainey, I really tried," she said. "I don't blame her for being angry. She lost both parents so young. I didn't know how to help her."

I remembered how Spencer told me that Melinda kept all of George's money after he died. For years I had just taken it at face value, believing that Spencer had been screwed over, but now I could see that Melinda really cared about her.

"Melinda, I'm sorry if this sounds insensitive," I said. "But did she have access to a lot of money?"

Melinda heaved a sigh. "You mean the inheritance," she said.

"That or anything else?"

"No," she said finally. "No, she didn't. George set aside money for her, of course, but when she dropped out of high school and got into really heavy drugs, he knew he couldn't let her have it. All that money is set aside in trust. Rainey, don't get the wrong idea. We told her that it was hers as soon as she got clean. I don't know if that was the right thing to do. She got so angry . . . I don't know. I just don't know."

"You can't give an addict an endless amount of money," I said, trying to reassure her. "She would've been dead years ago."

Melinda began to softly weep.

"Thank you for saying that," Melinda finally said.

"Let me know if there's anything I can do," I said.

"There's going to be a service," she said. "It's in two days' time. That might seem fast, but my daughters and I have discussed it. I know the news cycle can be vicious, and we want to remind people that Spencer was a person."

"I'll be there," I said. "Of course."

"We'll hold the funeral at our house," she said. "That way we might have a chance at some privacy."

Once I was back home, I took out my phone and called Cameron.

"Hi," he said. "How are you?"

"Not great. Have you seen the news about Spencer?"

I heard him sigh. "Yes, I saw," he said. "It's awful. The whole thing makes me sick. I thought about calling you, but I didn't want to disturb you."

"You wouldn't be disturbing me," I said. "Are you going to her funeral?"

"Yeah, I reached out to Melinda," he said. "I'm surprised she remembered me, because we only met a handful of times, but I used to be friends with Nathalie."

I hadn't seen Spencer's stepsister in years, and I wasn't sure she would remember me.

"Are you going to the funeral?"

"Yes," I said.

"I'll see you there."

Once I got off the phone, I brought out the contents of Spencer's bag. I felt annoyed all over again at how unproductive the visit to Casa Nopales was—Lola was right, I had recklessly exposed myself to someone who was happy to sell information to the highest bidder. I stared at the items and tried to imagine what Spencer had been doing for money and how she had gotten herself into this mess. I knew from firsthand experience that addiction was counterintuitive, that a drug could be both the shovel and the hole, and it was easy to judge from the outside without understanding why someone would keep on digging themselves deeper. Still, it was hard to fathom that Spencer could continue living in a shithole like the Casa Nopales when she had the entire inheritance at stake.

I organized the contents of her bag in front of me. Gum wrappers, a crushed cigarette pack (Marlboro Reds), spent matches, and crumpled receipts. I smoothed out the receipts to see where she had been. A gas station in Hollywood for cigarettes and candy bars. A Ralph's in Glendale. A dry cleaner in Koreatown. I scanned the receipts, trying to construct some kind of narrative, and then something clicked.

This is an estimated cost and may not reflect final total for cleaning, the cleaning receipt read. I stared at it for a moment longer, then took out my phone and called the number at the bottom of the receipt.

"Park Cleaners," came a man's voice on the other end. I could hear the chatter of customers in the background, and something that sounded like steam.

"Hi," I said. "I'm picking up some clothes for a friend. I wanted to know if they were ready."

"Last name?"

"Collins," I said. "I have an order number here, too. RFK-89."

"Checking now."

He put the phone down and I realized that I was holding my breath. I didn't know what I was hoping to find, or if Spencer was a regular customer and the man would refuse to hand over her clothing when he saw I wasn't her.

He came back on the line. "The dress is ready," he said. "The stain was very hard to get out, but we did our best. Extra charges for deep cleaning. Forty dollars."

I felt a wild stab of hope. "I'll be there in half an hour."

Park Cleaners was a tiny, narrow shopfront squeezed between a ramen restaurant and a bakery. My heart was pounding as I walked up to the dry cleaners and let myself in. Nobody was behind the counter, but a tiny bell rattled as I entered. After a moment a Korean man emerged from the back.

"Yes?"

"I spoke to you on the phone," I said. "I'm here to pick up for Spencer Collins."

"Yes," he said. "You have other things to pick up, too. I checked. Are you Miss Collins?"

"No, a friend," I said.

"Well, you can tell her that she needs to pay in advance next time," he said. "Too many things. I think she forgets."

He went to a rack hanging behind the counter and pulled off about six or seven items, all wrapped in plastic. He draped them over the counter, then collected all the chits and added up the total.

"One ninety," he said.

"Do you take cards?" I asked.

"Cards are okay," he replied.

I slipped him my card, trying to look at the clothing without being too conspicuous about it.

"Oh, one more thing," he said. "Some items fell out of the pockets when we were cleaning. We put them in a bag."

He handed me my receipt and a paper bag. I glanced inside and caught sight of a mess of items, including a tube of lipstick and some coins.

"Tell her payment up front next time," he reminded me.

"Understood," I said, then gathered everything up in my arms and elbowed my way through the front door.

I waited until I was back in my car to start going through the stash. Even through the filmy plastic I could see that the stack of clothing was expensive: there was a dress made of blue feathers, and one of black lace and silk. Two thin wool coats made the bundle heavy, and there was a double-breasted Chanel blazer. I laid everything on the seat next to me and opened up the bag of items that had fallen out of Spencer's pockets.

I removed each item one at a time, feeling like an archaeologist. Two tubes of lipstick—both Chanel—as well as a nearly empty bottle of Narciso Rodriguez perfume. A stack of movie theater tickets that had been bound with a rubber band. A jumble of hair ties, tangled with knots of hair. A paperback copy of Iris Murdoch's *The Sea, The Sea*. A miniature set of paintbrushes inside a tin. My hand closed on metal. I withdrew the item. A key.

Oh, hope beyond hope. I felt lightheaded. I was holding another key from the Hotel Stanislas, identical to the one I had found in Alice's pool. The only difference was the room number.

I didn't want to linger in front of the dry cleaners in case someone realized I shouldn't be there, so I waited until I got home to call my office. As soon as I parked and got out of my car, I took out my phone and dialed.

Blake answered after a few rings. "Left City Consultants," she said.

"Spencer had a key," I said. I was almost vibrating with excitement. "The same key that Alice had. The one I found in the swimming pool."

There was a pause. "Let me put you on speakerphone," she said.

"Hi, Rai," Lola said.

"Spencer had a key," I said. I walked up to my front door and unlocked it, then stepped inside. "You remember the key that I found in Alice's pool, for the Hotel Stanislas? Spencer had one, too."

"How do you know?" Lola asked.

"I picked up her dry cleaning."

There was a long pause on the other end of the phone. Lola finally laughed. "We can talk about that later," she said. "I'm not sure I want to know. Let's go back to the key."

"It's the same as the key that Alice hid in the swimming pool," I said. "Just a different room number."

"Okay," Lola said. "What do you think it means?"

"I don't think it's code, if that's what you mean," I said. "I think the keys correspond to rooms at the Hotel Stanislas."

"You already checked that out, though. You want to go back?"

"Yes. That creepy manager knows something. I had a feeling at the time, and now I'm even more certain."

"Okay," Lola said. "I'll go with you, then. When do you want to go?"

"You sure you have time? I'd feel safer with you there, but I can probably manage without you."

"No," she said. "If this is as big and complex as you think it is, we need two of us. Nonnegotiable."

"I agree, Rainey," Blake echoed.

"Okay," I said, feeling relieved and thankful. "Thanks, Lo."

"Not a problem. When do you want to go?"

I hesitated. "Tomorrow," I said. "After Spencer's funeral. We'll go straight after that."

"Hold on, let me just double-check my schedule," Lola said. I could hear her flipping through papers. "I've got something in the morning, so I can't go to the funeral with you. Are you okay to go by yourself?"

"That's fine," I said. "I'm sure I'll know some of the people there."

"Call me afterward," Lola said.

"Before I forget," Blake said. "Someone asked for you specifically, Rainey."

"Oh? Who?"

"No idea," Blake said. "It was sent to the general email address. They've included their email, but no name. Probably a burner account."

"What does it say?"

"Hold tight . . . *This email is for Rainey Hall, please get in touch with me. I have some information about Spencer Collins. Urgent.*"

"Forward that to me, please," I said.

"Done."

"While I have you," Lola said. "We have the meeting with Zo's lawyers in a couple days. Are you ready for that?"

It took me a moment to remember what she was talking about. "The slander lawsuit," I said.

"Yep. I can go alone, but I think you should be there, too."

"No problem."

"I've sorted all the paperwork," Lola said. "You just have to sit next to me and look strong."

"Not a problem." I glanced out the window at the garden. "Look, I should tell you guys that I ended up meeting up with that journalist—Max Hailey? He's looking into artists who've gone missing, and I thought we might be able to exchange some information."

Lola sighed. "I hate to be the voice of reason but is there a connection to the cases that we're already working on?" she said. "We can't go off on a tangent just because we get a whiff of something evil."

"I think there's some overlap between Ricky, Chloe, and the artists he's looking at," I said. "Blake, can you have a look and see what you can find about Rhodes? Eiko Mars, too, if you get a chance."

"Sorry," Lola cut in. "Can you clarify the relevance, Rainey? I don't see a connection to our case."

"Because once we find Spencer and Alice, we might be able to find Chloe," I said. "I think. There's a connection between these people—missing artists, people who used drugs."

I heard typing on the other end of the phone. "Is Rhodes Ian Rhodes?" Blake asked.

"That's right. I think he just goes by Rhodes."

"Well, I can't find any property or rental records for Ian Rhodes going back two years," she said. "It looks like he either moved back in with his family or else got someone to pay his bills."

"What about his family? Can you find out who they are?"

Blake typed again. "Parents are both deceased," she said, reading from her screen. "It looks like he has an older sister in Burbank."

"Send me that address, would you?"

"Done," she said.

"Can you keep looking into him?" I asked.

"Not a problem."

"And see what you can find on Eiko Mars."

"Done," Blake said. "Don't forget to check that email I sent to you."

I went to my email and found the message Blake had forwarded to me. The sender was someone called Reseda99.

I have information about Spencer Collins.

I hesitated for a moment, then fired off a response.

This is Rainey. What do you have for me? I included my phone number at the bottom, then sent it off.

NINETEEN

⎯⎯⎯⎯⎯⎯⎯⎯⎯⎯⎯

The morning of Spencer's funeral arrived. I was jumpy and paranoid, and not only for reasons pertaining to the key I had found in Spencer's things. I had gone to great measures to change my life since high school, cutting out anyone who might trigger me to start engaging in self-sabotaging behavior. I had done therapy and spent a lot of time working on myself. I had gotten better. I feared what seeing Spencer's body and all the people in her life might do to me.

My phone pinged with a text message. The number was one that I didn't recognize.

Thanks for getting back to me yesterday.

Who is this? I wrote.

I have information about Spencer Collins.

I'm guessing this is a burner phone, I wrote after a pause.

Correct.

That's reassuring. Why should I trust you?

We have some friends in common, came the response. *And you don't need to worry. I mean you no harm.*

Tell me who you are, I wrote again.

There was a long pause. Finally—*I'm sorry, I can't do that right now. I would be in a lot of danger. I'm putting myself in a bad position even reaching out to you like this.*

What do you want from me?

There was a five-minute interval without a response. I put my phone down a few times before a message came through.

I want you to find out what happened to Eiko Mars.

Eiko. *This feels really weird,* I wrote, then changed my mind and deleted it. Instead I wrote, *Why do you want me to look for Eiko?*

Another short pause. *Because nobody else is looking for her.*

How do you know? I wrote. *What's your interest in Eiko?*

She's a friend.

Try the police, I suggested.

The police can be bought. I've already tried.

I've looked for missing people before, I wrote, *but I do have limited resources. If the police can't find her, I probably can't, either.*

I can give you information that I didn't share with the police, came the response.

I felt a surge of annoyance and wondered if I was wasting my time even talking to this person. There was a chance this was all a practical joke, just someone trying to fuck with me and waste my time. We had encountered a fair number of these people over the years, bored trolls who thought nothing of giving up false information with little idea of the damage that they were doing. Still, we had to chase them down on the off chance they could offer up real intel, which they sometimes did.

What information are you willing to share with me? I wrote back. *What do you know about Spencer?*

Another pause. The response didn't come through for ten minutes.

Eiko was using drugs, came the response. *Something bad.*

What drugs?

I don't know. Something new. Pills.

I felt a little thrill as I read the message. *I can't take you on as a client if I don't know who you are,* I wrote, grasping at straws.

I'm not asking to be a client. It's not for me. I just need to know that she's safe. There was a pause. *If it's an issue of money, I can wire you some right now.*

It's not about the money, I replied.

I don't know when I can speak again. Here's something that might help you find Eiko. Eiko's sister's name is Hana.

A moment later, the name of a business came through.

Sweet Moon Bakery, Mercury, CA

I showered and got dressed, then jumped when my phone started ringing again. For a moment I thought it might be the anonymous contact, who I had saved in my phone as *Eiko's Friend.* When I picked up my phone, though, I saw that it was Hailey.

"Hey," I said. "What's up?"

"I was just wondering if I would see you at the funeral," he said.

I paused. "Spencer's funeral?"

He laughed, surprised. "You going to another funeral today?"

I blushed. "No, I'm just surprised that you know about it. How did you find out?"

"Give me a little bit of credit," he said. I could almost hear him smiling on the other end of the phone.

"I guess I'll see you there, then," I told him.

"I won't blame you if you want to walk in separately," he said. "My presence might raise some eyebrows."

"Fuck 'em," I said. "I'm happy to walk in with you."

After getting off the phone with Hailey, I wandered into the main house to make coffee. Sadie was sitting at the kitchen table, and she looked up and smiled.

"Coffee's just brewed," she said.

"Thank you!"

"Oh wow," she said. "Who is he?"

"Huh?"

She looked at my face and burst out laughing. "I was wrong about you," she said. "I thought you worked all the time. There's a dude!"

I flushed bright red and distracted myself by grabbing a coffee cup. "No, no, no dude. It's all work."

"Girl, please," she said. "I've been in love. It's been a while, but I still know what it looks like."

I was about to protest again, but then I burst out laughing.

"See? *See?*"

"Oh my god," I said. "I think you're right."

"Who is he?"

"First of all, it's definitely not love," I said. "I've only spent time with him once."

"Sometimes that's all you need."

"And it's a work thing," I added. "And you *definitely* can't tell anyone."

Sadie spread her hands. "Who would I tell?"

"Oh, god." I buried my face in my hands. "This is really inconvenient because we're going to be working together a bit."

She raised an eyebrow. "Client?"

"Oh, *god* no. I've made that mistake before. Never again."

"I learn something new about you every day," Sadie said with admiration. "Have fun with it. Life is supposed to be fun, you know? Sometimes people forget that."

———

By the time I reached Spencer's neighborhood, the day was scorching hot. I had allotted myself plenty of time to get to Pasadena, but traffic was oddly forgiving, and I arrived early enough to find parking and get myself emotionally situated to face the event. The street was lined with cars, and as I moved down the sidewalk toward the house, I spotted a familiar figure glancing down at his phone.

"Hailey," I called, and he glanced up, shielding his eyes against the sun. When Hailey saw me, he waved.

"Morning," he said. He wore a simple black suit and expensive-looking shoes. I felt a little thrill at seeing him, even though I knew it wasn't appropriate to the occasion.

"You scrub up nicely," I told him.

"So do you," he said. "I'm sorry about your friend."

"Spencer?" I frowned. "Thanks—but we haven't been friends for a long time."

"Still." He shaded his eyes.

There was a surprisingly big turnout for the memorial, and I caught a few people looking at me and Hailey as we walked into the house. I found that I didn't care, though—there was something comforting about Hailey's presence, something that made me feel safe. He was a good six inches taller than me, and he held himself with a respectful but quiet confidence.

I felt eerie about being in Spencer's house again after such a long time. We hadn't spent much time here back in high school, but I had visited on a few occasions, and it was strange to see that not much had changed. Melinda had kept everything almost exactly as I remembered it. I glanced around, taking in all the guests and trying to see who I recognized. Cameron Alder was in the corner of the room, talking to Nathalie, one of Spencer's two stepsisters. I had never had a close relationship with either Nathalie or Odessa. They were both older than Spencer and had moved out of the home by the time Melinda and George got married. From what I remembered, Nathalie had moved back to Singapore for university, then stayed on and took a job.

"I'll be right back," I told Hailey.

Cameron looked up and smiled when he saw me. I gave him a quick hug, then turned to Nathalie, suddenly nervous.

"Hi, Nathalie," I said. "I'm not sure if you remember me—Rainey Hall?"

To my surprise, she gave me a warm smile, then leaned in for a hug. "Of course I do, Rainey," she said. "I'm sorry we have to meet again under these circumstances."

I was relieved. I hadn't been sure what kind of reception I would get from Spencer's stepsisters—I wasn't sure how much they blamed me for Spencer's eventual downfall.

"I'm really sorry for your loss," I said, getting emotional again.

"Thank you." Nathalie's face was clouded. She swallowed hard, then nodded. "My mum's in complete shock. Obviously, I mean, she's the one who found Spencer. Odessa's been home for the last few months, so at least they had each other."

I had so many questions, but I needed to tread carefully. This was a funeral, after all, not a postmortem. I didn't want to open old wounds from back when we were in high school. Fortunately, though, Cameron spoke up.

"I haven't seen Spencer in such a long time," he said. "I guess I always thought she would get better. Stupid of me, really."

Nathalie gave a weak shrug. "I guess that makes me stupid, too," she said. "I thought the same thing."

Someone touched Nathalie's shoulder, and we both turned to see Bradley Auden. He looked exhausted, with dark circles under his eyes. Nathalie started weeping at the sight of him, then collapsed against his chest. He wrapped her in a tight hug and kissed her hair. I was surprised that they knew each other, but then remembered that their families were linked through Edith Frances and Emmett Auden.

"I'm so sorry," Bradley said, when Nathalie had taken a step back. "Violet and I have both been up all night. We feel sick about it."

"You did so much for her," Nathalie said.

"She's family," Bradley said. "I would do anything for her."

I hadn't seen Bradley since the Orphans' Ball, which had been before I broke into Spencer's apartment and heard Lucas rooting around, throwing furniture. Looking for something. I felt a hot flash of anger at the memory, and wondered how naïve Bradley was about his assistant.

Nathalie turned to me. "Sorry, Rainey—do you know Bradley Auden?"

Bradley gave me a sad smile. "Yes, we've met a few times. I had forgotten that you knew Spencer." He turned to Cameron and extended a hand. "I'm Bradley."

"Cameron Alder."

"Bradley was like Spencer's older brother," Nathalie told us. "They used to be close, at least."

"Not so much for the last few years," Bradley said. "I haven't slept at all since I heard what happened to her. I feel responsible—Violet and I told her she couldn't come around and see the kids anymore if she was high. Spencer was so angry the last time we spoke."

"You can't blame yourself," Nathalie said.

I glanced around the room and saw Violet Auden speaking to Simon Balto. He was nodding sympathetically at what she was saying, giving her long sad looks. I felt a surge of anger as I remembered seeing him fight with Spencer outside the Orphans' Ball.

I wanted to keep asking questions, but there was microphone static at the front of the room, and I turned to see Melinda standing on a makeshift stage where some instruments had been assembled. It took her a moment to collect herself before speaking.

"Thank you," she said. "Thank you all for coming on such short notice. I wanted to gather here instead of a church because George and Spencer both hated funerals. We'll think of this instead as a gathering of friends. Instead of speeches, I've decided to have musicians perform some of Spencer's favorite songs. Please mingle and reminisce about the good times. There's food in the next room."

When she stepped down, a group of musicians made their way to the stage and started playing jazzy covers of contemporary songs. When I turned back to talk to Bradley, he had moved across the room to be with his wife. There was no sign of Simon.

I walked back to where Hailey was standing with his hands in his pockets. "Sorry for abandoning you," I said.

"Please. You should be with your friends."

"I didn't mean to leave you to the wolves," I said.

"There's only one wolf I'm concerned about," Hailey remarked. I followed his gaze across the room, to where Lucas, Bradley's assistant, stood. Lucas stared back at us, his face contorted with anger.

"That's Lucas Mankerfield," I muttered. "Bradley Auden's assistant. Do you know him?"

"No, but he seems to know me," Hailey said.

Lucas had parted the crowd and approached us.

"This is a funeral," he told Hailey. "You shouldn't be here."

"He's with me," I cut in. I was appalled at Lucas's entitlement, and it took every ounce of my self-control not to reveal what I knew about him.

Lucas rotated his head to look at me with such contempt I almost shuddered. "Excuse me, this conversation does not include you."

I felt a surge of indignation. "This isn't your house," I said. "You can't kick people out."

He moved his eyes over my outfit with a look of disgust. One of the things that irritated me about him most was that we were probably the same age, and I would be surprised if his resume were much more impressive than mine, but he still assumed an air of authority and condescension.

"Did you hear me?" Lucas asked Hailey. "Are you deaf?"

"Rainey," someone called, and I turned to see Melinda coming toward me.

"Melinda," I said, then reached out and gave her a hug. "Melinda, this is my friend Max Hailey. Hailey, Melinda is Spencer's stepmother."

"I just told him to leave, actually," Lucas butted in. "He's a journalist. He's here to dig up dirt on Spencer."

"Is that true?" Melinda asked Hailey.

Hailey held up his hands. "I left my notebook at home today. I mean no disrespect to you or your family."

Melinda gave him a sharp look, then nodded. She turned her attention to Lucas.

"You, I don't know," she said. "Who are you?"

"I'm Bradley Auden's assistant."

"Did Bradley instruct you to act as security guard?"

Lucas looked flustered. He smoothed his tie and gave an uncomfortable laugh. "I'm looking out for your best interests," he said.

"And yet we've never met," Melinda said. "How kind of you to take care of me."

Melinda stared him down until he took the hint and went scuttling back off toward Bradley and Violet.

"I don't know most of the people in this room," Melinda said. "I want to go up to all of them and shake them. *Who are you? How did you know her? Did you sell her drugs?* I'm trying to give everyone the benefit of the doubt, but it's hard."

I turned and saw that Hailey had vanished.

"I don't know what I'm going to do, Rainey," Melinda said. "I'm so angry all the time. I feel like I could have done more to help her."

"You couldn't," I said. "It's not your fault. You can't save an addict who doesn't want help."

"Maybe." She looked close to tears.

Hailey reappeared, holding a cup of tea and a plate of food.

"Here," he said to Melinda. "Take five minutes and eat something."

She looked like she might weep at the unexpected kindness. She allowed Hailey to guide her over to a table, then sat down and took a bite of sandwich. I gave him a grateful look.

"I'll be right back," I said to him, motioning across the room. He nodded.

I knew that what I was about to do was morally objectionable on about a dozen different levels, but I felt like I could justify it, if anyone were to catch me. I wanted to find out what happened to Spencer just as much as her family did, and it didn't seem like the police were looking into it.

Spencer's room had been transformed since the last time I saw it. When we were at school, the room reflected Spencer's grungy European aesthetic: new wave film posters and advertisements for punk bands, jewelry hanging from hooks on her wall. Sometime in the last several years the wallpaper had been replaced and all the furniture swapped out for expensive-looking antiques. The room had obviously been cleaned since Spencer's overdose—the bed was freshly made, and I could see lines in the carpet where a vacuum had been—but an open suitcase and some boxes of her possessions sat in the corner of the room.

I slipped on a pair of gloves from my purse and started going through Spencer's things. Most of the contents were innocuous: expensive-looking clothing, some jewelry, a box of photos. There were some books, too, mostly European classics from the twentieth century. A box of art supplies, colored pencils, gesso.

The sounds of the funeral were muffled. I could hear the jazz band and the sound of laughter, but there was nothing in particular that jumped out from the blurry wash of noise. Information-wise, there was nothing of value in Spencer's things, and I wasn't so insensitive to ask Melinda if I could look through Spencer's phone. Even if she gave it to me, I doubted I would be able to get into it.

I was wondering whether I should go back downstairs when I caught sight of the fireplace, and a memory of sitting with Spencer and Alice on the floor of that same room came back to me. Spencer had pointed out the fireplace as one of the most ridiculous features of the house. "Such a status symbol," she had said. "Nobody burns fires in California."

The space had become instead a repository for Spencer to hide drugs or things she had stolen from the houses we broke into. This was facilitated by a brass insert that slipped into the space where the wood was intended to go, blocking the flue. I wondered briefly if anything was still there from that time, so many years ago, or if Spencer had cleared it all out.

I knelt before the fireplace, rolled up my sleeves, and then grabbed the edges of the brass insert. The fireplace was lined with green tile, and I didn't want to damage anything, so I tried to be careful. The insert was firmly wedged into the fireplace, and it took me a few goes before I managed to wrench it loose.

I didn't see it at first. I reached up inside the fireplace and felt around, half expecting to encounter plastic bags or even pieces of jewelry. There was nothing, though. After a moment, I turned to put the insert back into place.

It was there, wrapped in thick package paper and taped to the inside of the insert. A rectangular package. I felt pinpricks of sweat all over my body. My pulse sped up and I sank to my knees, feeling lightheaded. A flat book, or maybe a painting. I felt dizzy, contemplating the possibilities. Was it too much to hope that I was looking at *M.E. Stands Before the Mind of God*? The last time I saw the painting, it had been tucked under Spencer's arm as we fled Laszlo Zo's estate.

I felt exposed then, sitting on the floor of Spencer's room. I hadn't locked the door, and even though I didn't anticipate Nathalie or Melinda coming upstairs and questioning me, there was a reason why Spencer had hidden this, and there was a reason why she had moved back home only a few days before.

"Spencer said she's scared of someone," Melinda had said.

I was scared, too. I picked up the package and slipped the insert back into the fireplace, then dug through Spencer's things until I found a black T-shirt. I wrapped it around the package, then tucked it under my arm and slipped out of Spencer's bedroom, back into the upstairs hallway. The downstairs din resolved itself into a few clear voices, but I satisfied myself that nobody had become suspicious of my absence or decided to seek me out.

A text came through on my phone. It was from Hailey.

Where'd you go?

Meet me outside, I wrote back.

My body was a mess of nerves as I made my way downstairs, keeping an eye on the crowd. Nobody was looking at me. I still remembered the layout of Spencer's house, and I knew that if I made it to the kitchen undetected, I could slip out through a back entrance, into the old herb garden, then down the side of the house, and make it to the car. I didn't know who might be watching, and I felt like I couldn't breathe as I moved through the crowd, then reached the kitchen. The yard was a glint of light and color just beyond. I held my breath, clutching the package to my chest, slipped across the room and darted out the back, and then I was free.

Hailey was already by the front fence when I got there. He gave me a quizzical glance, and he looked amused when he saw the package under my arm.

"Did you just rob a funeral?"

I walked down the sidewalk toward my car, then nodded for Hailey to follow me.

"Get inside and I'll tell you." I climbed into my car and waited until Hailey was in, too, before I locked the doors.

"Did I miss something?" Hailey asked, perplexed.

I unwrapped the paper-wrapped package from the T-shirt and showed it to Hailey.

"What's that?"

"I don't know," I said. "It was hidden inside Spencer's fireplace."

He looked so surprised I almost laughed. I was still a mess of nerves, though, and I felt like someone might come out of the house to interrogate us at any moment.

"Are you going to open it?" Hailey asked.

"Not here. We'll go to my place. I need scissors, there's too much tape. Also, I don't want anyone to see what I'm doing."

He was looking at me with both amusement and what looked like new-found admiration. "Do you want me to come with you?"

"I said I would share information with you as long as it didn't compromise my clients," I said. "I don't see why not."

"My car's just down the street," he said. "Send me your address and I'll follow you there."

———

I drove quickly, slipping through lanes of traffic and going five miles above the speed limit all the way back to my house. Sadie's car was gone and the property was quiet, so I decided to open the package in the main house.

I was so excited at the thought of what might be inside it that I almost didn't notice the envelope stuck to the front door. I had just registered that my name had been misspelled—Rainy—when my phone rang. I set the package down on the ground and glanced at the screen. It was Lola.

"Hey, I just got back from Spencer's memorial," I said. "I have to tell you what I found—"

"Rainey, we got robbed," Lola cut in. She sounded anxious, and Lola rarely got anxious.

"*What?* What happened—you mean the offices? Are you okay?"

"I'm okay," she said, but her voice was shaky. "I'm okay."

"And Blake—is Blake there?"

"We went out to meet a client," she said. "The former accountant from the film studio. We were only gone for an hour, maybe ninety minutes. It's a mess, they went through all our files and took our computers. The cops are here now, looking for fingerprints, but I don't think they'll find anything."

"Why do you say that?" I stared at the envelope. Suddenly the misspelling of my name seemed ominous. I was acutely aware then that the house was quiet, that Sadie was gone. "Lo, who do you think broke into the offices?"

"Pick a card, any card." Lola's voice was grim. "We deal in deadbeats. They took our computers, but I doubt they'll get through Blake's security setup."

"Damn," I whispered. "I'll come meet you."

"I think you'd better," Lola said. "Get here as soon as you can."

"I have something to tell you, but I'll wait until I get there," I said.

"Fine."

I let her go before I remembered that Hailey was on his way over to my house. I had the sense that I could trust him, and he had had some good insights on our case, but inviting him to witness the destruction of our office was a different matter. Before I could decide one way or another, though, I heard footsteps on the path and then Hailey appeared in front of me.

"Are you okay?" he asked, seeing the look on my face.

"Someone just broke into our office," I said. My voice sounded strange to my ears. I couldn't believe what I was saying.

His forehead creased and his eyes went wide with alarm. "Just now?"

"In the last hour or two, yeah," I said. My hands were shaking.

"Are you going over now?"

"Yeah, I am," I said. "I wanted to wait until you were here, so I didn't leave you hanging."

"I'm happy to come," he said. "Strength in numbers and all that. Unless you don't want me to."

I felt resolved then, looking at Hailey. He seemed unflappable, resolute, and determined, and seeing that made me feel the same way.

"What's that?" he asked, nodding at the envelope taped to the door. "Don't you spell your name with an *e*?"

"Yes." I took the envelope off the door and flipped it over, then opened it with care. I had to read it twice before the meaning sank in.

This is your only warning. Stop looking or you will get hurt.

TWENTY

———

I felt sick when Hailey and I walked into the office of Left City and I saw the damage: furniture was smashed and overturned and the computers were missing. It was violation writ large.

Lola and Blake stood in a corner of the room, surveying the destruction. They both looked shell-shocked, uncertain of their surroundings.

"The cops just left," Blake said. She was clutching the arms of her wheel-chair as though she were trying to hold still. She folded her arms across her chest, and I saw that she was shaking.

"I'm glad you're okay," Lola said when she saw me. "In one piece, at least."

"Are *you* okay?" I asked. I started to cross the room, then stopped and glanced around, making sure I wouldn't step on anything. "Both of you?"

"We're fine," Blake said, even though she didn't look fine. She kept taking off her glasses and rubbing her eyes, and her mouth was turned down at the corners. She glanced at Hailey. "Who's this?"

"Max Hailey," I said. "He's the journalist I mentioned to you."

Lola closed her eyes and pressed her fingers to her temples. "I don't mean to be rude, but this probably isn't the best time," she said.

"It's fine, I understand," Hailey said. "We can catch up later, Rainey."

"No, wait," I said. I turned to my team. "He's a journalist, but he won't write about this. Not unless we ask him to."

"And why would we do that?" Lola asked, furrowing her brow.

"We're getting close to something," I said. My nerves had stopped jangling, and I was starting to feel angry. "I don't know what's at the heart of this mess, but all of these things are connected. The keys. Alice's disappearance, then her reappearance. Chloe, of course. Spencer's death. And this."

I put the package on the table. It looked small, innocuous, almost like something that had slipped through in the mail.

"What is that?" Lola grimaced and looked at it from the corner of her eye. It looked like she almost didn't want to know.

"I don't know yet. It was in Spencer's room. My point is that *someone* is killing people to protect themselves. Killing people or making them disappear. Something is at the heart of this, and we could be next, if we keep looking."

I brandished the note I had found taped to my door. Lola made no move to take it, so I crossed the room and handed it to her. She read it, then glanced up, her face pinched.

"I want someone here to observe this," I said, then pointed at Hailey. "In case someone comes for us. Someone needs to write about it and make sure that it stops."

Lola and Blake didn't say anything for a long time. Blake turned to look at Hailey, then back at me.

"You've discussed this, the two of you?" she asked.

"No," I admitted. I looked at Hailey. "Is that okay with you? I mean, you're writing about it anyway . . ."

He smiled and gave me a small nod. "Of course. I don't like to let people bully me into staying quiet."

Finally, Lola nodded.

"Okay," she said. "Okay, I hear you. But we need to know that we can trust him. You can't write about this—about any of this—unless we say it's okay."

"Or unless someone kills us," Blake chimed in.

"Understood." Hailey raised both hands in a gesture of supplication.

Lola closed her eyes and for a moment looked completely exhausted. Then she leaned against the wall and slowly started laughing.

"Right," I said, going over to my desk. "At least they left scissors. Am I allowed to touch things? The forensics team is done?"

"It's all done," Blake said, wheeling her chair toward me. "They came and took some fingerprints, but we're not holding out hope."

"There were two of them, we checked the security footage," Lola added. "They looked like men, based on their body types, but they were wearing black masks."

My mind immediately flashed to Lucas, and then did the mental math: Pasadena to Culver City without traffic was half an hour, bare minimum. I hadn't seen where he went after he tried to kick me and Hailey out of the funeral, but if he had left right then, he might have had just enough of a head start to make it to my office and fit the time frame. I still didn't know who the second man was, though.

"What do you think it is?" Blake asked, nodding at the package. "Why did you take it?"

"I took it because it was hidden inside her fireplace," I said. "And because a few days before she died, Spencer told her stepmother that she thought someone was after her."

I picked up the scissors and slowly cut through the tape on the package. Hailey picked up a chair from where it had been kicked over, then sat down, watching me. It took a few minutes to cut through all the tape. The package was wrapped in cardboard, and I lifted pieces away to reveal something wrapped in fabric. It looked like a pillowcase.

"Gloves, Rainey," Lola said, coming over to offer me a pair. I slipped them on, then very gently reached into the pillowcase.

I could feel something smooth, like a Ziploc bag. I removed it from the pillowcase and set it on the desk in front of me, and everyone moved in around me to see what it was.

It was an enormous bag of purple pills.

"Drugs," Lola said softly.

"You don't know that," Blake pointed out. "Keep an open mind."

Lola reached out a hand to touch the bag, then realized what she was doing and withdrew.

"I think we should go to the police," I said. "We have two hotel keys now. That's more than a coincidence. It's enough for them to go into the hotel. Melinda said that someone was threatening Spencer. And now we have this."

"Hold on," Lola said. "Where did you get these?"

"Spencer's room. I already told you that."

"Did you have permission to go in there?" She raised an eyebrow.

"Why do you always assume the worst?" I was annoyed. "I'm bringing it to the police. They're not going to look sideways at me—"

"What about the family?" Lo pointed out. "Grief does crazy things to people. If the police come and tell them that you found the drugs in her room, Spencer's family might turn on you. They could claim you planted the drugs."

"Oh, for god's sake—"

"She's right, Rai," Blake said. "Sorry. I think we should wait. Let's go back to the keys, though—where does the Hotel Stanislas fit in?"

I glanced at Hailey, who had remained quiet this whole time. I had been thinking about his theory of artists using drugs, and the pieces were just starting to fall together.

"You told me that you think someone is giving drugs away to artists," I told Hailey. "Right?"

Lola shot a quick look between me and Hailey. "Hold on, I'm still catching up. What now?"

Hailey cleared his throat. "I have a list of missing artists," he said. "I think someone is giving them drugs—well, it's a new kind of drug."

Hearing him say it out loud jogged my memory. I clapped my hand on my pocket, then reached inside and pulled out my phone.

"That reminds me," I said, opening up my messages. "Blake, remember that email you sent me yesterday, the one about Spencer Collins?"

Blake frowned, then slowly nodded. "Okay, yes?"

"I got in touch with them," I said, then held up my phone so they could see the screen. "They mentioned Eiko Mars—one of the other girls who's missing. They said she was on drugs—it was something new. Pills."

"Who is it?" Lola asked, pointing at my phone.

"Anonymous. I know, I know," I said, holding my hands up. "Suspect. You have to admit, though, this is a little fortuitous."

Blake seemed to be gnawing on a thought.

"So, who broke into our office?" she finally asked. "And what were they looking for?"

"The keys to the Hotel Stanislas," I said. "Or maybe they just wanted to steal our computers and see what we had found so far."

"All of the above," Blake added. "So, what's our next move?"

I thought about the second man who had been in Spencer's apartment when I visited, a man I hadn't yet identified. There was a possibility it had been Simon Balto, even though I couldn't really picture him getting his hands dirty. There had also been the time that I saw him shouting at Spencer at the Orphans' Ball. He was starting to seem more and more realistic as a suspect.

"I think we need to go back to the Stanislas," I said. "Tonight, if possible. Let's start there and see what happens."

TWENTY-ONE

———— ✥ ————

Downtown Los Angeles takes on a new energy at night. It isn't the same shift that other landscapes undergo when day slips away and the sky darkens, where color tones flatten to a neutral palette, and everything goes quiet as business winds down. There's something about the Downtown streets that take on new meaning, flip sideways and grow more sinister in the nighttime. People you would never see during the day emerge from the shadows, and the streets belong to them. Downtown Los Angeles was a heightened version of the disparity that existed elsewhere in the city, wealth creeping in to displace the damp and the rot. The two could not exist without each other.

At the corner of Cheney Street and Downey Avenue, the Hotel Stanislas glowed like a dark, wicked castle. Lola and I each parked in the lot down the street, and then she came and joined me in my car, from which we could watch the comings and goings of the hotel.

"It's beautiful," Lola said, after a few moments.

"It really is."

"I looked at all those articles you sent me," she went on. "The *Architectural Digest* stories and all about the restoration. I can't believe they'd put so much effort into it and be stupid enough to run a criminal enterprise behind the walls."

I glanced over at Lola. "You've been doing this long enough that it shouldn't surprise you," I said. "Criminals always think they're smarter than everyone else. Don't you remember the guy who covered himself in lemon juice and robbed a bank?"

Lola snorted, and I started laughing, too. One of Lola's favorite stories from law school had been from her criminal psychology class, in which the professor had explained the origins of the Dunning Kruger Effect: the psychologists who came up with the term did so after reading about a man who covered himself with lemon juice to rob a bank, believing that the acidic fluid would render him invisible unless he exposed himself to heat.

"You can't make that shit up," Lola said.

"We haven't proven that they're hiding anything," I said, nodding toward the Stanislas. "Not yet."

"How do you want to do this?" Lola asked.

"I think one of us should wait out here," I said. "That way, if something goes wrong, the other one can go for help. Besides, the two of us will be more conspicuous if we go in together."

"Who has to wait out here?" Lola asked. I could tell by the look on her face that she already knew what I was going to say.

"Lo, come on," I said. "I'm the one who found this place, and Alice was my friend. Spencer was, too, a long time ago. It's not fair for me to ask you to go in there and start poking around."

"I can counter that," she said. "You've already gone in and started asking questions. They know what you look like. They'll be on the lookout for you."

"Rock paper scissors?" I offered, holding out a fist.

The flat look on her face told me she wasn't amused.

"What's your plan, anyway?" Lola asked. "You've tried asking around. You've walked through the hotel, and there was nothing obviously out of place."

I was quiet, my attention focused on the theater next door. "I think there's something in there," I said.

Lola followed my gaze. "The theater?"

"Yeah," I said. "I think they're hiding something. It's the perfect disguise when you think about it. A decrepit old theater, run down and stagnant because of some city regulations. I think there's something in there. It used to be connected to the hotel, right? What if the hotel rooms that we're looking for were on that side of the hotel?"

Lola had a strange smile on her face. "I just got chills," she said.

"Me too."

We looked at each other for a long moment.

"If I could get inside there and somehow get access to those rooms . . ." I said.

"Hold on," she said. "We haven't agreed that you're the one who gets to go."

"Come on," I scoffed. "It was my idea. You stay out here and keep an eye out."

She chewed on her lip. "Fine," she said. "Fine. Do you have the keys with you?"

I reached into my pocket and produced the two old keys that I had found in Alice's pool and with Spencer's dry cleaning.

"Do you think it's a good idea to take them in? What if someone catches you in there?"

"It's a fair point," I said. "I think it's worth the risk, though. I need to see this through. If I can get access to those rooms, I need to see what's inside."

"Why don't you take one and leave the other?" she suggested.

I thought for a moment. "If I get caught, though, it won't matter if I leave a single key behind. They'll close up shop and we'll never get a chance to see what's in the second room, anyway."

"Good point," she said. "Take both. How are you going to get in?"

I pointed to the roof over the hotel bar. "I think that's how people have gotten in in the past," I said. "It's the only possible point of entry without stairs."

Lola's eyebrows shoot up. "You're going to jump across the alley?"

"It's a small space. I'll see if I can find something to lay across, like a ladder or plank. People have obviously done it in the past, if there are photos of the inside of the abandoned theater."

Lola sighed. "How long will you be?"

"Two hours, tops."

"Let's say an hour—if you're not out in an hour, I'm calling the police."

"Don't call the police," I said. "I'll get arrested for breaking and entering."

"What's the plan, then?"

"Come in and find me," I said.

The hotel was busy, full of young couples and well-dressed businessmen bustling through the lobby and heading to the bar. I could see all the activity just from standing on the street; all the brightly lit windows appeared like miniature living tableaux. I felt an unexpected pang of longing to be a part of the festivities, all the excitement and bustle of a night out on the town.

I didn't know what kind of security was in place to protect the Red Door theater, but I had to take my chances. If anyone caught me on the roof above the bar, I would just play dumb and say I was trying to get a good photo of Downtown Los Angeles. I took a deep breath, then followed a group of well-dressed women into the hotel lobby.

I didn't want to take the elevator because I wasn't exactly sure which floor had roof access to the space above the bar. It looked like the third floor, based on the window count from the lobby, so I decided to start there. I glanced around and saw the sign for the emergency access stairs near the elevator. When I thought that nobody was looking at me, I walked over to them and slipped inside.

The stairwell was concrete, a no-frills passage to provide emergency access. I took the stairs quickly, hoping that I wouldn't run into anyone, and to my good fortune, I reached the third floor unobstructed. I opened the door leading out into the hallway, then gently closed it behind me.

The third-floor hallway yawned before me, hushed and quiet. I was standing in a small area with the elevators, but even here, great detail had gone into the design: the dark wooden floors were protected with a rich-blue rug, and potted palms stood against a wall. The flocked wallpaper looked like it was either the original design or a very good vintage imitation. I walked away from the elevators and turned down a hall lined with doors. Lamps hung from the ceiling, and I felt like I had stepped back in time, back to when the Golden Age starlets had come out here to visit studios and audition for parts.

At the end of the hallway was a window. A small sign at the bottom read No Access—Staff Only. I peered through the window and saw that my guess had been spot on: access to the roof was through the window, and beyond, I could see the dark shape of the theater. I glanced around me to make sure that nobody had appeared in the hall, then pressed my hands against the glass and pushed upward.

To my surprise, the window was unlocked, and after a little groan of wood against wood, it slid open. I stuck my head outside and looked down at the roof, then saw why access had been easy: it was a ten-foot drop onto the roof below, which was probably enough to deter guests from venturing outside.

After a moment's hesitation, I climbed through the window, then lowered myself down. I had a moment of panic and indecision while I dangled there, gripping the windowsill. The roof was only four or five feet below me now, but dropping was still scary. I finally let go and dropped to the roof, falling onto my knees. Once I stood up and dusted myself off, I felt a thrill of exhilaration. *I had done it.*

I walked toward the edge of the roof and glanced over at the dark windows of the theater beyond. The windows had recessed ledges, some of them two feet deep, which meant that a ladder would have somewhere to land if I could find one. I was about to start looking around when I heard something. From behind me came the sound of a depressed latch, hinges creaking. I turned to see an open door at the edge of the roof, and emerging from it, a female security guard holding a flashlight.

Fuck, fuck, fuck.

She shone the light at me, then spoke into a walkie-talkie on her shoulder. "I've got eyes on her."

The woman started to advance on me. "What are you doing up here?"

My excuse about taking a photo of the city sounded too stupid to even mention.

"I just wanted to see what was up here," I said.

She peered at me and got close enough for me to read her name tag. *Paula.* "How did you get out here?"

I hesitated.

"You set off the alarm," she said. "Do you know how dangerous it is up here? There are weak spots in the roof. You could fall through . . ."

I raised my hands in defeat. "I'm sorry. I'll leave."

"Hold on a second." Paula shone the light in my face. "What's your name?"

I sidestepped her and started walking toward the door. I had only taken a few steps before she grabbed my arm. I immediately threw her hand off and then whirled to face her.

"Don't touch me," I said.

She stepped backward and unsnapped her gun from her hip holster.

"You need to come with me," she said.

"You have a gun?" I was incredulous. "What are they trying to hide?"

"Come with me," Paula repeated. "I don't want to shoot you."

"Why would you?"

"If you attack me or threaten me in any other way," she said. "You've already laid your hands on me."

"I shook your hand off," I exclaimed. "You think I don't know what you're trying to do? Make up some bullshit narrative?"

She gave me a look of pity. "I don't want to shoot you," she repeated, "but you're coming with me."

"Where?"

"My manager wants to see you."

I considered my options, but I didn't seem to have very many. I thought about grabbing my phone and trying to call Lola, but it wasn't worth the risk.

"Fine," I said. "I'm coming."

Paula led me back through the door. It looked like a service area, full of tools and mops.

"Straight ahead," she said. There was a door, and when I opened it, I saw another set of service stairs. A fluorescent bulb illuminated the path downward, and I started to have a bad feeling.

"Where are we going?"

She didn't respond.

"I haven't done anything illegal," I said.

"You're trespassing."

"So call the police. Have me arrested."

"Keep walking," she said, pushing me with a meaty hand.

"Paula," I said. "My friend is waiting for me outside. I'm going to go out there right now and find her. If I go missing, she's going to come looking for me."

There was no response, but Paula pushed me again. My heart pounding, I made my way downstairs. We had gone down three flights of stairs before they ended in another door.

"Go ahead," Paula said.

I opened the door and stepped through. To my relief, a boring hallway stretched away from the door, lined with doors that looked like offices. I could hear soft conversation and laughter, the sound of dishes.

"First door on the left," Paula said. A plaque on the door read JUAN RAMIREZ, GENERAL MANAGER. I opened the door and stepped into a cluttered office dominated by a big desk.

"Have a seat," Paula said. She moved to stand in front of the door, blocking my exit.

"I'll stand," I said, hoping that I sounded more confident than I felt.

She shrugged, and something like a smile flickered over her face. I slipped my phone out of my pocket, thinking that I would quickly call Lola or send her a text message—if the security guard tried to stop me, I would dive beneath the desk and fire off the text before she could stop me. To my surprise, she made no move to do so. She only smirked.

"Call whoever you like," she offered.

"All right," I said, trying to hide my surprise. I found Lola in my phone and called her, then lifted the phone to my ear. My heart was thudding in my chest, and I felt the edge of a panic attack coming on. *Don't overreact,* I reminded myself. *Lola isn't far away. She'll come soon.* After about ten seconds, I realized that there wasn't a dial tone. I glanced at my phone.

"We don't get service back here," the security guard told me. She looked like she was trying to suppress laughter, and her eyes danced with merriment.

I tried to call Lola again. *No available service network,* my phone told me.

"I'm leaving," I told the woman.

"In a minute," she replied.

The door opened behind her, and a man stepped into the office. It was Juan, the creepy manager. He smiled and pressed his hands together when he saw me.

"Rainey Hall," he said, with an incline of his head. "How can I be of service?"

"I was just leaving," I told him. Once again, I hoped I sounded more confident than I felt—my heart dropped when I heard him say my name; I had never given it to him. He must have looked into me somehow, perhaps because he knew that I had one of the mysterious hotel keys.

"Oh no, please. Have a seat! Let's talk this through." Juan gestured to the seat in front of me. His obsequious manner was grating, and I briefly wondered what he was like when he took his mask off, when he went home and had no audience. Maybe he had been doing this for so long that his previous personality had been overwritten entirely. When he saw that I wasn't going to sit down, he shrugged, then undid a button on his coat and took a seat behind his desk.

I glanced at Paula.

"Did you check her pockets?" Juan asked her.

Paula moved toward me and reached for my pockets. I pushed her away, and she slapped me.

"What the *fuck*?"

She twisted my arm behind my back and reached into each of my pockets. When she discovered the pair of hotel keys, she smiled and handed them to Juan. I felt the loss like a punch in the gut. Juan sighed and looked very disappointed.

"You don't know when to give up, do you?" he said. "These are nothing. They mean nothing. Is that why you broke in here?"

I didn't answer.

"Where did you get them?" He tried again. "Huh?"

I held his gaze but remained quiet.

"Did you hear me, Rainey? Do you understand the English language? Where did you get these keys?"

Adrenaline surged through my body. If Paula didn't have a gun, I would have tackled her.

"I take no pleasure in this, Rainey," he said. The features of his face didn't quite match: his teeth were too small, his eyes too big, and his smile looked cartoonish.

"Pleasure in what?" I asked. I tried to sound more confident than I felt. "You can't detain me for no reason. This is unlawful restraint. My lawyer is waiting outside right now."

Paula took out a pair of handcuffs. My eyes went wide.

"Are you serious? This is false imprisonment," I repeated. "Do you know what kind of jail term you'd get for that?"

Paula hesitated—only for a moment, but that was enough.

"My lawyer is outside," I repeated. I was eyeing the door, wondering if I should try to make a break for it. I looked at Paula's physique and tried to figure out her weak spots—stomach, knees, neck—in case I needed to attack her.

There was a knock at the door, and that moment broke the tension. I gasped so loudly that Juan and Paula both stared at me. When nobody went to answer the door, there was another knock.

"Yes, what?" Juan snapped. His anger contorted his face into something ugly.

The door opened a crack, and a man in a hotel uniform poked his head inside.

"There's a woman in the lobby," she said. "She claims her client is somewhere in the hotel, but she isn't answering her phone."

"Client?" Juan sneered.

The man gave a helpless shrug. "She said she's a lawyer and . . . and . . . Look, don't blame me, but she said something about calling the police if she can't find her client."

Juan shot me a look of such withering hatred that I actually recoiled.

"We'll just be a minute," he told the young man. The man started to close the door, but I leaped forward, grabbing his arm.

"I'm her client," I blurted, and my voice betrayed how anxious I was. The man stared at me, stunned, then glanced at Juan for direction.

"It's fine, we were just finishing up here," Juan said, plastering on a smile. "You can go, Rainey."

I followed the young man down the hallway, and once we emerged into the lobby, I scanned the room for Lola. She looked worried, and when she saw me, she came running.

"Let's go," I urged. "Let's go, now, let's get out of here."

I managed to hold my composure until we were back outside, and then I crumpled. The adrenaline had finally worn off, and my legs were weak. I leaned against Lola and heaved a few breaths.

"What happened," she asked, alarmed. "Rainey, what happened?"

"They're hiding something," I said. "We're really close. There's something in that other building."

I quickly summarized what had happened when Paula found me on the rooftop. Lola's eyes went wide, and she glanced back at the building.

"Maybe we should call the police," she said.

"No," I warned. "They'll just tell the cops that I was trespassing—which is true, when you think about it. I don't want them to clamp down their security. The worst thing that could happen is that they get a restraining order against me. Then I'll never find out what they're hiding."

"I must have called you twenty times," Lola said. She sounded annoyed. "Didn't you see?"

"There wasn't any service in the dungeon," I said. "This place is fucked."

I took out my phone for the first time since being in Juan's office. There were a dozen missed calls from Lola, as well as a few calls from Hailey. Hailey had texted me, as well:

Call me.

Then, *It's Rhodes. Did you see?*

I showed the phone to Lola.

"What do you think it means?" she asked.

"I'll find out." I called Hailey and waited while the phone rang. It didn't take long for him to answer.

"Hey," he said. He sounded breathless. "Did you see the news?"

"No, I've been tied up," I said. My heart was pounding. "What happened?"

"He's dead," Hailey said. "His body was found in an abandoned warehouse in Eagle Rock. The medical examiner said it looked like he overdosed on drugs."

TWENTY-TWO

I slept badly that night. I couldn't stop getting up to check all the locks on the doors and windows, and even when I had reassured myself that everything was secure, I jolted awake every twenty minutes. It was a windy night, and small branches kept falling onto my roof.

I finally fell into a deep sleep around four in the morning, then dreamed about Alice and Spencer, dark hallways and looming mansions, sprawling lawns that ended at the lips of ravines. I didn't wake up until eleven, when my phone rang. It was Isabel, Marcus's assistant. Isabel and I were friendly, but there wasn't much reason for us to talk outside of our relationship with Marcus. I was immediately concerned. I picked up the phone and took it outside, because the reception in my cottage was bad.

"Hi, Isabel," I said. A blue jay tangled with a seedpod on the ground. "Is everything okay?"

"Oh, of course," she said, then laughed. "Didn't mean to alarm you."

I closed my eyes and sat down on one of the chairs by the pool. "It's been that kind of day."

"I can tell. Well, this can wait," she offered.

"No, what is it?"

"I'm going to be in your neighborhood. I have the premiere package for you and some friends."

307

It took me a moment to remember the conversation with Marcus from a few days before. "Right, *Hogarth*. Of course."

"Are you still going to be able to make the premiere?"

"Yes, I should be," I said. "But I don't want to make you drive over for nothing."

"Oh, it's no problem," she said. "I'm going to meet my sister for a walk in Griffith Park."

"Great," I said. "I'll text you the address."

Isabel was at my house fifteen minutes later. I came down to the front gate to meet her, and she handed me a fancy-looking gift box wrapped in gold ribbon.

"What's this?" I asked, frowning.

"One of the top-tier boxes the executives give out to film critics and people who vote for the awards," she said, then gave me a guilty smile. "I swiped one for you."

"What's inside?"

"Chocolate and other bullshit," she said. "Some spa passes. Expensive trinkets nobody needs."

"Thanks, Isabel!" I said, hugging her and taking the box. "Come in. I'll make you a coffee."

She nodded in approval when I let her inside the house. "Very Norma Desmond," she said. "I love it."

"*Sunset Boulevard* is my favorite. Remind me how you take your coffee . . . ?"

When Isabel didn't respond, I glanced up.

"Isabel?"

She was looking at the box of plants that Noa had given me. One hand rested on the table, and she reached out to touch one of the white blossoms.

"Be careful," I said. "Those are poisonous."

She startled, then looked up at me. There was a strange look on her face. "I know," she said. "Why do you have these?"

"It's for work," I said, confused. "What's wrong?"

"You shouldn't keep these inside," she warned. Her voice had a tense note that I had never heard before. Isabel had always been so easygoing. "Really, Rainey, they're very dangerous."

"They're just morning glories, aren't they?" I gave her a perplexed look. "They grow all over the country. People grow them for the flowers. They're so common."

"Sure, but people are idiots," she said. "These are some of the most dangerous plants you can grow."

"How do you know so much about them?" I asked.

"Rainey," she said, giving me an exasperated smile. "I studied biochemistry, remember? I used to work in pharmaceuticals."

I closed my eyes. "Of course, it must have slipped my mind. Sorry."

She was looking at the plants with a kind of reverent fear. The morning glories were innocuous enough, but the other plants—the ones with spines and knotty fruit—looked like something out of a nightmare.

"Why do you have these?" she asked again.

"It's a case I'm working on," I said. "What can you tell me about them?"

She shuddered.

"They do horrible things to a person," she said. "Hallucinations. You see things that aren't there. You can completely lose your mind."

"Lose your mind how?"

"These plants belong to a family called datura," she said, then pointed at each one individually. "Jimsonweed and nightshade are relatives. They're used in religious ceremonies, but people who don't know what they're doing take them recreationally. I knew one guy who never came back, not all the way—he just completely lost his mind. That was back in high school."

"Can you use them to poison people?" I asked.

"Sure, of course, at the right dosage," Isabel said, shrugging. "But it's not the first plant I'd use if I was going to poison someone. I'd use foxgloves or oleander. The poison in those is more effective, and they're in gardens all over the city."

"Back to datura for a second," I said. "Can you tell me why someone would have these plants in large quantities?"

"Well, it's a drug," she said, heaving a sigh. "Not a drug I'd want to take, but it gives you a cheap, awful high."

"Why would someone do datura instead of, say, pot?"

"Oh, they're completely different," she said, giving me a wide-eyed look. "I mean, I don't do drugs at all, but when I still worked in pharmaceuticals, I knew people who experimented. Some of them were scientists." Isabel twisted her lips and thought for a moment, then shrugged. "Then again, if someone found a way to reduce the bad side effects of datura . . . well, they might corner the market. Wild hallucinations without all the terror? It'd be like acid, but you could grow it in your backyard."

"Is it addictive?"

"Almost never," she said. "Most of the time, when people take it, they never want to do it again. It's too awful. A living nightmare."

The neighborhood around Boneseed was quiet when I pulled up and parked out front. I marched straight up to the front door and rang the doorbell, then banged on the door for good measure. I had brought one of the datura plants with me, and I set it down on the porch.

"Hey!" I called, peering into the window. "Travis! We need to talk!"

The house was silent; I couldn't hear any noise inside. I glanced up at the camera above the door and waved, then rang the doorbell again.

"I know what you're hiding," I said, looking up at the camera. I pointed at the datura plant on the porch.

The intercom crackled. "Go. Away."

"You're making drugs," I said. "Datura. Jimsonweed. Nightshade. Open the door!"

There was a flurry of sounds from behind the door, and then the front door flew open. Travis poked his head out and glowered at me.

"Are you *crazy?*" he hissed. "My neighbors could hear you. You need to get out of here!"

"Let me in," I said.

"Leave," he said again, looking over my shoulder. I suddenly realized that he was scared. "Please leave. You're going to get us both killed."

I wavered, but only for a second. "I'm not going anywhere. If you don't want your neighbors to know what you're doing—"

"Jesus, Jesus, fine," he said, opening the door. He practically dragged me inside. "You've got a death wish."

Once Travis had locked the door and peered out through the window, he turned to face me. "What do you want?"

I felt some of my confidence evaporate. The adrenaline was still surging through my body, but now that I was alone with Travis, I realized that I was in a dangerous position.

"Do you read the news?" I asked.

He squinted at me in disbelief. "Do I . . . do I read the *news?*"

"Rhodes is dead," I said.

"Yeah," he said, his voice guarded. "I heard something about that."

"That's it?" I looked at him with mild disgust. "You don't feel responsible?"

He looked at me like I was crazy. "Why would I feel responsible?"

I took out the bag of purple pills that I had found in Spencer's fireplace and thrust them at Travis. His eyes went wide, and I knew I had him.

"Okay," he said finally. "Okay. It wasn't me. I had nothing to do with this."

"That's convenient."

"Really," he said, in a low voice. "I sell plants. Decorations. A taste of the jungle. I don't *kill* people."

"You sell *poisonous* plants," I said.

"You ever see a scary movie? Go on a rollercoaster? Maybe drink a little bit too much just to test your limits? It's the same thing," Travis said, waving a hand around the room to gesture at all the plants. "People nowadays lead sanitized lives. They wake up in a safe bedroom and watch TV while they brush their teeth. They sit in traffic and listen to music on their car stereos, then they spend all day in their air-conditioned offices. A lot of my customers spend ninety percent of their lives indoors. There's nothing dangerous anymore. We have everything figured out. I give them a little taste of adrenaline every morning so the animal part of their brain doesn't die out entirely. So we don't become pieces of Styrofoam."

The speech was so convincing I almost believed him.

"So who are you scared of?" I asked, looking at the front door.

Travis frowned in confusion.

"You're scared of someone," I said. "You keep looking around, like someone's about to burst in. Is it Ricky?"

He actually laughed. "Ricky? I'm not scared of Ricky."

"So? Who is it?"

Travis gave me a long look, then burst out laughing again. "I'm sorry, I can't right now. Are you serious, Nancy Drew? I don't owe you anything. You don't know anything about me. You're seriously about to bust up in my place and start asking questions?"

I forced myself to take a deep breath, then closed my eyes for a moment. "I'm looking for some missing artists," I said. "One of them is nineteen. This is important."

"I don't know anything." He turned away.

"What's your connection to Ricky?"

"I'm done with this," he said. "I'd like you to leave. I asked you nicely, and I'm about to stop being nice."

"You know what, I don't care!" I exclaimed. "I'm done being nice, too. I've got plants that you grew—poisonous plants, plants that kill people—and I have a bag of pills. I also have a video of Ricky shouting at you from a few days back. If you throw me out, I'm going straight to the cops and turning over all my evidence."

Travis looked scared again. "Did someone ask you to come here?"

"I'm on my own," I said. "I'm a private investigator. I'm looking for the artists, that's all."

"What artists?"

"Eiko Mars and Chloe Delmonico." I tried to soften my tone. "I just want to find them. I don't care if you're selling drugs."

"I'm *not*," he snapped. "I don't do that shit."

"I need your help," I said. "Ricky has protection. His dad's really powerful, and he's got a team of lawyers breathing down my neck."

Travis looked at me and shook his head. "Ricky's dad? He's not involved in this."

"I can't tell you who he is—"

"Laszlo Zo," he said. "I'm not entirely sure I believe it, but that's what Ricky keeps telling everyone."

I was nonplussed. "You know about that?"

"You know Ricky, right? You think he's the type of guy who can keep a secret?"

"Zo has some really powerful lawyers—"

Travis shook his head a few times, then muttered something under his breath. "You've got this all wrong," he said.

"What?"

"Zo isn't the one you need to worry about. Zo? Same dude who sells microwave ovens? Zo's harmless."

"Who are you scared of?" I pressed.

When Travis hesitated, I took out my phone and showed him the video of Ricky standing outside Boneseed, screaming threats.

"The cops are going to want to talk to you," I said. "You're worried about what your neighbors think? What about when the cops show up and ask questions?"

"I don't know anything about missing artists," he repeated. "Really. Ricky's a piece of shit, that's why we stopped working together."

"When?"

"Look, he had some extra cash and said he wanted to invest in my business," Travis said.

"Extra cash? Where did he get that?"

"Who knows?" Travis said, shaking his head. "Dude's a slimy hustler. He's always got money coming in from somewhere, you know. Maybe his dad. Anyway, I took a loss last year and needed an influx, *rapido*. We knew each other from around the traps. There's this café. We'd get coffee sometimes."

"Article 19?"

"Exactly. He seems like a really harmless dude. Kind of stupid in an endearing way. I never thought he'd drag me into this . . . this . . . *fuck*."

"Manufacturing drugs?"

His face crumpled then, and I watched the blood seep down into his neck. He leaned against the wall and put a hand up to his eyes, then shook his head.

"I just grow plants," he said. "I'm completely straight. I don't even drink alcohol. No pot, no cigarettes, nothing. I never thought . . . I want to cut myself off from this. From whatever's happening."

"If you tell me what you know, I might be able to help you," I said.

"It's datura," he said. "But it's a strain. He's been growing his own strain and mixing up the seeds or shit. He calls it Morphy."

"Morphy?"

"Morphy, Morphy, like Morpheus, the god of sleep, you know? You're really creative for a while and you have this surge of inspiration. But then you black out, you know, and it's like you're a sleepwalker."

I waited for him to go on.

"Datura's really dangerous. That's why people stay away from it," he said. "Ricky's good with plants, and he likes to mix shit up. Grow different hybrids. He figured out a way to make datura into this crazy trippy high. You get this wave of creativity. That's why artists started taking it. He didn't have the thing all the way cracked, though, because after the creative bit wore off, the artists were like the walking dead. Zombies, man."

"You seem to know a lot about it," I pointed out.

"I've got friends who witnessed it," he snapped. "I stay away from that shit."

"Your friends witnessed it?" I pressed. "How?"

Travis hesitated, and I held up the bag of pills again.

"And he's selling it?" I pressed. "Ricky's selling it?"

Travis stared into the distance for a little while. "I don't think so," he said. "He tried to bring me in on it, man. He had one buyer. Someone was paying him to make it. I don't know who they are."

"Morphy," I repeated. "How deadly is this stuff?"

"It's bad," Travis said. "I don't know how much he calibrated it, but datura is a dangerous fucking weed, man. People go crazy, and they never come back. That's why I told him I didn't want anything to do with it. I swear, you can ask him yourself. He wanted my help in growing the plants, and I wouldn't do it. That's what we were fighting about."

"When did this happen?" I asked. "How long has he been making it?"

Travis gave an expansive shrug, then frowned and scratched his chin. "Like . . . four months? He tried to grow pot for a while, but ever since they legalized it in California, it's hard to make a profit. He wanted something that no one else was offering. Ricky's dumb, but he's good with plants."

"I believe you," I said. "But why didn't you go to the police? If you bring them all this information, they might actually do something about it."

"I told you," he said. "Someone's protecting him. I don't know who. I wouldn't tell you if I did, though—I don't want to wind up dead."

TWENTY-THREE

—◦◦◦—

The morning of our meeting with Zo's lawyers arrived. Their offices were in one of the sleek buildings at the lower end of Sunset Boulevard, near the Comedy Store. These corporate offices were the kinds of buildings that were so bland you never even noticed them until you were inside the lobby.

A young receptionist in a suit buzzed me and Lola in and directed us to the third floor. Lola reached over to tuck a strand of hair behind my ear, then gave me a worried smile.

"Remember," she said. "It'll be over in a few hours. I've got a solid case."

"Okay," I said, trying to match her smile. "Thanks, Lo."

"We can get ice cream afterward."

"Thanks, mom."

The elevator seemed to take forever to reach the third floor. Lola walked down the hall two feet ahead of me. I felt numb as I took in everything around me—the thick carpet, the art on the walls, the muted white noise around us, and the quick snatches of conversation. Windows looked out onto Sunset Boulevard, and I observed the movement of cars and pedestrians on the sidewalk below, suddenly wishing that I hadn't lobbied so hard to be a part of this meeting.

We reached the glass conference room. Three people sat in the room; they stood up and smiled when we entered. There was a woman in her thirties and two men who looked like they might be around sixty. All of them looked moneyed, entitled, and somehow already bored with our presence.

"You must be Lola," the woman said.

"That's right," Lola said, her voice pleasant. "And this is my client, Rainey Hall."

"I'm Cheryl Reading. We've been emailing each other. Nice to meet you in person. This is Todd Feldman and Robert Gross."

She indicated a man with thinning blond hair—Todd—and Robert, a squat bald man with a deeply lined face. The men nodded as their names were mentioned. Todd picked his nails.

"Have a seat," Cheryl said. "Can we get you anything? Coffee, water?"

"We're fine," Lola said, and we took seats across the conference table.

"Well, I think we can wrap things up quickly," Cheryl said. "I think you'll be quite pleased. We've spoken to Mr. Zotkotski, and we're prepared to drop the defamation lawsuit if certain conditions are met."

I had forgotten Laszlo Zo's legal last name. There was something humanizing about it, something that made me remember that he wasn't untouchable.

"Conditions?" Lola echoed, then sighed. "All right, enlighten me."

Cheryl laid a sheet of paper in front of her and read from it. "All your client has to do is sign a nondisclosure agreement regarding any discussions or events tangential to their meeting," she said. "And as you approached Mr. Zotkotski on behalf of Noa Cohen, you would need to sever your professional relationship with her."

Lola bit back a smile. "Our client is in the process of getting a restraining order against Mr. Goff," she said. "*Your* client claims to have no connection to Mr. Goff, but he also wants us to drop Miss Cohen as a client. Something smells off to me."

Cheryl gave her a tight smile. "It's not for me to decode meaning in his requests," she said. "I'm just the lawyer. It's an excellent offer, and I would heartily encourage you to sign and get this whole thing behind you. I'm sure you've already told your client how expensive a defamation trial can be." She glanced at me.

"We're not worried about this going to trial," Lola said, folding her hands in front of her. She was preternaturally calm, and it was in these moments that I loved Lola the most. You couldn't bully her or intimidate her into doing anything; she made legal decisions based on facts, not emotion. "You can't convince me that you'd allow things to proceed that far. I know you wouldn't be here today if he even considered that a possibility. It's your job to illuminate *your* client on how bad that would make him look—how many things we could trot out in court."

Cheryl's look was hard to decipher. When she spoke, her voice was cold. "Maybe I wasn't clear," she said. "Defamation proceedings can drag out for months, if not years. All you have to do is cease business transactions with a single client. One client. That's it."

Lola was impassive. Cheryl gave a frustrated laugh and spoke up again.

"We've looked into your firm," she said. "You have no idea how much I admire you, actually. People have small problems that mess up their small lives, and you come in and you fix them. There's a kind of nobility in guarding the little man. We're not the little man, though—not by a long shot. If you had stayed at Darby and Ellis instead of dropping into the backwaters and working as a private investigator, you would know that."

Lola's face was still impassive, but I could see the tiniest hint of a smile at the corner of her mouth. She had something up her sleeve, something she hadn't shared with me. Also, I knew Lo better than anyone, and as much as she pretended to hate legal posturing, I knew she loved the fight.

Cheryl turned and spoke to me for the first time. "I can't make your lawyer see reason, but ultimately, this affects you," she said. "People don't realize that it's incredibly privileged to be able to take a case to court. I mean—think about it!—a court case messes up your entire life. If you've got a full-time job, forget about it. You never know when you might get called in, or scheduled to appear in court, or have it canceled and rescheduled, or if there might be an appeal, dragging things out months into the future. And it's not for a week, or a month—a case can take years. Think about the trauma of digging into this thing that hurt you, providing all the details, then getting put on the stand and having your character assassinated by the opposing counsel. On top of all of that—the trauma, the time, the stress, the instability of the schedule, canceling work—you've bankrupted yourself to pay legal fees. There's one of Lola, but we have an entire team of lawyers with nothing but time."

"It's not going to happen," Lola said.

The trio of lawyers fell silent, and Cheryl gave Todd an uneasy look. Finally, Robert spoke up. He had a red face and three chins, and I imagined that he wanted to finish this as soon as possible so he could rush off to lunch at the golf course.

"Maybe you don't get it," he sneered. "Drop the fucking client and sign the papers."

"I'll handle this, Robert," Cheryl snapped. She turned back to Lola, exasperated. "Can you tell me what the issue is?"

"Because this is a bullying tactic," Lola said, her voice level. "This is exactly why women like Miss Cohen don't proceed with restraining orders against their ex-husbands. We know who Mr. Zotkotski is—what his relationship is with Ricky Goff. He's the illegitimate father. If you want to take this to court, we can order a paternity test and have the entire world know. I'm surprised you'd allow him to suggest it as a condition of litigation. How much do you know about Mr. Goff?"

The lawyers exchanged a glance amongst themselves. Cheryl smiled.

"Okay," she said. "If that's the way you want to play things, I'll show you the other information that we have. Todd?"

Todd opened a folder in front of him. I could see some big black-and-white images. He passed the folder over to Lola, whose face remained neutral. She finally looked up. "How is this relevant to the case at hand?"

"We have grounds to sue for a legacy case of stalking and harassment," Cheryl said in a smooth voice. "We can go for felony burglary charges as well."

I took the folder from Lola. When I opened the flap and saw the photos inside, I felt lightheaded, and for a moment there was a very real possibility that I might faint. The photos were of me, Alice, and Spencer. The photo quality was grainy, and I knew immediately that these were stills from security footage, but still, there was a strange artfulness about the images. In one, Spencer strode across a lawn lit by recessed lights, her legs a dark isosceles blur. In another Alice knelt by the pool and traced her fingers through the water. And then there I was, caught in profile by a window, looking out into the night.

I thought it was over right then, but Lola didn't bat an eye. "Who's this?"

Cheryl scoffed. "It's your client," she said, pointing to my likeness. "Don't play stupid."

"You can't prove that," Lola said with a shrug. "These stills are grainy."

Cheryl gave us a grim smile. "We have dozens more photos," she said. "And we can pay to have them restored to higher quality."

"Let's see here," Lola said, picking up the photos. "Oh, good, they're time-stamped. Nine years ago. Wow, that's a stretch. The statute of limitations for felony burglary is three years—I might solve little problems for little men, but I know that much."

Cheryl's face went red.

"What else? Let's see . . . while I still dispute the veracity of your claim that this is actually Rainey"—she turned to me—"because you were a concert violinist, right? From a good family?"

I nodded eagerly.

"That's right. Not the type to break into houses. Let's say that you did go down that route, though—nine years ago, Rainey was seventeen. Even if you could prove that this is Rainey, Rainey was underage. That changes things."

"The burglary charge is an addendum to the larger case at hand," Cheryl pointed out, flustered. "It indicates a lengthier history of an obsession with my client."

"Let's look at this a different way," Lola said. "Can you prove that your client didn't *invite* these girls to his house? There have been rumors about Zo's predilection for underage girls. A jury might wonder why they knew the security code, but this is the bigger question: Why didn't Zo call the police after he found that they had broken into his house?"

Cheryl was starting to look irritated, and her mouth twitched. I felt a surge of love and gratitude toward Lola, but I didn't want to look triumphant, so I glanced down at my hands.

"Let's move on to our next point," Cheryl said, looking down at the sheet in front of her. "You're obviously versed in certain elements of the law, but the fact of the matter is that my client has more time and money than you do. He's one of the most powerful men in the entertainment world. I see that you're the only lawyer representing Left City. Zo has a team of associates behind him, and a drawn-out court case won't impact his life in the slightest. We'll do all the heavy lifting for him."

Lola gave her a resigned smile. "We both know that's just posturing," she said. "Zo was powerful in the seventies, when Dogtooth was still one of the biggest bands in the world, but the discerning consumer is invested in the misdeeds of their favorite artist. Any kind of court case would impact his clout, and since he hasn't performed in years, Zo's income stream isn't endless. Let's move past minor parries and get to the real issue at hand: Zo is hiding some dark shit, and you're obfuscating. You forget that we've got one of Los Angeles' best hackers. You think we haven't found all that dirt that you've been hiding?"

"I know a bluff when I see one," Cheryl said, but her voice was quiet.

"How much has your client told you about his son?" Lola asked. "Ricky Goff, the deadbeat he pretends doesn't exist. Did you know that Ricky has been selling drugs?"

Lola let that comment rest for a moment, then went in for the kill.

"If this goes any further, we won't have to come after you," Lola said. "All we have to do is present all our evidence to the police—evidence that directly links Ricky to a series of missing and endangered young women. It'll take a day for them to look into all the money that Zo has given him for the last two years."

Cheryl's poker face couldn't hide her shock. She cleared her throat a few times and glanced at the men beside her, who looked equally gobsmacked.

"Those are some very serious allegations," Cheryl finally managed.

Lola tapped her fingers on the table and glanced at her watch. "We've got another meeting," she said. "You think the three of you can huddle and come to some sort of agreement on this?"

Cheryl's lips were white. "We need to regroup and discuss. We'll contact your office and let you know when we can schedule another discussion."

"That's fine," Lola said. "I'll get my contact at the police to join us next time. I'll make sure she's caught up on all our information."

Cheryl glanced at Todd. There was a long silence.

"Can you give us the room for a moment?" she asked.

Lola nodded, then stood. "Come on, Rainey."

We walked outside and I kept my face neutral until we were out of sight of the conference room.

"I love you," I said.

"Don't get cocky yet," Lola said. "They haven't agreed to anything. And keep your mouth shut. You don't know who's listening in."

We waited for about five minutes before Todd emerged and beckoned to us. I tried to keep my face down as we filed back into the conference room and sat at the table. To my surprise, Cheryl's face went smooth, and she gave a thoughtful nod. She looked like the fight had gone out of her.

"We've spoken to our client and drawn up a new agreement," she said. The venom had disappeared from her voice, and she seemed tired. "We're willing to drop the lawsuit if your client signs a nondisclosure agreement regarding everything that we discussed today."

She handed Lola two copies of a printed agreement. We all waited in silence as Lola sat back and read through the document. It was short, so it only took her a few minutes.

"Fine," she said. "We're ready to sign."

Lola set the document in front of me and handed me her pen. I signed both documents, then handed them back to Lola. She tucked one in her briefcase and slid the other one across the table to Cheryl.

"Okay, Rainey," Lola said, standing. "Let's get out of here."

<hr />

I didn't take a deep breath until we were back on the street. Once I was sure that nobody from the law firm had followed us, I turned to Lola.

"Thank you," I said.

"Don't mention it."

I looked up and down the street. "What about the restraining order hearing?" I asked. "Do you think this is all going to backfire when Noa goes up against Ricky?"

"No, I don't," Lola said. She wore a look of grim satisfaction. "I suspect that Mr. Zo's lawyers are about to enlighten him on the wisdom of keeping some distance from his warty little offspring. For the foreseeable future, that is."

"And what about Ricky's application for a restraining order against Noa?"

Lola heaved a sigh. "One fire at a time, my friend."

My phone buzzed with a text alert. I opened the new message. It was from my anonymous contact, Reseda99.

I heard about the break in. I hope you're okay.

My heart started pounding.

How did you know? I wrote back.

They're scared, came the response. *You're getting close.*

Stop being mysterious and tell me what I need to know. I wanted to throw the phone across the street.

If I had everything myself, I wouldn't need you to keep looking. I do have some information that can help you, but first, you need to help me.

How, I wrote back.

Find Eiko and I'll tell you.

"Rainey?" Lola was staring at me.

"Sorry, Lo," I said. "What?"

"Do you want to come into work, or should I drop you back home?"

I hesitated. "Would you mind taking me home? I might head out again," I said.

"Where to?"

"You remember the anonymous source who asked me to find Eiko?" I said. Our team meeting with Hailey had only been a few days ago, but it already seemed like a year had passed.

"Sure."

"I'm just going to drive out there. If I get a whiff that something seems off, I'll head back." I took out my phone and texted her the address for Sweet Moon Bakery.

Lola hesitated before she spoke. "I want to trust that you'll be okay," she said.

"Come on, Lo," I said. "What's the worst that could happen?"

"I don't want to think about it."

"So don't," I said, putting my hand on her arm. "This could be the break we need."

TWENTY-FOUR

It was nearly noon by the time I got on the I-10 heading toward Mercury, which was just at the edge of Palm Springs and Joshua Tree National Park. There wasn't much information about the Sweet Moon Bakery online, other than a Google Maps tag with dozens of reviews.

My anxiety dissipated as Los Angeles disappeared behind me and the desert began to materialize. The sky was white with heat, and the highway unfurled under shimmering mirage lines. The little bit I had read about Mercury made it sound quaint, and the images available online confirmed this: old-timey wooden buildings that looked like they were straight out of *Lonesome Dove*, saloons and barber shops from the 1800s. Once a year, there was a retro car show, during which time vintage Mustangs and Ford Model Ts cruised up and down the main drag.

I consulted my map again once I hit the turnoff for Route 62 and saw that I was only ten minutes away from Mercury. The mountains rose up on either side of me, tawny and sparse, and even though my air conditioning was on full blast, I could feel the heat beating down on my car. The sign for Mercury was so small I nearly missed my turnoff. I switched lanes just in time to take the exit.

A thin cluster of buildings formed the outskirts of town, but as I continued down the street Mercury began to take shape: squat houses leading up to an antiquated church, a row of shops, a gas station, and a visitor's center. At the end of the main row of shops was a kitschy diner called the Thorn Tree, and next to that sat a bar. I hadn't seen Sweet Moon Bakery, even though my map said that it was at the center of town, and when I glanced at my phone again, my reception had disappeared.

I pulled over on the side of the road and stepped out of my car into a heat wave. A pair of men in cowboy hats sat outside the diner, and one of them nodded to me. "Need help?"

"Hi," I said. "I'm looking for Sweet Moon Bakery. Do you know where that is?"

"Sure do," the man said. "It's just on the other side of the gas station."

The day was hot, and everything had a feeling of being baked and faded beneath the sunlight. There was a kind of quiet to the place, a sleepy rumble that came from the nearby highway. Mercury seemed to have been forgotten by the passage of time. The world had moved on without it.

The main street was so small I could see all the way to the end. Past the gas station was a little library, which looked like it was still open for the day. I saw two antique stores, and as I walked down the sidewalk, I caught sight of a hand-painted sign that read SWEET MOON BAKERY.

The outside of the shop was retro, and I could see how it would appeal to wealthy people driving down from Los Angeles to visit Palm Springs. The exterior of the shop was the faded pink of cake frosting, with rounded windows that were somehow dust-free. I took a deep breath to steel my nerves before I walked up to the entrance of the shop and stepped inside.

The interior of the cake shop felt like an authentic 1950s diner: a chrome counter stretched along the length of the back wall, complete with tall stools. The black-and-white linoleum floor was clean and shiny, and the wallpaper was pink-and-white stripes. Framed along the length of the shop were black-and-white photos of celebrities who had come out to Joshua Tree. The shop was empty.

"Be right with you!" called a woman's voice from the back.

I walked along the shop and read the captions on the photos. To my surprise, they weren't professional photos clipped from magazines: these were celebrities who had actually stopped at Sweet Moon and posed in the room that I was standing in now: Barbara Stanwyck, Lucille Ball, Rock Hudson.

"Can I help you?"

I turned around to see a young woman in an apron dusted with flour. The woman was older than Eiko—probably mid-twenties—and there were other differences, like height and weight, but I could still see the family resemblance to the photos that I had seen of Eiko. She must be Hana, Eiko's sister. Hana was smiling, waiting to help me, and I felt stuck on how to proceed.

"Hi," I said.

"What can I get you?"

I walked over to the counter and looked in the glass display case. Everything looked fresh and delicious, and I wondered why they consistently put so much effort into preparing baked goods every day when so many of them must go to waste. Mercury didn't seem like a place many visitors passed through.

"Do you have coffee?"

"Filter," Hana replied.

I turned back to the pastry case. "What did Rita Hayworth get?"

Hana frowned, then her face softened into comprehension. She gave a sudden, short laugh. "Oh, wow," she said. "I think it was a bear claw. I've heard all those stories for decades. Most people look right past those photos."

"I'll have a bear claw, then."

"To go?"

"I'll have it here," I said. I took a seat at the counter and waited for Hana to get everything ready. She came back a moment later and set the pastry and the coffee in front of me.

"Passing through?" she said.

"I'm just here for the afternoon," I said.

"Palm Springs or Joshua Tree?"

"Neither," I said. "I'm actually just on a bit of a road trip from Los Angeles."

Hana nodded and scrutinized me but said nothing.

"Things seem quiet around here," I said, looking around. "Do you still get many customers?"

"Not a lot of tourists, not during the week," she said. "But we've got two AA meetings in town and a bowling league. There's a local book club at the library, too. They clear out most of the pastries at the end of the day."

"It seems like the whole town is pretty quiet," I said.

Hana shrugged. "Some businesses have folded over the last few years, but we get a lot of the construction crews and engineers lately. Sometimes we sell out of everything before noon."

She glanced behind her, into the kitchen. I could smell honey and rising dough.

"Give me a shout if you need anything else, okay?" Hana said. She turned to go, but I cleared my throat.

"Actually, I should probably introduce myself," I said. "My name is Rainey Hall. I'm a private investigator from Culver City."

"Okay?" There was a new edge to Hana's voice. She lingered in the doorway of the kitchen.

I took a deep breath and wrapped my hands around the cup of coffee before me. "Would you be willing to talk to me about your sister?"

When I glanced up at Hana, I could see her whole body tense up. She looked confused, but she also looked disgusted. I had seen the look before, of course; one of the worst parts of my job is existing as an omen of bad tidings. I know it's not personal, of course, but I always need to take a deep breath whenever people look at me like that. In Hana, though, I saw something that surprised me: fear.

"What are you doing here?" she asked in a low voice. Her body was almost entirely inside the kitchen now. "What do you want?"

I produced a business card and held it out to her. She made no move to accept it.

"Have you heard of Spencer Collins?"

Hana gave a bitter laugh. "Oh, sure I have," she said. "She's the one who got Eiko hooked on drugs. Are you one of Spencer's friends, too?"

"No," I said. "I called her a friend in high school, but she was never really nice to me. Now I'd probably call her a bully."

"That's the word."

"Spencer died a few days ago," I said quietly. "I don't know if you heard."

"I didn't hear. What does this have to do with Eiko?"

I thought carefully about how to phrase my next comment. "I think something is happening to these girls. Missing isn't dead, of course, but if something happened to your sister, it might help me find out what happened to the others. It's not just Eiko, and it's not just my friend, either. I have another client named Chloe Delmonico who has been missing for a few weeks."

Hana let out an ironic laugh. "So, you don't actually care about my sister. It's just a means to an end."

"That's not true," I countered, but just then, a timer went off in the kitchen. I could smell something like burnt sugar.

Hana cursed and disappeared out back. I could hear an oven door banging open and then the sound of something metal clattering on the floor. More cursing. A few minutes passed and Hana made no sign of reappearing. I picked up my bear claw and bit into it. It was perfection.

Hana finally reappeared. She walked over to me and picked up my business card. "What would you do if you found my sister?"

I considered the question. "I mean, that's a hard question to answer. If she were in trouble, I would try to help her. If she's struggling with drugs, I'm not going to report her, if that's what you mean. I'm not law enforcement."

"And what if she's dead?" Hana asked. "What happens then?"

"I'll try to find out what happened to her," I said.

"I can't pay you."

"I'm not asking you to."

"So why help me?"

"If she's dead," I said carefully, "then it may confirm a bigger theory that my colleagues and I are working on. I can't share more than that, not right now. I'm sorry."

Hana looked like she was considering whether or not to share something. "Eiko hasn't lived here in years," she said. "Our parents died when we were little. It was our aunt and uncle who raised us."

I waited, listening.

"Eiko started running away in high school. She was a great artist, but she was always getting in trouble at school. She couldn't sit still, so my aunt had her see a doctor. Got her on these pills, but I think they made it worse. Anyway, she dropped out when she was fifteen and started taking art classes up in Los Angeles. She'd take the bus or catch a ride with one of our neighbors who worked out there."

She looked out the window and fell quiet. A big gust of wind sent a dusty cyclone down the sidewalk outside, but here, inside the shop, we were insulated. Safe.

"She never got off drugs," Hana said. "She changed her last name to Mars and actually became kind of successful. I mean, her stuff was *good*. My aunt and uncle were pissed, because she was so unreliable, but I think they were proud, too. And then a few months ago, she came back and said she wanted to give it all up."

"Give what up?"

Hana didn't respond. She picked up a rag and a bottle of cleaning fluid and started wiping down the counter, even though it was sparkling clean. Finally, she wiped her hands on her apron and looked at me.

Hana nodded, then walked around the counter, and went over to the front door. She locked it and switched the sign from OPEN to CLOSED. She walked over to a table and sat down, then gestured for me to join her.

"Is this about Morphy?" she asked.

I was surprised. "That's part of it," I said. "How do you know?"

"That's part of the reason she came back," Hana said. "She was part of a group of artists in Los Angeles. They lived in a house in Glendale, and sometimes there were parties. Eiko didn't have a problem taking drugs, but once Morphy came on the scene, she was done. It was too scary, even for her. She wanted to move back home."

"Where did it come from?"

Hana thought, biting her lip and frowning. "She was pretty paranoid the last time I saw her," she said. "I dismissed a lot of what she said, because for the last few years she got into all these conspiracy theories. She said they were trying to sell her brain."

"Right."

"She told me about these parties," Hana went on. "They'd pick her up in a limo; she had to wear a blindfold and everything. The parties were always in the same place. She had no idea what part of the city it was in, but it was somewhere in Los Angeles."

"A hotel?"

"No, a mansion," Hana said. "At least, that's what Eiko told me. An enormous house with velvet walls."

The hairs on the back of my neck went up. "How did she know it was in Los Angeles?"

"She said it only took half an hour to get there," Hana said. She was looking at me closely again, and I could tell she was wondering whether or not I was trustworthy.

I took out my phone and opened it up to a photo of Alice. It was a photo I had taken on a disposable camera in high school, me and Alice with our arms slung around each other and grinning. We had just been to the Huntington Gardens, and Alice had a flower stuck in her hair.

"This is Alice," I said. "She went missing when we were in high school, and I thought she was dead. She's still alive, though, and Spencer knew what happened to her. Spencer's gone, though, so I have to find some other way to track her down. I think she might have been involved with those same parties. She's older than Eiko, but she's still vulnerable."

Hana examined the photo and nodded. "Don't take it personally, but I'm wary of anyone who comes here asking about Eiko."

"Why?"

She sighed. "You're not the first one," she said. "When she first left Los Angeles and moved back home, two men came out here and said some threatening things."

I felt chills all over my body. "Do you remember what they looked like?"

"I'm not good at describing people," she said. "Average size. Dark hair."

I thought desperately for a solution. I took out my phone and looked up Simon Balto, then showed a photo to Hana. She nodded, her face grim. "I think so," she said. "He wasn't dressed like that, though."

"What did they want?"

"They wouldn't tell me," she said. "They just wanted to know where she was. I didn't tell them, but they went to our house and talked to her. She left a few days later."

I nodded and put my phone away.

"I asked Calder if he knew anything about them," she went on, and it seemed like she was almost thinking out loud. "He told me that I was probably imagining things."

"Wait—Calder? You don't mean Calder Reyes, do you?"

She glanced up. "Yes," she said. "Do you know him?"

"I know a bit about the art world. How do *you* know him?"

"Calder was going to show Eiko's work," she said. She was staring at me. "Someone introduced him to Eiko, and he agreed to show her work. He was really excited, said he could make her career happen."

I was having trouble putting my thoughts into words. I felt a stab of anxiety in the pit of my stomach. I felt like Calder had lied to me, even though I had never asked him about Eiko; indeed, he had been the first one to mention her name to me.

"Have you talked to Calder about Eiko since she went missing?" I asked.

She shrugged. "He said that I shouldn't go looking for her. That he didn't want anything bad to happen to me."

The hairs on the back of my neck stood up. It was eerily similar to what Calder had told me when I had first gone to see him about Spencer.

"I didn't listen, of course," she said. "I went to the police. Both here and in Los Angeles. Didn't do much good, though."

"You have my card," I said. "Please call me if you think of anything else. Okay?"

She nodded. I got up and walked to the door of the bakery. Just as I was about to leave, she called after me.

"Just one more thing," she said. "There was a woman, too. She came a few weeks later."

"A woman?"

"She was Black," Hana said. "British, I think. She seemed really angry."

Hana must have read the shock on my face, because she looked surprised. "What is it?" she asked. "Should I be worried?"

I didn't know what to tell her. "It's possible," I said. "I'm sorry, I don't have any more information to give you right now. Until we find out who's behind this whole thing, you should be careful, though. Make sure you lock your doors at night."

As I made my way back down the street toward my car, I felt the ground beneath me quaking. I had grown up with earthquakes rattling the walls and knew that they came as a sharp swell, a big dip with occasional aftershocks: this was something else. It was a persistent rumble that seemed to thrum through the air itself. As I turned the corner and my car was in sight, I saw where the vibrations were coming from: outsized construction vehicles were pulling into the gas station to refuel. The main street was full of them, as far as the eye could see, long trucks loaded with metal beams, concrete mixers, and bulldozers.

I walked back to the diner and saw that the two men in cowboy hats were still sitting outside. The man who had helped me with directions earlier waved.

"You find Sweet Moon?"

"Yes, thanks," I said. I squinted toward the gas station. "Do you know where all those vehicles are going?"

"Sure do," the man said. "It's for the new museum out by Mission Creek Preserve. Out thataway." He pointed east, toward the desert.

"They're putting a museum out there?"

"Sure are."

I walked back down the street, toward the gas station, trying to get a look at all the vehicles. They were so big they dwarfed everything around them, making Mercury seem even more antiquated than it already was.

I reached the library at the end of the street and shaded my eyes to see a local community board covered in flyers. The flyers were all the same, and they fluttered in a dusty breeze that sent tumbleweeds across the road.

PROTEST THE MUSEUM, the flyers read. DON'T SELL OUR FUTURE.

TWENTY-FIVE

It was close to seven p.m. by the time I got back to Los Angeles. I had planned to go straight home after visiting Mercury, but when I saw the turnoff for the 5 North heading toward Burbank, I took it.

It was still light outside when I drove down the street where Rhodes's sister lived. I didn't know what I had been expecting when I went to look for the house, but I was still surprised when I parked outside the address and found a small post-war house with a front lawn paved in cement. Two pit bulls lay on the cement and came charging toward the fence when I approached. They were both leashed, but lunged at me as I skirted around them and made my way to the front door. Everything smelled like baked dog shit.

Someone in the house must have heard me coming, because I saw movement behind the curtains before I even had time to knock on the door. When I knocked, I heard three different locks undone before the door opened a crack and someone peered out at me behind a chain lock. I could discern faint features: frizzy hair with an uneven dye job, olive skin, knobby fingers.

"Yes? What is it?"

I glanced down at the information that Blake had sent me a few days ago. "I'm looking for Dolores Rhodes," I said. "Is that you?"

"I don't have to answer that," she said, nervous. "Not until you tell me why you're here."

"I'm a private investigator," I said, handing her my card. After a moment of hesitation, she accepted the card and peered at the text before glancing up at me.

"What do you want?"

I glanced at the dogs snapping behind me and felt a sudden wave of pity and compassion for the woman standing before me. It must have been a tough existence, living with suspicion and paranoia, always waiting for the danger to come. Anticipating it at any moment.

"Have you heard of Spencer Collins?" I asked.

"No," she said, then started to shut the door. "I can't help you."

"What about Eiko Mars?" I said, desperate. "Simon Balto?"

The door closed, and I heard the locks turn.

"I just need five minutes!" I called out, knowing that it was probably futile. Frustrated, I turned around and saw both dogs staring at me. No longer angry monsters, they now looked forlorn and pathetic. I saw that one of them was showing signs of mange, and the other was rail thin. He whined and looked up at me with big eyes, then licked his mouth a few times. I thought about knocking again, but there was something so pathetic about the whole situation that I couldn't bring myself to do it. I walked back to my car and glanced at the house one more time before driving away.

As I left Burbank, however, I passed a large supermarket. Before I was even conscious of what I was doing, I pulled into the store, thought for a moment, and then got out. Feeling a bit foolish, I got a cart from the front of the store, went to the pet aisle, and loaded up my cart with two jumbo-sized bags of dog food. I told myself that I was being a meddling idiot for what I was about to do as I walked through the checkout aisle and then back to my car. Even as I drove back to Dolores's house, I was trying to talk myself out of it.

Still, when I got back to the house and saw the two pitiful dogs on their chains, I knew that I had made the right decision. I hauled both bags up to the front door, one at a time, then knocked and walked back to my car without waiting for her to open the door. I had unlocked my car and was about to climb in when I heard the door of Dolores's house open.

"Hey," she called. "Hey, you!"

I turned. She had emerged from the house enough for me to see that she was a small woman.

"What do you want?"

I hesitated. She still looked fearful, like she might be scared off at any moment, and I didn't want to come on too strong.

"I'm trying to find my friend," I said. "Her name is Alice, and we used to be close. I think that Ian—I think your brother might have known her."

There was a moment's pause while she considered. Finally, she sighed. "Well, come on, then," she said. "You'll have to carry these bags in yourself. I can't lift them."

I hauled both bags inside and Dolores pointed toward some dog food bowls at the edge of the kitchen. I filled both bowls, and Dolores went outside and brought the dogs in. They lunged at the ends of their leashes, aiming for the food. I jumped back when she released them, but they ignored me, their attention firmly riveted on the food.

"I do feed them," Dolores said, sounding defensive. "I love my boys. It's down to once a day though since they cut my disability check."

I followed Dolores through the dim house and took a seat across from her at a little table. She lowered herself down and ran a hand through her hair. She took out a packet of gum and retrieved a stick, then offered it to me. I accepted one and unfolded it from the foil.

"Ian wasn't a drug addict," she said. Her voice was tired. "I need you to know that, first of all, because people keep saying it. And if you're going to write something about him, I don't want it to be that."

It took me a moment to understand what she was saying. "I'm not going to write anything," I said. "I'm not a journalist."

She didn't seem to hear me, or maybe her thoughts were elsewhere. She glanced out the window and then looked back at me.

"Ian was good at other things, too," she said. "Not just art. He helped me around the house. He'd build things. He put the bars on the windows." She nodded up at the window, and I saw that there were bars across it.

"When was the last time you saw him?"

"A year ago." Her voice was resigned.

"I'm so sorry for your loss," I offered. "I know how hard it is to lose a family member."

She unwrapped another stick of gum and slipped it into her mouth. "He changed once he started hanging out with them. I don't want you to write about him being gay, either, because he wasn't gay. I know he started sleeping with men, but that's just the things that happened at the parties."

I was about to protest again, remind her that I wasn't a journalist, but something told me to keep quiet.

"He was always generous with his money, though. That was Ian," she went on. "Bought me a new fridge and all. He used to take the dogs to the vet's. Don't know how I'll afford that, now."

"Dolores," I said. "I hate to ask, but how did you find out that he had died?"

She smoothed the gum wrapper out on the table. It took her a long time to answer.

"Someone came and offered me money," she said. "Last week it was, before he died. I saw him in the news, you know, I try to keep up."

"Who offered you money?"

"It was a man. He wouldn't tell me his name. Now, why would they offer me money unless something bad had happened to Ian?" The dogs started up a howl in the kitchen. "Quiet! *Hssst!* Bad dogs."

"What did this man look like?"

Dolores blinked a few times, then rubbed her eyes and leaned back in her chair. "He offered to buy Ian's artwork," she said. "He didn't need to look at it first. He said he would buy whatever I had."

"Did he tell you his name? Or do you remember what he looked like?"

"I didn't sell Ian's art," Dolores went on. "I've still got it. As soon as he came by to buy it, I knew something must have happened. He was so eager."

Asking her more questions seemed to be pointless, so I just waited for her to share whatever it was that she was ready to tell me.

"He was bald and fat," she said. "He had one of those silk dresses that Japanese people wear."

It took me a moment to realize who she was talking about. I hesitated, then took out my phone and looked up a photo of Calder. Dolores glanced at it, then nodded.

"Sure, that's him." She got up and left the room without saying anything. I could hear movement in another room, and a few minutes passed before she returned, carrying a scrapbook bursting with papers. She set it down in front of me, and I opened the cover. Inside were news clippings, dozens of them. At the beginning of the scrapbook were articles about Ian and his artwork. As those began to taper off—as the space between dates began to grow, and he showed up less in the news—a different kind of article began to appear. These were news of politicians and powerful people in Los Angeles, mostly men.

"He wanted to get off drugs," Dolores said, standing over my shoulder. "He could have been so big. They just kept sucking him back in."

"Who kept sucking him in?"

"Ian had it hardest, harder than me," she said. "He was so young when our parents died. I couldn't take care of him by myself. It's not my fault he had to go into foster care, you know, but who knows what happens to kids there. They paid him good money, and I think he liked it. He wasn't supposed to tell me about the men, but whenever he saw one of them in the paper, he'd show me."

I continued flipping through the scrapbook. An idea was starting to form in my head, a dark image that made me feel dirty. Drugs, prostitution. The image was made worse by Dolores's sad little house and the fact that she had started to rely on Ian for his hush money, but now that he was gone, she couldn't afford to feed her dogs twice a day.

I stopped at an image of a man that I recognized. He wore a cowboy hat and smiled at the camera. The caption beneath the photo read DAN EVERSON MAKES MAYORAL BID FOR PALM SPRINGS.

Dolores slammed the scrapbook shut, making me jump.

"You have the wrong idea about Ian," she said. "He had real talent."

She disappeared again and came back with another scrapbook. When I opened this one, I saw that it was full of sketches, done in pencil, then photographs of Ian's artwork. I got chills when I saw the images because they were so powerful, even the ones that were unfinished. I remembered seeing them for the first time a few days before, being startled at how cynical they were.

I turned the page and stopped. I was looking at a photograph of a woman leaning against a brick wall. I knew her, but I couldn't remember why. She looked dazed, dressed in white, a cigarette held between the tips of her fingers. She wore a white gown. It looked old-fashioned, like something you might see from the early 1900s.

Dolores saw me looking at it and tapped the page.

"Mary," she said.

"Who is it?"

"She was his first," Dolores said, and she sounded proud. "That's why I remember. Mary Ecclestone. She was sick, in and out of hospitals. Look."

She turned the page of the scrapbook, and I breathed in so sharply that Dolores jumped. The dogs ran in and started barking. I grasped the photo album and started shaking so badly Dolores took it out of my hands and looked at me, scared.

It was a rough draft, but all the elements were there: the tunnel, the wind, the wild hair. The white gown, the hand raised up to the face. Ian had written the title of the painting at the bottom of the page.

M.E. Stands Before the Mind of God.

TWENTY-SIX

⸺

I called Calder as soon as I left Dolores's house. It was eight o'clock, but Calder was a night owl, and I knew that he would still be working.

"Rainey?"

"Calder," I said, trying to keep my voice even. "You didn't tell me that the museum in Joshua Tree was going ahead."

There was a long silence on the other end of the phone. When he spoke, there was a feigned kind of nonchalance in his voice. "Why would I? I had nothing to do with it."

It took everything in me to hold back the anger and accusations I wanted to lobby at him. "I've heard some rumors," I said. "I know Simon Balto was trying to get that museum off the ground for ages, but he kept hitting roadblocks. Looks like he got his way in the end."

"Where'd you hear that?"

"Ian Rhodes," I said.

There was a long silence on the other end of the phone. "That's a sick joke," Calder said. "Rhodes is dead."

"It's definitely sick," I said. "The question is, Calder, how much do *you* know?"

He hung up immediately. I took out my phone to text Lola, and then I decided to call her instead.

"Rainey? Are you okay?"

"Simon Balto has been using artists as bait," I said. "I think he gets them high on Morphy and puts them in compromising situations with powerful people. Then he blackmails those same people into getting his way."

There was a long silence. "Are you still in Joshua Tree?"

"The Balto museum is going ahead," I said. "I think that's part of the reason that Ian Rhodes died. He fucked a council member from Joshua Tree and that's the only reason they were able to get the museum to go ahead."

"Okay, slow down," Lola said. "Some of this is going over my head. Do you want me to meet you somewhere?"

I took a deep breath and closed my eyes. "No," I said. "It can wait. Let's meet up as a team tomorrow."

Sadie's bedroom light was on when I got home, and I could hear oboe music drifting out the window. She had moved on from the Morricone and was playing something new. It was light and beautiful, and even though my day had been heavy, I felt a surge of gratitude toward my roommate for always seeming to exist on a happier plane. For a moment I thought about entering the house and calling out to her because we hadn't caught up for a few days. I didn't want to interrupt her, though, so I went straight out to the guesthouse.

I unlocked the door and went to switch on the light. I barely had a moment to register movement before a shadow detached itself from the wall, and then there was a hand on me, a flurry of fingers, someone scrabbling for a hold on my arm.

I whirled, spun around at the same time as an elbow came up. There was a moment of darkness as bone met bone. Blood surged to my head, and I gasped, then tried to lift a hand to feel my nose, assess the damage. As I lifted my hand, though, someone grabbed my arm again and then I felt a foot connect with my stomach and I stumbled backward, gasping for breath and wincing with pain. I couldn't breathe. I collapsed in the corner, then tried to inhale. I couldn't breathe, I couldn't breathe—

"Rainey," came a man's voice, from somewhere above me. "Rainey, Rainey, what are you *doing*?"

A flashlight clicked on, and someone shone it right in my eyes. It was a Maglite, heavy and bright, and I couldn't see anyone beyond it. Blood was coursing freely from my nose, and I could taste it in the back of my throat. Too much adrenaline was coursing through my veins for me to feel the pain; I knew it would come later. I finally managed to sit up and take a breath.

"We warned you, didn't we?" came the voice again. It sounded chiding, almost sorrowful. There were two of them, I could see that much: beyond the corona of light that nearly blinded me I could see the outline of a hand holding the flashlight. The man who spoke was farther back; someone else was holding the light. The room beyond was dim, too dim to see anything, but I thought I could see the black shapes of balaclavas, covering the heads of the intruders.

"Fuck you," I said, then wiped the blood from my nose with the back of my hand.

"There's no need to be vulgar," came the voice. I could almost place it, and then I realized why I knew it—it was the low growl of the man I had heard in Spencer's apartment, the one who had been with Lucas.

"Who are you?"

"Believe it or not, I'm a friend," he replied.

"Simon Balto," I said. It was a guess, but I hoped I sounded confident enough to make them hesitate. "Lucas Mankerfield."

This statement was met with laughter from both men. I thought quickly: I had recovered enough breath that I could try to defend myself. I didn't know if they had guns or knives, but that wasn't something I could think about right now: I had to seize the moment, the element of surprise. I leaned back against the wall and used both feet to kick out below the beam of the flashlight, where I imagined the nearest assailant's chest was.

I got lucky. There was a surprised *whoof!* as he got his breath knocked out of him, and the flashlight went flying. It hit a lamp, which fell off the shelf and shattered. My vision was severely impaired from having the light shined in my face—I was almost blind—but I dived toward the front door, felt the doorknob in my fingers. My hand was covered in blood and the doorknob slipped in my hands as I tried to turn it. I felt it click and there was a slat of bright light as I turned the knob . . .

Someone grabbed me from behind and kicked the door shut.

"You bitch," came a growl from the first assailant, the one I had kicked in the chest. My vision had adjusted to the dim interior of the apartment, enough that I could see the man in front of me, his hands balled into fists. He was wearing a balaclava; both of their faces were masked. He punched me in the stomach, and I doubled over but managed to stay on my feet.

"It's her left hand," came a pinched voice. I was right; the voice belonged to Lucas. "Her left hand is the one that matters."

The second man grabbed my hand and turned it over, looking at it almost gently.

"It's not enough," he said.

"She's a musician," Lucas urged. "Break her hand."

I felt delirious, lightheaded. I almost laughed then because Lucas had done enough research to find out I had once played violin but not enough to realize I hadn't touched a violin in years. I almost felt relief because I wasn't going to die; they were just going to break my hand . . .

"What are you doing?" Lucas asked.

"What does it look like?" the other man said.

The glint of a knife.

"We can't kill her—"

"Shut up."

My heart started to beat very quickly. I felt like I was going to faint. All the relief from earlier was gone, and I wanted to scream. Instead, I brought my knee up as hard as I could. It connected with the groin of the second man, and he screamed. He dropped the knife and I heard it skitter across the floor, but then he grabbed my left hand and yanked it backward. The bone snapped. I screamed.

"Let's go, *let's go*," Lucas hissed. "She has neighbors!"

"Give me the knife," growled his companion.

"We're getting out of here."

"Give me the fucking knife," the other man growled. "She's going to come after us."

There was a moment of hesitation on the part of Lucas. I was in so much pain I was having trouble keeping my eyes open, but I knew that I needed to retain consciousness. I was going to die, I was going to die . . .

I slipped down to the floor as the man dropped me and went to find the knife. The guesthouse door burst open behind me. I heard glass shatter and wood banging on wood. I lay on my side and could see a pair of feet standing in the door of my apartment. There was a moment of stillness before I heard Sadie's voice.

"What the *fuck*," she snarled. Her voice was flat and angry in a way I had never heard before.

"You need to go back to your house, ma'am," the second man warned. His voice was dangerous and calm. I could see him advancing toward her, his feet stalking across the floorboards.

"I don't think so," Sadie said. I heard a *crick-snick* and glanced up to see her holding a gun. I was momentarily stunned—I didn't even know Sadie owned a gun, and I was even more surprised to see how coldly confident she looked holding it. She wasn't even looking at me, but straight at the men.

"Get the fuck out of my house before I cap you," she said.

"Real tough talk," the man said, then laughed. "You're cute, you know—"

The sentence was cut short as Sadie shot him in the knee. He howled in pain and indignation, then dropped to the floor. The room was full of the sound of his labored breathing.

"I'm going to shoot your friend next, fuckface," she said. "God Bless America and the second amendment. I really don't want to drag your ugly ass outside and bury you, though, so I'm going to count to ten. If you're not gone by then, I'm going to have to chop you into pieces and put you in the compost."

Lucas hesitated, but only for a second. He raised his hands above his head and walked backward toward the open door. He slipped out, into the night.

"You too, shithead," Sadie told the injured man. Even though he was wearing a mask, I could see his eyes narrow into slits of hatred. "Leave the knife."

He threw it across the room, aimed at her. The blade narrowly missed her leg. Sadie didn't even flinch but fired a shot at the assailant's foot. He screamed, almost an animal moan, then shuffled sideways toward the door to join his friend. Sadie waited until they were gone before rushing to me and kneeling to look in my eyes. She looked frantic and scared, all signs of her bravado fading.

"Quick," she said. "Let's get into the main house and call the police."

I let her assist me across the foyer. Once we were inside the door, she bolted and locked the door, then took out her phone.

"No, no," I said. "Don't call the police."

"Don't be an idiot."

I walked over to her sink, ran the cold tap, and stuck my face under it. I hissed in pain, then took a few paper towels and dabbed my face dry. Sadie was watching me with a look of concern.

"I'll get you some ice, for your hand," she said. "It looks really bad."

She took an ice tray out of the freezer, filled a plastic bag, and pressed it to my hand. I winced in pain and felt fresh tears spring to my eyes.

"I'm calling the police," she said, her voice gentle. "And then I'm going to take you to the hospital."

"You can't call the police," I said. "Just give me a moment. I need to call someone, and then I'll explain."

Sadie waited quietly as I called Lola. Lola picked up on the third ring.

"I need you to come get me," I said. "It's an emergency. I'll explain everything when you get here."

"Where are you?" she asked.

"My house," I said. "Stay in your car when you get here. I'll come out and meet you. Keep your doors locked."

After I hung up, I closed my eyes for a moment, then turned to look at Sadie.

"I don't like to lie to the police," I said. "It makes things very difficult for me in the future, because we often have to work together. I can't share all my theories about who might have come to hurt me tonight, because it will endanger my case. If they find out I'm withholding information, though, I could get arrested."

Her face was a mess of conflicting emotions.

"I didn't realize you were such a badass," I said, and tried to smile. "You probably saved my life, you know. I'm really sorry I put you through this."

"What did those people want?" she asked.

"I can't get too specific," I said. "But I'm working on a case that implicates some pretty powerful people. I'm guessing I'm on the right track."

"I don't understand why you can't go to the police," she said. "If you've found something."

I winced and looked down at my hand, which had swelled to twice its normal size. "I don't have enough evidence for them to convict or arrest anyone," I said. "Just enough to tell me that I'm going in the right direction."

"Fine," she said with some reluctance.

"I'm really sorry to do this to you, but do you have somewhere else you can stay tonight? Otherwise, I can arrange something. I would prefer that you didn't stay here by yourself."

"I can stay with my sister," she said.

"I didn't know you had a gun," I said.

"It's not mine," she replied. "The old woman who lived here had them stashed around the house. She used to shoot rats in the garden."

—⋘—

Lola was at my house twenty minutes later and texted me to say that she was outside. Sadie helped me out to her car. When Lola saw my hand and the blood all over my clothes, her face went white. "What happened?"

"Take me to the hospital," I said through gritted teeth. The adrenaline that had kept the pain at bay was dwindling, and I could feel the faint throbbing in my fingers. It felt like something was broken, and I didn't want to stay at the house for longer than necessary in case Sadie called the police and I had to stick around to answer questions.

"Rainey, *what happened*?" Lola repeated.

Tears started running down my face, mostly from stress and fear, more than anything else. Lola put the car in drive and eased down Loma Linda Lane, then glanced back over at me.

"Rainey," she said, her voice urgent.

"Two men broke into the guesthouse," I said through pained breaths.

"Did you get a look at their faces?"

"They were wearing masks," I said. "But I recognized one of the voices—Lucas Mankerfield, Bradley Auden's assistant—the same guy who broke into Spencer's apartment. When I was there."

"And the other?"

"I think it was Simon Balto," I said. "But I'm not sure on that one, and if I'm wrong, we could screw up everything. I'm guessing they're the same guys who broke into our office."

"We have to go to the police," she said.

"Let's go to the hospital," I said. I winced in pain and squeezed my eyes shut. "We can decide what to say . . . before we go . . . to the police."

We had to wait an hour at the emergency room before I was called back to see a doctor. Lola managed to bully someone into giving me a bag of ice chips, which prevented me from passing out from pain. I was in too much agony to discuss a plan of attack with Lola, but I resolutely refused to let her call the police until I had decided what to say.

Finally, after what felt like a small eternity, my name was called, and Lola escorted me down a hall and into a room where a doctor stood waiting. The doctor was in her mid-sixties, her long dark hair streaked with gray. She had brown skin and large dark eyes behind small glasses.

"Have a seat," she said, gesturing to the table. "I'm Dr. El Khoury. Do you want to tell me what you're doing here today?"

I lifted my hand. "Something's broken. It hurts like hell."

"And the blood on your clothes?" She glanced at me over the top of her glasses.

"It's unrelated."

Dr. El Khoury gently lifted my hand and examined it. I winced and gritted my teeth, then sucked in air. She looked at me.

"How did this happen?"

I hesitated a moment too long, then cleared my throat. "Sports injury."

Dr. El Khoury kept her gaze on my face. "What sport?"

"Volleyball." I winced as she gently touched my wrist. I was in too much pain to think on my feet.

"You know that I'm required to speak to police if I suspect a crime has been committed, right?" Dr. El Khoury's voice was firm. "I don't even have to ask your permission."

"I'm fine." I was sweating bullets. I thought I might scream if she touched my wrist again, and I desperately wanted this whole thing to be over.

Dr. El Khoury glanced at Lola again. "Do you mind waiting outside?"

"She can stay," I said quickly.

"I would prefer to ask you some questions on your own."

"I'm here to support Rainey, so yes, I do mind. I'm staying right here."

"Lo," I said, gritting my teeth.

"Rainey," she replied.

"It's fine, Lo," I said.

Lola walked outside, pissed.

"Lie back," Dr. El Khoury told me. "I'll get you some pain relief, and then we can talk."

She disappeared and then reappeared a few minutes later, holding a paper cup with two pills. She handed me the cup and a glass of water, then waited as I swallowed the contents.

"Now," she said. "Tell me what really happened."

To my infinite shame and self-loathing, I started crying. It was mostly from the pain and the exhaustion of the last few hours, but it was partly the stress, too. If I had to be completely honest, though, the last straw was the kind way that the doctor was looking at me, the concern written on her face. I hated my own weakness in that moment, but I couldn't help myself.

"I'll just be a moment," she said. "I'm going to call someone in to talk to you."

"No," I said, more forcefully than I meant. "This isn't what you think. Please, I need you to listen."

She gave me a wary look.

"It's not a sports injury," I said. "It's a work injury, more or less. I'm looking for a missing girl. That's why this happened."

Dr. El Khoury frowned, then opened and closed her mouth a few times before speaking. "Are you police?"

"I'm a private investigator," I said. "Please, *please* don't make that call. If you call the cops, then we'll have to stop our investigation, and the girl that we're looking for could wind up dead."

"So, it wasn't volleyball."

"Two men got into my house and broke my hand," I said. "I just need you to fix it so I can keep working."

She let out an exasperated noise and held up my hand again. The pain-killers were doing their job, and it wasn't as painful.

"Are you left-handed?"

"No, right."

"It's weird they broke your left hand, then," she said. "It's an expert job, I can see that. Three different fractures."

"I used to play the violin," I said. "They knew that. It would have stopped me from playing for a very long time."

She was quiet, assessing the damage. "You know that sounds really bad, right?"

"I'll be fine."

"And your friend . . . ?"

"She's my lawyer. We work together."

She snapped off her gloves with a kind of efficiency, then sighed. "Okay," she said, finally. "I won't call the police. Not this time. But if you show up here again with more injuries, I'm going to have to rethink my position. You can't save anyone if you keep putting yourself in this kind of danger."

TWENTY-SEVEN

It was the early hours of the morning by the time we finally pulled up in front of Lola's house. She was yawning so hard she couldn't keep her eyes open, and I followed her up the front steps, fiddling with my phone.

"I'll see you in the morning. Make sure you lock the front door."

She vanished into her bedroom. I was too wired to sleep, and I took out my phone. I didn't care how early it was; I realized that I needed to tell Hailey what had happened to me. There was a chance that they were going to come after him next, if they hadn't done so already.

"Rainey?" Hailey's voice was thick with sleep when he answered the phone.

"I'm sorry about the hour," I said. "I wouldn't call you if it wasn't an emergency."

"Hold on." I heard the snap of a lamp switch, then the creak of a bed. "Okay. I'm listening. What's going on?"

I quickly filled him in on what had happened at my house. The words sounded strange coming out of my mouth, and I realized I was still in shock.

"Oh my god," Hailey said. He sounded wide awake. "Rainey—I'm so sorry. That must have been terrifying. Have you called the police?"

"Not yet. I'll do it in the morning."

"Where are you now?"

"I'm at Lola's house." I was full of anxiety all over again. "Are you safe, Hailey? I'm so worried about you—what if they come for you next?"

He cleared his throat. "I'll be prepared."

"There are things I have to tell you," I said. I suddenly felt extremely paranoid, wondering if they had managed to hack my phone. "I think I should wait, though. Tell you in person."

There was a pause. "Maybe I should meet you," he said. "Would that be okay?"

I hesitated. "Okay," I said. "I'll send you the address."

Hailey looked worried when he climbed out of his car and saw the condition I was in. I still hadn't changed my clothing, and the blood had dried on my shirt.

"I'm glad you're okay," he said, walking up the steps. "Do you want to go inside?"

"We should stay out here," I said. "Lola's asleep. I don't want to scare her."

Hailey sat down next to me. "Who was it?"

I took a deep breath. "You're going to think I'm crazy," I said. "But I think one of them was Simon Balto."

His face was partially hidden in shadow. The moonlight was so bright that the street was lit from above, and the shady outlines of trees were visible on the pavement. When Hailey turned his face into the light, I saw that he was biting his lip and frowning. He finally shook his head.

"I don't think you're crazy," he said. "I believe you completely. You said there were two men—do you know who the other one was?"

"Lucas Mankerfield," I said, my voice grim. "That one I'm more sure of."

He frowned. "The guy who tried to chase us away from Spencer's funeral?"

I gave a surprised laugh. "Yeah. He works for Bradley Auden."

Hailey reached out and gently touched my cast. I couldn't feel his fingertips, but my body thrilled at the contact.

"I went out to Mercury yesterday," I said. I quickly filled him in on my visit to see Eiko's sister and then mentioned my visit to see Dolores Rhodes.

"She said that Calder Reyes had tried to buy all of Rhodes's art from her," I said. "I think Calder's the one who sent those people to my house."

"Why would he do that?"

"Because he's involved with this whole scheme," I said. "Right, I left out the most important part. Simon finally got his approval for the museum in Joshua Tree. I think they're using artists as blackmail against certain politicians."

Hailey listened as I spelled out my theory, starting with what Hana had told me about the parties that Eiko had attended and ending with Rhodes's scrapbook. His face looked pale in the moonlight, and for the first time since I had met him, he looked worried.

"I know this sounds crazy," I said. "Now that I'm saying it out loud."

"It's not crazy," he said. "I believe you. We just have to prove it."

I shivered and looked down the street. The shock had made me feel numb, but now that the adrenaline was leaving my system, I felt cold. Hailey saw me shivering and took off his sweater, then handed it to me.

"You don't want me wearing that," I said. "I haven't showered since the . . . since we got back from the hospital."

"Just put it on."

I shrugged myself into it and felt warmer.

"You know, it's not too late for you to walk away from all this," I said. "If they're killing people, then it's pretty bad. We're looking into some powerful and twisted people."

"I'm not walking away," Hailey said quietly.

"Why is this story important to you?"

He sighed and rubbed his arms. "I'm an orphan, too," he said. "My parents died when I was eleven. Several months apart. My gran took me in."

"I'm sorry," I said.

"My childhood was kind of hard," he said. "I don't want to go into it too much now, but my gran turned things around. All I'm trying to say is that when I see these stories of vulnerable young people, I feel really powerless. I know what it's like."

I didn't know what to say, so I just listened.

"I lied to you about something," he said, then glanced over at me. "I knew who you were before I started looking into Rhodes."

"Oh?" I tried to keep my voice light. "When did you find out about me?"

"I didn't recognize you at first," he said quickly. "It was only when Marcus introduced you at the party that I started to put the pieces together. I was researching a story a few years ago—Theodore Langley, do you know him? Anyway, I was looking into old Hollywood and I saw some things about your grandmother. I know a little bit about your father. I followed the path until I saw you—you were a concert violinist."

I was cold again, even though I was wearing Hailey's sweater.

"I haven't looked at you since," he said. "Really. It was years ago."

"I'm not my family." I was having trouble meeting his eye.

"I know," Hailey said, nodding. We watched a cat snake its way between two cars. "I'm not, either. My parents used to fight a lot. It got really bad sometimes. My grandmother was the best parent you could ask for, but I always felt like there was something wrong with me. Like my parents' deaths were my fault."

He looked so sad that I wanted to hug him. I reached out and took his hand instead.

"Have you ever felt anything like that?" Hailey asked, his voice soft. He looked so vulnerable in that moment that my heart melted. Before I could question the wisdom of what I was doing, I leaned over and kissed him. The kiss lasted for about five seconds before Hailey pulled away. He was blushing.

"I shouldn't," he said. "I'd be scared I was taking advantage of you. You're probably still in shock, right? From what happened earlier."

"I don't think so."

He hesitated. We were still holding hands, and he hadn't moved his body away from mine.

"Are you sure?"

"I'm sure." I leaned in and kissed him again.

In that moment, with the moonlight making lacy patterns of the leaves on the sidewalk, with the night melting into morning and the stars fading away, I felt something that I hadn't felt in a very long time: hope.

TWENTY-EIGHT

I didn't mention Hailey's visit to Lola when she woke up the next morning, but she gave me a meaningful look when she came out of her bedroom.

"Anything you want to tell me?"

"No." I turned my attention to the eggs I was making for both of us.

"You sure?"

"Sure."

"How much sleep did you get last night?"

"An hour."

Lola snorted. "Good to see that you're taking care of yourself," she said. "Take the day off and get some rest."

"I'll have a nap later," I said. "We have too much stuff to discuss with Blake. I'll go in with you this morning."

She heaved a sigh. "Is it worth my time to argue?"

"Almost never."

Lola parked in the shade half a block from our office and we got out and started walking. We had almost reached our office when I noticed a familiar car sitting out front. I was so consumed with my thoughts of Eiko and the men who had broken into my house that I didn't register why I recognized the black SUV. It wasn't until the driver's door flew open and Serena Goff hopped out that I realized who the car belonged to. My stomach flip-flopped.

Lola and I glanced at each other, and Lola shook her head. "Don't," she warned me.

"Oh, yes," Serena said, marching toward us. "You and I are going to have a little chat."

"This isn't the time or the place," Lola said, but Serena ignored her. Her entire body was a flexed muscle, and her hands were clenched. She looked like she might tear me into two pieces, given half a chance.

"Do you know what you've done?" she jeered. "You stupid, *stupid*, fatuous little girl. You stupid woman."

I knew I shouldn't engage with her. I knew I should walk past her and go into the office, close the door, and lock it. After the last twenty-four hours, though, I had run out of patience.

"Why don't you tell me," I retorted. "Tell me what I've done."

Serena's eyes lit up. "You fucked it," she said. "I was building a relationship between Ricky and his father, and now you've fucked everything up. He just called me and said that because of you, he's ending the relationship with Ricky. What's this obsession with his father, anyway? Why do you care who Ricky's father is?"

I laughed, indignant. "Do you know anything about your son? All the drugs, all the times he's been fired? Have you seen the emails he sent around when Noa left him? Your son is a *narcissistic* . . . *psychopathic* . . . *piece of shit*. Just like you."

Serena was like a wildcat, pacing and jabbing her finger at me. I thought she might actually burst into flames.

"I'm going to ruin you," she spat, her eyes angry slits. "I will ruin everything you stand for. You stupid, fatuous little girl. You stupid, stupid woman. You think we don't know about you? About your family, how your own *parents* didn't want anything to do with you? Maybe you should just kill yourself."

Lola placed a hand on my arm, but I shook it off. I was suddenly full of hatred for this woman, for everything she stood for. Some people would look at her and see bravery, a woman who was willing to attack someone who had come for her family, but I saw the cowardice. If she were brave, she would sit down and have a rational conversation, instead of ambushing me when I was unprepared.

"Rainey, please," Lola pleaded in a low voice. "Don't engage."

"Oh, no, I want to do this," I said. I turned to Serena. "You want to chat? Let's have a *chat*."

She looked surprised for a moment, then narrowed her eyes again. "You are a stupid, silly—"

"Yes, yes, let's skip past that bit," I said, irritated. "I'm stupid and I'm fatuous. You've said all that. Let's get to the crux of your argument. Let's have it. Tell me why you're really here."

"You don't know who you're messing with—"

"Again, I've heard all this. Move past the threats and the insults."

"Look at your face," she said, jabbing her finger toward me. "Look at that little smirk."

"You know what I think?" I said. Lola was standing at my shoulder, ready to restrain me, but I ignored her. "I think that decades ago, when you were very young, someone told you that you could be special. That you were a little bit prettier and shinier and smarter than everyone around you. And you grew up thinking that you were better than everyone else, that you were going to be exceptional and that your life was going to be good, and you set your sights on big things. And you almost had your chance when you met Laszlo Zo, and you fucked him, or let him fuck you, and for about five minutes you thought, *This is it. I've made it.*"

I watched Serena's mouth open as she tried to respond, but I cut her off.

"But then he threw you away. He didn't want you; you weren't special. And you weren't a normal person, you were a narcissist, and your brain couldn't accept this. And you were left with this little baby who reminded you *every single day* that you had been treated like trash, and this was unacceptable to you. And so, you took out your rage, and your shame, and your disappointment on that little boy. And then Ricky grew up to be just like you. And that made you hate him even more, because this little boy started acting like he was better than everyone else around him. Better even than you."

Serena's face went white as she took in what I was saying. Her lips had gone bloodless, and her hands curled into claws.

"You couldn't let it go. Could you? You wouldn't let Laszlo Zo treat you like this, and you constructed a fantasy where the only reason you couldn't be together was that he was touring the world, and you were stuck here, caring for your child. And from what I've heard, you never told your son who his real father was, not until a few years ago. You only told him that he wasn't wanted. You always straddled this line between punishing your son and punishing anyone who retaliated against him. You hated him, and he hated you, but you were both all the other one had, and so while you were busy tearing each other apart, you also had to destroy everyone who threatened your little existence."

I thought she might hit me, but I kept going. I was too worked up, and I wasn't only talking to her anymore, I was talking to my own mother, who had chosen to walk away from our family.

"The worst bit is that you've decided to punish the world for how much you hate yourself," I said. "It's the worst kind of contradiction, isn't it? Hating yourself and yet thinking you deserve so much more than what the world has offered you? It must tear you apart at night, every single night, when you're alone and you have no one else to punish, and the world has left you behind. Because you've alienated every single person who has made the mistake of entering your poisonous little orbit."

I glanced behind her and saw the outline of Ricky's head in the passenger seat of his own car.

"There he is," I said. "Your beautiful little boy. You must be so proud of him. What a fucking coward, though—he sends out hundreds of threatening emails, promising to hurt everyone who crosses his path, but in the end he's too much of a fucking coward to do anything about it. His mommy fights all his battles for him. Let's go have a word."

"Rainey, *please*! Jesus Christ, stop!" Lola grabbed both of my arms, but I threw her off me. I was so full of adrenaline I thought I could have torn Ricky's face off with my bare hands. He was sitting in the car, watching me approach, like some tranquilized bear. When he saw me coming his eyes skittered around, looking for his mother, but she was still too stunned by my vitriol to break out of her trance.

"Hey! Hey, fuckwit!" I shouted. "Why don't you get out of the car and tell me about how you're going to destroy everything I hold near and dear? Huh? Too scared?"

I reached the car and grabbed the door handle, then yanked it open. Ricky just sat there, staring at me. He didn't even react.

"Are you scared of me now? You send all these emails, and you just sit there waiting for your mommy to take care of me?"

"Rainey," Lola hissed. She was standing next to me, and I hadn't even heard her approach.

"*What?*"

She led me away from the car. "Look at him," she said. "He's out of his mind on drugs. He doesn't know what you're saying. Let it go. *Let it go.* We'll beat them in court."

I glanced back at him and saw that Lola was right. Ricky's eyes were skittering around in his face, and his hands were twitching. A bit of drool dripped out of his mouth. Serena was watching us with fear. I felt a wave of disgust, both at them and myself.

"You're right," I said. "I'm done."

<hr />

Blake was waiting for us inside the office. Her eyebrows shot up when she saw my cast.

"What happened?"

"I'll explain everything," I said. "Just give me a moment."

I sat down at my desk and rested my head on my good hand. I felt disgusted at my own rage and the way I had treated Serena, even though she deserved it, even though she had tried to provoke me.

"I'm going to pretend I didn't hear all that shouting outside," she said. "But for the record, the security system has been updated, and if Serena tries to claim that you attacked her . . . we've got footage that says otherwise."

Lola came over and rubbed my back. "So we can add old-lady bashing to your set of skills now, eh? Blake, update Rainey's profile on our website."

"Go away," I mumbled.

"I told you not to say anything," Lola said, then added, "Although I will say, Serena was asking for it—she and her son keep showing up and trying to start fights. It was only a matter of time until someone gave them a beatdown."

"I can't believe I said all that." I rubbed my temples. "I'm exhausted."

"I told you to stay in bed," Lola warned.

"That's Ricky's mother?" Blake asked, leaning back in her chair. "Boy, she's . . . well, she's a piece of work."

Lola nodded. "You can say that again."

"Do you think she knows who her son is?" Blake grimaced. "I mean, she *must*. She must know. So why would she defend him?"

Lola sat down in her chair and rubbed her temples. "The pathology of narcissism is quite fascinating," she said. "Serena probably can't separate herself from her son, even though, on some level, she hates him—he still belongs to her. She sees him as an extension of herself, and if anyone attacks him, she sees it as an attack on herself. She has to defend him. In a way you almost have to feel sorry for Ricky, because he never had a chance. Monsters create monsters."

"They actually hate each other," I said. "Ricky and his mother, I mean—it's a fucked-up relationship. Noa told me all about it."

"Codependent," Lola agreed.

Blake watched me for a moment, biting her lips, then burst out laughing. She ducked her head. "I'm sorry."

"What's funny?" I asked, annoyed. "You're welcome to go out there and take a crack at her, if you like."

"I'm not laughing at you." She closed her eyes and pressed her lips together, then shook her head again. "It's really inappropriate. Please don't ask me to explain."

"Blake," Lola warned. "What's going on?"

"Okay," Blake said, wiping her eyes with the edge of her shirt. "Don't think I'm an asshole, though. You guys keep leaving me at the office and I have way too much free time." She pointed at me. "You said Ricky talks shit about his mom, but she's the only one who keeps showing up to break him out of jail, right?"

"Yeah," I said. "And?"

"I wrote a little rap yesterday," Blake said, adjusting her glasses. "But stop me right here, if you think it's inappropriate."

Lola was struggling not to smile. "Oh, go ahead."

Blake picked up a piece of paper and started softly rapping. "*Call your mom a bitch then you call her for bail, counting them dimes, can't do the time; grew up in the suburbs thought you shoulda been rich. Now your mom's retired, scraping that pension, she laid down for Zo and you call her a ho; Rick—stay in prison, bitch, you're going to jail.*"

Lola clapped, then pointed a stern finger at Blake. "Burn that piece of paper. Ricky's the type to sue."

"Aye, aye," Blake nodded. She tapped her head. "I think I've memorized it, anyway. In more important news—are you guys gonna tell me what happened last night?"

I laid my head down on my good hand and listened as Lola gave Blake a quick summary of everything that had happened after our meeting with Zo. It felt like a week since I had seen Blake, even though it had only been a few days.

When Lola was finished, I raised my head.

"There's a few other things," I said. "Blake, I need you to see if you can find out anything about someone named Mary Ecclestone. I don't have much information about her, but I know that she spent some time in hospitals. She was an artist, and at some point, Ian Rhodes painted her."

Lola and Blake listened, stunned, as I mentioned my visit to Dolores Rhodes and Rhodes's scrapbooks of all the men he had slept with.

"You think someone paid Rhodes to sleep with these politicians and blackmail them?" Lola finally said.

"I think they got him hooked on drugs, and when his art career faltered, he didn't have many other options," I said.

The room was silent for a moment, a calm that was broken by the sound of Blake typing.

"There you go," she said. "I found your Mary."

I sat up straight, stunned. "Jesus, I think that's a new record for you."

"Not really!" Blake laughed. "I just typed her name plus 'artist' into Google."

Lola and I crowded around Blake's computer. Her screen showed an archived article from the *LA Times*.

Artist Creates with Animal Bones, read the headline.

Mary Ecclestone lives in a former chapel overlooking a cemetery, the article read. *She draws a lot of inspiration from her perished neighbors, she claims, but her inspiration also comes from living in a chapel that was once a safehouse for women running away from abusive relationships. The Glendale neighborhood hosts many other historic buildings that most people might not know about, including a former dentist's office run by a man who gave abortions in his basement. Further down the road is a one-time stable; you can still see the wooden outlines where the horses were kept.*

There was a single photograph of Mary, and it was black and white. She stood in front of her house, cupping one elbow, smoking a cigarette. Her eyes were downcast, and she looked frail. Her skin was pale, almost translucent, and there were shadows under her eyes. Her arms were thin, too thin in relation to the rest of her body.

"I'll see if I can find anything else about her," Blake offered.

"Thanks, Blake," I said.

"I'll call the forensics team who were here a few days ago," Lola said. "We'll see if they can get prints from your house. They might be the same people who broke into our office."

TWENTY-NINE

I didn't have proof that Calder had been the one who sent Lucas and Simon to my house to rough me up, but the timing was suspicious because they had shown up right after I called him. Even if Calder was innocent of that particular infraction, though, I had more questions for him.

I wanted to drive straight over to Calder's studio and question him, but to be safe, I decided to wait until evening. Business hours would be over, and there would be a better chance of catching him alone. I didn't want a stray customer listening in to our conversation.

"I'll drive you," Lola said. "You're fresh out of the hospital, and I don't want him to come at you sideways when you start making accusations."

"Have you ever seen Calder?" I raised an eyebrow. "There's nothing menacing about him."

"Still."

We hung around the office until seven, then headed over. Calder's neighborhood was quiet when Lola pulled up outside his studio.

"Do you want me to come with you?" Lola asked.

I thought for a long moment. "I'm not sure it's a good idea," I said. "If there are two of us, Calder might not be willing to say anything. If I go in alone, I might be able to get him to talk."

She glanced at my broken hand. "You sure?"

"I've known Calder for twenty years," I said. "Even if he wanted to kill me, I know where all his soft spots are."

I took out my phone and opened a recording device.

"You know that won't be admissible in court," Lola said, then sighed. "I hate to be a lawyer right now, but it's actually illegal to record someone without their consent."

"Calder doesn't need to know that," I said. "There are people he's more scared of than me."

I walked up to the front of the studio, then opened the door and stepped inside without knocking. I could hear humming out back and followed it to the workshop, where I found Calder sitting at his desk.

I cleared my throat, and he jumped, nearly falling out of his seat.

"Hi, Calder," I said.

When he saw me standing there, he calmed down slightly, but there was still something wary in his look.

"Oh, Rainey," he said. "It's you. You scared me."

"Expecting someone else?"

"I'm in the middle of working on something," he said. "It's not a great time."

He looked pale. There were dark circles under his eyes, and it looked like he hadn't slept well in days. I knew Calder was fond of parties and staying out until daybreak; it was part of how he maintained his grip on the social aspect of the art world in Los Angeles. This was something else: Calder looked haunted.

"You look tired," I pointed out. "Everything okay?"

"I'm on some new medication," he said, irritated.

I waited for a few seconds, then held up my injured hand. "You're not going to ask about this?"

He blinked, then looked at me. "Okay," he said reluctantly. "What happened?"

"I think you already know."

Calder immediately whirled on me. "If you're going to come in here and start leveling accusations, leave! Just leave!"

I flinched at his anger but reminded myself that Calder potentially had information I needed. I had worked with enough artists to have seen dozens of adult tantrums—people throwing a fit because they couldn't handle their emotions, because they were triggered and wanted to lash out—and I wasn't going to be put off by it. There was too much at stake. I walked past him and sat on his couch.

Calder went to his fridge and grabbed a can of Coke. He was keeping his distance.

"I didn't see you at Spencer's funeral," I said.

Calder scoffed. "Why would I go? I wasn't friends with her."

"There were a lot of people from the art world there," I said.

"So it was a networking event? Big deal. As if I need the connections."

"I think I can imagine why you're scared," I said. "There have been some deaths, and you're wondering if you're going to be next."

"Threats won't work on me, Rainey."

"We've been friends for a long time, Calder," I said, trying a softer tone. "You helped my mother with her career."

"And?"

"Sometimes I don't think you get enough credit," I said. "The gallerist is always in the background, isn't he? The artist gets all the accolades, but what most people don't realize is that an artist couldn't exist without a platform. Without someone who believes in her."

Calder sniffed, but I could see the praise was working. "Matilda was a brilliant artist," he said. "Broke my heart when she gave it all up."

"You put so much work into shaping her career," I said. "And then she gave it all away."

"It was ungrateful," he said.

"The same thing happened with Spencer," I said. "You tried to help her, didn't you?"

He was watching me, guarded.

"Calder," I said, leaning against his counter. "How much do you know?"

He didn't move or say anything for a long moment. "I'm sorry, Rainey," he said. "But you need to leave. And maybe you shouldn't come see me for a while."

"I think the police might be interested to know why you tried to buy all of Ian Rhodes's artwork just before his death was reported on the news," I said. Calder scoffed.

"You and I know that artwork becomes more valuable after the death of the artist," I said. "They'll probably want to know how you knew that he was dead before it was announced."

"You need to leave," he said.

"Did you know that she had security cameras?" I asked. "Rhodes's sister, I mean." It was a bluff, but I could tell by the look on Calder's face that he believed me.

"I don't know anything about Ian's death," he said. "I knew talent when I saw it, that's all. That's why I went to her house and tried to buy the artwork."

"The timing's off," I said.

Calder's mouth twitched. "I heard rumors," he said. "That's it. I wanted to protect his legacy. Make sure nobody forgot him."

"And Eiko?"

"I don't know anything about that," he said, raising his hands in self-defense. "I heard rumors about that, too, but I try to keep out of it. I'm here to sell art, Rainey. You should know that better than anyone. I made your mother into a star."

"Eiko's dead, though, isn't she?"

"Those kids were idiots," Calder said. "They should have kept their noses clean and focused on their art."

I nodded, not trusting myself to say anything else.

"I can help you," I said.

He burst out laughing. "Help me how? I don't need your help, Rainey."

I took my phone out of my pocket. It took him a moment to understand, and then his face collapsed.

"Fuck you, Rainey," he said. His voice was quiet, dangerous. "You come into my studio and threaten me?"

"It's not a threat," I said.

"I know a threat when I see one," he said. "You know, they wanted to kill you. I told them that you were off-limits. I *protected* you. And this is the thanks I get?"

He was moving toward me. I held my ground, even though my heart had started pounding a crazy rhythm.

"We can help each other," I said. "You know too much. It's only a matter of time before they come for you, too."

Calder was quiet for a long time. "What do you want from me, Rainey?"

"I know about the parties," I said. "I need you to get me in."

His face went pale as he listened to me. "I can't help you," he said.

"No?"

"They'll kill me first," he said. "Look what happened to you. What do you think is going to happen when I help a private investigator break into their little club? They'll do worse than kill me, Rainey. You have no idea . . . *no idea* what you're messing with."

"What happens if I walk away? This is going to keep happening. People are going to keep going missing—vulnerable people, Calder. Poor artists. Street kids. People like you and me."

Calder burst into nervous laughter. "We have nothing in common, Rainey—*I* did it all by myself."

I didn't take the bait. I knew that Calder was lashing out because he was scared, and I couldn't blame him. My phone rang, and I glanced at the screen. *Noa Cohen.* I hesitated, then rejected the call.

"You're fucking nuts, you know that?" His voice was low, scared. "You can't get in there. What are you going to do once you get past the doors? You'll never walk out again."

"Let me worry about that. Can you get me in?"

He narrowed his eyes and frowned, then looked down his nose at me. "What if I can't? What are you going to do?"

I waved my phone at him. "Go to the police, I suppose. Play them the recording of our conversation."

"You would do that to me? Really?"

"If you're going to let these people keep doing what they're doing, I don't know why I should protect you."

The phone rang again. *Noa.* I hit Reject.

He was quiet, thinking about what I had said.

"They're at the Stanislas, aren't they? The parties."

He glanced up sharply. "Where did you hear that?"

"It doesn't matter," I said. "Yes or no?"

Calder chewed on his bottom lip and sulked. "Yes. You didn't hear that from me!"

I thought for a moment. "When did they start? How long have these parties been going on?"

"You give me a lot of credit, Rainey," Calder growled. "I already told you, I've never been to one of these parties."

"But you know."

He threw his hands in the air. "What do you want?"

"You really don't care, do you? That people are dying or going missing, and a few rich people are getting away with it?"

He gave me a long, hateful look. "I've heard rumors for a few years," he said. "Some rich people get together, do drugs. Sometimes they wear costumes. It's not as bad as you're making it out to be."

"Why the secrecy?"

He laughed, incredulous. "You think they should sell tickets? So anyone off the street could walk in? It's a group of friends. Do you have any idea what kind of debauchery goes on in most of the houses in Los Angeles? Don't be a prude."

"I'm talking about these specific parties," I said, tapping the palm of my hand. I refused to let him rile me up. "Between artists and wealthy patrons. There's a power dynamic there. You can't deny it."

He waved a dismissive hand at me.

"Do you know who Ricky Goff is?"

The look of confusion on Calder's face was too convincing to be fake.

"He makes drugs," I prompted. "Morphy."

Calder snorted. "Okay."

"You've heard of it."

Calder was having trouble meeting my eye. "Fine, so what?"

"People are dying because they're taking an unregulated drug," I said. "And the people who are dying don't have anyone to fight for them, because some of them don't have families. This is going to keep happening."

Calder chewed a fingernail.

"When's the next party?"

"I don't know anything about it."

"*Calder.*"

"Tomorrow," he said. "It's not enough time to get a plan together."

"You let me worry about that." I scrutinized Calder's face. He looked defeated, and I knew I had him.

A text from Noa came through. *Emergency.*

"What are the keys?" I asked, glancing up at Calder.

Calder glanced up. "What?"

I took out my phone and opened up my photos. Even though the keys had been taken from me, I had had the foresight to take a few photos. When Calder saw the image, he closed his eyes and shook his head.

"I can't believe you've gotten this far," he said. "You're good, Rainey, I have to give you that."

"What are they?" I asked. "What do they unlock?"

"Nothing," Calder said, then shook his head and sighed. He looked deflated. "They're a passcode to get into the club. They're from the old hotel, years ago, before the reconstruction."

"So they have nothing to do with rooms?"

"I don't think so. I have a key. They gave me a key because I represent so many artists, but . . . I've never *gone* to one of these parties. It's not my scene."

"So you've got a key? You can get us in?" I asked.

"They'll kill you," he said. "They'll kill me, too."

"You'd better make sure I get them first," I said. "Can you do it?"

Calder looked gray. For as long as I had known him he had looked ageless, but now it looked like the years had caught up with him. Everything about him drooped: his skin, his neck, his posture. He finally nodded. "I can do it," he said.

I called Noa back as I walked toward the front of Calder's studio. Her phone went straight to voicemail. Concerned, I tried calling back. Voicemail again.

I stepped outside and saw Lola standing on the curb, outside the car. She was talking into her phone, animated, and when she glanced up and saw me, something like terror contorted her features.

"She's here," she said into the phone. "I'll tell her. We'll come and meet you."

"Lola, *what?*" I asked, already fearing the worst.

"That was Noa," she said. "It's Ricky. His house is on fire, and he and Serena are locked inside."

THIRTY

———❧———

I could hear the sirens before we even got off the freeway. It was just past sunset, and the heat of the day still lingered. The sky was a bruised indigo, the dying sunlight tangled in the clouds over the horizon, and the whole tableau blended into a kind of nightmare landscape before my eyes. Lola's hands gripped the steering wheel and she stared straight ahead. Neither of us had to speak to articulate what we were both thinking: *They did this, they did this, they did this.*

We neared Ricky's street, and then I could see the flames. A barricade of fire engines and police cars blocked off the section of road near the fire, and neighbors drifted out of their houses to witness the inferno. I was having trouble breathing. The smell of smoke brought me back to the summer Alice disappeared, when people convened in public places to look around with dazed expressions. *What would you save, Rainey?* Shared catastrophe stripped away the illusion of distance.

"I'll park here," Lola said, and she had to repeat herself twice for me to hear her. Everything was too loud—the sirens, the cacophony of voices, and the fire itself. You can't realize how loud fire is until you're confronted with it—more than the heat and the terror of the thing, the noise is the most confronting element of a conflagration. It's a wild, hungry snapping, a destructive roar.

Lola kept her hand on my arm as we moved down the street, toward where the police had made a barricade to prevent anyone from getting closer.

"There she is," Lola said, pointing. "There's Noa."

Noa stood by the barricade, her arms wrapped around herself. She rocked from side to side, then pressed her hands to the thin metal stands that had been set up to block access. There was no movement from inside the house, and a trio of firefighters aimed their hoses at the lawn, trying to contain the flames. I couldn't hear anything but snatches of voices, truncated words that flew about with no clear source.

We reached Noa and I touched her shoulder. She spun around, eyes wild, her mouth a dark square. Her skin was flushed with the heat, and she almost didn't seem to recognize me. We were a safe distance from the fire, and yet it seemed that at any moment the flames would reach out and consume everything around us.

"Ricky!" Noa yelled. She grabbed my arms. "It's Ricky! He's still inside!"

I felt sick then, looking at the house. The structure of the house was still visible, though flames covered the roof and poured out of windows. It looked like a pencil sketch, a child's idea of a house, and it seemed impossible that the foundations could withstand such powerful flames.

"And Serena? Where's Serena?" I yelled back. I had a sickening thought, then—Taylor, Noa's son. "What about Taylor?"

Tears coursed down Noa's face. "He's safe, he's with a friend!" she had to repeat herself before I could make out the words. "Serena's still inside!"

"Why aren't they trying to save them!" I could hear the strain in my own voice.

"The doors!" Noa yelled. "Someone nailed the doors shut! They can't get inside!"

She locked eyes with me for a moment, and then turned and vomited on the street. I felt it then, too—the awful reality of what was happening all around us. Ricky and Serena were trapped inside a burning house. We were watching them burn to death. I looked at Lola, then dropped my hands to my knees and closed my eyes. *Don't do it, don't do it*—I vomited at the edge of the barricade. Lola immediately rushed to my side and grabbed me. Noa moved away from us, toward the house.

"We need to get out of here," Lola said.

"No," I said, squeezing my eyes shut. "We have to stay with Noa."

When I had regained my strength, I stood up and walked to the edge of the barricade, standing next to Noa. The three of us watched the house gradually buckle and disintegrate, folding beneath the weight of the flames, until finally there was nothing left.

Two hours later, when the flames had dwindled down to a manageable blaze, Serena's house was nothing but a crumpled heap of stone and shingles. I had dry heaved two more times before the nausea abated, but even then, I felt hollowed out and achy. Noa looked shell-shocked, and even though Lola kept trying to get her to leave, she refused.

"I have to know," she said. "I have to see it for myself."

It was almost ten P.M. before the firefighters brought the fire down enough that they could break through Serena's front door. I waited with bated breath as a team of four people in protective gear barged into the remains of the house. The smoke swallowed them whole, and it felt like a small eternity elapsed before they came out again. Each pair of people carried something between them, black and twisted. It took me ten whole seconds before I realized I was looking at two human bodies, charred beyond recognition. One large—Ricky, I could only assume—and one smaller form—Serena.

"Noa," Lola snapped. "We're going. You don't need to see this."

But it was too late; she had already seen. The gasp that came out of her mouth started as a whining keen, like a breath blowing over a reed instrument, high and nasal. As Lola grappled with Noa and tried to usher her away from the scene, the scream became inhuman. It was a devastated roar. She scrabbled against Lola's grasp, trying to get away.

A female police officer saw what was happening and approached. She was young, with a smattering of freckles.

"Everything okay, ma'am?"

"She's having a panic attack," Lola said, her voice taut with worry. "That's her ex-husband."

The police officer slipped an arm around Noa's waist and nodded to Lola, who stepped back. The woman escorted Noa toward the ambulance parked just beyond the police barricade, and we watched as a paramedic helped Noa sit down.

Lola turned to look at me. Exhaustion was written across her features, and her hair had gone wild with the smoke and heat.

"Talk to me," she said.

I gestured toward the house. "We already know that Ricky was the one making drugs," I said. "Morphy. The only thing we don't know is who his client was."

"Well, Simon Balto, right?" Lola rubbed a hand across her face. "That's what all the evidence points to."

I nodded. "Yeah," I said, even though I wasn't quite sure. "Yeah, I think that's pretty clear at this point."

"And he's started killing people off," Lola said.

"Him or someone else," I pointed out. "We can't be sure either way, not yet."

"Do we think he's responsible for all of it?" Lola sounded doubtful. "Spencer, Rhodes—now this?"

"I think it's out of our hands now," I said. "I think we have to go to the police."

Lola gestured toward the officers standing around the barricade, but I shook my head.

"No," I said. "Let's talk to Casey Lennon. I don't want to have to explain this from scratch."

The next morning we headed to the Hollywood police station to see Casey and tell her everything. It was hard to read Casey's expression as Lola and I told her about what had happened the previous evening. Lola pitched in with the occasional detail but, for the most part, let me explain everything. Casey waited until we were finished, then nodded and folded her hands together.

"Okay," she said. It looked like she was weighing her reaction. "That's quite a story. You're saying that two men have been leaving you threatening messages and breaking into private property—and now you think they might be responsible for the fire in Sherman Oaks last night?"

"That's right." I glanced at Lola.

She spread her hands on the table and raised her eyebrows. "First—none of this is in my jurisdiction. I work in Hollywood. The burglaries happened in Culver City and Griffith Park. The fire was in Sherman Oaks. Also, I'm not a detective. Why are you coming to me with this?"

"Because I know you," I said. "Kind of. We've already spoken about the cases that I'm working on."

"Fair call," Casey said. "But all I can do is report it up the ladder. It's a different jurisdictional matter."

I nodded and tried to tamp down my frustration.

She glanced at my hand. "What happened there?"

"Self-defense during the break-in."

"Why not report it at the time?"

"I had to go to the hospital," I said.

"There are police at the hospital."

I glanced at Lola, then looked back at Casey. Her expression wasn't unfriendly or forbidding but perplexed.

"We had to weigh the consequences of what might happen if we called in the police," I said. "We didn't want to be premature. There are people's lives at stake."

Casey's face was hard to read.

"Have you ever heard of a drug called Morphy?" I asked.

The look on her face was indecipherable, and for a moment I thought she might not answer.

"The better question," she said slowly, "is how *you* know about Morphy."

"I know that it's a drug made from the datura plant," I said. "It's made in Los Angeles. Popular with artists and other creative types."

"Uh-huh." She scrutinized me for a moment. "Anything else?"

"Are you looking into it already?"

"We sure are," she said. "Not many people know about it."

I glanced at Lola. We had quickly talked about all the things that we would mention to Casey, and had disagreed about Morphy. She hadn't wanted to bring it into the conversation, thinking I might get in trouble, but had reluctantly agreed when I argued that it was part of the bigger picture.

"This is a dangerous drug, and not just for the people who use it," Casey went on. "One of the unfortunate side effects is a tendency toward violence. It's when the brain goes to sleep. The user gets a surge of cortisol, and some people lash out."

I remembered the article about Rhodes biting someone on the street in Venice.

Casey took out a folder and then removed a picture. She hesitated before setting the photo in front of me. It was a dead woman, flat on her back in a kitchen. Her face had been smashed so badly that all that remained were the edges of her face—skull, ears, hairline—and a lower rim of teeth. Her body looked so relaxed I wondered if she had died instantly. It took me a moment to realize that her dress had originally been pale green, not crimson. It was stained with blood.

"Rosie Wilson," Officer Lennon said. "A waitress with three children. Married to a tennis instructor. This was from three days ago."

"Why are you showing me this?" The photo made me feel ill; I wanted to look away. I wondered how they had identified her, since there was nothing left of her face.

"Because you're not a cop," she said, and her voice was very gentle. "I don't want you to get in over your head. This is what happens to people who get wrapped up in this stuff."

"Okay," I said. I was rattled. "Understood."

I took out my phone and retrieved the texts from my anonymous informant. Casey took the phone and read through them, her brow furrowing as she went down.

"What's this?"

"I think I'm on the edge of something really big," I said.

"Who are these texts from?" Casey asked.

"I don't know."

"And Eiko Mars?"

"She's an artist who went missing."

Casey exhaled and leaned back in her chair. "You know you sound like a conspiracy nut, right?"

"You've already been looking into Morphy," I said. "You must already know there's a link between the drug and dead artists."

Casey handed me my phone.

"Okay," she said. "I'll send some people over to your house this morning and get some forensic evidence. Is there any other information you're willing to share with me? Anything that can help me with a search warrant or an arrest?"

I glanced at Lo. Her expression was closed, and she gave me a little shake of her head.

"That's it," I said.

Casey looked disappointed, but she finally nodded. "You have my number," she said. "Try not to get killed before we talk again."

When Lola and I emerged into the sunlight, I blinked and shielded my eyes.

"It's not enough," I said. "I don't know what they're going to be able to do without solid proof."

"We had to try," Lola said.

"We need to call Max Hailey," I said. "I'll call him and arrange for him to meet with us and Blake this afternoon."

"Why Hailey?" Her tone was skeptical.

"Because if we get killed, I need someone to write about it."

THIRTY-ONE

Hailey suggested we meet up at his office that afternoon to go over the details of our plan. The *LA Lens* was on the second floor of an old Spanish Colonial building just off Sunset Boulevard, in the heart of Hollywood. The courtyard was shaded with palm trees, and the whole complex had a pleasant air of decay.

"It's haunted," Hailey told us when he met us at the front door.

"What's that now?" Blake asked.

"A few people have died here," Hailey said. "Old Hollywood types. We get the occasional Haunted Hollywood tour. No one's here on Saturdays, so we should have the place to ourselves. Other than the ghosts, of course . . ."

We followed him into the lobby, and he punched the elevator key. "Good timing," he said, looking at Blake's wheelchair. "We only got it fixed last month. Damn thing breaks twice a year."

Hailey was right; the *Lens* offices were empty. The publication took up the entire second floor of the building, and I glanced around with curiosity as we walked through the lobby. The rooms were an odd hodgepodge of aesthetics and artifacts, with posters and news clippings all over the walls.

"In here," Hailey said. "We can use the conference room."

Even though I had taken a nap that afternoon, I was still tired. "Do you have coffee?" I asked Hailey.

"Oh, yes," he said. "Of course, I'll go make some."

Lola and Blake got settled at one side of the conference room table, and I sat down across from them. I was too nervous to sit still, though, so I stood up and walked over to the window. Venetian blinds partially hid the street from view, but I could see two women on the street below. One was posing as the other one took photographs of her.

"Here," Hailey said, returning with a tray of coffee cups.

"Thanks," Blake said, reaching for a cup.

"Right, then," Hailey said, rubbing his hands together. "What's the plan?"

I hadn't told him much on the phone, because I was still paranoid that someone might be watching us.

"There's a trail of bodies now," I said. "Spencer, Rhodes, and now Ricky. And his mother, I guess, but I doubt she was involved. That's only confirmed deaths—we might have to count Eiko Mars and Chloe Delmonico, but I'm hoping they're still alive."

"And you're operating on the theory that they're all connected?" Hailey confirmed.

"I think the same people are behind all of this," I said. "Making and distributing Morphy, then killing people off once they become an issue."

"And what are we going to do about it?" Hailey asked.

"There are parties," I said. "Where artists do Morphy. I talked Calder into taking me along as his guest."

Hailey's eyebrows shot up. "Jesus, how'd you manage that?"

I gave him a grim smile. "I made a strong case."

"Where do I fit in?"

"I was hoping you might want to come to the party," I said. "It's really dangerous, though, so I understand if you don't want to."

Lola glanced at Hailey. "There's a chance you'll both be killed."

He nodded, listening, and then whistled. "Where are the parties?"

"The Hotel Stanislas. It's in Downtown Los Angeles."

Hailey thought for a long moment. "This is a chance for us to witness the parties where artists keep overdosing," he said. "We can find out if our theories are right."

"And who's behind them, hopefully," I said.

"I don't think I can turn that down."

"Calder's taking us," I said, relieved and gratified that he had agreed. "We'll meet him at the studio at six, and we'll head over to the Stanislas together."

"You heard me say you might die, right?" Lola asked.

"Yes."

"Covered all my bases, then," Lola said.

"There's a dress code, obviously," I said. I felt skittish, listening to every sound and creaking stair as though someone might be about to jump in and attack us at any moment. "It's black tie. Anything less formal and you'll stick out. Is that an issue?"

"I've got a tux," Hailey said.

"Have we decided on timing?" Blake asked. "At what point do we call the police?"

"We're going in at nine," I said. "We'll be in and out in an hour. Calder will be there too. I don't think we'll be able to keep our cell phones with us, because I imagine they'll be confiscated at the door. We'll get in touch as soon as we're back outside."

"And if we don't hear from you after an hour and a half, we'll get in touch as soon as we're back outside."

"Maybe give it a fifteen-minute window," I suggested. "Just in case."

"You have a contact with the police, right?" Hailey asked.

"Yes," I confirmed. "Casey Lennon at the Hollywood station. We'll call her first if things go sideways."

"Does she have any idea that you're doing this?"

"No," I said. "Because I think she'd have to stop it from happening. She's a cop, after all."

"You know why we can't go to the cops now, right?" Blake asked Hailey. "Because police have to do things in a certain order, and if any part of that gets fucked up, we'll lose our chance to find Alice—and Chloe too, if she's still alive. Right now, the cops don't have enough to get a search warrant, and if they start scrabbling around to get one, the people running this thing will have time to cover their tracks."

"We've told them a small bit of the story," I said. "We told them that we think Simon might be behind the arson at Ricky's house. We just left out the part about the Hotel Stanislas and the secret parties."

"Got it," Hailey nodded.

"I feel the need to reiterate one more time that you might die," Lola said.

Hailey bit back a smile. "Understood," he said. "I need to go home and change."

Three hours later, I pulled up in front of Calder's studio. I was nervous, but also excited: there was a chance that I was finally going to find out what had happened to Alice. I wore the floor-length silk dress I had worn to the opening gala of the Kloos Museum, and even though I hadn't worn it in years, I was pleased that it still fit me like a glove. Disguising my cast had been an irritating issue—I tried to wear a pair of black gloves, but they wouldn't fit over the plaster. I ultimately decided to go with a drapey shawl that only detracted from my outfit in a minor way.

As I walked toward Calder's studio, I noticed that Hailey was standing outside. He leaned against the building, one foot up against the wall, and frowned down at his phone. He wore a tuxedo and expensive-looking dress shoes, in contrast to the T-shirts and slacks he normally wore, but it still took me a moment to realize why he looked so different. He looked up and saw me, then smiled.

"No glasses," I said. "And you parted your hair on the side . . . ?"

"Right," he said, patting his pockets. "I can't see anything. I hope the disguise is worth it."

I blushed, trying to think of a response, but he laughed and waved his hand at me. "I'm kidding," he said. "I've got contacts in. I didn't think the glasses went with the tux. You look nice," he added.

"So do you." I smiled and looked at my feet. I didn't know if it was appropriate for me to hug him. I settled instead for squeezing his hand, and to my surprise, he laced his fingers through mine.

"Are you okay?"

"I'm nervous," I admitted. "I'm scared I'm going to mess this up."

"You won't," he said.

"What if we die?" I asked, feeling my chest constrict. "Who's going to write about this?"

"I sent an email to my editor and let her know what I was doing," he said. "She knows everything that I do now. The police will have enough to go in and look for us."

The studio door opened and Calder stepped out. The dark circles under his eyes had gotten even darker, but at least he had made the effort of wearing a nice suit.

"Calder, do you remember Max Hailey?"

Calder gave Hailey a withering look. "I shouldn't be surprised," he said. "I knew you were bad news the moment I saw you."

Hailey gave a modest shrug. "You have good instincts," he said.

"Yeah, yeah. Let's go."

Calder was unusually quiet as he drove us to Downtown Los Angeles. I was too nervous to make conversation, and Hailey looked like he was lost in his thoughts. I finally spoke up, looking at Calder.

"I know you resent me for this, but I wouldn't have gotten you involved if I had another choice," I said.

Calder just glanced at me.

"These aren't good people," I reminded him.

Calder scoffed. "You're one to judge?"

"I didn't say that," I said. "But I'm not doing this for me."

He was shaking his head. "You're both going to die tonight," he said. "We're all going to die tonight."

"Calder," I warned. "Calm down. *Calm down.* This is almost over."

"You don't know that."

"It's almost over," Hailey said from the backseat. "All we need is one thing, one sign of illegal activity, and we can get the police involved."

I watched Calder hover on the edge of a nervous breakdown for the entire drive into Downtown Los Angeles. By the time we reached the Hotel Stanislas, I was a wreck of nerves myself. Calder parked, and Hailey took my arm and squeezed my hand.

"Are you okay?"

"He's making me nervous," I said.

"We'll be fine," he said, and his voice was so decisive that I almost believed him.

⸺

It felt like a dream. I was so high on adrenaline that I thought I might faint, and my heart was pounding so hard that I felt like I might collapse. I held onto Hailey's arm just to have something to ground myself, and even though I was grasping him so tightly it must have hurt, he didn't say anything. I was convinced that Paula and Juan would pop out at any moment and grab me, and so I tucked my head down and hid behind Hailey. The crowd made me feel almost invisible.

Calder led us through a side entrance of the bar and then pointed to a table.

"Sit there," he said. "I'll go give them the password."

"I'll go with you," Hailey said.

Calder gave him a sour look. "I don't need babysitting."

"Nevertheless," Hailey replied, his voice kind.

"I'm coming too," I said.

"Jesus Christ. Fine, we'll all go. Happy?" Calder threw his hands in the air.

We approached the bar, and after a moment the bartender materialized. It was a young man I hadn't seen before, which was a relief. I was altogether too aware of the fact that this plan was tenuous; if someone recognized me, there was a chance the whole thing could crumble, irretrievably broken.

"What can I get for you this fine evening?" the bartender asked. I watched his face—smooth, impassive—and wondered how much he knew of what went on behind the walls.

"A sidecar and two French 75s," Calder said. "Can you have them delivered to our room?"

"Which room is that?"

Calder reached into his pocket and placed something on the counter. It was an old key, identical to the ones that Juan had taken from me. The bartender glanced down at the key and gave a slight nod, but other than that, there was no recognition. He was good; I had to give him that.

"Very well, sir," he said. "I'll make the drinks and then escort you up to your room."

I tried to focus on details of the room while the bartender made the drinks. *It couldn't possibly be that easy*, I thought; I must have missed something. There was the possibility, too, that Calder had managed to slip a code word in and alert the bartender to the fact that we were spies. Any minute now, Juan was going to swoop in and force us back into his office, or maybe they would just shut the bar and kill us there, oh god, *oh god* . . .

"Here you are," the bartender said, placing the drinks on the tray. "I'll escort you to your room so you don't have to carry these."

We followed the bartender down the narrow hall leading to the kitchen. To the right were the bathrooms, and to the left was a narrow, old-fashioned elevator I hadn't noticed before. The bartender pushed the Up button, and we waited in silence for the elevator to appear. After what felt like a small eternity, the doors yawned open, and we stepped inside. Once the doors closed again, the bartender handed the drink tray to Calder and took a set of keys out of his pocket. He unlocked a panel below the illuminated floor buttons, then inserted a second key into a lock with a number pad, into which he typed a code.

"Drink?" Calder asked, offering the tray to Hailey. Hailey shook his head, and Calder shrugged, then downed both coupes of champagne. He sipped the sidecar and leaned against the back of the elevator as we began to descend. It took me a moment to realize that we weren't going up, even though I was sure that the bartender had pressed the Up button.

The bartender was watching me with a little smile. "First time?"

"What makes you say that?"

"Oh, I can usually tell."

The elevator stopped moving and the doors opened once more. The darkness of the basement yawned into the distance, and the temperature dropped a few degrees. I couldn't hear anything, no voices or music, nothing to indicate we were about to attend a secret party. Everything felt wrong, and my body went cold with dread.

"I'll need your cell phones," the bartender said.

Hailey glanced at me.

"Nonnegotiable," the bartender added.

Hailey hesitated, then took his phone out and gave it to the man.

"Go on," the bartender said to me. "I have to get back to work."

With a sense of dread, I took my phone out of my pocket and gave it to him. Calder finished the sidecar, then handed the tray and the empty glasses to the man, followed by his cell phone. His face was flushed, and I realized how nervous he was. I didn't want to know what was waiting for us in the darkness beyond. I felt myself collapse back against the wall of the elevator, and the bartender made a small sound of irritation.

"Well?" he said.

Hailey's hand was on my shoulder then, and I glanced up at him. He nodded, almost imperceptibly, and for some reason I felt just a tiny bit fortified by the gesture.

"Okay. Okay, Calder." I stepped out of the elevator, and a moment later Calder and Hailey followed behind. A vast space telescoped into the distance, and somewhere water was dripping. I watched the bartender disappear as the elevator doors slid shut, and then there was a mechanical hum as it ascended once more, back into the hotel.

"How do we get back out of here?" Hailey asked.

Calder gave a nervous chuckle. "You're worried about getting out? Maybe you should be more worried about staying in one piece."

Hailey slowly exhaled through his nose. "Okay," he said. "What's next? Where do we go?"

"That way," Calder said, pointing into the darkness. A single light was illuminated on the far side of the room, a faint lamp that seemed to float out in midair.

"We'll follow you," Hailey said.

Something occurred to me then. "Calder," I said. "You told me you've never been to one of these parties. Why does it seem like you've done this before?"

He shot me a look of disgust. "I'm an art dealer, Rainey," he snapped. "People tell me stories. I've heard about the parties, I told you that. I can assure you that's the extent of it."

My entire body felt like an electrical conduit, highly aware of the slightest sound or movement. If something was going to happen to us—someone springing out of the darkness with a weapon, for example—Calder didn't seem too concerned. He weaved slightly as he moved through the darkness, toward the light, and then finally we were standing in front of a metal door.

"Last chance," Calder said. "Last chance to back out."

"Go on," Hailey said.

"Suit yourself," Calder said, then opened the door. A set of carpeted stairs unspooled beyond, leading up. I could hear the faintest sounds of music, jazz or big band, something sweet and lively. For some reason the joy in the music made the fact of what we were about to do all the more haunting. I shivered.

"You okay?" Hailey asked quietly, putting his hand on my elbow.

"I'm fine," I said.

The music grew louder as we reached the top of the stairs. I knew the song, too: "Deep Purple" by Artie Shaw. It was a song I had always loved, and as the music got louder, I knew I would never again be able to listen to this song without thinking of this night.

We reached the top of the stairs and I realized where we were. We were standing in the lobby of the old Red Door theater, but it wasn't derelict at all, not falling apart as I had thought. It looked like we had stepped back in time to the 1930s: all the carpet was new and fresh, and the ceiling swelled above us with twinkling lights meant to look like stars. Double staircases led up to an upper level, and a young woman in an old-timey theater uniform and cap stood in the glass ticket booth. She smiled when we approached.

"Welcome and good evening," she said. "You won't mind if I search you?"

I nodded and she stepped out and patted us down efficiently.

"Go on through," she said. "The party's in full swing."

THIRTY-TWO

—❦—

I could see the bones of the old ballroom as we entered through the swinging doors and the party materialized before us. It was almost too much for me to take in—the ritual of the keys, the underground passage, the old theater present behind all the decay—but I tried to glance around and remember as much as I could, so that if we made it out of there alive, I would be able to share as many details as possible with the police.

The decaying front of the Red Door was clearly a façade to keep prying eyes away from the heart of the old theater, which had been restored to its previous glory as an old ballroom. I had seen the photos in some of the articles during my research; the Edwardian ballroom with its stained-glass ceilings was once the pride of the Hotel Stanislas. Valentino had danced here, as had Fred Astaire and Ginger Rogers. Now, though, the stage was occupied by a lively band that was dancing to entertain a crowd of well-dressed people and beautiful young men and women.

Hailey and I followed Calder to the edge of the room. The music and dancing were loud enough that I didn't think we would be overheard, but I kept my voice down just in case.

"Let's split up," I suggested.

"What's the plan?" Hailey asked.

"I'm going to see if I can get upstairs," I said. "That's where the old hotel rooms were."

"I thought they were gone," Hailey said. "Didn't they all burn down years ago?"

"Maybe," I said. "But whoever went to all the trouble to restore the old ballroom obviously had enough cash to restore the hotel rooms, too." I turned to Calder. "Do you know how to get up there?"

He raised his hands in a helpless gesture. "I've never been here," he said. "I have standards, you know."

"What do you want me to do?" Hailey asked me.

"Keep an eye out," I said. "If you see anyone coming after me, try to stall them."

Calder was watching the dance floor.

"You stay here," I told him. "Help Hailey, in case things go sideways."

I thought he might shoot back a sarcastic remark, but he seemed relieved not to have to do anything. I detached myself from the wall and walked around the edge of the party, scanning for a way to get upstairs and also for anyone who might recognize me. So far, I had only seen strangers, mostly older men dancing with younger men and women. Some couples had broken off from the crowd and gone to drape themselves along couches at the edge of the room, where they were openly fondling each other. There was something nightmarish and grotesque about the scene in front of me, and I reminded myself to stay focused: get in, get out, stay alive.

I was almost to the bar when I spotted Simon Balto speaking to a young woman who stood against the wall. I ducked and spun around to face the other way, then crouched behind a pair of ornate armchairs by the wall. Simon's face was bruised, and he was using crutches. He wore a cast that covered his entire leg. I felt a surge of triumphant anger: I had been right; he was the person who had broken into my house, the one that Sadie had shot. While I watched, Simon turned and limped away, in the direction of the band. The woman he had been talking to glanced around the room, then walked over to the wall and opened a door. Behind the door I glimpsed a set of stairs.

My heart was in my throat as I made my way across the room. *It's now or never*, I told myself. I glanced around once more as I opened the door and then started to climb the stairs behind it.

The stairs were old and narrow, made of a dark kind of wood. The wallpaper was musty, and the lighting was poor, lit at stages by dim lamps along the wall. They must have been from the original building, maybe for the staff a hundred years ago. I continued walking up the stairs until I came to a landing and saw the first door. I tried the handle, but it was locked, and so I continued climbing until I got to the second floor.

This door was unlocked. My throat tightened as I listened for sounds on the other side, but it was silent. I took a deep breath and then opened the door a crack and stepped through.

It felt like stepping back in time. The hallway that stretched beyond looked like it was straight out of the 1930s, full of palms in pots and flocked wallpaper. A Persian rug runner ran the length of the hall. It looked like a mirror image of the hallway I had seen in the Hotel Stanislas a few days before, but somehow much darker. It was very ominous that there was a complete hotel—furnished, in use—that existed behind the crumbling walls of an old theater that everyone thought was abandoned. It was haunting to know that people simply disappeared here, especially because, taken out of context, the image before me might seem inviting.

I walked down the hall, listening with trepidation for the sound of footsteps or voices. The hallway wasn't entirely silent; the building was old, after all, and there were creaks and moans running underneath the floorboards, behind the walls, in the ceiling above me. I could hear the faintest sound of music down below. I turned to the first door along the hallway and tried the knob. It was locked.

The second door was locked as well, and the one after that. I was beginning to despair about my plan to get into one of the rooms when a door opened behind me. I only just had time to press myself against the recess of a doorway before someone stepped out into the hall. I waited a moment and then peeked around the corner and saw the receding back of a different woman. She reached the end of the hall and entered the stairway, closing the door behind her.

I waited a moment and then approached the room she had just left. The door was unlocked, and I poked my head inside, half expecting to encounter someone in the room. The bed was rumpled, sheets pulled back, and I could hear the shower going in the bathroom. A pair of men's shoes sat by the door. The room, just like the hallway attached to it, looked like it had been perfectly preserved from the 1930s.

I softly closed the door and made my way down the hall. I thought desperately of Alice, of Spencer, and tried to visualize their keys. Alice's room key had been 323. There must have been a reason why she had left it in the pool, I thought. The rooms on this floor were a lower level. I needed to go upstairs.

Holding my breath, I made my way back to the staircase and went up to the next level.

This hallway was somehow even darker, and a musty smell hit me as soon as I left the stairs. There was a sense that nobody had been up here in a long time—the carpet was dusty and the wallpaper looked grimy.

I looked at the room numbers as I walked along the hall. *Room 301, 302, 305, 309.* The smell was getting worse as I moved down the hall. *Room 315, 318, 320.* The smell was almost unbearable as I reached the door in question and stood in front of it. I didn't want to know what was inside anymore; I only wanted to run. It took everything in me to reach for the doorknob and try to open it—locked—and then to stay there and figure out another plan when what I desperately wanted was to turn and run for the stairs, go back and find Hailey.

Time was running out. Someone was going to come looking for me, or else they were going to come into the hall and realize that I wasn't meant to be there. I tried the handle once more; it wasn't going to budge. It had been a long time since I had picked a lock—one of the many things that

I had Spencer to thank for—but I didn't have small pieces of metal that could perform the functions of a pick or a tension wrench. With no other options, I took off my high-heeled dress shoes and aimed a kick at the door.

The first kick did nothing, nor the second. Lola took martial arts and she had shown me the trick to kicking in a door: you aimed for the lock mount, just below the doorknob, with your foot flat. It helped if your leg was bent. I had practiced it with success in the past, but never with bare feet.

The door finally splintered around the doorknob, and I aimed one final kick at it before it crashed inward. At this point, the smell was unbearable. I reached for my phone to shine the flashlight into the room, then remembered it had been taken from me. I reached into the room and felt around for the light switch. The light was shocking, far too bright, and when I stepped into the room, I clapped a hand over my mouth to keep myself from screaming. A body was laid out on a single bed.

⁂

I felt like I was flying as I made my way back down the stairs. I had almost gotten to the door leading into the ballroom when I realized that the music had stopped, and there were loud voices in the next room. I burst into the ballroom and saw two people fighting at the edge of the room—and then a moment later I realized that one of them was Lucas and that he was struggling with Hailey. Lucas pulled back and swung out, hitting Hailey in the face.

Everything after that happened very quickly. I scanned the room and caught sight of Calder, who stood next to the bar. His hand rested on the wall beside him. He was watching the fight between Lucas and Hailey, and—almost as though he had sensed me watching him—glanced over and caught my eye.

He nodded, then, just once. His hand moved and then my thoughts came all in a jumble as I realized what he had done. He had flipped the fire alarm. It wasn't a fire alarm or anything that sounded familiar, but a horrible long bleating noise—*BONG, BONG, BONG*—that reverberated through my skull and echoed in my marrow.

The chaos was overwhelming. Suddenly it seemed like there were far too many people in the room. I tried to move toward Hailey but then there was a gunshot, and then another—*one, two*—and the sound was far too loud for the small room. People started screaming and I thought that I might faint. I was disoriented, confused, and terrified.

Everyone was fleeing in all directions. The strangest thing about it was that there almost seemed to be a lag between the sounds and the commotion—I heard things moments after I saw them happen. I felt claustrophobic. I couldn't breathe. I moved toward what I thought was the exit, but it was just another shadowy doorway leading deeper into the hotel. I was about to turn around, when I saw the girl sitting on the floor.

She had long dark hair and thin shoulders. She was holding her knees, rocking back and forth. *Hey,* I called, and I couldn't hear my own voice above the din. *Hey!*

I knelt down and shook her shoulder. *You have to get out of here—can you hear me?*

The girl looked up at me, and even though she looked different from her photographs—more gaunt, spectral, hollowed out—I recognized her. It was Chloe Delmonico.

I knelt and took her hands in mine. *Chloe—we have to get out of here! We have to get going!*

Her eyes were enormous black pools. Her face was impassive; she didn't understand anything I was saying. I dragged her off the floor and slung an arm around her waist, pulling her forward, across the dance floor. She was almost dead weight.

Someone was calling my name. *Rainey. Rainey!* Calder's face swam into focus above my own. He looked worried, and he kept glancing over his shoulder. He grabbed my hand and started pulling me through the crowd. I held on to Chloe with my other arm.

Hailey, I called up to him. I still couldn't hear my own voice; I had to trust that my mouth was producing the noises. *We have to find Hailey! We have to—*

He's gone, Rainey, Calder was saying. *Hailey's gone!*

What do you mean! I screamed. I wrenched my arm away from him. *We have to get him!*

He's already gone!

Calder grabbed me with both arms and shoved me down a dark hallway, away from the light and sound, away from the chaos and the horrible alarm, and I thought, *He's going to kill me, he's going to kill me,* but then we burst out into a stairwell and I nearly stumbled over my own feet as we descended, and then we were outside, we were outside, and Hailey was there, and once I heard the sirens I realized that I was finally safe.

THIRTY-THREE

"Rainey. Rainey?" Lola's voice brought me back into the room. "Do you need another break? You okay?"

It was six hours later and I had talked for so long that the words no longer had any meaning. A part of me felt like I was still in a dream, like the entire thing had been a dream, and I was running on fumes. My head was ringing with exhaustion and the shock of everything that had happened in the old theater. For the first hour, I described what Hailey and I had seen: the costumes, the decoration, the sense that everything existed in a time warp and we were trespassing. There were only small interruptions: Casey asking for clarification, or Lola confirming something, but for the most part I spoke uninterrupted.

When I mentioned finding the room with the body, Lola reached over and squeezed my arm. I had almost forgotten about how Juan and Paula, the security guard, had forcibly detained me in Juan's office days ago.

"We'll talk to them," she said. "I think they've already gone to bring Juan in for questioning."

Every once in a while, Casey would stand from the interview table and go outside to talk to someone. Lola never left my side, not even once; when I went to the bathroom, she escorted me through the police station and stood outside until I emerged. I didn't know whether she was making sure that nobody accosted me or if she was just reassuring herself that I was okay. That I was alive.

Even after all the commotion and chaos—after all the shock I had gone through—I was still able to pay attention to everything that happened at the station. I was paying attention when Casey told me very clearly that they had sent in special forces to raid the hotel and go through all the rooms, looking for bodies. That Eiko's family was coming in that afternoon to make formal identifications of the body I had found upstairs, and that later, once the horror had worn off, they might want to thank me.

"Chloe," I said suddenly. "Where is she? Is she okay?"

Casey looked at me for a long moment, then nodded. "She's in the hospital," she said. "She was on a lot of drugs, and they're monitoring her vital signs. She's lucky you were there, though, to pull her out. I'm sure she'll want to thank you herself when she comes down from all of this."

I was paying attention when Lola informed me that Simon Balto and Lucas Mankerfield were both taken into the station in handcuffs, both looking worse for wear. I was paying attention because even when all the reports came trickling into the station, there was still nothing of Alice. There had been no sign of her.

At some point my phone was returned to me. The battery was low, but I saw a dozen missed calls from Marcus and Cameron. I held up the phone and showed Lola.

"Did something happen? Why are they calling me?"

"The bust has been all over the news," Lola said. "Most of the details are still under wraps, but you can't keep something like that private. All the cop cars showing up outside the Stanislas—"

"But how do Marcus and Cameron know I was there?" I glanced down at some of my text messages from them. *Are you okay? Rainey—call me. Please let me know you're okay.*

"The cameras must have already been there when you got out of the hotel," Lola said. "I haven't watched any of the footage, to be honest. It's just too much for me."

I glanced up at Casey. "Can I step outside for a second? I need to make a phone call."

She demurred, and Lola gave me a worried glance.

"I'll be fine, Lo," I told her. "You stay here."

Marcus picked up almost immediately when I called him. "Rainey," he said. His voice sounded worried, and I knew that his mental state must be bad because Marcus was famously stoic. "Where are you?"

"I'm at the police station Downtown," I said. "I'm okay, really."

"You were on the news, and people kept calling me," he said. "It's become a major story."

"Marcus, I have to go," I said.

"Can I come see you?"

"I'll find you afterward," I told him. "I don't know how long this is going to take. Where are you?"

"I'm at the Farm, but I can leave whenever you're ready."

"I'll call you," I told him. "I promise."

I was deliberating about what I should say to Cameron when I got a text from my anonymous source. I hesitated, then opened the text.

I heard what you did. It was really brave.

I felt a flash of anger.

Who are you? I wrote back, exasperated.

I'm sorry. I still can't tell you.

Stop sending me messages then, I wrote back, irritated. I closed the conversation and called Cameron. He picked up after one ring.

"Rainey, I saw you on the news," he said. "Are you okay?"

"I'm fine," I said. I pinched my eyes shut. "I'm so sorry, Cameron. I thought we might find Alice when we went in there, but so far, they haven't found her. They've gone through all the rooms. There's no sign of her."

He murmured an acknowledgment. "It's okay," he said. "Really. I was going to call you anyway, because I think it's time for me to go home. I can't keep putting my life on hold, and that's what I've been doing."

"I'm so sorry, Cameron. I'm sorry we couldn't do more."

"You've done more than you know," he said, and his voice was gentle.

My throat closed up. I felt like if I said anything else, I might start crying.

"I'm going to head back to Paris in a few days," Cameron said. "But don't be a stranger, Rainey."

⁂

When I returned to the interview room, Lola was sitting by herself. She glanced up at me and gave me a tired smile.

"Casey had to take another call," she said.

"Is she coming back soon?"

Lola shrugged. "We'll see," she said.

After a few minutes Casey came back. She told me I was free to go.

"You're not a suspect," she said. "Yet. But don't take the lack of indictment as any kind of encouragement. You're not a cop, Rainey, so don't act like one."

"Got it." I tried to look contrite.

"You have my number," she said. I watched her face and thought I saw something like the hint of a smile. "Now get out of here. I've got enough on my plate."

I stepped out into the morning sunshine and blinked. Lola put her hand on my back.

"Do you want me to take you home?"

"I need to see Marcus," I said. "I want to let him know that I'm okay."

"Rainey!"

Lola and I both turned to see Hailey and Blake coming toward us. I hadn't seen Hailey since we had both entered the police station several hours earlier, and he looked just as exhausted as I felt: his hair was sticking up and his tuxedo was torn, but he looked oddly invigorated as well. As he moved closer, I could see that he wore the beginning of a black eye.

"Are you okay?" he asked me, pulling me into a hug.

"Shaken," I said. "I'm not really sure how I feel yet. Hey, Blake."

I leaned down to give her a hug.

"We can debrief later," she said, squeezing my hand. "You look like you need rest."

"Wait a second," Hailey said. "I want you guys to meet someone."

On the sidewalk behind him was a woman with dark hair shot through with gray. She was tall and statuesque, but she looked stressed: her hair stood on end, and she kept folding and unfolding her arms. Her mouth was set in a thin line.

"Alexa," Hailey called. "Come meet Left City."

The woman strode toward us and offered her hand, which I shook. "I'm Alexa Levine," she said. "I'm the editor of the *Lens*."

"Rainey Hall," I said. "And this is Lola Figueroa. And Blake Harris, but it looks like you've already met?"

"A few minutes before you came out," Hailey said.

"Very brave, what you did," Alexa said. "Hailey and I will be at the office for the next few days, pulling together a story. We can't print everything until we get confirmation of the identities, and we can't bring in too much of the criminal side of things until everything has gone to trial, but we can mention arrests."

"We've been speaking with a police officer named Casey Lennon," Lola told her. "She's been in front of all of this."

"She'll probably make detective if she knows how to play this," Alexa said. "I'll call her to confirm the arrests of Lucas Manderfield and Simon Balto, the discovery of the body, the ownership of the club and hotel, and the discovery of drugs in one of the upper rooms."

"She probably won't confirm any of it," Lola said with a grim smile. "But you can always try."

"I'll need to look into Ricky Goff, as well," Alexa said. "Anything you're willing to share on that front?"

Lola glanced at me, then looked back at Alexa. "We'll call you later," she said. "Right now, there's someone we need to go see."

Lola and I were both quiet as we left the police station and got on the freeway heading out to the Farm. I felt numb, exhausted, and disappointed all at once. Walking out of the hotel had been like walking offstage after a big performance was over: once the music had died and the lights came up, you could see everything for what it really was, just a room and a stage and people doing sleight of hand.

"We don't have to do this right now," Lola said, looking at me.

"I want to see Marcus. You can drop me off and go home. I'll be fine."

"No, I'll wait for you." She squeezed my knee. "I'm glad you're okay."

The Farm was quiet, and it took me a moment to remember that it was a Sunday. Marcus was waiting outside his office when Lola and I pulled up. He walked over to the car and pulled me into a hug as soon as I stepped out.

"I saw you on the news," he said. "I didn't know what to think—it was horrifying, Rainey—are you okay?"

"I'm okay."

Lola stepped out of the car and gave Marcus a weak smile. "Where is everyone?"

Marcus rubbed his jaw and looked dazed. "The production team called an emergency meeting at the offices Downtown," he said. "They're looking at Lucas's involvement with what happened at the Stanislas. Bradley and I are the only executives here today—we're holding down the fort while the producers figure out the extent of our culpability."

Marcus's phone rang. He glanced at it, exhausted.

"Take it," I said. "We can wait here."

"It's been ringing all morning," he said.

"Go put out your fires," I told him. "Go, go."

Marcus answered the phone and walked inside the office. The dull exhaustion that had been hanging over me all morning felt like a fog, a veil, a gauzy weight on my brain. The gnawing anxiety that had lingered on in my stomach hadn't abated since the previous afternoon when Hailey and I were getting ready to go meet Calder. I glanced down at my phone, and then I had an idea that seemed so wildly improbable that I almost didn't say anything.

I turned to Lola.

"Lola," I said slowly. "I just had a crazy thought, and I need you to tell me whether or not it's impossible."

She looked pale, exhausted. "I don't know if I can handle crazy right now," she said.

I glanced inside to where Marcus was talking on the phone.

"The person who's been texting me," I said. "We never figured out who it was, right? They were worried about Eiko, and they had some knowledge of what was going on inside these parties."

"Rainey . . ."

"I know who it was," I said. The fog was starting to dissipate. "It was Bradley. Bradley's been texting me this whole time."

Lola opened her mouth, then seemed to reconsider what she was about to say. She sighed and shook her head.

"He knew about the parties," I went on, warming to my own theory. "But Lucas was his assistant, so if he came right out and told the police, he might be implicated. You see what's happening right now—the Auden empire is at stake because people at the studio were involved in these parties."

"Rainey, Rainey," Lola said. "You might be right. You have great instincts. But please—*please*—can't this wait another day? We're both too tired to think this through clearly."

"We might not get another chance," I said. "The whole production lot is empty, but Bradley's here. I need to get him alone without making it obvious. I need to give him a chance to reveal himself to me."

"It's not a good idea," Lola said.

"Tell me I'm wrong. Tell me this is outside the realm of possibility."

Her mouth twisted up, and she sucked in a breath. "You could be right," she said, but her voice was doubtful.

"Let's just go see him," I urged. "We don't have to say anything. I'll just see if he offers up any information."

She glanced inside. Marcus was still on the phone.

"Fine," she said. "But let's make it a quick visit. I'm tired."

THIRTY-FOUR

We took one of the golf carts that was sitting outside the recording studio. I waved at Marcus and pointed toward the back lot, then mimed driving. He nodded and continued talking to whoever was on the other end of the line.

Bradley's office building was quiet, and I wondered if he might have already left. Lola and I were silent as we walked down the hall. When we were halfway there, I turned to her.

"Let me go in alone," I said. "I don't want to spook him."

She laced her fingers together and glanced past me. Her forehead was creased. "Do you want me to wait outside at the car? "

I thought about it for a minute. "Yes," I said. "I don't think he'll admit anything if we're both there."

When I reached Bradley's office, I heard quiet murmuring. I hesitated, then knocked. The voice fell silent.

"Yes—come in," Bradley called.

I opened the door and stuck my head in. Bradley was sitting behind his desk. There were dark circles under his eyes, and his hair looked like it hadn't been washed in several days. He held his phone to his ear and held up a finger when he saw me.

"I'll call you back, sweetheart," he said. "I'll be home in a few hours. I love you, too."

He put the phone down and gave me a wan smile.

"Rainey, hi," he said. "How are you? I mean, you don't have to answer that. You must be exhausted—we all are. I'm just in shock about Lucas."

"Yeah," I said. "It's pretty bad. I don't know what to say."

"Come in," he said, then motioned to a seat in front of his desk. The room was full of pleasant clutter, with papers all across his desk and Post-it notes stuck to his computer. A stack of books occupied a corner of the desk, and posters from old movies occupied the walls.

"How are you, though?" I asked.

He seemed taken aback by the question. "I'm okay," he said. "I was just talking to my daughter. I'm going to try to take some time off and see my family more. This whole affair puts things into perspective."

I studied his face, looking for some sign of recognition or acknowledgment.

"You had no idea this was going on?" I asked.

Bradley rubbed his chin. "I've been accused of being naïve," he said. "But this makes me think I don't deserve to oversee anyone. I have a bad fault of looking for the good, long after the bad is evident."

I waited, hoping that he would go on, out himself as my anonymous correspondent. Nothing.

"It's a shame, really," Bradley went on. "When you think of all the artists who died. We live in a sick world, Rainey. You must be especially angry—your mother was an artist, right?"

I stiffened involuntarily. "She was," I said.

"Why did she give it up?"

"You'd have to ask her," I said. "I haven't spoken to her in years."

"I'm sorry," Bradley said, and he sounded chastened. "Family estrangement is a lot more common than most people realize. It might surprise you, but I wasn't close to my dad. I think I disappointed him."

I didn't want to listen to what he was saying, no matter how heartfelt it might be. I wasn't in the headspace to talk about my mother, and I felt a little resentful that Bradley had mentioned her. Instead, I glanced around the office: the posters of the movies he had worked on, the stacks of scripts.

It was sitting on a shelf, tilting sideways under the weight of some books that had slipped against their bookend. I saw the dull glint, the bronze gone dull from lack of care, the small knot of a mouth and closed eyes. A dead woman resurrected in sculpture. It had been so long since I had seen the head that I almost didn't recognize it, but it was something I had thought about so many times that I had never quite forgotten it. I was looking at *Lille, Après*.

Bradley stopped talking long enough for me to realize that he was looking at me, waiting for me to say something. I covered with a lengthy yawn, closing my eyes and stretching, then glanced up at him with bleary eyes.

"I'm so sorry," I said. My heart was hammering so loudly in my chest that I thought he could hear it. I felt almost delirious. "It's not you. It's just this week, I haven't been sleeping at all. This chair is so comfortable, I think I almost fell asleep."

Bradley laughed. "You wouldn't be the first to fall asleep there," he said.

I felt lightheaded in a way that made me question whether or not I could do this. I had plenty of experience confronting people through Left City, but this was different: if I was wrong, I was risking further victimizing someone who had already been through a great deal of trauma. I was putting my job at risk, my relationship with the studio, and I was potentially putting Marcus in the line of fire.

If I was right, though, there was a chance that I was putting my life in danger.

"I don't mean to cut things short, Rainey, but I might head home soon," Bradley said.

"No, of course," I said. "Hey, how old's your daughter?"

"Nine," Bradley said.

"Does she watch your movies?" I asked.

"Sure," Bradley said, smiling. "We try to limit her screen time. She loves to read."

"You guys play games as a family?"

Bradley laughed, surprised. "Oh, yeah," he said. "We play some board games. Both of my kids are pretty competitive."

"Oh yeah, me too," I said. "I was so good at hearts when I was a kid. Nobody would play with me. I can only remember losing once."

"No kidding," Bradley said. There was a glint in his eye. "I used to love hearts."

"What's your strategy? You play it safe?"

"Never," he said. "It's no fun unless you Shoot the Moon."

"Risky," I said. "Because if you miss even one card, you go down hard."

"What's life without a little risk?"

My blood pressure was off the charts. I almost didn't trust myself to speak, because I knew that my voice would start trembling.

"It's a bummer we didn't get to hang out more when Spencer was still alive," I said. "I know you guys used to be close."

"Yeah, I always thought of her as a kid sister."

"She could be rude, though," I said. "She gave people really nasty nicknames."

Bradley squawked with surprised laughter. "You're right! She could be a little shit."

"She called me Foster," I said, lying through my teeth. "Because my mom left and my dad basically started treating me like a foster kid."

"That's really twisted." A little smile played around the corners of his mouth. "I guess she could be kind of mean."

"What did she call you?"

He twisted his wedding ring. "I'm not sure I ever had a nickname," he said. "At least, not one that she called me to my face."

"Wait a second—you weren't Tall Boy, were you?" I cocked my head to the side and gave him a perplexed smile.

He laughed, stunned. "Hold on," he said. "How did you know that?"

"She must have mentioned it at some point." I shrugged, pretending to be nonchalant. In reality I felt like I was going to pass out from the blood flow going to my head. "I didn't get it, though. No offense, but you're shorter than me, and I'm not exactly tall."

"Ha-ha . . . no, none taken. It's not because of my height. I used to drink tall boys in college—you know, shitty beer? My frat brothers called me Tall Boy. I must have forgotten that Spencer started using it, too."

He was gathering his things, standing up. He was about to leave. It was now or never.

"Did you kill Spencer?"

His face dropped, but only for a moment. The mask returned almost immediately.

"You're a funny girl, Rainey," he said, resting his hands on the desk. "Such a jokester. I'm heading home, but I'll catch you later, hey?"

"What do you think happened to her?"

He tilted his head to the side. The glint in his eye was back. "I know it's tempting to look for answers at a time like this," he said.

"Weren't you close?" I asked.

"Not *that* close. She was a kid." Some of the friendliness in his tone had evaporated.

"Passing acquaintances," I offered.

"Rainey, what's this all about?"

"You were her boyfriend," I said. "Back in high school. You visited her at rehab. She told me about you."

Bradley was quiet, watching me.

"Spencer stole a piece of art called *Lille, Après*," I went on. "It went missing from a private residence about nine years ago. I would know, I was there. Spencer wouldn't have given it up for anything. And yet there it is, sitting on your shelf."

I pointed, and Bradley craned his head to follow the direction of my finger. He did an exaggerated double take and then picked up the metal head.

"Oh, this?" he said, then started laughing. "This was a wrap present from a film I worked on a few years ago. It was a gag gift, probably cost three dollars at the LACMA gift shop. Here, have a look."

He set the bust down in front of me. I didn't touch it; something about it seemed cursed.

"You're very convincing," I said. "I think you missed your calling. You should have been an actor."

"I'm going to go home, Rainey," he said. "You're grieving, and you don't realize the weight of what you're saying to me. I forgive you, really, but please don't bother me with your theories again."

"*M.E. Stands Before the Mind of God*," I said, and he stiffened. "It started with Mary Ecclestone, didn't it? All those artists taken away from their families. But there's only so much power in art. You started going after politicians."

He stood very still.

"I know you told Spencer to steal the painting," I said. "It all makes sense now—you were her boyfriend. She would have done anything you asked. How long do you think you can hide? They're going to come after you eventually."

Bradley had not moved. His hands were gripping the back of his chair, so hard that they had gone white.

"Did your father know? Is that why you guys had problems?"

Bradley wasn't looking at me. His gaze was turned inward, and his eyes were unfocused as though he was completely lost in his thoughts.

"He didn't even notice you, did he?" I asked, trying to make my voice kind. "You worked so hard for him, and it was like you were invisible."

"I *saved* our family legacy," he said, and his voice came out a growl. "The Auden Foundation wouldn't *exist* if not for me. All my father's bad investments, terrible ideas . . . I brought us back. I did!"

"I know what it's like." I nodded. "To be abandoned. My own mother walked out on me. It was because of me—not my father."

"It's the same for all of us," he said, finally looking up to meet my eye. "Spencer, you, me . . . our parents have impossible expectations. We can never meet them, of course. We're just bound to be disappointments, no matter what we do."

"Spencer was a good artist," I said. "She was great. It's too bad she got caught up in all the drugs. She could have been more successful than any of us."

"You didn't know Spencer at all," he continued. "I know you were friends, but she wasn't a good person."

"I never said she was a good person," I said. "But I know talent when I see it. I always thought she was a bitch."

"Exactly. A bitch who was addicted to drugs and money."

"You cultivated artists," I said. "I bet you tried to help her."

He gave me a wry smile. "Don't patronize me, Rainey."

I was treading water, trying to keep up with my own thoughts. I needed to ask him so many questions, but at the same time I knew that if I betrayed my own ignorance of the situation, Bradley was likely to shut down.

"Why did you stop?" he asked, watching me.

"Stop what?"

"Playing music," he said. "You could have been great. You *were* great."

"It was never for me," I said. "All the praise went to my parents because they were the ones who made it happen. They got all the credit. I was just a dancing monkey."

"They build this world and force you to live in it, then expect you to act grateful," Bradley said, nodding. "I didn't ask for any of this, either."

"I always wanted a quiet life," I said. "I hated being onstage."

"Me too," Bradley said. "Me too! I never knew which version of myself to be. No matter what you do, you get scrutinized. I hated it."

I rested my chin on my hand and tried to relax. If I tensed up, I knew that Bradley would sense it. The worst thing you could do with a predator was run, act scared.

"You found all those artists," I said. "You have an eye for art."

He snorted. "Tell that to my dad."

"It takes real skill to mentor an artist," I said. "Artists are so flaky, so temperamental. Impossible to deal with. I should know."

He was watching me. "Did you ever find out what happened to your mother?"

"She changed her name and started a new family."

"Huh." He nodded and fell quiet for a moment. "Why?"

"I guess we were too heavy for her."

"I heard you fell out with your dad," he said.

"That's what happens when you disappoint people," I said.

"Who disappointed whom?"

I nodded and gave him a knowing look. "Exactly."

There was a long silence.

"What happened to Alice?" I asked, trying to keep my voice light.

His jaw tensed, just slightly. "Who?"

"Come on, Bradley," I said. "I think we've gone too far for that. You must know what happened to her."

"I don't know who you're talking about."

"Alice Alder," I said. "Alice. Spencer's friend Alice."

His face had gone so still that it looked like he was made of wax. "You've clearly put a lot of thought into this," he said. "But again, you have the wrong idea about all of this."

"Well, enlighten me," I said.

"I foster artists," he said, and his voice had a note of condescending anger in it. "I find creative people from rough backgrounds and give them the resources they need to become successful. There have been some great success stories—look at Paula Morales, for example. She was one of ours. Trai Nguyen? And what about Roderick Miller—he just signed with William Morris."

"What about Ian Rhodes?"

He pressed his lips together, then gave me a thin smile. "This conversation is over."

"You found vulnerable people without families," I said, and I couldn't keep the tremble out of my voice. I was becoming emotional, as hard as I tried not to. "You found stray kids with drug habits and exploited them. You were using them to fuck powerful people and then blackmailing those people into helping you."

"I wouldn't expect you to understand," he said.

"Where does it end, Bradley? When does it become enough?"

"Get the fuck out of my office." His voice was low and ugly.

"I will," I said, "once you tell me where to find my friend."

The movement was so fluid that I didn't even register the gun at first. Bradley's hand moved under his desk, and then a moment later, he was pointing a gun at me.

"You could have been great," he said. "I was rooting for you. We were all rooting for you. That's what you do, Rainey—you throw away the people who try to help you."

I felt a cold wave of panic. I cleared my throat and tried to speak, but I felt frozen to my seat. Bradley gave me a look of pity.

"I'm a patron," he said, talking to me as if I were stupid. "I am a patron of the arts. The relationship has existed for centuries—artists and their patrons. It's a symbiotic connection, something you obviously wouldn't understand. Artists need their patrons. People like you ruin it for the rest of us."

"Are you going to shoot me, Bradley?" I asked.

"You haven't left me much choice," he said.

"How will you explain this?" I asked. "What happens when they find me?"

"I don't have to explain anything," Bradley said. "I have people to do that for me."

He aimed the gun at me. There was no emotion on his face, not even reluctance.

"You're an obstacle, Rainey," he said. "You're standing in my way."

It sounded like a hammer against corrugated iron. There was something afterward, too, a kind of echoing reverberation that was almost visual. It felt like it was happening in slow motion, and by the time I thought to raise my hands to cover my ears, it was already over. There was a ringing sound then, tinnitus, and all I could think was how annoying it was—I couldn't hear anything Bradley was saying, although his lips were moving. I shook my head a few times to clear the sound, but it didn't help.

I didn't realize that he had shot me until I felt the liquid on my hands. *Oh*, I thought. *Something must have spilled.* A stupid thought, really, but the first one that came to mind. When I raised my hands to look at them, they were covered in a shocking red liquid. I glanced up at Bradley and laughed, confused.

"Bradley?"

I felt the word leave my mouth, but the ringing in my ears was still so loud. The blood started to spread, very quickly, soaking my shirt. Bradley gave me another look of disgust and then he grabbed his things and walked out of the room, moving past me, and this time I heard what he said:

"I told you not to stand in my way."

THIRTY-FIVE

There was a faint beeping sound, always a beeping somewhere down the corridor, a sound that invaded my brief snatches of dreams whenever I drifted off.

"Stay with us, Rainey," someone kept saying. It was a different voice every time—a man, a woman, faces blurring together over the haze of morphine. The lights above were so blinding that I pulled my pillow over my face, but when I woke up the pillow was underneath my head again.

"Rainey, can you hear us?"

For the first time in a long time, I dreamed of Alice. There was a memory I had gone back to so many times over the years that it was polished to a perfect shine. The details were arranged so neatly I could almost recite them without closing my eyes. The days leading up to Alice's disappearance. The things I must have missed. *Alice.*

A week before Alice went missing, she made a comment that scared me. We were at my house, and I was taking photos with my dad's old film camera, which I had found while going through some boxes in the attic.

"Stop it," Alice said, covering her face with her hands.

"You're beautiful and I love you. Move your goddamn hands."

She laughed, one hand still covering her eyes.

"You'll thank me for this one day," I said, taking a photo. The light through the window made patterns on her long blond hair.

"You're a creep." She sat up and looked out the window. "It's weird, but sometimes I wish this summer would never end. There's been so much bad stuff, with the fires and my mom, but there are nights when I wish it could stay like this forever."

I put the camera down. "I know what you mean."

"I wish everyone would stay away," she added. "I wish we could keep the city to ourselves. It doesn't seem fair that they can return, you know? They fled so easily."

The last of the fires had been extinguished—finally, *finally*—three days before, and we had been in a mood of giddy celebration ever since. The mayor had made an official announcement that evacuation orders were lifted, and people were welcome to return home. There was still some lingering smoke haze above the mountains and in the crooks of the valleys, but for the most part, people walked around the city with smiles of relief. There was a communal sense of well-being, a feeling that we had been spared. We had a second chance.

"Do you think we'll stay friends?" Alice leaned her head against her knee and looked at me.

"When we're older? Of course, idiot." I flicked her.

"When I leave LA." Her voice was calm and clear.

"Who said you're leaving?" I was caught off guard.

"When my mom dies, I won't have a choice. I'll go to New Hampshire." Her voice was distant. She seemed resigned, almost devoid of emotion. "My aunt and uncle have been talking to Monica. Everyone seems to think it's the best course of action."

It took me a moment to respond. I thought that Alice and I told each other everything, but she had clearly managed to hide this from me. I didn't know why.

"Alice," I said, coming over to wrap my arms around her. "Why don't you stay with us? If it's a matter of paperwork, I'm sure my dad could sign something."

"I have a friend," she said. "He has a house where I can stay. I've seen it—it's beautiful. There are roses in the garden."

"In Los Angeles?"

"There are stained glass windows," she said. "The house is really beautiful. You'd like it."

I was annoyed and a little hurt. "Why wouldn't you just stay with me?"

She was looking out the window. "Do you ever wonder how long it would take for someone to notice you were gone? I mean, some people just slip through the cracks, right? My dad's gone, my mom soon will be, too . . . I only talk to Cameron once a week or less. He's so busy with school."

"You're scaring me, Al."

She glanced up and gave me a pale smile. "I'm sorry. I'm really going to miss you, you know. When I leave."

It was in those moments when I felt closest to Alice, because it was easy to see how much our lives overlapped. My mom had walked out on my family the previous summer, tearing a hole in the fabric of our lives that felt like it would never go away. From an outsider's standpoint it might have looked like my life was perfect: I lived in a beautiful house off Mulholland, I went to one of the best private schools in the city, and I never wanted for anything. Every morning, though, unbeknownst to anyone but Alice, I woke up with a sense of existential dread. It was a weight that only abated when I was with my best friend. I lived with a sense of self-loathing and despair that I quelled with minor rebellions, small acts of self-sabotage, like breaking into strangers' homes.

Alice kissed my hand. "Let's order a pizza," she said. "We can watch movies until we fall asleep."

─────

When I woke up again, Lola and Blake were sitting by my bed. They were having a quiet conversation, but Blake caught my eye and shook Lola's arm.

"She's awake," she said. "Rainey's awake!"

Lola gasped and then started crying. She rushed closer to the bed and grabbed my arm.

"Rainey," she said. "Oh my god, Rainey. You scared me to death. I thought—I thought—oh my god, I'm so glad you're okay—"

"Hey, punk," Blake said, smiling at me.

"Hi," I said, feeling groggy from the drugs. "What's going on?"

"You're in the hospital," Lola said, enunciating each word.

"I'm not brain-dead, Lola. I know that," I said. My voice was slow. "I've woken up a few times, but I keep falling back asleep. I'm so tired."

Blake and Lola exchanged a glance.

"What do you remember?" Blake asked.

"Bradley shot me," I said. "I didn't think he was going to do it. He was pointing a gun and he shot me."

I didn't feel emotional about it at all. I was disconnected from my body, numb from all the drugs. Something occurred to me then, for the first time.

"Where *is* Bradley?"

Another glance between Lola and Blake.

"Stop doing that!" I said. "I can see you looking at each other."

"We don't know," Lola said, her voice soothing. "The police are looking for him."

"But . . ."

"I heard the gunshot," Lola said, and then she was suddenly overcome with emotion. Her eyes glistened, and she had to clear her throat before she continued speaking. "I heard a bang. I thought something had fallen, like a tree branch or something. I saw him run out, and at first I thought he was going to check it out . . . but then he drove away and you were still in there. When I went to look for you . . ." She stopped and pinched the bridge of her nose.

"I'm okay, Lo," I said. "Thanks for saving my life."

There was a knock on the door, and I looked over to see Sadie. I hadn't seen her since that night when she had intervened with the people who had broken into our house.

"Well, damn," I said, trying to smile.

Sadie's face was creased with worry. She ran over to the bed and grasped my hand. "Oh my god," she said. "Rainey. What *happened*? Is it the same people—the guys who tried to hurt you before?"

"No," I said, then attempted another smile. "Seems a lot of people want to kill me."

A nurse bustled in and checked his clipboard. "Glad to see our patient is awake," he said. "We need to run some tests, which means I need all of you to leave."

Lola started to protest, and he held up a hand. "You can wait in the visitors' lounge," he said. "We'll take good care of her, I promise."

Later that day I met my doctor for the first time. Dr. Minari was a small woman with long, dark hair and creases around her eyes. She had burnished olive skin and a healthy complexion, and even though she bustled through my room with a practiced efficiency, she still radiated a sense of calm.

"Hi, Rainey," she said, coming over to check my heart monitor. "How are you feeling?"

"Numb."

"That's to be expected. We've got you on a morphine drip. You've got a lot of friends who care about you."

"I'm lucky."

"You're a very lucky girl," she said. "It's nice to finally meet you. How much do you remember?"

I was feeling sharper than I had when Lola had asked me. "I didn't pass out right away," I said. "I remember bleeding a lot, wanting to go to sleep. It didn't hurt at all—I just felt cold."

She was nodding. "That's normal."

"I remember Lola coming to find me," I said. "And that's when things get fuzzy. I was really tired."

"You lost a lot of blood," she said. "We had to put you under in order to operate. So far it looks like everything went well—we should be able to release you in a few days."

"What day is it?" I asked. Sunlight streamed in from outside.

"Monday," she said. "It's Monday afternoon."

"I've been in here a week?" I asked after a moment. Lola and I had spoken to Marcus and Bradley on Sunday afternoon. "Was I in a coma?"

Dr. Minari looked at me for a moment, then burst out laughing. "You've been here a day and a half," she said. "That's all."

She checked something on her clipboard, then turned to go.

"There's someone waiting to see you," she said. "A woman. I didn't catch her name."

I closed my eyes. "Is she coming in?"

"I said she could come back tomorrow. Visitors' hours are over for the day."

I slept for fourteen hours. When I woke up again, one of the nurses glanced at me and smiled. "Good morning," she said.

"Morning."

"You up for a visitor? There's someone out there who wants to see you."

"Sure," I said, trying to sit up. I was still on painkillers, so I couldn't feel the wound in my side as anything more than a dull pressure.

"I'll go let her know."

The nurse disappeared. A moment later, there was a knock at the door. I looked up, and to my shock, Violet Auden was standing there.

"Oh, no," I muttered.

"Rainey," she started, but I cut her off.

"You need to leave."

She nodded and gave me a look of sorrow. "I'm so sorry," she said, and she sounded close to tears. "That's all I came to say—I tried to come earlier, but then I thought you might need some time."

I struggled to sit up.

"Is this what you wanted to see?" I gestured at the tubes in my arms. "I came after your husband, and now you want to make sure I'm in pain?"

Tears slipped down her face. "No, Rainey, you have the wrong idea."

"Leave," I said. I started shaking so badly that I thought I might set off one of the monitors.

"Rainey—"

"*Leave!*"

A nurse poked his head in, a look of alarm on his face. Violet raised her hands in a gesture of defeat.

"Okay," she said. "I'm going."

Lola came by an hour later. She sat by my bed, then reached out to tuck a strand of hair behind my ear.

"How are you feeling?" she asked.

"Not great."

"Yeah. Obviously."

We both burst out laughing.

Dr. Minari came in then and startled when she saw Lola. "Oh!" she exclaimed. "Another visitor. You're lucky to be supported by so many friends."

"Rainey's very popular," Lola agreed.

"Liar."

"One of the nurses said there was a bit of a scuffle in here earlier—some shouting? Everything okay?" Dr. Minari peered down at me.

Lola raised an eyebrow. "Shouting?"

"Nothing happened."

"Rai."

I cleared my throat. "Violet Auden came by."

Lola looked confused. "What did she want?"

I glanced at Dr. Minari, who smoothed her shirt and avoided my eyes.

"I don't know," I said, failing to suppress my frustration. "I think she wants to apologize."

"Oh, okay," Lola said. "And you won't let her?"

"Why should I?" I said, my irritation rising to meet Lo's. "She's complicit in all of this, too, even if she hasn't been arrested yet."

Lola's expression was vague. She turned to look at Dr. Minari, then back at me. "Fine," she said.

"What about the story?" I asked.

"What story?"

"The story Hailey is writing," I said. "Does he know about Bradley?"

"I haven't talked to him," she said. "Not yet. I've been too worried about you."

"Call him, please," I said. "Let him know."

She looked at me and squeezed my hand. "Talk to Violet," she said. "Let her apologize."

———

Four days later, Dr. Minari finally allowed me to go for an exploratory walk outside accompanied by a nurse. If everything went well, she would release me the next morning, she told me. I was exhausted, but it felt good to breathe fresh air and step away from the constant beeping and hushed voices of the ICU. As we walked away from the hospital, I saw someone sitting on a bench under a tree. It was Violet Auden. Her neck was tilted to the side, and a book and some wilted flowers rested in her lap. She looked like she had been asleep for a while.

I stood there for a moment, thinking about what Lola had asked me to do. I watched Violet sleep, trying to summon the hatred I had felt earlier, but at the moment, all I felt was pity; all the polish and grace Violet had exhibited when I had seen her before was gone, and she looked so unguarded.

I turned to the nurse. She was a young woman with glasses and braces, someone who looked like she was still in high school.

"Do you mind if I have a moment alone?" I asked.

She gazed at me placidly. "I'm not supposed to leave you unattended," she said. "Dr. Minari's orders."

"I'm just going over there," I said, pointing toward Violet. "I won't leave your sight."

The nurse shrugged and nodded, then took a seat. I approached Violet. "Hey," I called. Violet didn't stir. Her mouth was open, and she almost looked sweet, vulnerable. "Violet," I tried again. Nothing. I hesitated, then walked over and touched her shoulder. She jerked and sat upright, then looked at me in shock.

"You fell asleep," I said quickly.

Violet glanced around in a daze, trying to get her bearings. She looked scared, disoriented, and then seemed to calm down.

"Oh," she said. "I had no idea where I was for a moment. Sorry."

"What are you doing here?"

"I guess I was hoping you'd change your mind," she said. "I must have drifted off." She gazed at the flowers, then shook her head. "They're ruined, aren't they."

A thin gold band adorned her wrist, but other than that, she wore no jewelry.

"No wedding ring," I said.

Violet nodded, gave a single quick burst of breath that sounded like surprised laughter. "Right," she said. Everything about her was graceful—the way she tucked one ankle behind the other, reclined slightly in her chair, touched a finger to her chin. She had recovered whatever composure she had lost falling asleep on a hospital bench.

"You move quickly," I remarked. "Trying to distance yourself from Bradley?"

She sighed. "I haven't worn my wedding ring for the last month, Rainey," she said. "We've been living separate lives for quite a while."

"Forgive me for being blunt, but it seems like convenient timing to come out with that statement."

"I haven't made any statements yet," she said. "Even though my lawyer keeps pressing me to. I have to think about my children."

I was quiet for a long time. I wasn't even angry, not anymore. I just felt empty. I wanted it all to be over.

"I'm sure you have a lot of questions," Violet said.

"I don't flatter myself to think you'll answer any of them," I said.

"You might be surprised."

"When did you realize that your husband was a monster?" I asked.

Violet's eyes rested on my face for a long moment before she broke my gaze. "If you're asking when I realized how bad he was," she said. "That was three months ago, when Eiko disappeared. But there were things that I chose to ignore for years, naïvely thinking I could somehow help him. Make him better."

"I can't absolve you of that," I said. "You don't need to convince me of anything."

"Fair enough," she said. "So why did you decide to come talk to me?"

"I'm here as a favor to Lola," I said. "My friend is writing an article about what happened. I wanted to give him the full story, but Lola said that I should talk to you first. I just came to let you know that you'll probably be implicated, but it's not my job to see what happens to you."

To my surprise, Violet didn't look surprised or even upset. "Fair enough."

"That's it? Fair enough? Your husband tried to kill me. I got really fucking lucky, which is the only reason I'm sitting here right now. You know, if it was up to me, I wouldn't have even bothered to talk to you. Jesus Christ, the things that Lola talks me into. I've said what I needed to say. I'm going back inside."

I had made it about ten feet when Violet called out. "You love her a lot. Lola."

"Don't say her name," I said, turning around to face her. I had momentarily forgotten my injury, and the movement caused me to grimace in pain. It took me a moment to recover, and then I said through clenched teeth: "You have no right."

"You're lucky you have someone that you love so much," she said. "Friendship is important."

"You know nothing about it."

"I know more than you think," she said, with a calm that I found infuriating.

"You were married to a monster," I said. "Some might say that makes you one, too."

"I've been where you are," she said. Her eyes were glistening with tears. "Someone I loved was taken from me. Someone I loved very much."

"Yeah? This should be good." I could feel a familiar tightness in my throat and I wished very badly that I wouldn't start crying. The two went hand in hand for me, anger and sadness, because growing up I had never been allowed to express anger without experiencing punishment in the form of silent treatments and anger from my mother.

"Eiko Maramoto," Violet said.

My drugs were wearing off, and I could feel the tingling sensation that precipitated sharp stabbing pains. The pain was making me more irritable, and I had very little patience for Violet's stories.

"Eiko? What did you have to do with Eiko?"

"The Auden Foundation gives money and resources to orphans, even when they've aged out of foster homes. Eiko had applied for an art grant, and I saw that she had real talent. We've got friends in the art world—well, you already know *that*—and I made the mistake of introducing her to Simon. I thought Eiko might make a career of it."

I thought for a moment. "You weren't in love with her, were you?"

She gave me a scathing look. "Absolutely not. It wasn't like that."

"Forgive my skepticism," I snapped. "I've just dug through layers of filth to find that you and your foundation were at the core of it. What was your relationship, if it wasn't sexual?"

"She reminded me of my little sister," Violet said. "Or maybe she just reminded me of me. I wished that I'd had someone to look out for me when I was her age. I was *trying* to look out for her."

"I don't believe you," I said after a beat. "You must have known. You knew something."

"By the time I figured it out, it was too late," she said.

"Too late for what?"

"Too late to save her."

"So go to the police," I said, through gritted teeth. "That's *what they're there for.*"

"I did," she said, and a few tears slipped down her cheeks. "They were no help."

"Find another way!"

"I did," she repeated, her voice soft. "I went to you."

I stared at her for a very long moment. She took out her phone and typed something in. A moment later, my phone pinged with a text.

New message from Eiko's Friend, the screen read. I opened my phone. *I didn't know what else to do*, the message read.

I wanted to throw my phone onto the pavement.

"It's not good enough," I said. "It's not enough!"

"I know. I know, *I know*." Tears were streaming down Violet's face. She brushed them away angrily with the back of her hand.

"Why didn't you go to the police when you realized she was in trouble?"

"I told you, I *did*," she said, and for the first time that day, her voice sounded angry. She reached into her bag and pulled out a fat folder. "I kept notes, you know. All the times I went to the police. When Eiko went missing,

I called them. She was an adult, legally, and she wasn't my family. They looked into her, saw that she had drug problems. That was thanks to Spencer, by the way—Spencer got her hooked on drugs. Did you know that? Spencer's family was looking out for her, but Eiko was on her own. I kept going back. Kept making phone calls. I went out to see her aunt and uncle, and they slammed the door in my face. I still went back. They said it was my fault."

"There are other ways of getting attention," I said. "You could have gone to the news."

She laughed, angry, and rubbed away her tears in two rough strokes. "Try to think about this from my perspective for two minutes," she said. "I have a family. I have two children that I need to protect. But you have to understand, Rainey, I was scared of my husband. I've been scared of him for a long time. When I met him, I didn't have any friends—I was only meant to be out here as an exchange student. He swept me off my feet and we got married straightaway."

For some reason I thought of Noa, of her relationship with Ricky. *Not all monsters start as monsters.* For the first time that day, I started to feel some sympathy toward her.

"I know that I look bad," she continued. "I know that I deserve to be punished for my ignorance, for not doing more. I've been punishing myself already. Whatever you need to do—do it. I don't care anymore."

"Why did you do so much for Eiko?" I asked. "You help so many orphans."

"She was determined and so talented," Violet said. "She could have been exceptional. I thought I could help her, that I could save her. How fucking stupid of me."

"When did she go missing?"

"It was about three months ago."

I remembered my visit out to the bakery to see Hana. "Hana thinks you had something to do with the disappearance," I said.

"I don't blame her."

"Why didn't you hire an investigator yourself?"

"Again, I couldn't do anything that ran the risk of catching Bradley's attention," she said. "He had me watched all the time. We have children together. He comes from a very powerful family, and even though the Auden Foundation has always been my project, there was a chance that he could take it all away from me."

"What are you going to do now?"

"I don't know," she said. "I don't know. I'm going to take a break from work to look after my children. I can't think about any of this right now."

I sat down on the bench next to Violet. She was clutching the bouquet of flowers so tightly that the stems were bent. I suddenly felt a wave of compassion for her, and then guilt as I realized that Violet was a victim, too. I was attacking her because she was accessible to me, and Bradley had disappeared.

"Okay," I said quietly. "I believe you."

She looked at me, wary. "Really?"

"Bradley's at the heart of this. He's the bad actor. I shouldn't punish you for that." I looked back at the hospital. "Did you know that Bradley was involved with Spencer?"

She gave a bitter laugh. "We fought about it constantly," she said. "He was a very good liar, and he was very good at making me think that I was crazy."

"I think they first got involved when we were in high school," I said. "Spencer had a boyfriend, someone who visited her in rehab, and she wouldn't tell us who he was."

"In high school?" Violet's face was tight.

"When we were seventeen," I said.

"Seventeen," Violet echoed. "You know . . . no, never mind."

"What?" I turned to look at her. "What were you going to say?"

"It's so stupid," she said. "I've spent the last few days wanting to die, because I feel like I should have known. When I first met him—when we first started dating—he had a friend staying with him. He said that she was an actress who had come out from New Hampshire, and she had nowhere else to stay, so he was letting her crash. She was just a kid."

My body felt numb. "What did she look like?"

"She was blond," Violet said. "She wasn't an actress, I know that now. I've never seen her in any movies or anything. I don't know if she was sleeping with him or what their arrangement was. By the time we got more serious she had disappeared. I don't know where she went."

I pulled out the photo of Alice and showed it to her. Violet squinted at the photo, then nodded.

"Yeah," she said. "That's her. Who is she?"

"She was my best friend in high school," I said. "She's been missing for a long time."

We sat there, side by side, and the silence felt almost companionable. I was too exhausted to feel the anger that would come later, and I already knew that it would come. I thought of Spencer as she was at seventeen: lying on the ground next to my pool, tying her hair back at the base of her neck—Spencer, who had more talent than anyone I knew, who could have become a famous artist if she'd had someone to believe in her, the way that Violet believed in Eiko. For the first time I realized that Spencer was a victim, too.

"Can I ask you one more thing?" I said, turning to Violet.

She sighed. "Go ahead."

"Does the name Mary Ecclestone mean anything to you?"

"I don't think so," Violet said.

"Let me show you a picture," I said, then took out my phone. I had managed to take a few photos of Ian's scrapbooks the evening I had visited Dolores Rhodes, and had saved the images in a folder.

Violet took the phone from me and looked down at the woman in the white gown. For a moment she looked confused, and then the confusion was replaced by something like sadness.

"Bradley's sister," she said. "I knew her name was Mary, but I didn't know her last name."

It took a moment for the words to register. "Bradley's sister?"

Violet turned the phone to look at the photo from a different angle. "Half sister, actually," she said. "I only met her once. She had a lot of problems—both health problems and mental afflictions—she was in a hospital for a long time, and then Bradley's father bought a house for her to live in. He paid a nurse to live with her full-time. I only met her once, and then Bradley told me that she died. We weren't ever to speak of it, of course."

"This is going to sound crazy, but was she an artist?"

"Sure," Violet said, and then to my surprise, she laughed. "That's part of the reason why Bradley and his father fell out, I suppose. Bradley wanted to have his own art gallery, you know, when he was young. He found out Mary could paint and tried to encourage her. I think it was all very well intended. He got in a lot of trouble, though, when he convinced her nurse to let her go off the meds. There was a big row . . . and when James found out, he threatened to disinherit Bradley."

I couldn't help thinking of the parallels to Laszlo Zo and Ricky Goff. Ricky had spent his entire life punishing the world because he had been rejected by his father. Not all unwanted children turned out that way, though.

"So, James wasn't on the birth certificate, but he supported Mary financially?"

Violet gave an expansive shrug. "Once I took over all the financials for the Auden Foundation and hired new accountants, there were a lot of payments that we couldn't make sense of."

My mind was racing, trying to keep all the details in line.

"He bought a house for Mary to live in and hired someone to look after her, and he told himself that was good enough." Violet stood up, walked over to a garbage can, and tossed the bouquet of flowers inside. She stretched and rubbed her face.

"I'm going home," she said. "Tell your friend to write his story, and tell him not to leave anything out. I'm tired of lying."

THIRTY-SIX

Three days after I got out of the hospital, the police finally told me that they were done questioning me for the time being. Lola had sat with me during all of their questions, but she had ended up retaining outside help as well, because she could possibly be implicated if the police didn't believe us at any point of the story.

"I'm going back to music," I told Lola as we drove back to my house on Loma Linda Lane. "I'm out of the PI game for a while."

"You still know how to play?"

I grimaced. "I don't think so, but what else am I going to do? I tried applying to restaurants a few years ago, and I didn't even get called in for an interview."

"You're not serious, are you?" She glanced over at me. "I can't tell if you're being serious."

"I'm half serious."

With Sadie at her sister's place, the house seemed almost deflated. A scrim of jacaranda leaves and blossoms floated on the surface of the pool, and the entire place had an air of dust.

"Damn," I said. "I'm supposed to be taking care of this place."

Lola's phone rang, and she glanced at the screen. "It's Kathy Delmonico," she said, then answered. "Kathy, hi—is everything okay?"

She walked toward the edge of the yard to take the call, and I slowly lowered myself into a pool chair, wincing in pain. The ending of a case always left me hollowed out, even if we were successful in finding what we were looking for. By every stretch of the imagination, this case had been successful: We had found Chloe and, despite the lingering trauma she was bound to suffer, she was alive. Other than Bradley, we had found the people responsible, and they were either dead or in jail. We hadn't found Alice, but that was something I was going to have to let go.

"Rainey," Lola said, walking back to me. "How are you feeling?"

"Bad."

She nodded, her face sympathetic. "Yeah. Maybe you should get some rest."

"What did Kathy want?"

Lola hesitated. "Chloe wants to see you," she said. "But I told her it can wait."

I sat up with difficulty and looked at her. "What, now?"

"We can go in a few days."

"Why does she want to talk to me?"

Lola shrugged. "I think she just wants to thank you," she said. "But really, I think you need to rest—"

"No, I'm fine," I said. "I'm just going to sit here thinking about everything I messed up, anyway. Can you drive?"

⁂

The sunlight glinted off the ocean in diamonds. The highway was busy with cars and pedestrians crossing over to the beach, carrying surfboards under their arms. Every ten minutes or so Lola glanced over at me, and I tried to ignore the concern on her face.

"I still have questions," Lola said.

"What questions?"

She frowned and scratched her neck. "I keep going back to when Alice first disappeared," she said. "Bradley helped her run away and then housed her. Right? But where has she been hiding for the last few years? It's not like she can easily rent an apartment, at least, not in her own name. She'd be on a database somewhere as a missing person. She wouldn't have any credit. You can't just disappear and then come back from the dead. Not in this day and age."

"Maybe she was living with Bradley," I suggested. I was tired of thinking about Alice. I had been carrying her for the last nine years.

"But Bradley was married," she pointed out. "*Is* married, I guess. I bet Violet will have that annulled right quick, though."

"He's got loads of money. I'm sure he's got other houses."

"And Violet never knew?"

"I don't know." My voice was snappy, and I immediately felt guilty. Lola had been so patient. "Sorry, Lo, I just can't keep thinking about this."

She drummed her fingers on the steering wheel. "Why steal the painting? It all started with the painting, didn't it?"

I thought about it. She had a point. "Maybe that was the only connection between Bradley and Mary," I said. "She was supposed to be a secret, right? Bradley's dad didn't want anyone to know about her."

We reached the edge of Oxnard. Lola was quiet until we turned onto the Delmonicos' street, and then she turned and gave me a little smile.

"I'm proud of you," she said. "I don't know if I've told you that."

"Thanks, Lo," I said, reaching over to squeeze her hand. "I'm proud of you, too."

Kathy Delmonico looked like a different person when she opened the door to greet us. The dark circles under her eyes had vanished, and she had lost the vacant gaze I had seen the first time I showed up at her house. She didn't look like she had recovered completely—there was still a lingering edge to her features—but when she smiled, it looked genuine.

"Come inside," she said, smiling. "Chloe and Michael are in the living room."

The house had been given a deep clean, and the windows had been uncovered. Sunlight streamed in, illuminating sparkling surfaces. Chloe's paintings on the walls were on display once again.

Chloe stood up from the couch and lingered there for a moment, uncertain. Her long, dark hair was pulled off her face, and she looked a bit peaked, but like she was on the path to recovery.

"Honey," Michael said to her, "this is Rainey and Lola. The women who helped find you."

"Our colleague Blake was going to come, too," I cut in. "But she had to put out a fire back at the office. We couldn't have done it without her."

"It's nice to meet you," Chloe said. Her voice was deeper than I would have expected, less childish. It was the first time I had heard her speak.

Now that we were all in the room, an awkwardness descended. I watched Chloe lift her hands to her chest, fidget with them, then sit down again. She was uncomfortable, I could see that much.

"It's a beautiful day," I offered. "Why don't we go to the beach? I'm sure Chloe could use some fresh air."

"Sure," Kathy said, looking at Chloe for confirmation. "We'll follow you in our car."

<hr>

We met up again at Thornhill Broome Beach, which was twenty minutes away. It was a Thursday afternoon, but even so, the beach was dotted with a few dozen people. There was enough wind that we were assured of discreet conversations, though; words were tossed and erased by the sound.

The five of us left the parking lot together and walked toward the beach, but gradually, Chloe and I split off and sat down together in a quiet area.

"They told me that you saved my life," Chloe said. She cast a nervous glance in my direction, then squinted out at the ocean.

My side was starting to hurt—nothing more than a dull ache, but the sensation communicated its way down my legs. I felt tight and itchy and wondered why I had offered to meet on the beach.

"Who told you that?"

"My parents," Chloe said. "The police. The nurses and doctors at the hospital. Everybody, I guess."

"They're exaggerating," I said. "People say extreme things when someone comes through something like this." I itched around the edges of my cast and tried to stave off my cravings for a painkiller.

Chloe eyed me, then nodded at the cast. "Did that happen . . . did you get that when you came to the hotel?"

I lifted my cast and assessed it for a moment. "No, this was from something else."

She gave me a long, cool look. It wasn't unfriendly, but there was something unnerving about her gaze.

"What happened to you?"

"The cast? Someone broke into my house."

"You're limping," she said. "When we walked down to the beach, you were limping."

I wrapped my arms around my body and shivered. The beach had brought an assortment of conflicting physical sensations: the overwhelming midday heat, the cold gusts off the ocean, the diamonds of white that broke with each wave. I wanted to shield myself from all of it, wrap myself in a blanket and yet get away from the heat.

"Bradley shot me," I said. I couldn't look at Chloe; it was too hard. I didn't want to see her reaction. "He shot me. I think he meant to kill me, and he probably would have, but my best friend was in the parking lot. She heard the noise and came running."

When I finally looked over to see Chloe's face, she met me with the same cool, unflinching gaze I had seen before.

"I'm so sorry," she said. "I'm sorry you had to go through that. It's my fault. I know that. And I'm sorry."

"Why is it your fault?" I squinted at her.

"You wouldn't be here if not for me," she said.

"Chloe, that's not true," I said. "I called your parents because I thought Ricky might have been involved in your disappearance. I'd been following him for years, because I always thought he was involved in my friend's disappearance."

She wrapped her arms around her knees. "I'm sorry," she said. "Did you ever find her?"

I had almost forgotten that there was a connection between Alice and Chloe. Chloe had been close to Alice at one point, close enough to lie to her parents and move into a house with Alice.

"No," I said after a beat. "I didn't. I looked for her for years, and I just couldn't find her."

"Was she one of the girls at the hotel?"

"No," I said. I already knew there was a relationship between Chloe and Alice, because her roommate had told me as much. I didn't know how Chloe would react if I mentioned that straightaway, though, so I decided to broach the topic gently. "Her name was Alice. She disappeared nine years ago, when we were still in high school. She was my best friend."

Chloe's face hardened. "Alice?"

I decided to be honest. "You know her, don't you?"

"Alice Hill?"

It made sense that Alice would have changed her last name, since she had been on the police radar. I took out my phone and found a photo of Alice, then showed it to Chloe. She immediately nodded.

"Yeah, that's her. We were close for a while."

I didn't want to push her, since she had already been through so much. Chloe seemed to want to speak, though, and I let her.

"We met at Calder's gallery," she said.

"Calder?" I raised my eyebrows. "Calder Reyes? He knows Alice?"

"I guess so," she said. "There was a party. Bradley was there, too, and Spencer. But Alice was the one who convinced me to move in with her, said that if I didn't have to work and pay rent, I could spend all my time making art. That didn't happen, of course."

"What happened?"

"She started introducing me to older men," she said. "Really wealthy older men. I liked the attention, at first—I didn't always have to sleep with them."

"Sorry," I said, confused. "This was Alice—not Spencer?"

Chloe nodded, emphatic. "Spencer mostly sold drugs," she said. "Alice was the one who kept finding girls to pimp out to older guys. Not that it didn't have its perks."

My head was spinning.

"Did she make you do this?"

Chloe shrugged, and looked kind of uncomfortable. "I'll be honest," she said. "Not at first. I liked it. Not all the guys were bad. I felt really fortunate to be able to pay my bills. Buy things. But then they introduced this new drug—the purple pills. That was horrible. I needed to get out."

I was reeling from this new information. "Have the police talked to you yet?" I asked.

"We're going in to talk to them tomorrow," she said. "My parents wanted to make sure I was recovered first."

"Do you have any idea where Alice is?"

"She's probably long gone, right?" Chloe searched my face. "Don't you think she would have left the city?"

"Where were you living?" I felt nearly frantic. There was still a chance that I could find Alice.

"I don't know the address," Chloe said. "Or even the street. I just remember the stained glass windows and the roses. We didn't go out during the daytime. Oh, there was one more thing—it was near a cemetery. I know that, because Bradley talked about how traffic was a nightmare when they went past. All the dead people blocking the road."

Lola was deep in conversation with the Delmonicos when I limp-ran across the beach toward her.

"Lola," I called. "Lola! We have to go—I know where Alice has been hiding!"

Lola spun around to face me, then shielded her eyes from the sun. "What?"

"We have to go, now," I panted. "You drive. I'll explain everything on the way."

Once we were back on the highway heading toward Los Angeles—after we had made our hasty apologies to the Delmonicos and promised to return soon—Lola turned to me.

"Where is she?" she asked. "And how do you know?"

"Chloe made a comment about a house near a cemetery," I said. "A former chapel. It's the house where Mary Ecclestone was living. It's the house they all described—stained glass and roses. Near a cemetery. Don't you remember that article we read about Mary Ecclestone? She was Bradley's sister! He probably still has the deed to the house!"

"Did you get the address?"

"No," I said. "But there are only so many cemeteries in Los Angeles, right? Didn't she say she lived in Glendale?"

"I'll call Blake," Lola said, then dialed.

Blake picked up almost right away. "Hi, Lo."

Lola quickly summarized the situation. "Can you find that article about Mary Ecclestone?" she asked.

"Right away," Blake said. I waited in agony as she typed something. "So she lives in Glendale, near a cemetery. Probably Forest Lawn, but it doesn't say."

"What other information can you give us from the article?"

"Well, the house is a former chapel," she said. "No street name listed. I'll just do a quick check . . . There are a few streets that run along Forest Lawn and a few others that might have a view of the cemetery. I'll keep looking while you guys drive over there and call if I get any other information."

"What streets?" I could hear the edge in my voice. Heat rose in waves off my dashboard, and the sun slanting at an angle through the windshield was almost blinding. I couldn't get there fast enough, something was going to happen, something was going to happen—

"El Paseo Drive and Courtland," Blake said. "Call me back if you need more help."

Once we got to Forest Lawn, I told Lola to park.

"We'll split up," I said. "You go down this street, and I'll go down another."

"Rainey, you're in no condition to be walking around," Lola snapped. "We're going to drive up and down every street until we see the house."

"But if we split up—" I protested, and she cut me off again.

"If you were in your right mind, you would realize that a *car* moves faster than a *person*," she said. Her voice grated, and I could tell she was at the end of her rope. I slumped in my seat and looked out the window to hide how wounded I felt.

"Fine," I sniffed.

Outside the car, heat rose in visible waves off the pavement. My side was aching again, and I knew that I was going to have to go home and take more pills soon, but there wasn't any time for that. The houses here were postwar, modest two- and three-bedroom affairs. Ordinary. Nothing historic.

Lola reached the end of the street and scanned it, then turned left. A hedge offered a scant amount of shade next to a house with an archway crawling with jasmine. I needed to drink water. My head was starting to hurt . . .

And then I saw it. It was just as Alice had described, and Chloe too, a house that looked like a little chapel with stained glass and roses out front.

"There!" I yelled. "There it is!"

Lola slowed down to look, but before she had even stopped the car, I threw open the door and stumbled out.

"Rainey!" Lola screamed, but I didn't stop.

I didn't question the wisdom of what I was doing, not even for a moment. If I had more time to think about it, I might have called Casey Lennon or even just the Glendale police, but there was no time, there was no time. I had to find her. I needed to find Alice.

As Lola parked, I walked up to the front door and knocked. The heat was overwhelming, and my side hurt. Everything itched, and sweat dripped down my forehead. There was no movement from inside the house, at least, nothing I could hear. I knocked again.

"Rainey! Rainey, wait!" Down the street, Lola got out of the car and came huffing up the sidewalk.

"Can I help you?"

I whirled, startled at the sound of the voice. A diminutive woman with a deep tan and wrinkles stood on the path behind me. She was smiling, cautious, her hands clasped in front of her. She could have been anywhere from sixty to eighty years old, but it was impossible to say—her hair was pure white, but her eyes were sharp and clear. She couldn't have been more than five feet tall.

Lola finally reached me, and the woman glanced between us, her face uncertain.

"I'm looking for someone," I told her. I pointed to the house behind me. "This house, I need to get inside." I was aware that panic had made my voice into a quavery stutter, but there was nothing I could do about it. Everything in me was pressing to get inside the house, because I could feel that something very bad was about to happen and I couldn't stop it. The woman on the path stood smiling at me quizzically, but it wasn't helping, and I almost wanted to push her over. She couldn't understand my urgency.

"Now hold on," she said, then laughed. "You look like you're about to have a fit. Do you need some water? You can come inside with me; I live just there. Have a drink of water."

"No," I said, hiccupping. "I'm looking for my friend."

"Is your friend Bradley?" She peered up at me.

"What—yes," I said. "Yes, yes, I'm looking for Bradley. Have you seen him?"

The woman advanced and put a hand on my arm. She radiated strength and kindness, and her presence was soothing.

"Come on, now," she said. "Why don't you step inside for a moment—that's my house, right next door. Have a glass of water. It's baking out here."

I cast one last glance at the former chapel before allowing myself to be ushered across the yard, toward the woman's house. Lola followed behind, silent. I knew that she was angry with me, but hoped she would hold onto whatever she had to say until I had given the woman a chance to speak.

"I'm Nancy," the woman said, smiling at me and Lola. "I was born and raised here. Lived here all my life, Glendale. You from around here? I don't mind the heat, myself. Bakes away all the rot. Cleans the air. Nothing like clean, desert air."

She opened her front door and ushered us inside. It took a moment for my eyes to adjust, but when they did, I saw that the interior of the house was cool and spare.

"Just a quick glass of water," I said. "I can't stay long, really. I'm looking for my friend."

"Through here," Nancy said, slipping her shoes off and padding through the living room. The rooms were pleasantly bare of all but the essentials: mid-century furniture, a Bakelite phone, some modest paintings on the walls. The air was a lot cooler inside, and I put my phone away before following the woman into the kitchen.

She poured water into two yellow glasses and handed one to me and one to Lola. Her eyes crinkled as I drank, and she nodded when I was finished.

"Have one more," she said, pouring another glass. "I'm a nurse, so I want to make sure you're well enough to go out in that heat. Well, I'm retired, more or less, but I still keep an eye on people."

I drank the second glass of water, feeling grateful, then walked over to the sink and put the glass in the basin. Lola's phone rang and she took it out of her pocket, then frowned at the screen. She held it up so I could see the face. *Blake Harris.*

"I'll step outside," she told me, heading for the door. "I gotta take this."

"Thank you," I told Nancy, then turned to follow Lola. "Really. I have to go, now."

"Wait," she said. "Please."

I crossed the kitchen, wondering why this woman was so invested in what I was doing.

"Hold on," she said. "Let me give you my phone number. Please. You can call me at any time."

I stopped walking and turned to look at her. "Why would I need to call you?"

"I'm not here to judge," she said. "I've seen all kinds in my time as a nurse. I'm retired now, but I still like to help people when I can. Here." She jotted her number down on a pad of paper by the telephone, then ripped off the sheet and handed it to me.

"Do you think I need help?" I knew that she had the wrong idea about me, but I had no idea why. I was torn between the urgency of finding out what was inside the house and knowing what this woman was trying to tell me.

"Does your family know where you are?" Nancy asked, peering at me with concern.

I decided to be honest. "I don't have a family."

"You poor girl," she said. She looked like she was on the verge of saying something, but then refrained. Instead, she gave me a cautious smile and pointed to the scrap of paper. "Call me," she said. "Any time."

Through the front window I could see Lola leaning against her car, talking to Blake. Even from this distance I could see the tension in her shoulders. The little former chapel sat on the other side of the yard, dazzling in the sunlight. There was a static buzz in the air, the sound of electrical wires, and a distant lawnmower trundling away somewhere down the street. I had been looking for this house for years, but now that I had found it, I was almost scared to see what was inside. It felt deceptively peaceful, like I might be walking into a trap.

I turned back to look at Nancy. "You've lived here your whole life?" I asked.

She looked taken aback by the question. "Yes, I have."

"So, you knew Mary Ecclestone? She lived in that house, right?"

Nancy studied my face for a moment, trying to parse my question. "I did," she said finally. "Her father hired me to look after her."

"And Bradley?"

She lifted a hand, almost unconsciously, and started playing with a pendant that hung around her neck. A sour look crossed her open, pleasant face.

"I shouldn't say. It's not my place."

"She was his sister," I pressed. "Mary. Wasn't she?"

Nancy looked past me, toward the chapel. She looked almost frightened. "What did he do to her?"

Nancy shook her head and started to retreat into the house.

"You must see a lot of girls here," I said. "Right? Desperate girls with nowhere else to go. You wanted to help me—you said I could ask for your help. Please."

Her eyes still had a faraway look.

"He shot me," I said, lifting my shirt. "Bradley shot me." The words still didn't feel real to me. I hadn't really connected with what had happened to me, which I knew was probably a good indication that I was still in shock. Nancy's eyes went wide, looking at my stomach.

"He did this, too," I went on, holding up my hand. "Well, he sent some people to do it. He's going to go on hurting people unless someone stops him."

Nancy wrapped her arms around her stomach. "She was twenty when she moved into that house," she said. "Just a girl, really, so much younger than her age. Mary. She wasn't equipped to deal with . . . well, any of it. The real world. Adult problems. And they put her in this house and locked her away. It was horrible."

I waited, listening, for her to go on.

"I met him once, you know. Her father." Nancy shook her head in disgust. "Acted like he was so magnanimous, paying for all her bills. He ended up hiring me to look after her, because I was a nurse. I wasn't a doctor, mind, and I didn't have much experience with schizophrenia, but he didn't care about any of that. Hired me to make sure she was taking her meds and eating right."

"When did you meet Bradley?"

"He was in high school, I think," she said. "Maybe college. I can't be sure. I think he'd just found out about Mary. They were only half-siblings; Mary was older. Anyway, around comes Bradley, sweet as pie. He was so impressed with Mary's artwork, asked her why she wasn't doing it anymore.

"He was the one who convinced her to stop taking her medication," Nancy said. She looked almost near tears. "He said the drugs were holding her back. That she wasn't *creative* with them. Those drugs were saving her life."

I glanced back at the house, and Nancy grabbed my arm. "What are you going to do?" she asked. "Why are you here? You can't go in there, not after what he did to you. We should call the police."

"You said Bradley isn't here," I pointed out. "I have to know what's inside."

"Leave," she begged. "I'll call the police and tell them what I know. Have you talked to them? Do they know that you were shot?"

"They know." I gently extricated myself from her grasp. "When did you last see him?"

"I haven't seen his car in a while," she said. "The only one I've seen come and go is that girl. The blond one."

I felt a fist in the pit of my stomach. "Alice?"

"I don't know her name." She looked near tears again. "There were so many kids, so many of them. They all looked so desperate, like they had nowhere else to go. And I did nothing to stop it. I could have stopped it years ago."

"You didn't know," I said. "It's not your fault."

She brushed angrily at the tears that had coursed down her cheeks. "I'm going in there with you," she said. "It's the least I can do."

As soon as Nancy and I emerged into the sunlight, I felt cold fingers of panic, even though it was at least ninety degrees outside. Down the street, a pair of gardeners trimmed the hedge of a boxy house that looked out of place in the neighborhood of historic buildings. We were above Forest Lawn, looking down into the graveyard with its manicured lawns and avenues of cypress trees. A funeral was in progress, and nearby a man in a starched suit stood over a different grave, head bowed.

I walked up to the front of the old chapel, then knocked on the door. Nancy stood a couple feet behind me, and having her there was reassuring, though I wasn't sure how much protection she offered.

"Alice?" I called. "Alice, it's Rainey. Are you there?"

The words felt performative and silly. My voice sounded far too casual, even to my own ears: I had been looking for Alice for a decade, and she had been in the city the whole time. She obviously didn't want to be found.

"Alice?" I tried again. I reached out and tried the doorknob. It was locked.

"Let's go around the back," Nancy suggested. "The back door used to be busted. I don't know if they got it fixed or not, but it's worth a shot."

The smell of roses was almost overwhelming. Dense banks of flowers pressed in from all sides, filling the air with their perfume. I wondered who had been taking care of these roses for all these years; I couldn't imagine that it was Bradley.

The back entrance was protected by a small alcove. When we reached it, Nancy pushed me aside and jiggled the doorknob a few times. To my surprise, it creaked open. Nancy turned and gave me a smile of fiendish delight.

"Let me go in first," I whispered. "Just in case."

As soon as I stepped into the house, I smelled something like rot. It was the sweet, clotted scent of old food moldering into compost. The air was thick with it. I pulled my shirt up over my nose and moved farther into the house, which was cool and dim. The curtains had been pulled in all the rooms, plunging the space into darkness.

We passed through the kitchen at the back of the chapel, which had evidence of recent habitation: a cardboard pizza box full of crusts, a glass of orange juice.

"Disgusting," Nancy whispered.

I walked through a door, which led into the main part of the house, what had once been the chapel. Furniture was arranged in an odd configuration around the room: chairs dragged into corners, facing the walls, a sofa toppled over on its back. I had almost turned around to leave when I saw movement—a scrabbling, the movement of an animal, really—in the corner of the room.

I put up a hand to let Nancy know that something was there. She nodded as she saw it, then put a hand on my arm.

"Stay here," I whispered.

I moved toward the corner of the room, which was illuminated by a shaft of light that slanted in through the stained glass. I didn't want to know what was there, but I couldn't tear myself away. Panic seeped through my body, a cold prickle, and I couldn't feel my extremities. The thing moved.

I saw a flash of blond hair and then the thing turned to look at me. I didn't recognize her, not at first. Her face was contorted in a mask of agony and terror. When she saw me, she scuttled backward, trying to get away.

"Alice?" I whispered. "Oh my god, Alice . . ."

I knelt down and moved toward her slowly, arms outstretched. "It's okay," I said. "It's okay. It's Rainey."

When I got closer, I could see that her eyes were completely black. On the floor nearby were dozens of purple pills. I realized what had happened, and quickly stood up.

"Call an ambulance!" I cried, turning over my shoulder to look at Nancy. "Oh god, call an ambulance—"

But Nancy wasn't looking at me. Her attention was riveted just beyond my reach, behind one of the couches.

"There's someone else here," she said quietly. She looked transfixed, frozen in place. "It's a man, but I can't see his face . . . I don't want to move him, in case he's hurt . . ."

I ran over and saw who she was looking at. A man in a pair of jeans and an old T-shirt. One arm was over his face, but I could see his dark hair.

I knelt to take his pulse, which was weak.

"Can you hear me? Hello?"

I lifted his arm and then, just as quickly, dropped it. It was Bradley.

"He's still alive," I told Nancy, my voice frantic. I felt like I was disassociating, struggling to stay inside my body. "Call an ambulance. Call someone—we have to save them—we have to get them to a hospital . . ."

I ran back over to Alice and took her in my arms.

"Stay with me," I said, shaking her. "Alice—Alice!"

Her eyes stayed on me without blinking for five minutes, then ten. I didn't let go for a minute, not even when I heard the sirens wailing down the street, when the door burst open and Nancy was telling them where to go, when they finally took her from my arms, when they told me that she was already gone.

THIRTY-SEVEN

—⚬⚬⚬—

TWO WEEKS LATER

"Where do you go every night?"

For a long time I told everyone that I was fine. For a few days, it was the truth—people kept checking in on me, calling to see how I was doing. I didn't know what they wanted from me—some kind of reaction, *something*—but I didn't know how to give it to them. I could tell each time that I disappointed them, though, because I hadn't collapsed into a corner and started pulling my hair out.

I was fine when I went back to the house near Griffith Park and began pulling out weeds, even though Lola told me not to bother. I was fine when I started the process of cleaning the pool and fixing the pool cover so that Lola could go swimming, even though I wouldn't be able to get in the water for another six weeks. I was fine until I went to the hospital to get my stitches out.

When I heard the ambulance wailing outside the emergency room, it suddenly all came back to me. Lola had to sit in the car with me for two hours and was on the verge of calling a doctor out because I was having a panic attack.

"Bed rest," Dr. Minari told me. "This isn't negotiable, Rainey. I don't want you to work from home, either. Unplug. Read a book. You own books, yes?"

I might have been tempted to break the rules if not for Lola, who had moved in with me. She was the one who told me that Cameron was going to arrange a memorial for Alice and that he wanted to know when I was going to be able to make it.

"I can't go," I told her.

"Why not?" She sat on the edge of my bed and smoothed my hair off my forehead.

"Because the whole thing was her fault, wasn't it?"

A crease appeared in between her eyebrows. "I'm not sure I would say that . . ."

"She was finding girls for Bradley," I said. It was a thought that kept rising up, something that I couldn't push away, no matter how hard I tried. "She's the reason that Chloe ended up in that disgusting hotel. I want nothing to do with her."

"She's dead, Rai," Lola said gently. "The memorial is for the living. For Cameron."

My eyes filled up with tears. "I can't go. I'm sorry."

"It's not her fault, you know," Lola said, getting up to leave. "Remember that she was just a kid when Bradley took her. She was a broken person who didn't have anyone to help her."

The only reason I left the house was to sit in the garden and watch a family of stray cats appear every evening. It was a mom and her kittens, four little gamboling things that raced around the edge of the pool and caught mice.

"Where do you go every night, Rainey?"

I glanced up at Lola, who was watching me with the same baffled concern I had seen on her face since I'd gotten out of the hospital.

"I don't go anywhere," I said.

"We're living in the same house," she said. "Every night you slip out and go somewhere. I've heard you leave. You can tell me—I'm not trying to keep you prisoner."

I glanced out the window. "I just need to get out," I told her. "Nighttime is when I feel safest."

"You don't want me to go with you?"

"I need time by myself," I told her. "It's nothing personal. I just need to think about everything that happened."

The box of tickets to the premiere had sat untouched on the living room table, but three days before the event, Lola finally mentioned them to me.

"It might be a good idea for us to go," she said. "We've got four tickets, so we can take Blake and Hailey, too. What do you think?"

"I don't know."

She nodded and put the tickets away, out of sight, but I could tell that she was disappointed. She had been trying so hard, and all I could do was disappoint her. I felt a wave of disgust toward myself, and stood up.

"Lo?"

She turned.

"I might need help," I said, gesturing to the cast and the area where I had been shot. "Getting dressed. Putting on makeup. Would you do that for me?"

"Of course, Rainey," she said, coming over to give me a gentle hug. "Of course I'll help you."

———

On the morning of the premiere for Marcus's film, I got dressed in jeans and a T-shirt, then pulled a comb through my hair. I pulled it into a loose chignon and pinned it at the base of my neck and grabbed my keys, then slipped out of my house and walked to my car. I didn't want to think too much about what I was doing, because every time I thought about

Alice—about what I had seen in Mary's old house—I felt sick all over again. As much as I wanted to believe that what had happened to Alice wasn't my fault, it was a message I couldn't internalize. I kept flashing back to our last summer together, thinking of the ways it could have turned out differently: if Alice's mother had recovered and turned her life around, if we hadn't started hanging out with Spencer, if we hadn't broken into all those houses.

I made it all the way to Santa Monica before reality set in and I realized what I was about to do. I pulled my car over to the side of the road and turned off the engine, then closed my eyes and leaned against the steering wheel. My whole body was shaking, and I couldn't draw a breath. Sunlight broke in dappled shadows over the seats of my car, and the heat of the leather made the temperature almost unbearable.

After grabbing my things, I got out of my car and went to a bench in the shade. I could see Cameron's hotel a few blocks away, but the idea of walking over there and knocking on his door was too much for me.

When I had gotten my nerves under control, I took out my phone and called him. He answered on the second ring.

"Rainey," he said. "Hi—how are you? Is everything okay?"

"Yes," I said. "I'm sorry, I've been meaning to call you—"

"No, no, don't apologize," he said. His voice was solemn. "I came to the hospital twice, but they wouldn't let me see you. When I came back a third time, you'd already been released. I talked to Lola, and she said that you'd reach out to me when you were ready."

I nodded, even though I knew he couldn't see me.

"Where are you?" he asked.

"I'm at home," I lied.

"I'm leaving tomorrow," he said. "Is there a chance we could catch up before then? I'd love to see you—I'm not sure when I'm going to be in LA again. After the memorial, that is . . ."

"Really? No plans to come back?"

He sighed and fell quiet. "I'm selling the house," he said. "I know why I held on to it for so long, but she's gone, you know?"

"I know." My throat went tight.

"Are you coming to the memorial? It'll be in a few weeks, once I get in touch with everyone who knew Alice."

"I don't know, Cameron. I'm sorry. I really want to, but I don't know."

"It's okay," he said quickly. "I understand."

We both fell quiet for a long moment.

"Rainey, I'm so grateful for everything you did," Cameron said, his voice soft. "Really. I don't think either one of us could have saved Alice. We both tried, you know?"

Tears coursed down my face.

"She was lucky to have you, Rainey," he said. "I hope you know that."

I felt fine again until the evening of the premiere arrived. Lola got dressed in her room, and I pulled out my box of nice dresses and started to go through them. The simple action reminded me of the Orphans' Ball, when I still thought there was a chance of finding Alice, when she had still been alive and living in Los Angeles, only I didn't know about it.

When Lola called me to come out a few times and I didn't, she came in to find me.

"Rai?" she asked, then saw me sitting in the corner of my closet. "Rainey, what's going on?"

"It's all so stupid," I said. "It all feels completely pointless sometimes."

"You're right," she said after a moment. "I've definitely been there before."

"I can't go. You go without me."

She sighed. "Rainey, we're going to meet them in a few minutes. Just get dressed and have a strong cup of coffee. I promise you'll be glad you came."

"I won't," I said.

She glanced out the window. "Is there any point in trying to talk you out of this?"

"No, Lola," I said. "I'm sorry. Tell Marcus I'm sorry. I'll come to the next one."

—⁂—

Once she had left—when I had the house to myself again and my nerves started to settle—I grabbed my car keys and toyed with them for a minute, deciding whether or not I should go. In the end, I couldn't make myself sit still.

It was where I had been driving every night for the last week, even though I hadn't yet worked up the courage to tell Lola about it. There was an element to all of this that felt wrong, but I wasn't sure what it said about me, and I didn't want to know.

I coasted out of the driveway, then took surface streets until I hit the 134-W. I didn't listen to the radio, just drove in silence until I was on the 101 North, which I took all the way to Oxnard.

The Delmonicos' street was silent, just as I thought it would be. I found it comforting to see the little houses with their configuration of windows lit up against the night, each family tucked in safe from the outside world. I had started coming here after we met Chloe that day, after Alice died, because I realized that I couldn't sleep without knowing she was safe.

I hadn't seen any indication to the contrary. There had been no strange cars coasting down the street, pausing outside the Delmonico residence. It was a safe neighborhood, as safe as they came, but there was no telling what could happen when the outside world came crashing in. There were only so many things you could do to protect yourself. I wanted to be there in case of the unexpected.

So far, it hadn't come yet, but I was going there for myself as much as I was for Chloe. I didn't want her to know that I was watching from afar, but I knew what it was like to live without a safety net. I never wanted her to feel that way.

That evening I stayed there for three hours, watching the street and noticing all the noises and activity that happened where the squares of light cast by the windows ended. A part of me knew that there was nobody left, nobody left to come for Chloe; we had gotten all of them. There was nobody left to hurt her.

The reason that I couldn't tell Lola about this was that it was the last part of myself I had managed to keep secret. Even though I had grown up going to movie premieres and standing in front of the bright lights, there had always been a disconnect, because this was where I belonged. Just on the periphery of the action, watching from the outside. It was one of the reasons I was good at my job. I thrived in the shadows, existed on the fringe, lived in a way that others didn't understand.

When the last light on the street winked out, I finally decided it was okay for me to leave. This time I took the long way back to Griffith Park, driving down the coast, past Point Mugu and all the beaches that had emptied out hours before. There was nobody left, I reminded myself, nothing left to run from.

ACKNOWLEDGMENTS

My gratitude always goes first to Annie Bomke, my incredible agent, who is also my editor and sounding board. Thanks for seeing the good and weeding out the bad. Thanks for fighting so hard for my books.

Thanks to everyone at Pegasus: Jessica Case, Claiborne Hancock, and my generous and insightful editor, Victoria Wenzel. Thanks also to Maria Fernandez and Lisa Gilliam. I am always enormously grateful for the work you put behind my books.

As always, thanks to my family: Marsh, Tilda, and Huon.